# Praise for *FATE OF FLAMES*

"With its cast of diverse, well-drawn heroines, colorful world building, and action-packed story line, *Fate of Flames* is an immersive and monstrously fun read."
—Elsie Chapman, author of *Dualed* and *Divided*

"Raughley depicts the cost of power, the lure of fame, and the trauma of overwhelming stress in a compelling story with memorably flawed heroines. . . . An engrossing kickoff to the Effigies series."
—*Publishers Weekly*

"This series opener has it all: strong females, intrigue, a dash of romance, monsters, and a sequel in the wings."
—*Kirkus Reviews*

"It's a compelling concept, and the mix of fragility, defiance, strength, and utter exhaustion that plays out in the girls feels authentic. . . . A sequel will likely be eagerly anticipated."
—*The Bulletin of the Center for Children's Books*

# Also by Sarah Raughley

*Fate of Flames*

*Siege of Shadows*

Book Three in the **EFFIGIES** series

# LEGACY OF
# LIGHT

## SARAH RAUGHLEY

Simon Pulse

New York   London   Toronto   Sydney   New Delhi

SIMON PULSE

An imprint of Simon & Schuster Children's Publishing Division

1230 Avenue of the Americas, New York, New York 10020

First Simon Pulse hardcover edition November 2018

Text copyright © 2018 by Sarah Raughley

Jacket illustration copyright © 2018 by Craig Shields

For information about special discounts for bulk purchases,

please contact Simon & Schuster Special Sales

at 1-866-506-1949 or business@simonandschuster.com.

The Simon & Schuster Speakers Bureau can bring authors to your live event.

For more information or to book an event contact the Simon & Schuster Speakers

Bureau at 1-866-248-3049 or visit our website at www.simonspeakers.com.

Series design by Karina Granda

Jacket and interior designed by Steve Scott

The text of this book was set in Adobe Caslon Pro.

Manufactured in the United States of America

2 4 6 8 10 9 7 5 3 1

Library of Congress Cataloging-in-Publication Data

Names: Raughley, Sarah, author.

Title: Legacy of light / by Sarah Raughley.

Description: First Simon Pulse hardcover edition. | New York : Simon Pulse, 2018. |

Series: The Effigies ; 3 | Summary: "The Effigies must uncover the connection between

Saul, Blackwell, and the phantoms before it's too late"— Provided by publisher.

Identifiers: LCCN 2018014637 (print) | LCCN 2018021137 (eBook) |

ISBN 9781481466851 (eBook) | ISBN 9781481466837 (hardcover)

Subjects: | CYAC: Four elements (Philosophy)—Fiction. | Psychic ability—Fiction. |

Superheroes—Fiction. | Monsters—Fiction. | Science fiction. | Fantasy.

Classification: LCC PZ7.1.R38 (eBook) | LCC PZ7.1.R38 Leg 2018 (print) |

DDC [Fic]—dc23

LC record available at https://lccn.loc.gov/2018014637

*To every geek girl ever*

## Before

I'M DEAD NOW, SO IT'S POINTLESS TO REMEMBER.
But the last time I saw my twin sister, she was pissed at me.

What did we even fight about?

When I was alive, I'd think of the future. I figured I could be anything if I could dream it: doctor, president, firefighter. I believed in possibility.

The hubris of youth.

I thought I had time to figure it out. But time had other plans.

If I'd known, I wouldn't have fought with her that day. But what did we fight about?

I don't think I've been dead very long. I have a general sense of that. My body's gone now, but my memories still exist. Strange. My consciousness should have faded the second my soul left my body. But they were still part of me.

Memories.

Memories of pain.

Remember . . .

*Last year*

*Early April*

*Buffalo, New York*

"Hey—hey, I said stop!" Before she could escape up the winding steps, I grabbed the crook of my twin sister's arm and pulled her around.

"What?" she spat, but I knew my sister. She was all bark and no bite. She couldn't even look me in the eye—lots of attitude pointed like a dagger, not at me, but at the peeling paint on the walls of our two-story house. Typical.

"What do you mean 'what'? Really, Lil Sis?" I hoped I sounded as appalled as I was. "You don't have *anything* to say for yourself? After what you just did on the bus?"

She let her schoolbag slide off her shoulders. "I didn't do anything. What the hell do you want from me?"

"Yeah, that's the problem. You didn't do *anything*." I swept my long, curly brown hair over my shoulders, my too-long fingernails getting caught in the thick curls. "You were sitting right next to Jake and you didn't lift a finger when Austin started messing with him. You were right there and you didn't even tell him to stop. That's just messed up."

I let her go because I knew I had her attention.

She stayed put, fuming just as I anticipated she would. "It wasn't my problem to begin with."

"Wasn't mine either, but I still tried to stop him."

"Oh, gee." She rolled her eyes. "Well, aren't you Miss Perfect Little Mary Sue running into burning buildings to save kittens?"

This was rich. Stooping down, I pulled the day planner out of her schoolbag pocket. The Sect had made limited copies of these, and the two of us made sure we were among the only ones to buy it. It was nothing special—just your typical planner, except it had Natalya Filipova's face on the front and back, her battle stats printed on the first few pages before the memo section. A pointless but special item only a mega-fan would bother paying for. Lil Sis sighed impatiently when she saw me flap it in front of her face. She knew exactly what I was getting at.

"I mean, I'm just saying," I said. "The whole running-in-to-burning-buildings thing is pretty much what makes people worship them in the first place. Why else are you on that stupid forum every day?"

"That's them." She snatched the planner out of my hands. "We're *not* them. I don't have to get involved in some other kids' business if it has nothing to do with me. I don't have to care, and I don't."

But that wasn't true at all. She did care. I could tell by the slight tremor of my sister's hands as she gripped the planner. Trembling, just like they had done on the bus, when she'd pretended to listen to music while Austin was pushing the back of Jake's head into the seat in front of them. She did care. She did want to do something. She was just scared.

She'd always been like that, ever since we were kids. Walking down the sidewalk with her head to the pavement as if she were counting the cracks. Unable to stand up to the bully. Unable to stand up for anyone.

I folded my arms. "You honestly looked so dumb sitting there, and it's not like I was the only one who noticed you wuss out. Why don't you grow a spine for once?"

I left her bristling, passing her without a glance back, and began to climb the stairs.

"You love acting so superior," she whispered, and I could almost feel her shaking. We turned and faced each other at exactly the same time. "So self-righteous. You always have this thing where you think you're better than me."

"If what I just saw on that bus is any indication, I *am* better than you."

I regretted saying it immediately, only because I knew about my sister's complex. She already thought I was better than her, an assumption that kept her confidence on life support even if she'd never admit it to me. She shrank at my words, but stayed where she was, chin raised, her eyes wavering as she glared at me. An unsettling feeling always crept down my nerves, as if tiptoeing down a tightrope, whenever the two of us stared each other down like this. It was the mirror effect. As we looked into each other's dark brown eyes, we both saw in each other the image of ourselves that we didn't want to see. For me, it was a weakness I'd thrown away long ago. I could only imagine what it was for her—the image of who she wanted to be, maybe.

Anyway, it wasn't my problem.

"So what should I have done?" She'd asked it just as I started to swivel back around. I could see the silent plea she kept locked up behind that deceptively calm expression. "That's the lesson, right? When in doubt, I'm supposed to do whatever *you* would?"

"I don't know, Maia. But literally anything would have been better."

And those were the last words I told my sister.


Yes. I can still remember that fight.

But why *can* I still remember? Why am I still reeling from the pain of it all?

I shouldn't be able to remember anything—or *feel* anything.

Everything should go black when you're dead. Everything just vanishes as you wait for the next phase: a secret of life only the dead know. We who are dead can't "remember" anything because we don't exist in one temporal spectrum. We exist everywhere—past, present, and future. We exist as the *bedrock* of space and time, the raw essence of matter.

But here I am, remembering, feeling. That day, Maia and I didn't speak to each other after the fight. I'd spent the night in the living room knitting my cosplay outfit for Comic Con, and she'd locked herself up in our room, blasting music through her headphones and trolling the crap out of people on the Doll Soldiers forum again.

Mom and Dad had been so busy bickering about some stupid family thing that they hadn't even noticed we were in a cold war of our own. I'd assumed things would be fine by morning, so I didn't care, not even when I heard Maia sneak out of our room late at night. She'd left her phone on the desk, so I couldn't tell her to bring her butt back.

Maia would do stuff like that from time to time. Dad had caught her so many times, he ended up screwing the window shut when we were fourteen so she couldn't sneak out that way. But I don't remember being worried that night. I already knew she wasn't in any trouble. I was *damn* sure she wasn't out meeting guys or drug dealers or older neighborhood kids, even if that was what she wanted me to think. I was so sure then that Maia would come back in a couple of hours like she always did, with some chips, donuts, and soda from the twenty-four-hour convenience store, sufficiently satisfied with her rebelliousness—at least, enough to pretend that she didn't feel like a total loser.

That night I went back to sleep thinking I'd have the opportunity to set her straight. I'd tell her that there were better ways to feel good about yourself, to feel strong. I'd help her because that's what big sisters did—yeah, *big* sister. The two minutes that made me the "older" one, the two minutes I'd always used to justify calling her "Lil Sis," had generally given me a sense of responsibility that Maia had ended up interpreting as self-righteousness. But I'd hoped she'd come to understand me someday.

I'd hoped for a lot of things.

It wasn't Maia who'd woken me up again, but the smell of smoke.

The smoke. I remember the smoke. I remember how it'd stung my eyes, filled my lungs whenever I gasped and inhaled poison instead. I remember stumbling out of bed, unable to see. I remember pounding on the window, forgetting it wouldn't budge, courtesy of Dad.

Stumbling, stumbling. The smoke alarm not working. The smoke billowing, swallowing everything. My mom screaming, yelling for me. *Everybody* yelling:

"Where's Maia?"

"Where's the door?"

"Where's the fire coming from?"

The flames in the living room. The door out of reach, out of sight. A cough, deep and ugly from my throat. My clumsy feet losing their footing. My body falling down the stairs. Bones and organs bruised, head hitting the hard wood.

I remember it all. Every second. I remember lying on the staircase unable to move, thinking about Mom and Dad . . . thinking their names with my mouth open, but frozen.

*What will happen to me after I die? Where will I go? I'm scared. Please, god, I'm scared.* I can still remember each terror-filled thought racing through me. *I don't want to die. Not like this. Not like this. Please let a miracle happen. Someone save me! God, don't take me! It can't be me. I'll never accept it. Never! Someone! Anyone . . .*

The saliva pooling around my chin, slipping down my throat. Choking without feeling the physical pain of it. My body convulsing, then going lax.

A painful death.

In the moment of my passing, I saw a white light come and pull my soul from my body. It was supposed to go dark after that. That's the normal way. That's how people die.

But it isn't dark here, where I am now. I can see nothing except that which I shouldn't: white streams flowing, filling the world in an expanse of darkness. The same light that came for me in death. A white, almost silver sheen blanketing everything.

That's it.

I don't know where I am. I see no plains or rivers, no cities or buildings. No cobbled streets or the people to be found on them. No stars, no planets.

All I can see now are white streams.

The pathways of fate.

That's what they are. The knowledge simply exists inside me—one of many cosmic secrets withheld from us while we're still breathing. All matter is connected through the power of fate linking life and death in an endless dance. I and other souls are one with this energy, this ether. The substance of starlight and souls, the fated destination of all creatures: this nothingness from which other forms spring.

Forms. Space. Time. Life. Death. And the final mystery: fate. Fate is the culprit connecting us in the never-ending cycle of rebirth. All forms are destined to take another. It'll happen to me, too. All people, beings, life, and death are held together by this mysterious, magical force, this effervescent energy encompassing everything.

The skies, the sea, the earth, and the flames bringing us to ruin.

The ashes and the new breath rising from them.

Everything is connected. Predetermined pathways continuing the dance of life. Everything in order.

Everything . . . in order . . .

Except for them. Those girls. The Effigies: the ones who stand apart in a cycle of life and death all their own, the pathways of reincarnation twisted by a desperate wish . . .

The secrets of the world. I understand it all. I understand everything. I know that I'm supposed to be nothing. I'm supposed to see, feel, and remember nothing. I'm supposed to exist as part of this energy. I'm supposed to wait quietly as fate scoops me up and molds me into something else. A human newborn perhaps. Maybe a seedling. I'm supposed to be passive. I'm not supposed to feel this emotional. This scared.

This *furious*.

Why should I just wait quietly to be reborn? I shouldn't even be dead in the first place! It was a ridiculous accident. A fluke. An electrical problem in the walls. It shouldn't have been me. I should still be alive. My parents too. We deserve to be alive.

I may not be alive, but I'm frustrated. I want to tell Maia all the secrets I know now! I want to tell her about fate, about the Three who, with their eyes that see all, govern the pathways of destiny, deciding who lives and dies. I want to tell Maia everything, but I'll never see her again. That's how death works: Our souls will follow different paths. Once it's time for me to be re-created into a new form, I may not even have a mouth to speak, even if she does.

Maia. Mom. Dad. I will never see any of them again. And I hate it. I hate it so much. I can't stop wishing for that body of mine, already burned and rotting. I want to come back.

Is it all a game to them? Life and death? Maybe our lives mean nothing to those three *sadists*. Maybe my pain means nothing too. Why would it? I was born and then gone in an instant, just one life of the billions that'd come before me. Insignificant.

Why? Why must *any* of us die?

I hate it. I *hate* this. It's hate I shouldn't feel.

Hate I *wouldn't* feel if the pathways of fate were as they should be.

Something is terribly wrong with us souls. We're all supposed to find peace in death, but all I feel now is agitated. I know I'm not the only one. A bitter poison is flowing in the ether. The pathways of fate . . . As the energy itself is strained by unnatural forces, so too are we souls. Some of us are able to hold on . . . but others give in to their anger.

And when they give in to anger, *it* happens.

It's happening right now.

I can see a soul convulse and distend in agony. Smoke is rising from it as it darkens pitch black, growing like a tumor. A soul in chaos. It's descending now from the ether, its body funneling with the force of a tornado. Bones are sprouting from the smoke, encasing itself around dead flesh, rotted and stinking.

A phantom.

Its jaws are dislocated as it snaps open, revealing ivory teeth. As it breaks the barrier between life and death, I know it's not just the dead but also the living that can see it now. And then, soon, just the living. As it disappears from the ether, it leaves the realm of the dead. Elsewhere others appear. And more will appear after that.

Monsters birthed from anguished souls.

Phantoms are of soul. Souls are of ether. Ether is of the realm of the dead, though now, because of the twisting, poking, and prodding of this energy by human agents, part of its presence can be felt, can be *quantified*, in the world of the living. Like the tip of a submerged iceberg. Cylithium. The mystic energy that controls the cycle of life and

death and the fate of all matter. The source of an Effigy's magic, drawn
into their very bodies. The source of phantoms.

Phantoms are not natural to this world. They don't belong to the
cycle of life and death. They're aberrations. *Abominations*. Distortions
of fate. Distorted by the arrogance of those men. Distorted by the
cruelty of that girl.

That girl . . .

Because of her, I can't let go of my anger. I can't find peace. I just
keep getting . . . *angrier*. I can't stop it. What if I become like that *thing*
one day: a monstrous phantom, peering at the world through dead
eyes, snatching innocents into my ugly, rotted jaw?

It's that girl's fault.

But is it really?

Isn't it the fault of the Three? The cruelest ones of all. The ones
who'd decided to see with their own eyes the path humanity would
take when given the power of gods.

Yeah. The phantoms are *their* fault, in the end. Souls will keep rotting. Phantoms will keep appearing. People will keep dying. I can't stop
any of it. I can't protect anyone. I can't change anyone's fates. The dead
have no agency. The dead have nothing.

It's not fair. It's not *fair*!

It isn't fair. Three words. Just those three words. I repeat them for
seconds, centuries, eons, in the past, in the future, in the present, until
I no longer know words. Until the anger takes me over. Until my soul
begins to writhe in agony, a monster's rebirth waiting for it.

Until I awake again. In agony.


*What's happening?*

The first thought slipped into my consciousness like feeble, dying breath. Every cell in my body burned. Dirt slipped through the cracks of the opening casket as a pulley lifted it—lifted me—into the air. Where were my legs? I couldn't see them. I couldn't move. The box was too tight and my vision still black behind heavy eyelids. My dead flesh was slow to wake. Cockroaches scuttled across my skin looking for the detritus they'd been feasting on. Crawling, scratching, they traveled up my face and down my neck, into the loose dress I'd been buried in.

Something living slipped into my lips as I tried to crack them apart. I hacked. Writhed. Neck stiff. Arms twitching. Memories. Memories of burning.

There were other things I tried to remember. Important stuff—grand stuff. But they remained just out of my reach. Now all I could remember was fire, smoke, and the agony of an unfair death.

Now all that I could remember was that I was furious.

*It isn't fair.* The first clear words that formed in my consciousness. *It isn't fair. . . .*

A heavy thud against soil. The pulley stopped. The casket opened into the night. A young man grinned, silver hair brimming under the stars.

"Take her to Grunewald," he told someone behind him, before bending low, running his hand through my filthy, coiled hair. "The same as hers," he noted. "Hello, June. My name is Saul."

"Sau . . . Saul . . ." My voice was ash in my mouth. I was surprised he could even understand me. I looked at him, at his beautiful face, and for a moment I wanted to kill him. There was no reason for it. I didn't know him. I didn't have anything against him. I just wanted to kill.

I wanted to ruin.

It passed quickly, a curious rage that frightened me.

"You've suffered long enough." His sea-blue eyes sparkled as he let his hand rest on my desiccated cheek. "It's time. June . . . let's go see your sister."

# PART ONE

When shall I marry?
This year, next year, sometime, never.
What will my husband be?
Tinker, tailor, soldier, sailor, rich-man, poor-man,
beggar-man, thief.
What will I be?
Lady, baby, gypsy, queen.
What shall I wear?
Silk, satin, cotton, rags.
How shall I get it?
Given, borrowed, bought, stolen.
How shall I get to church?
Coach, carriage, wheelbarrow, cart.
Where shall I live?
—an English fortune-telling song

# 1

WHO AM I? WHERE AM I?

*Come on, girl, remember. Remember, dumb-ass . . . before it goes dark. . . .*

*Maia . . . Yes. My name . . . Maia Finley. Good. Good . . . I guess. . . .*

Lips shut against the water. No breath. Eyes stinging. The image of a rocky cliff rippling in the darkness, just above the waves of Dover Strait. I caught the reflection of the moon against the surface of the water, bright flashes in my dimming vision.

What happened? My chest was going to explode. Bubbles slipped from my lips when I moved them. The sounds of heavy, baritone, rumbling water battered my senses, cacophonic until it slipped into the recesses of my mind.

I was sinking.

Wow. It was for real this time. I was totally dying. This was me dying.

My body felt cold. It was a cliché, maybe, but still true. It had gone numb, even before breaking the surface of Dover Strait. The feeling in my arms had vanished. The water pressure's death grip on my skull . . . even that began to feel like a wistful caress.

Time was up. My life was over. But maybe it was what I deserved.

Those reckless decisions born out of fear. The secrets kept. Step by wrongful step until the steel of Belle's sword pierced through my sternum. This was the fate I'd paid for.

I was dying.

Oh well. At least I'd get to see my family again.

It went dark.

Darkness.

Darkness . . .

Then I saw that which I never could with living eyes. A mysterious white light swept through me, pulling soul from dead flesh. It surrounded me, filling me with a sensation I'd felt before. This power. The power that fed the Effigies and the existence of the phantoms. A spring that connected life and death in a continuous cycle.

A continuous cycle.

But I was not to be part of it.

My lonely white river was my own. The power of fate spirited me away on a journey just for me. I was a traveler and I was traveling.

Traveling to the next girl . . .


"So it's finally time, Maia."

Natalya Filipova. The Fire Effigy before me. A familiar panic hit me too suddenly, and for a moment I thought I'd faint. I'd been conditioned to fear this girl on sight. And why wouldn't I after the number of times she'd tried to take over my body?

But she was different now. It was her quiet, unreadable expression, devoid of the contention I was used to seeing. "You didn't last as long as I thought you would," she said.

I thought Natalya's voice would have some kind of mocking lilt to it. Like: "Ha, moron, you're dead! Look at you!" But her pale face was stone set into a somber expression.

Why would she mock me? She knew too well the pain of death.

I had to be dead, at any rate. I mean, what else could this be? I wasn't scrying. The weird thing was, I could still kind of feel it. My soul leaving my body behind to sink in the lonely strait. And yet here I was too, standing in this familiar white stream before Natalya Filipova, the once legendary hero.

"How does it feel?" she asked, genuinely curious, like maybe we'd had different experiences.

"What, death?" I thought for a moment. "It feels . . . stretchy."

Natalya tilted her head, her brown eyes narrowed. "Stretchy . . . ?"

I breathed in deeply, contemplating the odd sensation rippling through my "body," or whatever this was. "Yeah, stretchy. Like I'm being pulled in two places at once."

"It's all the same," she said in her intense voice familiarly inflected with a Russian accent. "Your life force, your consciousness, and the magic within you . . . it's all going to the same place. Searching for the next one."

"The next Fire Effigy . . . ," I whispered.

"It's only been seconds," she said. "But it'll start to feel like years. We experience time here differently. It feels slower. Much slower. You'll see."

Her expression darkened, and for a moment her gaze looked off-kilter, unfocused like one of her glass decanters sliding off an unbalanced shelf, alcohol spilling everywhere. *You'll see.* Her promise resonated like echoes in a graveyard.

I looked down at my feet shimmering beneath the waters. "And this place . . ."

"Everything is connected," Natalya said. "Life and death. Those that die tether to the life they will become. But not for us. For us, our souls don't manifest into new life. We are pulled into *existing* life. Our souls find refuge in the bodies of others. The channels of fate twisted only for us. We're bound only to each other. Like links in a chain."

Links in a chain. A dangerous game. I remembered the words but couldn't place where I'd heard them.

Natalya looked up at the endless sky. "If all life is bonded by chains of fate that lead one form to the next, then you could say this place is a manifestation of *our* chain. Every girl linked here, tucked inside the other like a matryoshka doll." She smiled. "A fitting fate for me."

Said the girl once called the Matryoshka Princess. I understood now—there were many layers to this girl, layers I never noticed as a fan. The legendary hero. The struggling alcoholic. The mentor. The vengeful spirit. Now she was the mentor again, like she had been for Belle, imparting her wisdom upon the girl whose mind she'd tried too many times to destroy.

"Where we are now is how we perceive our connection," she said, "how we see each other with eyes of the dead. Of course, we should be able to see each other when we share souls."

When I was alive, I'd have to meditate—*scry*—to get here. Natalya's tall frame guarded the magnificent red door as she always had, her hand on the hilt of her proud sword, her Zhar-Ptitsa, whose tip had disappeared into the waves at her feet. But this time, there was no fanfare, no shock or conflict. Nothing but pity and maybe a hint of disappointment—the kind my parents used to have whenever they knew I could have done better. June too. She'd given me that look more than once.

June . . . She'd smiled so prettily just before Minerva's dazzling stream of light hit the ground and obliterated her.

Minerva, the Sect's secret satellite weapon. And Rhys . . . Oh god, *Aidan*. I covered my mouth, stifling a teary gasp.

"It hurts, doesn't it, Maia?"

Too many memories came rushing back, but they were all in the wrong order. I couldn't piece them together. Why was June in Oslo? Why with Saul? What was this intense anger that drummed against my chest as I thought of Rhys's father, and the hopelessness when I thought of his son? Why was my sister gone again . . . ?

"It's hard to piece things together after dying." Natalya placed a hand atop her dark brown hair, cut closely to her head. "Memories fall to pieces, events become blurred. All this time you came to speak with me, wanting to know everything I knew, but I could only give you what I could muster in this state. Pieces and reflections. It'll become more difficult for you too soon. Perhaps you should let them go. Let it all go."

Natalya, the strongest Effigy in history, worshipped by all during her tenure. Worshipped by me too, until she began scheming to take my body. But now there was no body for her to take.

"Let it go?" I repeated. "That's funny, coming from you. *You* didn't let it go."

Natalya considered the golden hilt in her hand. "That was my decision to make. Now you have yours."

A gentle breeze grazed my cheek as I saw the red door behind me.

A door.

Mine.

As magnificent as Natalya's, with golden embroidery around the wooden edges. I guess each door was the "link" in the chain, then, opening itself into the subconscious and soul of the next girl in a path that stretched on for more than a century. A bronze doorknob waiting for my hand. When my soul found the next girl, I would walk through and stand at my station.

For eternity.

The Seven-Year Rule. That old Sect joke. Effigies were considered legendary if they could last seven years on the job. Natalya was the baddest of them all, having survived twice that. What was my number? Three months.

*What will be your number?* Ironically, it was Belle who'd asked me, three months ago.

Belle. The fear I'd usually reserved for Natalya gripped my chest in one exploding moment, an electric impulse that soon gave way to a silent, seething bitterness.

Cold steel breaking through bone. Mind-numbing pain. That moment when your heart stops—so painful in the midst of sweet release. The water crashing against my body upon impact like a speeding truck barreling into me.

I'd once stood outside a building for hours just hoping to catch a glimpse of her. My idol.

Now my murderer.

Natalya was watching me curiously. Another idol. Another disappointment. Another enemy—well, no, not an enemy anymore. Now that I was dead, she no longer had reason to harm me, though the fear I'd learned at her hands wouldn't let me trust her, wouldn't let me feel completely in control.

I stared at the door. Ruby, like blood on a blade. My beautiful gravestone bought and paid for by the combined efforts of my so-called heroes.

My *heroes*.

I'd tried to believe in them—tried to model myself after their strength, only to find myself crumbling under it.

When it came down to it, I couldn't beat either of them.

And now I was here, dead. Stuck for eternity in front of a pretty door. I was a failure. I was a failure alive and a failure dead.

June really should have been the one. She would have made a better Effigy than me.

I buckled over. Tears began to build, but Natalya was still watching me. I had to collect myself. Raising my chin, I kept up the ruse of nonchalance. It was all I had in this place. There was no point in being angry. Anger wouldn't do a damn thing for me. Not here.

"A door. Ah, that's right." My lips stretched into a smirk. "I guess this is what it means to be on the Dead Girl Squad now." I turned back around. "Wow, this effing sucks."

I wondered what death was like for regular people—where they ended up. What had it been like for June?

I could see very easily how one could go mad standing here. The worst part of it would be the loneliness, certainly. Unless the next girl came stumbling in here, in which case I doubted I'd have much to say—or maybe I'd say a bunch of confusing shit just to keep myself from being bored. Wouldn't surprise me if that had been part of Natalya's motivation.

That day I watched my family's coffins lower into the ground, I'd felt a secret solace in the notion that I might see them again in death. Instead, I was here. And I would never be able to see them again.

An image of June flashed in my mind. Her hand on the gun, pulling the trigger.

"No," I breathed. It was all barreling back. June. She was alive again. She'd been with Saul in Oslo, which he'd taken over with his gang of criminals and traffickers. June had been standing there among them. She murdered an agent. Rhys was there too, crouched in defeat, his fate sealed by his own father. I desperately held on to these memories, knowing that soon they'd shatter to pieces, leaving me with nothing but frustration, hate, and anger.

"Natalya, you were right about the corruption in the Sect. But I don't think Rhys's father knew. I think—" I remembered the dread etched into the saggy lines on Director Prince's red face as he stared at the cold blue eyes of Blackwell. "It was as if Blackwell had manipulated him into firing the Sect's satellite weapon. Like he'd meant for all of it to happen."

"And?" said Natalya.

"And!" I glared at her. Project X19. The traitorous Sect agents. Saul's plan wasn't just his plan. "This is bigger than Saul. Probably bigger than we could have ever imagined."

"A mystery for the next girl to solve, I suppose."

The crushing reality of my own helplessness made my knees buckle. "No. There's more I can do. Baldric!" The sound of the old man's name sparked something behind Natalya's steel gaze. "Baldric Haas. You remember him? One of the Council members with Rhys's mother, Naomi?" I immediately pictured the old man in his wheelchair, eyes sunken into his wrinkled face ashen with dread. "They sent you to get the volume Thomas Castor wrote in secret. The one in Prague. We went there. Naomi sent us too. We found it, but it was stolen."

By Vasily. I remembered his pale blond hair, wild around his shoulders. His wicked grin promising chaos.

"Baldric knew about the rebel faction within the Sect—and I know you met with him before you died. I scried it."

"Yes." Natalya tapped her temple. "I remember you milling around in there."

"Did he tell you anything else about what Blackwell was planning?"

"Maia, stop this."

"Stop what?" I bellowed, and I could hear my voice echoing. My fists were tight. "This is your mystery too! You were trying to solve this before I even stepped into the picture."

"I was trying to be something more," Natalya said quietly.

"More than what?"

Natalya's head turned slightly, her eyes downcast. "More than an empty shell." I waited for her to elaborate, but she wouldn't, not at first. She only shook her head, looking at me almost as if she pitied me. Somehow, the pity was more infuriating than whatever malice I'd seen whenever I'd come here alive. "It won't do you any good to know these secrets now. Believe me. I was like you too when I first died. No, even before. Desperate to know. After seeing Baldric, I scried to find Marian, thinking that if I could only reach her, she'd tell me everything I needed to know. I scried longer and harder than I ever had, to the point of madness. The chain—our chain—became blurred. All the doors opened at once. Memories assaulted me every which way. And in the end, what I found . . ." She shuddered. "Marian's death. And riddles. Teachings—Emilia's teachings. Her words, her symbols. Where it all began. It was too much, but I thought I could handle it. I thought I could bring all the pieces together, but it wasn't to be. I died. No—" Her gaze darkened. "I was killed."

The accusing tone was meant for me. It was I who'd protected her murderer, Aidan Rhys, even after I'd discovered what he'd done to her on the Sect's orders. We'd both paid with our lives, but that wasn't enough for Natalya. Her anger still quietly hummed.

"And now that I'm dead, the world continues as if my life never mattered. And I stand here for an eternity, Maia, unable to affect it, except through you. But now you're dead too."

My hands tingled from restlessness. My soul was still traveling. I could feel it.

"And so, what will it accomplish now if you knew the secrets of the world, Maia?" Natalya continued. "What can you affect from this place that has become our grave? There's nothing that can be done from here. Nothing."

I looked from Natalya's door to mine, silently calling me. There was nothing I could do from here in this prison. Nothing I could accomplish but to stand here, waiting for some stranger to show up so I could give her a few cryptic warnings based on faded memories.

"No, there has to be more I can do. . . ." I had to reach the others. Uncle Nathan and Sibyl, quietly working against the evil faction of the Sect in the shadows. Lake and Chae Rin, who'd driven off to meet them. I had to help somehow. I had to get back into the trenches.

"You could let it go," Natalya said again, thinking it over. "Or you could make the decision that I made."

She smirked, sharp eyes glinting maliciously. She didn't have to elaborate.

I glared at her. "No."

"I supposed it wouldn't be impossible for me to steal her body if she finds her way through your door to me. It wouldn't be impossible for me, but the consciousness of the one who died last is always stronger. You could—"

"I said no."

Silence charged with an intense hatred followed. Hatred and fear. Both mine.

"It would be easier to do it yourself, wouldn't it?" Letting her sword drag behind her, she walked closer to me, step by deliberate step. "Rather than trying to lead another frightened ingenue to the answers you couldn't find alive. Just pick up where you left off." The sword made no sound as it traced a line in the shallow waters behind her. "Wearing new flesh. It's what I would do. And I would do it again."

"Stop," I blurted out before she could come any closer. I had to remind myself that she wasn't a danger to me anymore. I was already dead. She couldn't hurt me if she had no use for me. As long as I was dead, I was safe. How ironic. I looked at the Effigy whose trading cards I used to collect. "God, I used to *admire* you. Don't you feel sorry for what you did to me? Don't you feel sorry for *any* of it?"

I was dead now, so I might as well take the opportunity to give her a piece of my mind. Ignoring the fear still bleeding into my flesh, I squeezed my hands into fists. "You made my last few months alive hell when you should have been helping me like I figured you *wanted* to be helped. My sister and I thought you were *everything*. We wanted to *be* you."

Though June was more like her than I ever was or could be. Noble, confident. Maybe that was why I'd idolized my sister too. Nobility was June's last act. I could still remember her chiding me. Telling me to do better. And I tried, June. I really tried. But that kind of strength was a hard skill to master. Effigy fans online always dragged me for it: "Why can't she just be the unflappably perfect bad-ass action-chick we *demand* her to be?" But that took courage. Even now my courage was shaking before Natalya. She must have known it too. But I just kept talking.

"I thought I could be stronger if I could act like you, Natalya. I thought if I got everyone to respect me like they did you, then I wouldn't have to feel so . . ."

I remembered those days I shut myself in my room and blocked out the world while June was out living life. That dreaded feeling of being left behind. Of standing still while others were running forward.

"So useless," I finished, biting my lip. "So pathetic."

"And how have you changed, Maia?" Natalya lifted her sword, studying her reflection in its familiar steel. "Or have you changed?"

Changed. Had I really?

I looked up at the never-ending white stretching upward and thought of flames burning. Burning down my house. Burning New York's La Charte Hotel, where Saul had attacked with his phantom-controlling ring. Burning the elevator that took a screaming woman I'd failed to save. Burning Oslo after Minerva's light obliterated my sister and the boy of my dreams and nightmares. I was still scared. I was still looking at this dead Effigy with fearful eyes. I was still looking to her for answers, for validation. Had I changed?

"I *will* change," I whispered, tears stinging my eyes. "I swear, I'll change."

"Nothing changes here," Natalya said flatly. She closed her eyes. "Change is only for the living."

"No. I will change." I stumbled back. "I *will* change. I just need a second chance."

Something desperate in me stirred. I couldn't stand still. A terrible truth began breathing fire. I wasn't satisfied. I wasn't ready. There was more to do, more to fix.

And Natalya . . . Natalya, who opened her eyes again, was smirking as she watched me squirm because she knew that what I was experiencing was the very thing that had driven her mad in here. I didn't care. There were too many mistakes to atone for. I couldn't be done. But my soul, my consciousness, and my power were on the move.

Panicked, I turned, facing the door. "No. *No.* Somebody has to give me a second chance."

"There's something I should tell you," Natalya said. "Now that you're here."

Ignoring her, I sloshed through the stream, pounding on the wood of my magnificent red door because it was the only exit I could see in this expanse of nothingness. "Please, you have to let me out. I can't be here!"

"You may have been disgusted with me in the past," Natalya told me. "But soon you'll come to understand me. The longer you're here, the more the silence drives you mad."

Links in a chain. The Effigies' fate was a fate worse than death.

"No." I stepped away from the door, looking everywhere that this prison with no bars would allow me. "No, no . . ."

"Eventually, you'll start to consider things you never would have in life. You'll start making exceptions to every rule you'd lived by . . . until the next one comes knocking on your door. This is our reward after living, fighting, and dying to protect humanity. The price of a twisted fate."

An ugliness had seeped into her beauty, her small features sharpening like the stretch of her blade. I saw it reflected there, reflected in the white stream. I saw my reflection too.

"You and I are the same now, Maia. Not heroes. Not even monsters," she said. "Simply shadows."

But it was not to be so.

Something was stirring in the land of the living. A silent force tugged at my soul, pulling it back.

Back toward my body.

Natalya, the door, the endless blank space—it was fading. Or maybe I was the one disappearing. I was being called back.

A second chance.

A surge of ecstasy stung my eyes like tears. A second chance. And I wouldn't screw it up this time. Though my vision blurred, I could see Natalya's features screwed up in fury.

"It isn't fair. . . ." Natalya'd whispered it. But before I faded, her face had calmed. And before disappeared, I could hear her whisper. "I told you I would do it again if I had the choice. And now I have that choice. You *will* see me again soon."

Her murderous promise receded until it was nothing more than a silenced echo. And I could still hear the last of its murmur as I shuddered alive with breath.

# 2

"LOOKS LIKE SHE'S BACK, DAD! THE MOUTH-TO-mouth worked!"

"Good, son. Get her onto the deck. Keep the pressure on her chest. We need to take this girl to a hospital."

I hacked all of the water in my lungs out onto the sand. An unspeakable pain shot from my chest. Coughing, I struggled to move my hand to the open gash in my chest oozing blood.

"My god." The young man who'd spoken first sounded English, like his dad. My eyelids were still shut from exhaustion, beads of water dripping through my lashes. "She can still move a little bit."

Air passed through my lungs once again. And though Natalya's grimace persisted like a shadow in my thoughts, I couldn't remember much else from my time as a carcass.

What did come back was the time I was missing. I'd just escaped the London facility with the other Effigies. After Director Prince of the North American Division made the blunder of firing Minerva on Oslo, we'd had to flee. Sibyl had arranged for our escape, and so we'd split up: Chae Rin and Lake in one van. Belle and me in another. The two of us were to meet up with a ship that would take us into France.

The boy and his father must be part of the crew. They'd come after all. Thank god . . .

The father's voice wheezed a little as he exhaled. "She can move? That's impossible. Her body's broken. Probably has a concussion. And this knife wound in her chest—"

"It missed her heart, Dad. I think she still has a chance if we can get her to the hospital in time—wait a minute." I felt a hot, large hand brushing the wet curls away from my face. "Bloody hell, Dad . . . This . . . this is an *Effigy*. She's *that* Effigy, isn't she?"

"What?"

"I recognize her. She's an Effigy."

"An Effigy . . . ?"

"The video's going around online. She was in that terror attack in Norway."

And I could feel the pressure of the two of them leaning over me. Something wasn't right. If they were Sibyl's men, they'd already know who I was.

"I see," the father finally said. "My hunch was right. So this was the cargo. . . ."

"Cargo . . . ?" The son sounded bewildered. "Dad, what do you mean by—"

"Si-Sibyl . . ."

The sound of my hoarse voice had clearly spooked the young man.

"W-what?" he said in a high, agitated pitch. "Who?"

"Take . . . me . . ." I didn't know what was happening or how to make sense of it. But I knew where I had to go. "Take . . ." I tried again, but it hurt too much to push out the air from my lungs.

There was a dog barking in the distance. Short, staccato, impatient.

"Dad, we have to turn her in. The police are looking for her."

"She needs a hospital—"

"Screw the hospital. She's a terrorist!" The son sounded more fearful than malicious. His weight shifted in the sand as he stood on his feet. "If she really is an Effigy, she'll be fine, right? Don't they heal really quickly? We can't wait around for that to happen. What if she attacks us? I saw on the news the police are raiding that Sect building. We need to turn her in. Maybe they'll even give us a reward!"

The old man took a second to think. "No," he said finally. "What happened in Oslo is recent. She can't be in two places at once. On top of that, the place was nearly destroyed. How did she escape all that and turn up here?"

His son had no answer.

"What's more," the father continued, "is that the Effigies aren't evil. They wouldn't work for a terrorist, least of all for the one they've been trying to catch for months. Something's not clean in the milk. Come on, Harry. We're taking her with us."

"So you can what? Investigate?" Harry scoffed. "Thought you didn't work for them anymore, Dad. You're *retired*."

"Harry . . . I didn't tell you this before we left. But there's another reason we crossed the strait."

"Dad . . . did you . . . ?" Harry paused, choosing his words carefully. "Did you know we'd find her here?"

"I need to know why she's in a place like this," the man said. "And I'm not going to get answers by giving her over to some bloody mob in uniform. Now, enough talking. Help me get her onto the boat."

Soon I was being lifted off the cool sand with no control over my dangling limbs. The shift of gravity and the sudden rush of pain knocked the senses from me.

*Whoever you are,* I begged, *just take me to Sibyl and Uncle Nathan. . . . I need to . . .*

After another second I fell unconscious again.

Waves crashed against the little boat. My broken body rocked back and forth on hard wood, consciousness slipping in and out. Harry and his father were whispering conspiratorially. About me. I couldn't make out what they were saying. My eyes remained shut.

Sloshing, sloshing. Slippery against my skin. A sticking smell. God, what was that? Smelled salty. Fishy.

Fish. I could feel their flopping against the left side of my body through the netting. I was just as much cargo. Where were those men taking me?

Effigy healing or not, it was still a struggle to breathe. My shirt was off, so that explained the light chill. One of them had placed a sterile gauze onto the stab wound and fastened it with a bandage under my bra. I was too relieved to be alive to feel embarrassed.

My consciousness was as volatile as the waves. A panting, barking dog brushed up against my leg, its little bell jingling as it trotted up to my face for a lick.

"Vader, get back here," the boy scolded.

The dog obeyed. Its saliva dripped down my cheek from where he'd licked my hair, just above the ear. I slipped out of consciousness again until the aggressive moans of a bullhorn jolted me awake, hot red lights washing over my closed eyelids.

"Dad, is it the coast guard?"

"Harry," said his father with urgency, "get my ID. And cover the girl."

"But—"

"Do it."

*Clomp, clomp* went Harry's boots against the wooden floor. "If you can hear me," he said, leaning in close, "now would be a good time to hold your breath, yeah?"

Before I could figure out what was happening, a rough burlap carpet fell onto my body with a particularly unceremonious *thwap* against my face. He dragged the net of fish over my body, mercifully leaving my head free. I get that being an Effigy made me more durable than a regular girl, but this dude was manhandling me as if I were nothing more than a broken action figure. Needless to say, Harry was far from a gentleman.

*I'm still wounded, you idiot!* That was what I wanted to say, but I'd fallen unconscious again from the sudden shock of pain. I slipped back into consciousness long enough to hear an exchange.

"What else do you need?" said Harry's father. "As I've already shown you, we're a licensed fishing vessel taking our cargo into France. You've already seen the cargo for yourself."

"Sorry, sir. We've been extra cautious tonight." I had to concentrate to hear the second man's voice through the wet sloshing of smelly fish. "There've been smugglers illegally crossing the strait, using anti-phantom technology to pass through unofficial routes from the North Sea. Not to mention there's also the Sect we're looking out for."

My fingers twitched.

"The Sect?" Harry repeated, and I swore I felt him staring at me.

"Not too long ago, an agent turned himself in to the police department in Dunkirk. Said he was part of a crew of Sect rogues planning to make their way to Dover from around the English Channel. They were supposed to rendezvous with some fugitives."

"And by fugitives," Harry said, "you mean—"

"The Effigies, of course."

A chill ran through the dull, throbbing pain in my body. Fugitives. We were fugitives. Luckily nobody could have noticed me squirm while I was buried in fish, but Vader made his way toward me, rummaging through the net, looking, maybe, for another slurp of my hair.

"So it's true that they're wanted?" Harry's voice was low. "The rogue agent turned himself in. What happened to the other agents?"

"Police picked them up after he told us where their hideout was," said the coastguard. "They never left the city. You've seen the news. Oslo. Those Sect rogues are out of control and so are the Effigies. We have to do what we can. There's more out there, I've no doubt."

I carefully swallowed the sweet, tangy saliva sticking to the roof of my mouth. Fugitives. My heart jerked along with the fish pounding against the wound in my chest. How many police officers and coastguards out there were actively trying to sniff us out?

Belle was probably long gone by now. Fled the murder scene. But what about the others? Lake and Chae Rin. What if they'd been caught? How did I even know they were still alive?

Belle. Lake. Chae Rin. Rhys. June. Alive. Dead. Oslo. The murder of Rhys by his own father. Saul's attack. June's obliteration. Belle's betrayal. It was too much. A sob choked somewhere deep in my throat. My thoughts flew everywhere at once. It was too hard to concentrate, too hard to breathe. The ship went on its way, but by the time the fish, the net, and the burlap slid off my body and my face once again kissed the clean air, I'd fallen unconscious once more.

# 3

THE SMELL OF FISH FRYING IN OIL SEDUCED ME
back into consciousness. Groaning, I pressed a hand against my throbbing head.

My hand. I could move it! I stared at it in awe, at my knees buckling
as I dragged them up to my chest. There was a weird dark bruise on my
arm. Everything was still sore, but I could move all the same.

I sat up in a bed. It was nothing fancy: clean white sheets, flat pillow. The mattress springs just barely had a little bit of life in them. The
window was closed to the darkening skies, and through the trees—and
there was *nothing* outside but trees—I just made out the sinking sun
streaking the atmosphere orange and red.

The small room had only a simple wooden desk and a chair to my
right, a pad of paper next to a desk lamp. Everything here was made
of evergreen or maybe cedar. Cozy as a camp. Except for the ominous
hoots outside, and the howls, and the cicadas chirping in the night.

Slipping my hand underneath my shirt, I traced a line across the
fresh bandages. A scar had definitely formed. The raised, hardened
scab tinged with pain as I pressed my palm against it. Had Belle

missed by accident, her brain too addled to make the death blow? Or had she simply chickened out of taking my life?

Once again my bitterness stung. The fangirl in me, the one who'd waited outside Lincoln Center just to catch a glimpse of her hero, still tried to make excuses. Belle had been tortured, the fangirl would say. Belle was an abused orphan. Natalya was her only friend, her mentor. Like family. She'd wanted answers so desperately, but once I found out that it was Rhys who'd killed Natalya, I kept it from her. She'd had every right to be pissed.

But did she have the right to *kill* me?

First Natalya. Then Belle. I'd already learned the hard way not to deify them. But during those shining days, as the four of us traveled across the world, searching for answers, I'd thought we'd all become greater than just the magic that bound us. We'd become one. The Effigies. A team. Friends. Maybe even family.

That was all shattered now.

If only I'd told her the truth from the beginning. I'd had so many chances. So many times when the words were on the tip of my tongue. But once again I was too scared. She was a monster for killing me, but she was a monster I created.

I shattered the team. I shattered it with my indecision. With my cowardice. Belle pulled the trigger of a gun that I placed in her hands and aimed at my own head.

Just another failure on my part. One that, for a time, had cost me my life.

A powerful ambivalence pulled me to the opposite extremes of anger—anger directed outward and inward. I stared at my sheets in silence until the sound of a dog barking outside snapped me back to reality. Vader?

*Okay, calm down, Maia,* I told myself. *First you need to figure out where you are—and who's been changing your bandages.*

Gingerly, I got out of bed, stepping across the wooden floor with swollen, bare feet. A stubborn pain needled my left hip, so I held on to it as I opened the door.

"Whoa!" Harry almost fell over the couch in the living room I'd just entered. His laptop crashed to the ground. Grabbing the back of the couch, he watched me shut the door to my room. It'd been a while since I'd seen someone truly terrified of me.

He was older than I originally assumed. Older than me, but probably not by much. Blond hair, shaved close to his skull, faded at the sides. A light golden beard was forming around his angular, flushed chin. He was scrawny, almost malnourished, but his arms were long, so I could tell he was tall even as he peered at me from behind his couch as the television blared in the background.

He stared at me for another second. "Dad," he yelled finally, "she's awake."

His words were directed at the old man cooking in the tiny kitchen quartered off from the living room by a pair of swinging half doors. The father turned off the heat on the stove, set down his spatula, and began toward me.

Looking at him in the kitchen reminded me of Uncle Nathan, though where Uncle Nathan was the long, gangly limbed type like Harry, this man was short and brawny, with wide-set shoulders draped by flannel. Uncle Nathan would have worn one of his goofy aprons too. I missed it. I missed him.

"Are you okay?" He must have noticed my body suddenly droop. He was blond like his son, though his hair was longer, more disheveled, his beard fully grown but unruly. His shirt was only half tucked in to his gray trousers while Harry had everything in order. I would have thought it'd be the opposite.

"I'm all right." The words were hesitant, a little painful, but clear. "Thank you, sir."

"Please, it's Harvey. Harvey Dawson."

I rubbed my neck. "Mr. Dawson . . ."

From outside the cabin, Vader's excited barking interrupted the silence stretching between us.

"You Effigies really do heal fast." Dawson casually pointed at my chest with a finger. My hand instinctively touched the bandages. "The way we found you in the strait, broken and bloodied, a normal girl would have been dead before we could do CPR."

"You saved my life." I looked over at Harry, who gave a skittish shift on the couch. "Thank you."

"Are you hungry?" Dawson waved me over to the kitchen. "Got some long-grain white rice and fish. Some string beans too."

Harry wouldn't look at me. He shrank back into his seat wordlessly as Mr. Dawson prompted me to follow him. He gave me a plate and the food was ready for eating. Smelled good. I still had no clue who these people were beyond their names, but if they wanted to turn me in, they could have. If they wanted to kill me, they could have. I sat down at the little table up against the wall—wood, all wood, yet again—and began eating. I had no idea how hungry I was until I tasted the fish, and then suddenly I was stuffing my face.

"Well, your appetite's back." Dawson swiveled the chair around so the back rested against the table and sat next to me. "That's good."

"Who are you?" I asked after forcing a mush of beans down my throat.

He smirked. "Pleasantries aren't your style, then."

"Where am I?" I dropped the fork onto the plate and wiped my mouth. "Thank you for the food, but where am I?"

"Just my cabin—our cabin." He nodded his head toward the living room where I knew his son was watching television. "Cabin in the forest near Calais. We stay here during the summer months."

"You fish?" I stared at the bones on my plate, picked clean by my greed.

"Luckily for you, yes."

Ironically, it was a fishing ship that was supposed to take me to France anyhow. But those Sect agents were all in jail. There was no way to get to where Sibyl and Uncle Nathan were if I didn't know *where* they were or how to reach them.

Well, first things first.

"What day is it?" I asked him.

"Thursday."

"Thursday . . ." I didn't even know what that meant, or if it was important.

"You've been out cold for five days, if that helps."

Five days? Well, with my injuries, that wasn't too hard to imagine. I stretched out my neck, swallowing the last bit of food in my mouth. Then I lifted my arms above my head, satisfied with the crack in my joints. *Oof.* My shirt stank, though. I dropped my arms quickly and gave a self-conscious look toward Dawson, who was too interested in his mug of coffee to care. How long had it been since I'd taken a shower?

I started to map it all out in my head. There was the awards show in Toronto. Then we went to Spain to meet Naomi.

I breathed in sharply. Naomi. I could see in my mind's eye the bullets flying through the window of Natalya's apartment, piercing her body. She could be dead for all I knew.

The more I thought, the more I realized just how much had happened. Going to Prague, losing Castor's volume, getting locked up in the London facility. This shirt had been through a hell of a lot, all things considered, and the funky stench was clearly its reward.

At least I was alive.

Dawson dropped his coffee mug back onto the table. "Now, I should let you know before this goes on that while I'm glad you're finally back with us, I didn't exactly save you just out of the goodness of my heart."

My eyes narrowed. "What's that supposed to mean?"

Mug in hand, Dawson stood and left the kitchen, beckoning me to follow. While the television played a French sitcom, Harry streamed the BBC news on his laptop, which he'd set up on the glass surface of the living room table.

SECT HACKERS ARRESTED FOR FRANKFURT APD DISRUPTION

Black letters printed across a red and white band at the bottom of the screen with the white flashing *Breaking News!* just next to it.

Hackers. I made my way to the couch in a daze, barely paying attention to Harry as he slid to the armrest so he could get away from me.

"George, I'm standing outside an abandoned building in Frankfurt where a police raid took place moments ago." The reporter swept his large hand toward the dirty red bricks, the winds battling with his clothes and microphone. "Four agents from the Frankfurt Sect facility were found hiding here in an attempt to evade officials. Now, as our viewers know, over the months, many antiphantom devices around the world have malfunctioned, causing large-scale destruction at the hands of the terrorist Saul and the phantoms under his control."

"But, Steven," said George, a tan-skinned news anchor with white patches of hair around the sides of his bald head, "have they been able to apprehend Saul?"

My fingers curled around the couch. I remembered Saul, his pale silver hair draped down his high cheekbones, his grin deep in wickedness as he brought forth my sister and announced her as a cold-blooded murderer in front of the world. I would never get out of my mind the sight of her empty gaze as she shot a Sect agent.

How had he brought her back? With the ring? The stone that controlled phantoms . . . that granted wishes . . .

"George, he and his associates haven't been seen since the disaster in Oslo that left a section of the city in ruins," said the reporter. "Authorities in Norway are assuming that everyone in the area had been killed by the blast from the Sect's satellite weapon."

It was almost bewildering how powerful the chilling effect of a single word could be.

"Killed."

Rhys. June.

The word was a gut punch. I pressed my lips against the moan building in me.

"In the meantime, one of the agents, after being apprehended by police, confessed that they, like others around the world, had been involved in aiding in Saul's terrorism efforts. While we won't know the details for certain until the German authorities have finished interviewing the offenders, George, this is a shocking development nonetheless."

We'd already assumed that the faction in the Sect responsible for freeing Saul from the London facility had also helped his attacks on all those cities. Freeing Vasily, ambushing us in the tunnels to steal back the ring. All of it led to the destruction in Oslo. But to what end?

"George, this is just one major arrest in a long string that have taken place all over the world during the last few days based on information given by rogue Sect agents currently in custody."

"Just how many are in custody?" I asked Dawson as he sat in the rocking chair near the window.

"Too many to count." He sipped his coffee, staring into its contents after setting it back down against his knobby knees. "It started with the directors of the European and North American Divisions. Director Prince and his son."

Brendan? My mouth parted in surprise. Last I'd seen him, he was in the London facility with the rest of us, watching helplessly as Prince fired Minerva. But even though he hadn't been able to stop his father from giving the fatal order, he'd tried to stop him. He'd tried to save his little brother.

"A friend of mine went down too, the night I found you. It's been a bloody witch hunt these past few days. Sect agents are being trapped like animals, thrown into cages, interrogated—not all of them, mind. Some Sect agents are even leading the charge—that is, after being cleared of any involvement."

Agent versus agent. Hopefully it wasn't the bloodbath it sounded like.

"Sect agents are brothers and sisters in arms. It takes a lot to turn one against the other." And he became very quiet. "Loyalty, for one." Dawson's pale green eyes shimmered from behind a curtain of rising steam as he gripped his mug tighter. "At any rate, Harry's been glued to the livestream these past few days, giving me updates."

Harry gave me a quick glance but remained silent. It wasn't long before a frenzied musical cue signaled yet another breaking news story flashing across the screen.

"We're interrupting that report—Deidra Kyle, our senior political correspondent, is joining us at the London facility. Deidra, what are you learning?"

Deidra stood beyond the second set of iron gates that blocked off the facility from the rest of Epping Forest. When the camera panned out, I could see the host of reporters there with her, speaking into their cameras in their own languages, stalling, perhaps, as they waited a few meters from an empty podium just beyond of the main building. The front doors of this wing were still totaled, courtesy of the car we'd driven through it. It was sealed off by some translucent construction sheets.

"George, we're being told that Senator Abrams of British Columbia resigned from the Senate of Canada this morning over his involvement in the Oslo disaster. In his resignation letter, he confessed to the ethics committee that as a secret member of the Sect's High Council, he unilaterally gave Director Prince permission to fire the Sect's weapon, which thus far has claimed fifty-three lives."

"Fifty-three," I whispered. A flash of light and a number didn't quite bring home the gravity of the devastation.

"It would have been more if not for the evacuation, but there were stragglers, agents, people who couldn't leave, people who weren't found in time," Dawson said. "Prince must have weighed his options and decided the loss was acceptable."

Including his own son. Including my twin sister. Lake, Chae Rin, Belle, and I were in that room. We could have stopped it. *I* could have stopped it.

"Of course, this is coming on the heels of new revelations about the Sect's involvement in Saul's terrorist activities. George, we're assuming these are just a few of the urgent matters Council representative Bartholomäus Blackwell promised to speak about in the press conference he'll be holding in ten minutes."

"All right, Deidra, we'll stay tuned."

Blackwell. My throat closed at the name. It was Blackwell who'd manipulated Abrams and Prince into firing on Oslo. What was he planning?

"They're dropping like flies," Dawson continued as Harry lowered the volume. "It's total chaos. And you, Maia Finley. You seem to be at the center of this firestorm."

Without looking up, Harry pushed the corner of his laptop to the side so I could see a grainy satellite image of my face on the news. My face . . . No, *June's* face. We were twins, but there were slight imperceptible differences that others could never notice, not even our parents. She had the same tanned skin, but her unruly curls of brown hair were always lighter than my own. And her jaw was a little narrower. Her frame overall was a touch thinner than mine.

"What were you doing there, anyway?" Harry finally spoke to me, his fingers curled around the back of the couch. "You really a damn *terrorist?*"

"No."

"That's complete bollocks!" His voice was louder than his dog's endless barking behind the log walls. "You were there with Saul. We all saw you. What do you take us for?"

How could I possibly explain it to him? No, it wasn't me, it was my dead twin who was alive and evil and is now back to being dead? The very act of trying to wrap my head around the thought made my brain feel as if it were caving in.

"Tell us the truth! There's footage of you shooting a bloke in the head!"

"Harry—" Mr. Dawson warned.

"It's true, Dad." He was on his feet now. I was right. He was tall. "You heard the coast guard—they're looking for her. For all of them. If one Effigy's a terrorist, you can't exactly rule out the others, can you?"

"I didn't do anything wrong. *I didn't do anything wrong,*" I repeated more forcefully. "The girl you saw wasn't me. It was someone who *looks* like me. But it *wasn't me.*"

"Oh, please!"

"Oh, come on! You don't think there could be a girl who looks like me out there? Probably a dozen guys out there who look like *your* dumb ass!"

Harry was breathing fire hotter than I could conjure. "Watch your bloody mouth! I saved your life!"

"I'm *telling* you that wasn't me. Believe me, there's all sorts of sci-fi bizarre shit happening that you couldn't possibly dream of. But I didn't kill *anyone*."

"Is that true?" Dawson's voice was steady and quiet. Somehow it frightened me more than his son's outbursts. I stood up straight, as if I were in the principal's office.

"It's hard to explain, sir, but I swear that wasn't me."

"Harry, even if it was her in that video," Dawson said, "how could she have survived the blast? There's nothing left of that area. Officials have been analyzing human ashes for five days, trying to identify the victims."

Human ash. I kept myself steady by holding on to the couch, trying to block out the plodding shudder up my body.

"Harry," Dawson said, "bring in the dog, would you? He's been barking for a bit now. And while you're out there, maybe take some time to cool your head a bit."

Harry readied a protest before thinking better of it and, with a frustrated sigh, stomped outside. Vader barked excitedly at the sight of his owner, his panting soon receding into the woods, along with Harry.

Dawson waited for the door to close. "If you were there, how did you escape? And how did you end up in the Dover Strait so soon after? I may not know all the answers," he said. "But what I do know is that for as long as we've been standing here, you could have killed us. And you haven't."

My legs felt too light and my torso too heavy. "I would never do that," I said. "Never. I don't want to hurt anyone. I just wanted to *help* people. That's all I ever wanted to do."

"I believe you," Dawson said, after a pause. "I've seen it. I was there in France that day. I was on that train."

My head jerked up. Saul's phantom assault on our train months ago. "I don't remember seeing you."

"We weren't in the same car. We were spared the phantom onslaught, mostly. But I remember the stench of fear." He closed his eyes. "The bodies spilling out of the windows like tumbleweed falling into the jaws of that . . . *creature* at the foot of the mountain. The phantoms petrifying around us. I thought the bloody walls would cave in when they wrapped around our car." He shook a little as he recalled it, snapping his eyes open again as if fearful of what else he might see behind the lids. "And all the while I couldn't do a damn thing. You and your friends—you're the reason I got back home to my son that night. So if you say you're not a terrorist, then I believe you. Tell me what happened and I'll believe that, too."

I looked at him, the trenches dug deep into his forehead as he raised his eyebrows.

"It's why I rescued you in the first place. Why I risked you coming here. Depending on what you tell me, I may decide to take my son's advice and turn you in."

"Who are you?" I studied him through narrow eyes. "Don't tell me you just fish."

He cleared his throat, sinking deeper into his rocking chair. "Right now I'm nothing more than a fisherman," he said. I opened my mouth to argue, but he cut me off. "But I *used* to be a Sect agent. I worked under Director Arthur Prince when I was stationed in Pennsylvania. And Director Bradshaw when I came back to London. I was gone before Langley took over. I've been out seven years and haven't carried a weapon since. Well"—he paused—"that's not entirely true. I have a few cases in the basement. Decided I couldn't be too careful when Saul was out there."

"Old habits die hard."

"Lucky for you." He pointed at my bandages. "If I hadn't injected you with that inoculation weapon, there'd be Sect agents swarming this place by now."

The bruise in my arm. He was right. I'd completely forgotten. We Effigies could be tracked by the frequency our magic gave off. Dawson really had saved my ass. Then again, with a man as vigilant as Dawson, I was sure the inoculation was double insurance to block off my powers in case I really was a rogue Effigy. Smart man.

"Like I said, hyper-preparedness. Saul was destroying cities. I still have connections with some people in the agency who dropped off a few things. But despite that, I live the civilian life now. A few decades on the job was enough."

And it definitely had not been a desk job, judging from the faded scars on the parts of his arm not covered in flannel. He had that worn look I'd expect out of a man who'd seen plenty of blood.

"Let me get this straight," I said. "You're a former Sect agent who just happened to be fishing in the same strait I died in?"

Dawson smirked at the hint of disbelief in my tone. "That friend I told you about. The agent who was arrested?"

"Yeah?"

"That night I found you, the man calls me out of nowhere asking to use one of my fishing boats. Didn't tell me why. Said it was a secret operation. I wouldn't give him anything unless he gave me a better reason than blind trust, even if we've been friends for ages. So he told me a little more: He was going to the cliffs with a team. Said he had to pick up some important cargo. Said he was risking his neck for it."

"Important cargo . . ." My back straightened as I realized. "Me."

"The group of agents, according to that coastguard, were supposed to rendezvous with you. We set up a time for them to pick up my boat, and when he and his team never showed, I knew something was wrong. I was going to take my boat out anyway the next morning, travel a little farther down the channel. Instead, I traveled to the cliffs in his place to see for myself what was worth the risk."

But Sibyl's team were in jail now. Redman, the man who'd driven us to the cliffs, may have been in jail too. Unless Belle did something to him.

Did something. Like kill.

Redman was knocked out when Belle attacked me. She wouldn't have needed to kill him, but who knew what she was capable of anymore. I sure as hell didn't.

If Redman was in jail, he'd be one of many agents. Dawson didn't look too pleased about his friend being in jail, but as he continued to tell me, there wasn't much he could do. Being retired didn't mean the police wouldn't question him or suspect him if he gave them a reason to—a reason like announcing to everyone that he was cozy with a "suspected terrorist." It was a dangerous thing to admit during a witch hunt.

"So what happened with you?" I sat down. "What turns a Sect agent into a kindly old fisherman?"

"Perhaps I'd seen too many of my friends die. But we all took the risk because we believed in the Sect and what it stood for. The Sect has always had rebels. Like in any organization, there will be those on the fringes, rejected or disillusioned, hurt by the very institution they'd dedicated themselves to. Those who resent the top brass of authority, the directors, the Council. Even, sometimes, the Effigies."

That didn't surprise me. Plenty of people liked to scapegoat the Effigies for various things. Something about girls with powers seemed to tick some people off.

"But what's happening now is beyond anything I've ever seen," Dawson said. "Leaks, hackers. Incarcerated agents." He sucked in a breath, steadying both his hands. "It's as if all the rogues came together to stage a coup. They're being arrested, yes, with other agents leading the charge in putting them away. But one part of me wonders if all those boots aren't just marching on the same road leading to the same destination. I don't know why—"

"Blackwell," I whispered, walking around the couch, my eyes glued on the thick black curls on the laptop screen that draped down the neck and broad shoulders of the Council's representative. The man who usually spared no expense in his appearance this time wore muted attire. His tailored suit was gray and simple, devoid of any adornments like broaches or pins. There was no silver Rolex hanging on his thick wrist, no silver rings fitted around his long fingers. He stood at the podium in front of the main building—the same pulpit he'd sabotaged us from just weeks ago.

I turned up the volume.

"—and the arrests that have been made recently under my supervision have made clear that the ongoing matters of the Sect cannot continue as they have. For the security and safety of people around the world, a major restructuring must take place."

He looked serious. He looked like a different Blackwell from the one who'd watched the London police swarm Communications and hold everyone inside at gunpoint at his command just moments after Director Prince had fired his weapon.

A different Blackwell? Yeah, right. Everything about this was a performance, no less so than the two times he'd taken a microphone to tell the world that the Sect and the Effigies had failed to capture Saul.

He took a question from a bespectacled journalist standing in the front. "A reorganizing of the Sect has been proposed before, particularly by those who've been fearful of the Sect's operating ability and firepower. Now that those fears have been realized, do you really think what you're proposing would be enough to ward off any future threats?"

Blackwell sighed, deep and heavy. It was the imperceptible hint of whimsy, like from a performer musing at the rapt attention of his audience, that confirmed my suspicions. He was enjoying this. Anyone who didn't know him, who didn't know what he was *really* capable of, wouldn't have caught it.

"Yes, many have feared that the Sect's far-reaching might would become the basis for their transition into an imperial power. Rest assured, many of us have seen the warning signs and are committed to attacking this problem from the root. That's why I have been working tirelessly on a proposal that I aim to submit to the United Nations soon. This proposal outlines a global project that would reorganize the resources of the Sect while placing its functions under international sovereign jurisdiction. It will be a system that handles the dangers of the phantoms without adding on the dangers of a corrupt institution or an untrustworthy and uncontrollable fighting force such as the Effigies. I've been writing this proposal with the blessing of the remaining members of the High Council. In two weeks a special three-day Assembly will be held in New York to discuss how to move forward. At the Assembly, the project will be unveiled to the public. The aim is to get a vote by the end of the three-day period. However—"

He squared his broad shoulders, straightening his back as he peered into the cameras with dark eyes. "When I became the representative of the Sect's Council, I took a solemn oath to use every resource I had to safeguard humanity against the threats that have plagued us for a century. I have regarded and continue to regard this promise as seriously as my own life."

What a joke. His useless position was inherited from his father, like all the Blackwells since the Sect began. Ceremonious and largely pointless, as Director Prince had once taunted him. But this was a man who believed in his own importance. I could see it in the breadth of his chest as he spoke in his low, baritone voice. His confidence in his own right to speak was the one part of this press conference that didn't feel fraudulent.

"And those of us still committed to the Sect's original aim of justice and peace can no longer turn a blind eye as those aims corrode from the inside. I am committed to putting the world first. Even if that means making a world without the Sect and the Effigies. Thank you."

Blackwell's penny loafers clicked on the pavement, taking him away from the crowd. A world where the Sect was obsolete. How had Dawson put it? Agent versus agent . . . boots marching on the same road leading to the same destination.

"The destruction of the Sect," I whispered.

And of us.

# 4

AN OBSOLETE SECT. IT'S WHAT VASILY HAD promised in Prague. Why he and so many others had joined hands with Saul, aiding his terror attacks against the world. It's what Sibyl had guessed that night we escaped the London facility.

Standing from his rocking chair, Dawson walked over to the fireplace, taking a framed picture of Harry as a child from the mantel. Moments passed where he considered the laughing face of his son in silence.

"I spent years training," he said. "Fighting to make a better world for him. I didn't dedicate decades of my life to this organization only to see it crumble in a few short days. I may not be an agent anymore, but I still believe what we did was right. That the Sect was just." He turned to me. "You were on the inside, weren't you? You've been in the Sect, following their orders, all while the walls were crumbling down. Tell me, Effigy. Is what he's saying true?"

Yes and no. There *were* traitors in the Sect who worked with Saul. But, as I'd learned, Saul's attacks were orchestrated specifically to lead to this conclusion. Saul. Blackwell. And agents like Vasily following them. They were a faction unto themselves.

Part of me, though, did wonder if the end of the Sect was really a bad thing. Get rid of the Sect. Get rid of us. We wouldn't have to fight anymore. But then what did "getting rid of us" entail? Locking us up to make sure we could never interfere with their affairs? And when we die, hunting the next girl down to lock her up the same? Would Blackwell really go through such lengths to keep power out of our hands?

"What do you know, child?"

I shrugged, exhausted. "Just that we were never the bad guys."

Dawson gazed down on the picture again before placing it back on the mantel with a heavy sigh. "Getting rid of the Sect would make a few people happy." His hand lingered on the mantel's wooden surface. "The problem is, even if you manage it, you still need to replace it with something else. It's a brave new world. Isn't it? But the fate of that world would depend on whether that new 'something' is better or worse than what came before."

I understood immediately what he meant as his solemn gaze fixed on me. If Blackwell was determined to tear down the Sect, then what was he going to replace it with? We Effigies had power. Power to fight the phantoms. With the whole world—no, with *his own safety* at stake, he wouldn't just get rid of us, would he? I mean, why? Why tear down the Sect in the first place? The Sect had been doing a fine job protecting the world before Blackwell and Saul teamed up to sabotage the organization. How many civilians and agents had died because of their actions? A needless waste of life, all to tear down an organization already working fine. If Blackwell did all this to tear down the Sect, it was for his own selfish reasons. How could I trust whatever system he'd come up with next?

An uneasy shiver ran through my skin as I thought of the secrets held back by Blackwell's malicious grin our last night in London. What was he planning?

"Brave new world," I said.

Blackwell's brave new world.

•  •  •

Everyone had retired to their rooms for the night. I was grateful for Dawson letting me shower, wash my clothes, and stay as long as I needed, but now that I was up, my body couldn't sit still. I had to go somewhere, do something. This incessant needling beneath my skin kept reminding me that something wasn't right. How had Dawson put it before? "Something's not clean in the milk." Well, he wasn't wrong.

Blackwell had caused an awful lot of pain and mayhem to tear down the Sect and build something new in its place, and Saul had helped him. I had to figure out why. And to figure out why, I had to put the pieces together.

I swiped the pad of paper on the desk in my room, then rummaged the desk for a pencil—oh, a pen. The black ink was a little thin, but it'd work. Pen on paper. It was the easiest way to organize my thoughts.

The forest was dense with trees. Dawson said you could get lost in here if you weren't careful, but I was going stir crazy inside. I needed air, and the window wouldn't do. I went out the back door I'd spotted in the kitchen, found a fallen trunk under a cluster of trees, and plopped down, ignoring the wet moss. I closed my eyes, allowing the cicada symphony to lull my heartbeat into a slow rhythm. The sky was so clear and dark: a starless abyss. The air was so crisp, like it'd been packaged fresh.

I placed the pad of paper on my knees and started putting together everything I remembered. Each shocking moment blasted into my brain. Naomi Prince shot, maybe murdered. Rhys and June obliterated. An Effigy's sword piercing my chest, nearly killing me.

The pen shook in my hand.

I forced myself to focus. Why? How did we get from A to Z?

I wrote "Blackwell" in the center of the page.

Blackwell wanted to tear down the Sect, and judging by his press conference, he seemed confident he could replace it with his own institution. But he couldn't replace the power of the Effigies without a backup plan ready to go.

Then again, he *had* a backup plan. Those fake Effigies. The Silent Children.

That had to be it. Drawing a line up from Blackwell, I wrote the words, slanted on a frenzied angle: "Silent Children." The faux Effigies had gotten their genetically engineered supernatural powers through the nanotechnology crawling up their spines. I'd faced them before, the beast-like dead boy in the tunnels of London and sociopathic Jessie, who'd manipulated his carcass with the power of her mind. And there were at least two more out there.

It was all part of their grand master plan: Project X19. Creating scientifically engineered Effigies, using Saul's attacks to stir global fear and support for his anti-Sect scheme. Blackwell was naive if he thought he could replace us with a bunch of copies who, if Jessie was any indication, had a few screws loose. But then again, they were loyal—or at least easily controlled by the wonders of science. Maybe that was what made the difference.

Still, why the hell create all this misery just to replace the Sect and the Effigies with substitutes? The only reason I could think of was power. Blackwell got to go from a bit player to the core of the new world order while his enemies were in jail or in hiding like Sibyl.

But he couldn't have done any of it without Saul.

I closed my eyes and pictured him, his sea-blue eyes and silver hair. Saul, the fifth Effigy, an amalgamation of two personalities battling for dominance. Alice was the stronger mind, the one who usually drove Nick Hudson's body like Natalya had twice driven mine. But the last time I saw him, Nick had made it clear that they both had the same goal: to grant a wish, one his tiny ring couldn't handle. And to do that, Saul needed me. He needed Marian, the Effigy inside me.

*Because she knows where it is,* he'd told me once. *The rest of the wishing stone . . .*

But then why didn't he take me in Morocco? He'd gotten the best of me, had me in his sights. But instead of grabbing me, he'd left me there with a few cryptic words and started preparations for Oslo, a move that would benefit Blackwell far more than himself. I'd figured working with Blackwell was some kind of quid pro quo deal: You help me screw up the world, and I'll give you something shiny in return—Maia Finley delivered on a platter, perhaps. Or a granted wish for power. But Saul didn't need Blackwell's help in screwing up the world, surely. So why help Blackwell at all? Somehow Blackwell had gotten a powerful, century-old Effigy—a *real* Effigy—to set aside his own plans and work on a stranger's behalf.

With what bait?

Sighing, I tore up the page and started a fresh one, drawing a line across the center of the paper. Saul, Vasily, and the remaining Silent Children. Blackwell and whichever Council members were supporting him. I wrote their names at the top. And on the bottom half of the page: Sibyl and Cheryl, her assistant. Uncle Nathan working with them, wherever they were. Lake and Chae Rin, who by now had hopefully met up with them. Baldric and Naomi, if she was still alive. Me. Natalya, once upon a time.

I hovered the pen over the center line, but left Belle's name unwritten.

A sense of loss came along with that. A friend, a mentor, a hero crumbled. Unmistakable disappointment lived at the core of the quiet fury that burned in me when I thought of her sword piercing my chest. A broken pedestal where Belle once stood.

And hers wasn't the only broken one.

June. My hands twitched. If Saul needed *me*, then why bring my sister back? Why bring June back just to let me watch her kill? Watch her die? Was it to psyche me out? To remind me of that year of crushing loneliness and grief I'd spent without her, only to take her away again?

And Rhys. The boy who'd once kissed me died confessing his crimes to the world. Died in front of my eyes. And in his last moments, he probably believed we thought him a monster.

But I didn't. And I couldn't tell him that now.

I squeezed the pen, trying to keep myself under control. He *killed* someone, yes. He killed Natalya. But did he deserve death at his own father's hands? Rhys was a pawn who knew nothing of Blackwell's plans. Frightened and abused into obedience by his father, he'd killed on orders alone. Killed his friend and then masked his self-loathing unto death. So what did he deserve? Maybe he deserved the disgust I'd shown him that night he admitted it all to me under the moonlit trees. Maybe he deserved public disgrace.

But did he deserve to be *obliterated by his own father*?

The pen almost snapped in my hand. I calmed down in time to save myself from a mess of ink, but the pain in my chest still throbbed, my bones weary, eyes still wet.

Rhys and June. Gone in the blink of an eye, like they were never even there. Death was such a strange thing.

I peered up through the tree leaves above me. Moonlight filtered through the branches as if refracted by a diamond. Squeezing the pen in my hands, I let it dig deep into paper where the ink blotted. Fallen leaves and branches cracked in the woods behind me.

Under someone's foot.

Sensing danger, I whipped around, looking for the source of the sound. Impervious darkness seeped through the trees but couldn't conceal the moving shadow that had slipped behind a tree trunk. I leapt to my feet. It was more than danger I sensed. My stomach felt as if it'd collapsed like a sinkhole, but my hands tingled in anticipation. Someone was out there. I could feel it.

Someone I knew . . .

The crunching of leaves drew closer. The shadow was out of sight but not gone. I stepped back, ready to take off, until a dog snuck out from behind a tree from the direction I'd sensed someone.

"Vader?" The dog barked once or twice before pawing at my legs. I bent down and rubbed his head, but kept scanning the trees. It was the dog all along. Maybe I was just too anxious, too weary, to make sense of things anymore. Exhaustion was really catching up to me.

The deep shudder I suppressed helped remind me that I was still alive. Yes, I was alive. I could do something about this whole mess. But what?

Where was I supposed to go from here?

# 5

*MAIA . . . MAIA . . .*

Again and again, Natalya's voice whispered of death in my sleep.

*I told you I would do it again if I had the choice. And I will.*

*Maia . . . You will see me again soon.*

I awoke in the morning with a violent start, Natalya's deadly promise ringing in my ears. I felt like a petrified phantom, a body mummified in cold crystal. I was starting to recall more details from my time in the Dead Effigy Realm, albeit gradually. For one, Natalya's eerie serenity as she told me she'd "kill" me once and for all.

My body seized up. *Calm down,* I told myself. *She isn't here. Calm down.*

No, that wasn't true. I took her with me wherever I went.

I had to pinch my limbs just to make sure they were still mine. She could get into my head more easily when my mind was in a weakened state. I had to stay strong.

I ate the breakfast Dawson made, ignoring the way Harry'd taken his plate of food into the living room before I could sit down. Eventually, I was able to tell Dawson some of what had happened to me over the past few days, sparing him the crazier details.

"So you were set up, then?" Dawson stroked his beard, black coffee steaming from his favorite ceramic mug.

"Now we're full-on bad guys as far as everyone's concerned." My gaze followed out the half doors to where I knew Harry was eating, the news from his laptop playing over Vader's friendly barks.

"All to tear down the Sect?"

"The worst part of it was not knowing whom to trust." I stared at my plate, empty but for a few smears of scrambled eggs and syrup.

"Maybe the lesson is you shouldn't trust anyone." Dawson sat back in his chair and folded his arms. "Not even me."

We looked at each other.

"I mean, if you're going to turn on me, you might as well have at it. Just let me finish my orange juice first."

Dawson laughed as I picked up my glass. "That's not what I meant, necessarily, though I must admit, that wasn't quite the reaction I was expecting."

"Guess this is what happens when you don't expect much from anyone anymore."

When Dawson nodded his head, his shaggy blond hair slid across his leathery cheeks. "Trust is like glass. Once it's broken it can never be put back the right way. You don't see through it the same. When I became a Sect agent all those years ago, trust was everything. Trust in your colleagues. In your superiors. And in the organization itself. Even after retiring."

"I had a friend like that too." I traced a line through the syrup with my fork. "He was raised in one of those Sect legacy families. He lived for the Sect, killed for the Sect and . . . died for the Sect."

The fork slipped out of my hands, and I was silent for a long time. Rhys's pain was forged long before he killed Natalya. His father. The abusive Fisk-Hoffman facility in Greenland. All of it part of an old institution that didn't value his life as it should have.

"There are times when I think maybe the Sect *should* burn," I whispered suddenly, without looking at him. "Maybe if there was no Sect—"

"If there's no Sect and no Effigies, then who would fight the phantoms?" Dawson rested his forearm against the table as he leaned in. This was the face of the noble Sect agent before he turned fisherman. "Who protects the world? The Sect wasn't a perfect organization, but for more than a century it safeguarded humanity. Justice and peace. Do you understand what that means, girl? *Really* understand? Do you understand the other side of it?"

Terror. Chaos. The kind of fear that sank into your bones and died there. "Yes," I said.

"Despite its problems, the Sect's one aim was and has always been to save lives—that is, before it was corrupted from the inside. So what do you think, then, eh? You think Blackwell had the world's best interests at heart when he called that press conference?"

Blackwell? No, not the Shit-Stirrer in Chief. Not he, nor Vasily, nor those murderous pretend-Effigies.

"And while the Sect is being torn apart, while bureaucrats are shooting its operations straight to hell to resolve the 'issue,' who is out there protecting the people who need it most?"

"I *would* be." I balled my hands into fists, jaw tight from the frustration building. "I would be if I could. But I need to find out the truth first."

I already guessed what Blackwell's goal was, but there had to be more to the puzzle. Even if he had grand plans of a post-Sect world, his plan could still be rejected by the international community of state leaders, or he could be removed from the project altogether. How could he ensure that he'd get—and keep—the power he wanted?

"Whatever Blackwell is *really* planning, I have to stop it. I have to stop him. Too many people have died for me to just let this go."

Smirking, Dawson pushed out his chair and stood. "Righteous. You remind me of some of the agents I once knew."

"Yeah." I stared at my plate. "I remind me of some agents I once knew too."

Despite everything, I couldn't forget how hard Rhys worked to slay phantoms, to protect civilians. Even after taking the life of his friend, even after donning a mask to hide his crimes, he'd risked his life to protect the helpless, and I knew it wasn't just because of the training burned into him by the Sect. Sibyl was the same. Howard and his wife, Eveline. Chae Rin and Lake. If any of them were still alive, then they were still fighting, so I had to fight too. I had to get to the bottom of all this or I'd never be able to live with myself.

But how?

I needed help.

"Mr. Dawson." I tried not to let my hesitation show. He'd taken me this far. I had to trust this guy. "You were once in the Sect. . . . That means you still have some contacts, right?"

Dawson tilted his head. "Looking to go somewhere?"

I had to get to Sibyl. She was like the rebel commander or something. She'd know what to do. The last I'd seen her, Brendan Prince had gotten her shipped off to Philadelphia. Maybe she was still at home. That was one option.

But wouldn't she be one of the main targets of Blackwell's faction? Sect agents were probably camping out there with s'mores and beer waiting for her to show up.

Well, if I was careful, I could still check it out. I had to start somewhere, right? "Listen, Mr. Dawson, I need to leave soon, but I don't have any transportation."

"Where are you looking to go?"

If Sect agents got ahold of him, it'd be better if he didn't know where I was. "Somewhere I'll need a plane to get to. Or a ship."

"A ship." Dawson scratched his beard. "There's not much I can do with my little tugboat. But I might be able to secure some people who can take you where you need. I had lots of contacts as a Sect agent. Official ones . . . and not so official ones."

Bingo. Going through underground channels would be safer. "How well versed are you in Europe's trafficking networks?"

Blinking, he jerked his head back, staring at me like I'd suddenly grown fangs. "Not the typical little girl, are you?" He laughed. "I know some people. It was good to have contacts in the underground world. Some of them made good informants when it came to who was trading what Sect technology. Others could tell you who had antiphantom technology from other development firms stronger than even that of the Sect—and there's always better technology out there. So we'd take that information back to our Research and Development department. From what I last heard, Saul blew through many trafficking camps on his way to Oslo. I recognized a few of those men in that footage. With the 'you' that wasn't you."

I shifted in my seat. "Do you know a guy named Jin?" I described the man I'd met in Spain, his flat black hair pressed along the back of his skull. Sweeping coat covering his large frame. A beard wilder than his. "He travels with his son, Derrek, a cute Irish guy named Lucas, a scary bald-headed woman named Abril. . . ."

"I've heard of a Jin. I may be able to draw him out with the right message. But you should know these aren't exactly trustworthy people. I don't want them knowing where I live."

"Gotcha. If you can, please get this message to Jin." Code messages. Uncle Nathan would be better at this stuff, with his geeky love of spy movies. I racked my brain. "Okay, okay, how about: 'The girl who saved your son in the Urbión Peaks needs to . . . fly over the pond.'"

Dawson crumpled his face as he held in a laugh, embarrassed for the both of us.

"Well, I didn't say it'd be amazing." I sucked in my lips in annoyance. "Please just tell him that it's a matter of life and death. I'll be waiting for him. Um, not here. Where?"

"Some traffickers have been known to do business in Sangatte. It's about a fifteen-minute drive southwest. I'll take you there tonight when you're ready. But after that, you're on your own."

On my own. "What can go wrong?" I shrugged with a struggling smile that flipped and fell on its head the moment I thought of every possible thing that probably *would* go wrong.

Dawson raised an eyebrow. "I'll start contacting folks."

Dawson had spent a couple hours on the phone following leads, but traffickers weren't exactly easy to find. Some contacts you had to go and find. Apparently there was one just outside town. Dawson told me to stay hidden while he left to find him. Meanwhile, Harry went to the docks. Since I was alone, I could plan. And pack.

I hadn't told Dawson yet that I'd need a few of the weapons he had stashed in his basement if I was going to keep inoculating myself to stay off everyone's radar.

Well, I'd pack first and tell him later.

I found an old backpack in Harry's closet—looked like a school-bag he used to use. If he minded, then oh well. There were only a few comics and candy bar wrappers inside. I dumped them out and went down to the cabin's basement. There were piles of used clothes and garbage bags marked for donation. I took out a few things I thought would help in concealing my identity: a big floppy fisherman's hat, sunglasses, and a handkerchief. I skipped past the stacks of magazines in the corner, looking for supplies. There were toolboxes on a shelf and some cleaning stuff. And—hello—tucked in the closet, three silver briefcases. They were low-tech, fastened with a simple lock, like he'd gotten them in an auction from a retired magician who'd used them to store his props and rabbits. I found a set of keys nearby and tried all of them until one worked.

Inoculation weapons. There were only two here, seven injections each. I took one. He'd collected this stuff for a reason; I couldn't eat him out of house and home. Smoke bombs. And this gizmo—an oddly shaped gun with streamlined, round edges and strips of glass on the sides through which I could see metal tubes—tubes that would buzz with blue energy when firing. An antiphantom weapon.

Wow, I was totally just raiding their stuff. Felt a bit icky. Of course, normally I wouldn't just help myself, but having my provisions *now* made me feel more in control. Hopefully, he wouldn't be too annoyed when he got back. Besides, this was all ultimately for the greater good anyway. Stopping Blackwell could only make things better for everyone, including Dawson and Harry—assuming I didn't mess things up.

I piled everything into Harry's backpack, along with a few cereal bars I found in the kitchen upstairs.

Now that I was packed, I had to find out if Chae Rin and Lake were all right. There was no way I could call them, though. What if their numbers were being traced? They'd probably gotten rid of their cell phones by now anyway. I checked the internet instead for any news on them, silently thanking Harry for not being paranoid enough to use a password. No news yet from major media except that they were still at large.

But sometimes major outlets missed things *we* didn't. The netizens.

I checked Doll Soldiers. The website was currently ravaged with debates over what they were calling EffiGate. The pinned Oslo Thread was still raging on, nearing its fiftieth page at the very top of the Popular Threads sidebar.

"Oh god, I shouldn't click," I whispered, cringing. But, of course, I did.

[+1500, - 560] But why the hell would the very people putting their lives on the line knowingly join hands with a goddamn terrorist? Y'all really think that makes sense? What would they even get out of it?

[+1000, - 1300] But is it really that hard to believe? Lake and Chae Rin were both basically screwups and flops before the whole thing in Argentina and France. Belle was a soulless bitch, and Maia is a complete question mark. Maybe they were recruited by Saul because they knew they couldn't hack it for long as a group.

[+800, - 600] Some of you are making NO SENSE. I'm done! Those pics in Oslo look FAKE! I bet it's some Russian shit!

[+1800, - 400] First of all, Icicles, Swans, and High Wires would like to be excluded from this narrative. Our girls didn't do ANYTHING. Maia was the one up there shooting folks in the head like they owed her money. At least we actually know the other girls. This Maia chick appeared out of nowhere like a month ago and nobody knew where the f she came from. She was probably a plant from the beginning, and now the rest of the girls are f'ed because of her!

I almost punched the screen. I knew it was a mistake. In between every comment defending me were fans of the other girls desperately trying to throw me under the bus to save their faves. It angered me, but I knew they could only make sense of what they could see. The pictures of the "me" who was in Oslo with Saul were convincing enough for the rest of the world to shove all the Effigies into the same category.

At least it was good to know where we stood with common folk. Threads were being made by the second, a few of them relaying more information about the ongoing Sect investigations, anti-Sect demonstrations, and even drudging up dirt on us Effigies, particularly about our pasts—anything that could explain why we may or may not be secretly sociopathic murderers. The thread titles said it all:

> **Maia Finley's sister died in a fire. Do you think that set her over the edge?**
> **Why is nobody talking about how Lake flaked in Milan? She's too WEAK to be an Effigy**
> **Reasons why I don't think Belle is a terrorist, but I think Chae Rin could be**
> **Lake donates to children's charities once a month. She is not terrorist material!**
> **That Blackwell guy was making legit SENSE. Sect is CRAZY. Glad he's taking control!**

I spent hours reading through them all. Blackwell would be pleased to know that public support overall was not in our favor, judging by some of these posts. Shaking my head, I refocused on my original plan, searching the site until I found a thread in the Conspiracy Section.

Effigy Sightings.

My heart jolted with hope and dread in equal measure. I clicked the link. Pictures were few and far between, blurry, many of them proven edited by creeps for kicks to send the thread into a frenzy, or else they were red herrings, photos of girls who only looked like us. But other images were not so easy to ignore. Someone had posted a picture of the crowd around the Kim family's restaurant in Vancouver, eggs and trash thrown at the windows, dirty garbage water streaking down the glass behind which hung a red-lettered CLOSED sign, left up despite the daylight. A closer angle revealed the words GO BACK TO CHINA scrawled in different colored chalk across the brick. The picture of the girl users originally thought was Chae Rin coming out of the restaurant a few days ago was actually her older sister, Ha Rin. The video of her short, tiny frame being pelted with tomatoes was too difficult to finish.

Down the thread, a user posted a tearful interview given by Lake's parents for Beautiful Naija, a website Lake frequented. Lake's mother in particular dressed like she was going to dinner with a robust, full face of makeup, curly crocheted braids down her neck, long earrings, flawless skin. A beauty marred by the dark circles under her swollen eyes.

"We don't know where she is," her mother insisted to the reporter in her Nigerian accent, "but we're telling you that our daughter could never be a criminal. Why would you just call her a monster before you even ask if there's evidence? It's unfair to my daughter, who risked her life."

This wasn't my fault, I had to remind myself, but the twinge of guilt stung anyway as I turned off the video. No sightings of them anywhere. Not Chae Rin, not Lake . . .

Belle. At least I thought it was her, though half her face was hidden behind the hood of the red coat she wore. There was a blurry photo of her checking behind her shoulder, maybe making sure she wasn't being followed. It was taken from above, maybe by drone or some other surveillance system. I'd have to be careful of those.

Users wrote that she was found near York, that British city destroyed when the phantoms first appeared. While we were all in Prague, that town was the focus of our fever dream as we scried together. I'd seen Marian—no, I *was* Marian, facing off against Alice on the crazed girl's family estate. Each of the Effigies had seen their own vision, but it all revolved around York, the arrival of the phantoms, and the fate of those five girls—Abigail, Emilia, Patricia, Alice, and Marian—who were at the center of it all. The only reason Belle would go there would be to scry. Like immersing herself in the atmosphere would give her a better foothold into those memories. Maybe she'd witnessed more clearly how Emilia, the first in her Effigy line, lived and died. Where you scry was sometimes just as important as the technique itself. She'd told me something like that once before. Back when she was my teacher and not my killer.

It was evening when the front door to the log cabin finally opened again. Harry returned before Dawson, slamming the door behind him. I stood from the couch.

Harry's eyes shifted from his laptop to his backpack at my feet. I knew he didn't trust me. He'd been tolerating my presence because of his father. But his father wasn't here.

"Where's Mr. Dawson?" I asked.

He didn't answer.

Raising an eyebrow, I tried again. "Is he around?"

"Out back," Harry answered, and then, avoiding my eyes, added, "I didn't tell him."

"Tell him what?"

With two short strides, he stalked over, grabbed the controller off the living room table, and turned on the news. I couldn't read French, so I couldn't decipher the frantic scrawl at the bottom of the screen. But I did see the same figure in each shot of the burning towns they showed. It reminded me of the pictures of citywide destruction Saul had shown me at La Charte before I knew who he was; pictures of *himself.* The only difference was that Saul attacked with phantoms.

This terrorist attacked with fire.

The figure was average height and wearing black pants, boots, and a faded jeans jacket with a hood that didn't bother covering her face— *my* face.

My lips parted in a silent gasp as I stepped closer to the television. It couldn't be. The pictures were blurry. I could have been wrong. "No . . . ," I whispered, because in some of the footage, I could see the figure snap her fingers and the flames erupting several feet away.

It wasn't true. Or was it?

It was.

It *was.*

I fell to my knees.

"Hey!" Harry barked because my nails scratched against the wooden log floor as I drew them in. I tried to bring my short breaths under control before I realized tears were blurring my eyesight. "Hey!" Harry said again, this time with an awkward hesitance. What to do with the monster you were trying to crucify sobbing in front of you?

"She's alive. . . ." I choked on the words and gulped in a breath. But it couldn't be true. How could she have survived?

My sister was alive. She was alive!

My heart soared. My eyes stung.

She was . . .

She was . . . alive. . . .

I looked up and watched the French reporter trembling at her newsroom desk as she discussed the mayhem in the clip they'd just shown: the one of people fleeing in terror.

My whole body was shaking. Why would she . . . ?

No, it had to be a mistake.

Slowly, I rose to my feet without realizing, my eyes helplessly locked on the screen. It was a trick. I was seeing things. I refused to believe it. I rubbed my eyes. "No . . . ," I whispered, shaking my head.

"Yes." Harry's glare was aimed, ready to kill, and I finally understood why. Who else could conjure fire out of nothing?

"It's not me," I told him as earnestly as I could with my head still reeling. "This isn't me. You have to know that." I held up both hands as if trying to stay a wild animal.

"Like that girl in Oslo wasn't you."

"She *wasn't* me! I was here the entire day!"

"Arras? Lille?" Harry pointed at the television. "Just an hour away. Maybe you grabbed a lift and did a little damage."

"Why would I risk exposing myself?" I was screaming now, instinctively moving away from him, but my eyes were still darting to the television screen. None of it felt real. "Why would I travel hours to burn cities nearby instead of burning down the one I'm currently in?"

"So you admit to thinking about burning this place down?" he spat in disbelief.

"No! This is—stop jumping to conclusions and calm down. Damn it, I don't have time for this—my sister is *alive*!"

I'd blurted it out in seconds. My eyes wide, my mouth gaping in air. I must have looked rabid. I *felt* rabid. Everything was beautiful and falling apart. I wanted to dance. I wanted to cry.

Meanwhile Vader was barking outside. Footsteps. I heard footsteps just outside the door.

"You really are mad, aren't you?" Harry finally spoke again, his voice low. "Unstable. And a *murderer.*"

Now he was staring at me, a wild kind of resolve, defiant as he gripped his phone like a gun. That was when I realized that it was already too late.

"Maia Finley!" Voices cried from outside the front door, authoritative voices yelling for my surrender in French and English. "Come out with your hands up! Slowly!"

"I called them earlier when I saw the news," he said as lights peeked through the window. "My mother's already dead. I have to protect my father."

I bent down to pick up the arm of his knapsack.

"Maia Finley, I repeat, come out with your hands up!"

Harry watched me, swallowing the lump in his throat. "I'm not sorry."

Staring at his sniveling, terrified face, I shook my head. "I wouldn't expect you to be."

"She's in here! Quick, help!" Harry cried.

I swung the backpack over my right shoulder and booked it to the kitchen just as the doors burst open. Dawson had just run in through the kitchen entrance, hearing the commotion. After hastily shoving a stuffed yellow envelope in my hands, he jerked his head toward the back door. "It's clear. Go to Sangatte—"

That was all he could manage before a bullet flew over the swinging half doors behind us, narrowly missing my head.

"Go!"

I ran out the kitchen door into the trees, leaping over fallen logs. The Dawsons' cabin was just on the outskirts, but I was rushing into the forest itself with no clue which direction I was heading in. The boots clambering behind me told me the police were in pursuit.

A bullet pierced the trunk of a tree next to me. I ducked, breathing in a gasp as another one flew and missed me by inches. A man was yelling. "Don't kill her!" maybe. I doubted they wanted me dead.

The bullets stopped, but the police chased nonetheless—until a wall of fire erupted behind me. I jumped to the mossy ground, using my arms to shield my face from the impact. The sky filled with frantic, confused yells. One man was screaming horribly. I looked back—oh god, one of them was on *fire*. But it wasn't me. It *wasn't* me!

The gentle rustling of a tree branch a few meters away from me drew my gaze forward.

There she was, standing on one of the branches of a tree. Her jacket hood up, her hair hidden, her face just barely concealed as she turned it away from me.

Maybe I was wrong. Maybe it wasn't her. No, it *couldn't* have been her.

But what if it was? I began breathing rapidly, the screams of the police officers ebbing away beneath the pounding of my own heart. That terrible sensation began pulsing through my veins, just like it had last night. A confusing mix that made me fearful and hopeful at the same time.

She was holding on to a branch, but seemed steady enough on her own, her small feet balanced on the wood. Her frame was more clearly delicate than I remembered. Skinny, like she hadn't eaten in days. Nails chewed up and ruined on slender, tanned hands.

She snapped her fingers again and another explosion erupted, scattering the police, before jumping down from the tree and walking forward. Powers. Powers?

No, it wasn't her. It *couldn't* be her.

I was paralyzed. She passed me without a word, feet barely making noise against the grass. Her presence felt heavy, electrifying, making the hairs on my arms stand on end. What was happening? Why wouldn't she say anything? Why was she helping me?

I wouldn't have time to ask her. The fire was spreading, flames licking up the trees. Dawson and Harry! What if the flames reached them? I had to go back and help them, but the flames were too hot and the inoculation hadn't faded enough for me to banish them. I'd have to run, but even after standing, my feet were glued to the soil.

All the while, she stood among the flames, unfazed when a burning tree branch fell down, separating us.

"Stop!" I shielded my face from the embers. "Stop this! You'll kill everyone!"

She took down her hood and turned. Long, messy, dark curls fell down her back just as the smoke billowed across her face and the hand she extended to me.

It was her. Tears dripped from my lashes. It was *her*. She was alive. Oh god, she was alive.

And she was killing people.

"June," I whispered, my body numb with joy, with terror. "Why?"

Another tree branch fell into the flames, the fire exploding every-where. My heart beating, I ran from the scene without another thought except the one of my sister burning down a forest to save me.

# 6

IT WAS JUNE.

June was alive.

June was a murderer.

I'd been walking along the D940 highway for more than half an hour, and for the entire duration, those words circled around and around like one of those spin-the-wheel games, except the wheel didn't stop. The painful part of seeing my sister was the knowledge that I couldn't drown myself in the relief welling up inside me. Not with what I'd just seen.

I shuddered to think of the terrified shrieking. I'm sure they were running for cover, running to escape death. But nobody had followed me since I escaped the forest. Pretty sure that was a good sign they hadn't. Yet more deaths I was going to be blamed for.

How could she kill? How could June Finley, June the Brave, June the Righteous, be so okay with *murdering* people? I needed to talk to her, needed to figure this out with her. But I didn't even know where she was now, and going back to see if she was still in town meant getting locked up in a jail cell.

At least she was alive. That truth, at least, filled me with a joy so crippling it nearly transformed to guilt. This wasn't the time to be celebrating. How could I not celebrate? How could I not be horrified?

My sister wasn't an Effigy. Where had her powers come from? It was hard to forget the numbing sight of her massacring people—with fire of all things. June could never do that. She knew full well the pain of dying in a fire. And now that she was here, breathing—

My feet stopped dead on the grass. "It *can't* be her!" I said suddenly, then snapped my lips shut with a gasp. A car zipped by on the highway several meters away. I'd concealed my identity using the oversized, floppy fisherman's hat I'd found in Dawson's basement, a muted dark green that wouldn't draw attention. I'd wrapped the white bandana around my mouth too. The disguise would have worked better during the day; onlookers would have thought I was trying to shield part of my face from the sun, hence the added sunglasses. Still, no one bothered too much with the weird "hitchhiker" either way, not that I would dare get into anyone's car.

Dawson had already said that it was only a fifteen-minute drive to Sangatte, which meant it was within walking distance. I just had to stick by the greenery and keep track of the highway and the signs, because otherwise I couldn't be sure I was going in the right direction.

I got here in the first place thanks to the old travel map Dawson had stuffed inside this manila envelope in my hands, along with a burner phone and some money. To my right was an endless stretch of shrubs and trees, the edge of which I clung to, though no doubt there were all kinds of animals lurking deeper within—and worse farther off. If I squinted I could hear phantoms crying in the distance just beyond what looked like a long fence. Antiphantom fence, set up far away just before the rolling hills. On the other side of the highway, there were rows of golden brown wheat swaying in the wind, and houses, all protected by a lower-level APD whose signal stretched only so far.

I started dragging my exhausted legs forward once again, adjusting the backpack over my shoulders. If June had survived, then maybe Saul had survived too. Maybe he'd saved the both of them by warping out of the area just before the weapon's beam had hit—but why would he need her? Why bring her back in the first place?

Why brainwash her?

Yes, brainwashing. It was the only way to explain what she was now. Just like Jessie, she most likely had a mind-control device placed inside her body by the same people who'd given her those powers.

The very fact that my sister was working with Saul made me want to scream into the night. Saul himself had told me that night in France that it was a simple task to bring back the dead. That stone. He'd used it.

Somehow, everything always came back down to that damn stone. The stone of wishes . . . With it, Saul had promised that he would reshape the world. Well, Blackwell was already doing that just fine on his own by tearing down the Sect with Saul's help. Was Saul promised something more?

I had to think. What did I even know about the stone? It was connected to the phantoms. The phantoms that had appeared suddenly more than a century ago. Nightmares. Demons. But there were some who thought the phantoms were spirits, once. The Deoscali.

I shivered just thinking of them. I didn't want to get back into Deoscali stuff. The Scales were weird phantom lovers and hated us Effigies, but Pastor Charles in London preached a different doctrine— the original doctrine created by Emilia Farlow.

Emilia, one of the first five Effigies.

If anyone would know the secret of the phantoms—and thus maybe even the stone— it'd be her, right?

Wait a second.

I thought back to my conversation with Natalya. She'd told me that she'd scried before she died—a *major* scrying session. She'd been trying to find Marian and ended up watching her death and more: symbols, riddles. "Emilia's teachings." She'd seen too much for any of it to make sense.

Symbols . . .

Like the flame she'd drawn for Pastor Charles in London while asking him about Emilia Farlow's teachings. This Emilia thing was certainly shaping up to be a possible lead. I wonder what else Pastor Charles said to her. More importantly, what could the man who worshipped phantoms tell *me* about this Emilia woman who started his cult all those years ago? He'd helped me before, so it would be safe contacting him. I hoped.

I pulled the burner phone out of the first flap of the knapsack where I'd stuffed the envelope until remembered I didn't have his number or a wireless connection. This would be tricky.

Two hours of walking and I entered the coastal town. The D940 took me straight into the commercial district, the simple, two-story houses clustered by the street with their mauve and maroon roofs. The town was quiet save for a few city buses passing by. Near me, a long brick wall separated the cobbled walkways from the wild shrubbery on the other side with helpful signs staked into the road. Some I could make sense of: OFFICE DE TOURISM; CALAIS. Both arrows pointed in the same direction, so I went the other way.

I noticed young people, mostly men, walking the streets in faded clothes, some loitering and some hanging around phone booths. As I kept my face hidden, I realized that I didn't set up a meeting place with Jin or whomever among their trafficking team Dawson had managed to contact. I kept my eyes peeled.

In the meantime, I was still determined to contact Pastor Charles, but that meant I needed a phone with internet access. I entered a small general store with my head down, weaving through the rows of random goods sold here. I stopped once to look over my shoulder. There wasn't anyone suspicious, but I was sure I'd felt someone following me the moment I stepped inside the store. This would have to be quick.

I searched for a phone to swipe, finding one in the shopping cart of a sick woman checking out some cracker boxes, hacking all over the merchandise. *Gross.* She moved down the aisle, leaving her cart behind her and her bag inside it. I waited for her to go into another coughing fit before digging into her purse and grabbing her phone.

Her data was on. Good, that saved time.

Pastor Charles. Friary Road, London. That was where we'd found his tall, stone church. The number blinked onto the screen. I couldn't trust myself to memorize it, so I input the number into my burner phone.

*"Qu'est-ce que tu fais!?"* A big, blond woman grabbed my wrist, holding up my hand where the phone was. *"Voleur!?"*

I didn't know what she was saying, but at the sound of her words, the woman whose phone I'd stolen swiveled around and gasped. I couldn't let anyone recognize me here. Ironically, they probably *hadn't.* The next stream of words coming out of the sick woman's mouth included *"Arabe!"* and *"migratoire!?"*

I let the phone drop from my grasp. "I'm sorry, I don't speak French—"

I think that made it worse. Yanking my wrist out of the woman's grasp, I bolted out of the store. Damn it. Having the police on my tail was the last thing I needed, even if they were called on false assumptions. I ran as fast and as far as I could, hopping the brick wall by the road, squeezing through shrubbery, ending up on a dry patch of sand separating me from the English Channel.

I collapsed onto the sand, sweat sticking to my body as I set the backpack down beside me. *Migratoire.* Migrant? I suppose that was the consequence of having a skin shade just brown enough to set off the alarm bells of those who tended not to trust darker shades. In those women's eyes, I wasn't an Effigy. I was just another oh-so-scary migrant milling around her quiet town. I guess it worked in my favor. It would keep the police confused enough to stay off my trail, not that I wanted to send them bothering people who didn't deserve it.

My feet were burning in these tennis shoes. I kicked them off, then my socks, and let my bare feet touch the cool sand. I had blisters everywhere. Sighing, I picked up the burner phone and dialed Pastor Charles's number.

Two rings. "Hello?"

I checked behind me. The last time I'd met Pastor Charles, he always sounded so zen when he spoke, like he was perpetually high as a kite. He picked up the phone, and when I hesitantly told him my name, the terror breathed out of his silence through the receiver.

"First things first, I didn't do whatever it is you think I did," I said. "Just know that."

I had to wait several seconds for his response.

"Y-yes, I know. Belle told me."

"Wait. *Belle?*" Lowering my voice, I checked behind me again, listening for police sirens. "She called you?"

"She was here."

Penance? Belle wasn't particularly religious despite being Catholic. And Charles wasn't exactly a Catholic priest. Somehow I couldn't imagine the Deoscali having a confession booth.

"She was here to scry," Pastor Charles added.

My eyebrows furrowed as I stifled a derisive chuckle. No penance required, then, for trying to kill a friend. At least she'd vouched for my not being a terrorist.

"Regardless of what Belle said about you, it's still dangerous for you to be calling me, Maia. And for me to be speaking with you."

I heard shifting, chair legs scratching the floor, and a door shutting in the background.

"I know, Pastor Charles," I said, "and I'm sorry. I'll be out of your hair soon. Now, you said Belle was there to scry in that weird chamber you have. Was it about Emilia Farlow?"

"I'm not sure what it was about. She didn't tell me what happened."

"Okay, well, the question I have is about her." I had to jog his memory about Natalya, how she'd visited him only after experiencing a scrying session so intense she needed someone to make sense of it. Going to Pastor Charles, for her, served only one purpose—to learn more about Emilia Farlow, the first Water Effigy and the creator of the Deoscali cult of phantom worshippers. The symbols I'd found in Prague on the concrete safe where we'd found the thirteenth volume had to be connected to her. They had to be connected to our origins. What were the words engraved there?

"'And among the shadows, you will find them,'" I said. "'For only in calm—'"

"'—can you hear them speak,'" Pastor Charles finished on the other end of the receiver. "Yes, this is among Emilia's teachings, the original Deoscali doctrine before it became twisted into the mainstream interpretation of phantom worship."

"Do you understand what it means?" I asked him. "I've been thinking about it. The shadows have to be phantoms, right? But who is 'them'?" Shifting on the sand, I drew up my knees to rest my elbow, propping up my chin with my free hand. "I mean, I wondered if it could be that traveling sect you told us about before—the one that gave you that scrying chamber in your church cellar."

The calm I'd felt there the day I'd scried in the chamber was the same I'd felt in that special room in Prague's museum, but those Deoscali nomads didn't fit the equation. *For only in the calm can you hear them speak.* But I'd heard nothing in the calm. What I felt, however, was a different story. Those invisible beings slithering past my arms as if the very air itself were a pond to swim in.

Spirits. Pastor Charles had told me of the existence of spirits, and when I was in Prague, I felt certain that they were in the room. Spirits . . . I'd died once already. Had I become one of them, floating about in the atmosphere?

"Remember," Pastor Charles told me, "Emilia's teachings are that the phantoms would not exist if not for the spirits. The spirits exist in the world as shadows, as agents of life and death. The phantoms should not exist at all. They are, in a sense, twisted spirits. That is what Farlow's teaching describes."

"But what can twist a spirit into a phantom?"

"I believe the same thing that transforms life into death, death into life, and one form into another," he answered. "Fate."

One form into another form. I stared out over the English Channel, watching the waves gently roll onto the sand and recede back toward the cliffs I'd fallen dead from. Life to death and death to life. For a moment I'd died and become a spirit. If Pastor Charles was correct, then a regular spirit would have to become something or someone else: a brand-new life. But it was different for Effigies. The chains of our destiny followed an off-beaten path. Wasn't that what Natalya had told me? It was coming back slowly.

"What did Emilia have to say about it?" I asked him. "What can you tell me about her?"

"Emilia Farlow was born in the mid-nineteenth century: the Victorian period. She was a genius, and though she had few opportunities to showcase it, I believe she was preparing to be a teacher. Like many during the time, she was a Protestant, but after the phantoms appeared, she seemed more interested in crafting and documenting her cosmological theory of our world before she died in 1868."

Three years after the phantoms first appeared in York. "So she spent the last three years writing a religious dissertation and teaching people?"

"Well, yes, she taught others, although this is where things become strange. Some say the first students she ever taught were not in England, but in the Antilles. The traveling sect I told you about, the one that passed on the original teachings to me? They say she taught in a small temple she helped to build on the Basse-Terre Island, in Guadeloupe. The temple still exists. I've never been there myself as it's in the center of a Dead Zone. But the temple was built from 1880 to 1882."

"Emilia was dead by then," I whispered.

"Now, I believe many things," said Pastor Charles, "but how can a ghost oversee the construction of a Deoscali Temple?"

"A ghost . . . ," I whispered, frowning.

"The temple was built by people who were somehow able to travel through a wilderness of phantoms without any technology to protect them. Without any protection, they spent two years building a temple that thus far hasn't fallen despite existing outside the field of Pointe-à-Pitre's antiphantom device. Back then the followers were accused of being devils and chased down. But according to Yulia, that temple is as sacred as its secrets."

"Yulia?"

"The leader of the traveling Deoscali faith. The ones who taught me the original teachings. She has traveled to the temple from time to time, once every few months—in fact she's due back in just a few days. When she goes, she stays for at least two weeks. But she doesn't believe in antiphantom technology. I'm not sure how she's been able to move around the world the way she has. Or how she could travel so confidently through the Dead Zone surrounding the temple. The only time I asked, she smiled and told me to simply believe."

Something in Natalya's memories had told her to seek out Charles and learn more about the mysterious work of this genius, Emilia. Its "sacred secrets" could be the key to unraveling this mystery. This was good. This was a piece to the puzzle Blackwell and Saul didn't have.

"Thanks, Pastor. I'll call you again if I need anything. Oh, and please don't tell the cops you talked to me or anything because technically they still think I'm a murderer, 'kay?"

"Wait, Maia," he said before I clicked off the phone. "There's something else I want to tell you. About Belle."

My hand tightened around the phone. "What about her?"

"Granted, I don't know Belle that well. But when she came to me several days ago, there was something very off about her."

"Guilt, maybe." I stared at the white cliffs in the distance. "Last time I saw her, she wasn't exactly doing the whole 'noble warrior' thing."

"Even still, I've never seen her so . . . detached. She's aloof, yes, maybe a bit cold. But this time . . . it was as if her humanity was gone. She ordered me to let her use my chamber that night. And when I didn't respond fast enough, she shoved me against a wall."

"Belle did?"

"She apologized afterward. But she'd hit me with such force it almost broke my back. To be honest, she felt to me more phantom than Effigy."

I'd seen it firsthand: a frigid inhumanity, the kind Natalya had shown in those instances she knew she would do and kill anything to live again.

"Maia," Pastor Charles said after a hesitant pause. "I know the news about you Effigies must be false. But that doesn't mean you can't be dangerous. I think . . . that if you can't reason with Belle, you may have to—"

He stopped, and during his silence my mind finished his thought for him. There was only one logical conclusion to his words. One I couldn't fathom without being overwhelmed by the distinct need to throw up.

"I'm sure it won't come to that," I said quickly.

It *couldn't* come to that. Or rather, I wouldn't let it. My blood still boiled thinking about what she did to me. She *killed* me. Killed me to punish me over a lie. It was impossible to fathom how she was supposed to come back from that, though if she were losing it, then fine. *Good*. Even with all the guilt screaming in my ear that I'd brought it on myself, I wasn't about to feel sorry for her when she murdered me of her own free will.

But as angry as I was, I wasn't particularly interested in trying to fight her back out of revenge. That wasn't me. I just wanted to be as far away from her as possible. Not just out of anger, but out of self-preservation. My death already proved that I couldn't take her in a fight. It was out of the question.

"I hope it doesn't. It's just that the last thing she told me had me worried," Pastor Charles said. "She said that things needed to change."

"Nothing wrong with that," I replied, my voice pitching up with hope.

"And that she needed to change it. She was *going* to change it. She swore it—to me, or to herself, I don't know—but she *swore* it," Pastor Charles said. "She swore that she would bring about the end of everything."

I didn't let on that I was shaking, but maybe he could hear it from the other end of the phone before I turned it off. The end of everything. The end of *everything*.

There was no way of interpreting that statement without flying into a panic. I pressed the phone against my head to stave off the flow, clenching my teeth in frustration, in fear. The chips were piling up and none of them were in my favor. Entropy. Order falling to chaos. As if things couldn't get any worse.

"Ici!"

The voice of a young man. I turned to see one, pale-skinned with scruffy black hair, peeking his skinny figure through the bushes that separated me from the stone wall behind me. Another man behind him stepped onto the sand with his black boots. The pointed cap and black shades obscured most of his face, but the blue cop uniform he wore and the badge he flipped quickly in front of my face was enough ID to know I was screwed.

"Maia Finley? *Vois êtes en état d'arrestation!*"

"Let me guess," I mumbled.

You're under arrest.

# 7

THE INOCULATION WAS WEARING OFF. MAYBE that's how the cop had found me, or maybe those two women in the general store saw which direction I'd headed in. Either way, I could feel the magic beginning to spark in me, but my body was far too worn out for me to make any big moves, as evidenced by my head's inability to duck in time as the cop pushed me into the backseat of the police car.

"Ow," I whined as the hat and bandana slid off my head. Much to my surprise, the officer bent down and picked both up, handing them back to me as I pulled my left leg into the car. He had my bag full of weapons too, but strangely, though he checked it and knew what was inside, he threw it into the car at my feet.

Was this cop naive or an idiot? He must have heard what "Maia Finley" had done to those cops just a few miles from here. Maybe because I was handcuffed, he didn't think I was a threat. I had to escape. But then, if I wanted to prove that Maia Finley wasn't a terrorist, using my powers to blast my way out of here wouldn't be the right way to go. Not that I had the firepower yet.

The cop thanked the young man before getting into the vehicle and driving off.

"You have been a hard woman to find, Maia Finley," he said in a French accent so obnoxiously thick I would have thought he were some actor playing a French cop in a comedy sketch. His wide, smarmy grin certainly fit the bill. Everything about this guy was weird.

At any rate, thank goodness he spoke English. "I'm not who you think I am," I started. "I swear, I'm not a bad person. I'm so tired of having to say it."

"Last I heard on the news, you have been enjoying, how you say, *burning* people alive like the duck flambé we French love to eat?"

I grimaced. Was this guy for real? "That wasn't me. Just someone who looks like me. I can explain if you let me go! Ugh—" I winced from the throbbing in my head from the bump. Even though I couldn't see the cop's eyes, I could tell he was watching me from behind his shades.

"Hurt? Ah, you can handle it. Don't you Effigies heal fast?"

There was something familiar about his laughter. I'd heard it before.

Shades in the dead of night. A bizarre fashion choice—except for those who needed to conceal their identity.

"I could let you run off and flounder around on your own again," he said, his hands reaching up to his shades. His terrible French accent had suddenly disappeared, replaced with a Scottish lilt. "But that's not the deal I had with Dawson."

I almost launched myself forward. "Lucas?"

I'd guessed right before he even revealed his deep brown eyes. Lucas, the handsome boy with the chestnut curls I'd met with the other Effigies in the Urbión Peaks. The sight of him almost brought tears of relief to my eyes. Actually, it *did*.

"Don't cry, lass. I was just taking the piss a bit." He flung his police cap onto the passenger seat.

I rubbed my wet face. "How did you find me?"

"Well, a friend of a friend who gave me your little message earlier this morning," he said, scratching his head through his curling, chestnut hair. "'The girl who saved your son needs to fly over the pond'? I'm so embarrassed for you."

"Yeah, I knew it was stupid when I came up with it."

"We headed west after you left our camp near the lagoon. Then up north. Jin and the rest are still down near the French southern border. We'll be crossing the pond ourselves soon enough to do some business in Canada. But I was already in France securing a deal about an eight-hour drive away. Not too far. Since I got into town, I've been asking around for a young 'refugee' with your description. Figured some of the locals would be more eager to help me if they thought I was here to round up some 'scary foreigner.'"

Well, I *was* a bit of a "scary foreigner." Though not the kind certain people liked to demonize, I too now knew the pain of being falsely accused of terrorism.

"By the way, Dawson—have you talked to him recently?" I clasped my fingers together, waiting for the answer.

"He called. He and his son had to leave home because of a fire in the woods, but they're all right. So's the cabin, overall. Fire trucks got there in time."

I soaked in the relief, but it still didn't stop me from feeling guilty. Neither of them deserved what had happened. If they hadn't found me . . .

"I didn't do that," I quickly added before I could sink further into my thoughts.

"I'm sure you didn't. It was someone else with wacky fire powers?" He laughed.

"But you're here," I pushed him. "If you didn't believe me, you wouldn't be here helping me."

"Not necessarily. I'm a criminal, after all. I've done business with murderers before."

The word "murderer" hit like a gut punch no matter how jovially he'd said it. "So you *don't* believe me."

"Whether I believe you or not doesn't matter. You're a pretty, complicated girl who needs a favor. My favorite kind. Let's just leave it at that."

Not the comforting answer I wanted, but it would have to do. As long as he wasn't turning me in.

Lucas stopped at a light.

"Where'd you swipe the uniform and the car?" I asked, leaning to the side.

"And the fake credentials!" Lucas added cheerfully, clearly proud of himself. "I know some people who know some people. The usual for someone in my line of work."

"Right . . . so since you're not really a cop, can you take off my cuffs?" I waved my chained wrists beside his head.

"Maybe I like them better on," he said in that slightly sleazy way that reminded me of how quick he was to flirt with us in Spain. "Don't worry," he added, upon noting my incredulous look. "I will after we're safely out of town. Then we can get to where we're going."

"Which is?"

"There's a port in Dunkirk. A few cargo ships are going to leave throughout the day and head west across the Atlantic. I know a guy who can smuggle you aboard one of the ships. I don't have 'wings,' but surely a few fins would do, right?"

Cargo ship. Well, that didn't sound too bad. I hated flying anyway.

"Where are you going, anyway?"

Good question. Finding Sibyl was still important, but I had no idea where she was. The other option—

"Guadeloupe," I said. "Or rather, close by there."

"Guadeloupe?" Lucas repeated incredulously. "Why there?"

I shrugged. "I have family in the Caribbean. Guess I thought with my life possibly coming to an end soon, I might as well go around the Lesser Antilles and see what's up."

"Well, you lie as badly as I figured you would, so I'd consider that a plus in terms of my character assessment abilities."

Perhaps, but telling him why I needed to get to Emilia Farlow's mysterious temple in the forest would take too long. Unlike Sibyl's unknown hideout, this was a concrete place I could travel to. Even without the secret volume, maybe there I could get a sense of what was in it: the phantoms. The stone. The original Effigies. If I could just get to the temple, maybe I could learn how they all factored in to Saul's and Blackwell's plans.

I saw his curious eyes watching me in the rearview mirror. "Maia, you sure you don't want to tell me—"

Frantic French babble came in from his police scanner. Lucas fell silent, listening in. The words were indecipherable to me but one: "Effigy."

"Is it about me?" I slid down the bench and leaned in. "It's about me, isn't it?"

"Yes," Lucas said. I noted the blood had drained from his face rather quickly. "But it's not what you think."

"They spotted us?" I sat against the back of my bench. "Oh, damn. Damn, we're screwed!"

"No," Lucas whispered. "They didn't spot us. At least—" He stopped at the red light, one lonely police van in an empty, dark street. But he didn't take his foot off the pedal, even when the light turned green. "They didn't spot us. They spotted you."

"Me?"

Lucas looked at me from over his shoulder. "They arrested you."

"Well, yeah, you just technically—"

"And they have you in custody in their town jail."

My cuffed hands rested limply on my lap. I swallowed the painful, heavy lump in my throat. "June."

"This is crazy!" Lucas shut the door behind him after striding out of the cop car, his little police hat sliding onto the ground.

"Quiet," I hissed. We were in a back alley somewhere in town in the middle of the night, but he still had to be careful. "I told you, I have to see my sister." He'd already freed me, the silver cuffs discarded on the backseat.

"I didn't even know you had a sister. A *twin*? An *evil* twin frying up cities?" He shook his head, looking up at the heavens as if only they could save him from my slipping sanity. "Wait, is being an Effigy genetic? How can she have the same powers you do?"

"That's one of the many things I'm going to ask her," I told him, "once you turn me in to the police."

"You're completely mad. Once they have you, they'll sure as hell never let you go. I mean, they apparently already have your sister, don't they? That's the perfect chance for you to get away clean."

I glared at him so viciously he stepped back closer to the car. As if I was going to leave my sister in jail, use her for my own gain. French police confirmed she was alive. I had to find out why. *Why?* My mind was flying too fast for me to think clearly, but I knew I had to get to her. I had to see her again. And since the world would soon know Maia Finley was in some French town, I had a limited window of time to do it.

"Okay, let's say I bring you in." Lucas folded his thick arms over his chest. "You're opening up another can of worms by heading there. How will you explain two Maia Finleys?"

I stared at my hands, the spark of magic flowing through them. "I won't."

Without a word, I brought up my sizzling hand, charged with the steaming heat I mustered from deep within me.

Then I clasped my right cheek, burning it. White-hot pain blasted across my face.

"Maia, what—*what the hell're you doing?*"

I'd learned while training in London that in our natural, steady state, we're protected against our own magic. We could hurt ourselves only if we specifically *focus* on hurting ourselves. We were told the story of a former Wind Effigy, Anastasia, who'd used this rule to cut open her own wrists. It was supposed to be a cautionary tale.

Lucas yanked my hand away, but it was too late. Gasping in pain, I collapsed, throwing up onto the concrete as my flesh continued to burn.

"Oh god," Lucas said as he bent down and parted my hair, surveying the damage. "*God.*"

I could feel the flesh tearing, raising into boils. "Effigies heal fast, remember?" I said within coughs, bent over from the vicious seething in my stomach from the upshot of acid.

Lucas's hand remained in my hair, pushing it out of my face. "But"—he swallowed—"but what if it leaves a scar?"

Even if it did, I could bear it. Walking in with my face intact and letting the police know it was my twin committing these awful crimes would clear my name. But that would mean forcing June—who had never asked to be resurrected, who wasn't in control of her own actions—to bear that blame herself. I wouldn't do that to her. It was help she needed, not a life sentence.

Admittedly, though, I wasn't exactly thinking straight. A year of suffering, of wishing I were dead myself. I now had what so few people did—a second chance to see a dead loved one just one more time. That need was so overwhelming, it was hard to set my thoughts in order.

Lucas babbled something under his breath, indecipherable Scottish slang I wouldn't have understood even if I did hear it clearly.

"H-help me put my hair up?" I asked him.

He did, his large hands working smoothly, softly through my tresses almost as if he wanted to soothe me with them. They were cool and gentle, the roughness of his palms sweeping over my head like a caress. But the bit of relief they gave me was followed by the painful realization that they'd reminded me too much of Rhys.

"I'm not going to lose anyone," I said to no one in particular, my lips curling into each other as I fought back tears. "Ever again."

"I know," Lucas whispered, though the trembling in his voice undermined his seeming certainty. "Let's get you up."

He helped me to my feet. My hands were still shaking as I got back into the car. On my orders, he drove, terrified and in silence, to the police station. Hopefully, the police would be too preoccupied with the burn scrawling across half my face to realize they had already locked me up. Lucas parked his car at the station.

"You know, this stunt is a risk for me, too," he said as he turned around and locked my wrists back into their cuffs. "Don't know if you noticed, but I'm not exactly a Boy Scout."

"I'm sure you can sweet-talk your way out of trouble if things go to hell."

"Yeah." His eyes lingered on my baked cheek. "'Cept I'm not really in the sweet-talking mood right this minute."

"Just get in and get out. Between June and me, we'll stage a prison break. You'll be driving our getaway car."

"That's all well and good. But that also begs the question—if your sister has the same powers that you do, why in the world would she let herself be kidnapped?"

The answer froze on my lips. This was a girl who'd managed to take down a police unit. Maybe she was injured. Or inoculated. But that would only work if she were an Effigy. I winced from the seething pain in my face, which shuddered down my neck. I guess I'd find out soon.

"Let's go."

Lucas dragged me out of the car and hauled me through the front door. He was all police-officer-gruff, and I could tell he was trying to sell it, but it was clear he was hesitant to hurt me further than I'd already hurt myself.

He spoke to the cops in French, telling them what we'd agreed he would: that he'd caught some messed-up kid attempting to commit arson a few blocks away. A bit of truth in the lie. They gave him permission to drag me over through the hallway to the right into the holding area.

I held my breath.

June Finley sat alone on a bench in her cell, her scrawny body chained at the ankles and wrists to the concrete floor. The only prisoner in the holding area. Her black pants and tucked-in white shirt were dirty with soot and ash from the fires she'd caused. Her curly hair, a bit lighter than mine, was a disheveled mess across her face, individual strands twisted and raised as if from static shock. She sat still, unflinching even when Lucas brought me in, even when he swore under his breath because the two girls he saw were carbon copies of each other. It was only when I called her name that she blinked and looked up at me, heavy bags under her eyes. She said nothing, studying the tears in my eyes with a dispassionate expression. Then, finally, she spoke.

"Your face," she said, letting the question ask itself.

My lips were trembling. "It'll heal."

Her eyes softened, the warmth of family brimming within them as she tilted her head to the side. "Don't cry, Lil Sis. It's really me. I've come here to get you."

# 8

LUCAS'S GRIP PINCHED OFF THE BLOOD FLOW under my arm, made worse by the amount of pressure he was using to keep me standing. June—my *dead sister*, June—stared at me through a wild, thick haystack of hair as if she'd just crawled out of her own grave with her bare hands. The dirt underneath her nails would certainly suggest it. She wasn't dirty anywhere else, aside from the signs that she'd been committing arson along the coast. Her sooty clothes otherwise looked new, simple but stylish even. June was always better dressed than me, more confident in her own skin, so she could switch between sleek outfits and geeky cosplay with ease when the opportunity arose. Always so sure of herself. Even now she didn't waver, didn't cower.

As if she hadn't just burned people alive.

My god. Shooting a Sect agent in the head in Oslo. Burning those French cities. Nearly engulfing Dawson's cabin in flames. She'd done it all. I knew it wasn't her fault, but it didn't change the fact that my sister was a murderer.

"Up ya go," Lucas said, because my legs had given up on me again. "And *you*—"

June was on her feet, walking toward the metal bars, her chains trailing behind her.

"You can stay right there, ehm . . ." He struggled for the words, too freaked to come up with something clever, so he settled on, *"Evil twin."* He pointed at her. "Just stay right there."

June raised her hands in mock surrender just as I heard footsteps and French chattering on the other side of the hallway. Lucas took a set of keys from his pocket.

"Swiped these," he told me, though I didn't ask. "It's a busy station, so I've been able to slip by, but eventually someone's going to realize they haven't seen me around here before."

There was another cell, empty next to hers. That was the one Lucas would have opened had I not pulled him back.

"This one," I said. "Open this one." And when he protested, I added carefully, "It's my sister."

His Adam's apple bobbed up and down in his throat, his defined jawline rigid. He did as I asked, though not before ordering June to take several strides back. The cage door rattled shut behind me.

"When you two escape," Lucas told me through the iron bars, gripping one with his hand, "I'll be waiting 'round the back. But you'll have to be fast." He let go of the iron and stepped back. "Well, that's it, then. I'll leave you two to your . . . twin mischief."

Finally, Lucas was gone.

June and I stood, sizing each other up, noting the bruises on each other's skin.

"It's really been a long time, Maia," she said simply.

It wasn't June who rushed forward first, but me. Like a dam had broken, I wrapped my arms around her, clinging to my twin sister's waist and letting my forehead rest against her shoulder. I cried until she told me to quiet down.

It still hurt to cry because of my face burns. On one side, the tears rolled down flesh I couldn't feel. "I'm sorry," I said.

June tilted her head to the side. "For what?"

For what indeed. For *everything*. I'd always dreamed about what I'd say to her if she were ever to suddenly walk through my front doors. Now, miraculously, I had this opportunity, whether bestowed from above or offered as poisoned fruit from below. But my mind was blank.

"It was awful." As I cried, I remembered that first terrible twenty-four hours after Mom, Dad, and June's burned corpses were sent to the morgue. The tears followed by a clean numbness that separated me from my own flesh.

The day they died, my life got divided into "before" and "after." Like a big line had been drawn, and suddenly everything behind the line was blurry and wrong, a makeshift distortion of reality that may or may not have happened. And everything in front of the line was darkness.

"It was awful," I repeated again, thinking of the funeral, the condolences from people who no longer contacted me. The food cooked by my parents' friends, some of whom followed up with ugly gossip once my back was turned. *You know his mother never accepted that he married a black woman.* I remembered that one distinctly. A frigid funeral hall where both sides blamed each other for their children's deaths and then never spoke to each other again.

"I went to live with Uncle Nathan," I explained, "but then all this happened. . . ."

"How is Uncle Nathan, Maia? He's doing well, isn't he?"

June looked at me quizzically. She'd asked as if she'd been away on vacation or something. I didn't know how to respond. I was too busy thinking about the time I was on the floor of his apartment crying and didn't know how I'd gotten there. And then Uncle Nathan was on the floor too, trying to hold himself together.

I let go of my sister's shirt and stared at her face in wonder, trying to remember what it was that I wanted to say, realizing that in that moment none of it mattered.

Except this.

"You've killed people."

"Because it was the right thing to do."

She'd answered too quickly. She didn't even ask "who." Just answered. The bags under her eyes were sunken pools. Her eyes weren't . . . They were the same brown as always, and yet they were screaming at me somehow. Screaming through the silence.

I frowned. "The right thing to do?"

As she shrugged I noticed how hard she scratched her jawline just below her ear. I was sure she was taking some skin off. "They were shooting at you." June stepped back, the chains jingling as she lowered her arms. "They were going to kill you. I had to save you."

*That* was the June I knew. Righteous. There wasn't a doubt in her mind that she was just.

But there was something too wild about this girl, no matter how controlled her words. She stopped scratching, her fingernails dirty, and cracked her neck from side to side. Eyes laser-focused on me.

"June, all those cities," I said slowly. "That girl in Oslo . . ."

"It's all to save you." For the first time, June's lips stretched into a little smile. She shook her head, teasing like she used to. "Trust me. This whole thing"—she spread out her arms—"it's all to help you. That's why he brought me back."

"He?"

"I mean, I know it sounds a little off." June rubbed her mouth as she sized up the jail cell all around her. She couldn't stand still. "Maybe I'm a little off for thinking it makes sense."

"By 'he,' you mean *him*, don't you? Saul?" I spat out his name.

Her gaze only continued to climb up the walls. "But this whole thing? You being an Effigy, having to suffer because of the Sect. None of it is fair, right?" She emphasized "fair." Her body twitched as she did. "I mean, you didn't ask for this, right?"

I grabbed her arm, snapping her attention back to me. "I have to make sure. Are you or are you not working with Saul?"

We stared at each other in silence for a heartbeat too long. Then June peeked over my shoulders and lowered her voice. "Yeah. I'm working with him," she confirmed, much to my dread. "He said he and his colleagues needed me. He said *you* needed me. And that I could help you by doing this."

"Doing what?"

"This."

She snapped her fingers. In horror I stared at the tiny flame that'd erupted there.

"The officers here really thought I was a bona fide Effigy." June showed me her other arm. "They even gave me this injection thinking it'd stop my powers. But it only works for you guys because you produce it naturally."

"And you don't." I was right. Like Jessie, like the dead soldier in the Sahara and the other Silent Children. I yanked her around, and sure enough, if I squinted I could see a red bruise at the back of her neck. "Nanotech? Did people experiment on you, June?"

"I got used to it. They even gave me a power like yours." June laughed. "I thought it'd be terrible, but I actually appreciate the irony."

This wasn't just about the powers. Like the other ones, like Jessie, they were controlling her somehow. But even though I'd guessed right, it didn't make me feel better. She'd still committed those crimes. And with that brain-controlling chip in her, she was capable of anything. How was I supposed to free her?

I shook my head and strode toward the bars, gripping the cool metal. This had to be a joke. A cruel joke designed to break me completely. And yet through it all, June was well behaved. A bit agitated, mind. And fidgety: I could see her feet bobbing up and down as she stood, waiting for me to understand. Her fingers were twitching as she kept her gaze on me.

"You've *got* to see the bigger picture, Lil Sis."

"Oh?" I whipped around. "And what's the bigger picture? You continually frame me for murder and arson and have the world treat me like a criminal? You wreak havoc and turn the world against the Effigies?"

"Yes," June answered simply, and straightened her back. "Because once the world doesn't need you anymore, you'll be *free*. Free from this bullshit."

She had a scolding air now, the kind she had whenever I wasn't on board with whatever good she wanted to do.

"Think about it, Maia. Why are you even an Effigy in the first place? When I was dead . . . what I can remember . . ." She shut her eyes for a moment, pressing her lips together as if trying to recall something important. She remained silent for a beat too long, her hands clenching and unclenching. "No. I can't remember everything, but I know I learned something important. About the Effigies. About the secrets of the world. Fates twisted . . ."

The words died on her lips. She was squeezing her lids too tight, her hands frozen in fists that were now trembling. "Fate," she whispered, a scowl deepening on her face. "Fate," she repeated, letting the heavy word fall between us. "Your fate was twisted, Maia, when you became an Effigy. My fate was twisted when I died. But who twists fate? *Who* controls fate? *Who* decides who lives and dies and suffers?"

Her eyes snapped open, but she wasn't looking at me at all. She was seeing past me, focused on an invisible enemy.

"No . . ." Her downcast eyes hid behind a mess of hair as she bent over and shook her head. "No, I don't remember. I don't remember. . . ."

"June . . ." I'd never seen June like this—agitated, frustrated, and unable to cope with it. *I* was usually the basket case of the two, guided by her calmer, cooler head. "What are you talking about?"

*"I'm saying it's not fair,"* June yelled suddenly, her words bolting up my spine, causing my body to seize up. "None of it was fair. It wasn't fair." Three words. She kept repeating them, lost in faded memories of death until I grabbed her shoulders to bring her back to reality. But it took her a moment. I could tell. I could see her eyes trying to work out where she was. Was it the effect of being alive again? The effect of the mind-controlling chip? Both?

She'd gone from fierce to frail in a second. She looked lost, at least until she'd sunk back into the here and now. That was when she inhaled a shaky breath. "I'm sorry," she apologized, wrapping her arms around herself, letting her fingers touch mine.

"June." I released my grip because I could tell I was hurting her. Saul had brought her back for a reason. He *did this* to her. I had to get to the bottom of it. "What did Saul tell you?"

"That with my help I could put you back on the right path," June said. "The fate of our choosing. Blackwell's plan is to make the Sect and Effigies obsolete: an antiphantom system that doesn't require either. No Sect. No Effigies. You wouldn't have to fight anymore. We could go back to our normal lives."

"You really think they're going to let a superpowered being just roam free without any kind of surveillance or supervision?" No way. If Blackwell's new order couldn't abide by free-thinking Effigies who could one day turn against him, he'd find a way to lock us up and keep us out of the way. But June was focused on something else. Her eyes brimmed, wet, as she answered me.

"Yes, I do." Her voice sparkled with a kind of childlike hope that made it somehow sound softer, higher. "Saul promised he would. And, Maia—Saul said he'll bring back our parents."

My hands dropped to my sides. Mom. Dad? My expression twisted in pain as I thought of them. Saul would . . . he would . . . ?

"With a stone that grants wishes. The same one that brought me back. Maia, don't you want that?"

I did. The idea of Saul dangling my dead parents above my not-dead sister's head like a doggy treat incensed me, but I still did want them back.

"What attachment do you have to the Sect anyway?" June continued. "Just a bunch of bureaucratic jerks. Why not get rid of them?"

But I wasn't sold. There had to be a catch. "And replace them with what? Or whom?"

June folded her arms. "That man, Blackwell. He does seem to be the center of it all. Saul's helping him, though he never told me why. I'm sure both have their reasons. If Blackwell thinks he has what it takes to lead everyone in a new, wonderful direction, then why not let him?"

I shuddered. If Blackwell was the Pied Piper of the New World, I doubted the direction he'd lead us in would be all that "wonderful."

"There's something else though," I said. "The stone that brought you back. There's more of it out there. Saul may be helping Blackwell right now, but the stone is his true goal."

"Oh, not just Saul's," June said. "Blackwell wants it too. Saul told me."

"Blackwell?" I searched her calm expression.

"Yeah. Though tearing down the Sect seems to be more of a priority for him, eventually Blackwell wants the stone for himself."

I blinked, trying to understand. "And Saul is just . . . okay with this?"

"Of course. Why not?"

June didn't seem to understand the conundrum. Not just Saul, but

Blackwell wanted the stone. Well, it was a stone that, with enough power, could turn someone into a god. It would be a fitting prize for a man like Blackwell, who already carried himself in that esteem. But surely Saul wasn't naive enough to think that Blackwell would play nice and share a power like that?

"I don't know much about the stone or what exactly Blackwell would do with it," June said. "In either case, Saul assured me that after everything's done, I'll get my reward. He'll use the ring to bring back our parents."

"But everything comes at a cost, June." I quickly checked behind me to make sure no one would barge in. "The stone grants wishes, but only when it's charged with . . . with death."

"Energy." June looked up at the sky. "Death and life are part of the same energy. I . . . I remember that much from being dead. I guess death energy is easier to manipulate . . . to harness. But then doesn't that make sense? Protecting is work. Isn't it so much easier to hurt someone?"

The eerie calm of her words matched the serenity in her eyes as she thought of it, her fingers twitching on the word "hurt." Like they were anxious. Maybe as anxious as I was.

"Yeah . . ." I trailed off, swallowing the uncomfortable lump in my throat. "But if just that little ring can do so much damage, imagine how much power the rest of the stone has. Only some kind of psycho megalomaniac would want to get their hands on that. June, doesn't this bother you?"

It should have bothered her. But what should have bothered her didn't, and what *did* bother her made no sense. June was upside down. She cupped my face in a pair of hands, one of which felt rough against my burns. "All that concerns me, Lil Sis, is getting my family back. And Saul's promised me that."

The mind control had completely destroyed her. It was the conclusion I'd drawn before even stepping into the station, and I was right. She was now some mangled version of herself. *That* was the reason for this fear building inside me, the beads of sweat forming on my forehead. That was reason for the shadows beneath her eyes.

"You can say what you want about that stone," she continued, "but Saul used it to bring me back. He . . ." She paused. "He conquered death. Yes." She was shaking a little, as if the very thought of it sent her bones into an ecstatic shiver. "With the stone, he conquered death. No. He surpassed *fate* itself, Maia. And soon we'll do it too."

"Fate . . ." I struggled to decipher her ramblings, but all I could concentrate on were the quick twitchings of her fingers. "June, what are you—"

"Enough talking. Come on," June said. "We have to go. It's why I got 'arrested' in the first place—to draw you out. Bring you here."

"Bring me here . . ." I considered her, noting the twinkle in her eye as she shared her brilliance. "How did you know I was in the city?"

"Dawson told me."

My body seized up. "Dawson?"

"After the fire trucks came . . . I guess he didn't notice Maia was wearing different clothes. He was upset, thought you'd escaped to Sangatte already."

The dread in me sank like a weight. "Oh god, please tell me you didn't kill him."

"What?" June made a face. "No! Of course not. Jesus, Maia, I'm not some psycho. I do what I have to, when I have to."

My mouth went lax as the words flew freely from her lips. "You mean you *kill* when you need to kill? Is that what you're telling me, June?" This was too much. I swiveled her around again, spotting the red bruise in her neck. "Okay, look, we need to get that chip out. Like, now. Maybe Lucas knows someone who can help dig it out of you. That has to go first and foremost."

"Maia—"

"It happened to me once," I explained, like I couldn't get the words out fast enough. "All the Silent Kids are being controlled. Grunehilda? No, Grunewald. It's Grunewald, right?"

June gave me a lopsided grin, shaking her head as if she found my terror amusing, almost cute. "Yeah, that's his name."

"And I know there's a lot that's confusing you right now, what with the being dead and coming back to life, but we can deal with that later, after we short-circuit whatever nanotech is controlling you. Then we—"

"Nothing is controlling me."

My lips froze in a part as my next words died in my throat. "What . . . ?" I swallowed, furrowing my brows as I tried to understand. "What are you talking about?"

"There is something in here." She tapped the back of her neck. "But it's different from what they put in the others. It's a simpler system they used due to time constraints, something more like a failsafe in case I don't follow orders. If I don't do what they say, they'll incapacitate me—maybe even kill me."

"They're *controlling* you!" I gripped her arms once more. "It's a damn kill chip. June, that's what that means. I'm telling you that *they're controlling you.*"

"And I'm telling you that I don't need it." June'd said it too simply, too calmly, with a pleasant shrug I felt like poison in the pit of my stomach. "I don't know why, Maia, but ever since I came back, I've just felt so . . ." She flinched again, stretching out her neck as if something inside her wouldn't allow her to sit still. "Agitated. Frustrated. But every time I use this ability . . ." She looked at her own hands, the whites of her palms flush with living red. "I don't know, it's like it fixes everything. At least for a moment. I thought I'd be terrified using fire, but I'm not. I feel strong. I feel free. It's ironic, isn't it? But with this power I can actually have a hand in my own fate. I can *change* our fate. It's crazy, isn't it?"

Her eyes were wide as she waited for confirmation, but I was too shocked to give it to her. I couldn't speak, couldn't think.

"Believe me. Maia, everything I'm doing is of my own will."

The statement left me shattered.

It was now clearer to me than it'd ever been. My sister hadn't come back—at least, she hadn't come back *right*. What was once her strong sense of justice had been strangled by the mortal coil. It wasn't science.

Death and resurrection had broken her.

"Come on." She grabbed my wrist. "I've got a ride waiting for me as soon as they see my signal. Now that the world is turning against the Sect and Blackwell's whole anti-Sect plan thing is almost done, it's time for me to take you to Saul. He knew you'd be hiding yourself from tracking devices, but he also figured that if I were out there, you'd come to *me*. And he figured you wouldn't fight if it was me asking."

June tugged on my arm, but it flopped lifelessly in response. She sighed impatiently. "Come on, Maia! All I have to do is bring you to Saul—and I guess burn a few more places down. All *you* have to do is tell Saul and his people what they need to know. Then that's it. We're free to go back to New York or wherever you're living now. With Uncle Nathan, right? We'll get our parents back, and we'll be a family. No Effigies, no Sect, no fighting and dying." True, genuine happiness emanated from her smile. "We will make our *own* fate."

Why was the villain's speech always so tempting?

Why was my *sister* the villain?

She was right. None of this was fair. It wasn't fair that she'd died so horribly. It wasn't fair that someone was manipulating her pain to control her. It wasn't fair that she'd become so twisted from the process of death and resurrection that she saw murder as nothing more than a means to an end. None of this was fair.

But . . .

"I can't go with you." Gently, I took my arm out of my sister's grasp.

June blinked. "What?"

"And I can't let you kill any more people."

She looked at me. Peering through her now slightly blank eyes, I could see a silent rage roll out of its slumber. "But, Maia . . . I did all this *for* you."

"You're a murderer now," I said. "And I can't let you kill any more people. I refuse."

Silence. A mixture of anger and hurt twisted June's expression into something slightly frightening. "You *refuse*." She was rigid. Her lips snapped shut as she stared straight ahead, *through* me. "I see. So, what now, Maia?" she said. "What are you planning to do?"

"We can escape together," I said quickly, letting myself hope that she'd just agree. "We'll still be on the run, but that's okay for now. First we can find out more about this stone and how it might fit into Blackwell's plans. Then we can meet up with the other Effigies and this agent friend I know. Well, 'friend' is kind of—" I was sure Sibyl would bristle at the word being used to describe her. "Project X19 is the 'plan' designed to get rid of the Sect, but we can't trust that what Blackwell and his faction of traitors have in mind will be any better. We have to get ahead of it. Once we expose them, we can clear our name! And then—"

"And then *what*?" June snapped, and for a moment she looked taller, larger, like the something *terrible* that lived inside her body had suddenly roused. "And then the status quo? We live without our parents? And you—you stay on as an Effigy until you die in some phantom battle? *That's* your *plan?*"

A kind of fury was building in her voice that didn't belong there. I stumbled back unconsciously as she approached me, step by slow step.

"It's the right plan," I answered quietly. "In your plan, you're a bad guy. In *my* plan, you're one of the good guys. Remember? Those games we used to play as kids?"

Pummeling our stuffed animals. Bathroom towels for capes flying righteously behind us.

"Yeah." June stopped. "I remember."

French chattering from the other end of the hallway. A door opening. A few cops were coming into the holding area.

"We were supposed to be the good guys, June."

"Yeah. But your plan sucks." June stepped back. "So I guess I'll be a bad guy."

I heard the snap of her fingers. The flames followed.

# 9

THE BACK WALL CRUMBLED IN SMOKE AND flame. I coughed, shielding my face from the smoke. The cops were on the ground, dazed but unharmed, but I couldn't guarantee the ones in June's path of escape would be as lucky.

I chased after her, jumping over mounds of rubble. Overturned desks, blood-spattered walls. June left chaos in her wake as she ran through the halls. The officers couldn't even get their guns out to shoot before there was another explosion.

She reached the front of the station. "Stop!" I cried out, but the sight of her through a wall of flames froze me to the spot. Suddenly I could remember seeing her charred corpse in a body bag. Then I was doubling over, heaving, breathing in too sharply.

"I love you, Lil Sis," she said. "But I'm going to do things *my* way."

Another snap of her fingers, and the floor exploded between us, sending me to the ground. I looked up just in time to see her confidently stride out the front door.

Once my head was no longer spinning, I stumbled to my feet, sucked in a breath, and stretched my arms outward, banishing the flames before surveying the damage. Dead bodies, some still alive but half burned. It was horrible. Inhuman.

June wasn't a Fire Effigy. She couldn't banish the flames. She could only destroy—or only wanted to destroy.

This wasn't my sister.

"Call for medical," I told someone I found quivering under his desk, and staggered out the door after June. The streets were empty because it was the dead of night, but the few bystanders nearby had ducked for cover. June was already halfway down the street, striding with determination, exploding the cop cars that tried to chase her. A flaming car crashed upside down onto the pavement, smoke billowing. Biting my bottom lip, I snuffed out those flames too. Chase after her or save them: June knew I wouldn't be able to leave the officers. She was keeping me busy. Maybe that's why she slowed down, checking the skies. She had no intention of running any farther. She was waiting for something.

I began tearing open car doors with my renewed strength, pulling bodies out onto the street, keeping stock of who was alive and who wasn't. I'd just successfully given CPR to someone when another police car pulled up behind me.

"Maia!" It was Lucas. The car had barely stopped moving before he swung open his door. Stepping out of the car, he looked at the damage down the street. "This isn't really what you had in mind, is it?"

Sirens in the distance, though they were almost too far away to catch. Ambulances were on their way. But something else appeared before they did, from the skies: a helicopter. It flew in from behind a column of smoke, wings chopping the air. June waved. Her ride had arrived.

"June!" I called. "June, don't—"

The helicopter door opened and a long rope ladder fell out. The one who'd dropped it came out from the darkness.

"Vasily," I rasped.

Seeing him again drove me into a rage I couldn't release. The murderous boy grabbed hold of the side of the wall to keep himself steady, his blond hair tossed by the wind generated from the chopper. As usual, his ribs could be seen through the loose T-shirt he wore, his long fingers flicking, indicating for June to climb quickly. She did. And as she did, he waited.

"June!" I screamed when she was already halfway up, a frantic energy pulsing through me. "Don't go!"

Not only June's, but Vasily's eyes were on me. Two pairs of eyes. Two very different emotions. I could have sworn Vasily arched his eyebrows in amusement, scoffing before receding back into the helicopter. It took off as June kept climbing.

I slapped the hood of Lucas's car. "We're going after her."

"Really? You want to end up like those guys?" He jerked his head at all the officers lying on the street.

"I can take her!"

"And how many people are going to get charred in the battle?" Lucas flung open the back door. "Get in. Stick to your original plan. Regather yourself. Go after her when you have more manpower—like your friends, yeah?"

I felt a sudden pang at the thought of Lake and Chae Rin. I tried to ignore the Belle-shaped hole in that group. "But I have no idea where they are."

The ambulance sirens grew closer.

"Look, we've got to go." Lucas tapped the door. "The ambulance comes, you get framed again. And next time they'll lock you up in a steel prison in the middle of Siberia and throw away the damn key."

"But—"

"You know why I'm helping you?" Lucas shook the car door in

frustration. "Because you saved Jin's son. Now, I like the kid, don't get me wrong, but it's *Jin*. Jin's the one who picked me up off the streets. He's the one who gave me a second chance at life. I respect the man. And he asked me to do this favor for you, so I'm here, but I am *not* going to die for you."

I let out the breath I'd been holding, my head pounding, as he straightened up.

"Now, you have two options," he said. "One"—he held up a finger—"you come with me and you get on that cargo ship. You regroup, figure out whatever weird shyte you have going on, and then, when all the cards are in *your* favor, then and *only* then do you go after your evil twin. Or option two"—he held up the other—"you chase after a helicopter on foot and get your arse thrown into that Siberian prison. Or dead. What's it going to be?"

I clenched my teeth, staring up at the sky where my sister and the helicopter carrying her were shrinking to a point. Yanking the door out of his grip, I shot him an angry look, but nonetheless got into the backseat of the car.

"Door number one. Good," he said, and sat in the driver's seat.

Even with the kill chip, June was doing everything of her own free will. But it was the experience of death and rebirth that had twisted her into this. She'd so much as told me herself. Her anger. Her frustration. She was lashing out, emotional, vulnerable to Saul's manipulative promises. She was a murderer, but not everything was of her doing.

And I was going to save her. Even if that meant saving her from herself.

I stared at my mutilated reflection in the window superimposed onto the horrible destruction of the station, seeing her scars instead.

*I will save you, June, I swear.*

# 10

I INOCULATED MYSELF AGAIN. DIDN'T HAVE too many of those left, but it was better than having an army chasing me, especially after the mayhem June had caused. It was only a forty-minute drive to Dunkirk, but before getting there, we stopped by the side of the road under the cloak of trees. And waited.

A beat-up little white pickup truck made its way down the road before parking a few feet behind us on the dirt shoulder. Two men exited and slammed their doors, one with a fat mustache that annexed practically half his face. Oil pasted his sallow skin and his gut hung over his belt, distending his flannel shirt. The other man was leaner, brown skin and curly black hair mushrooming from the top of his head.

The two men approached us with caution. On the way here, Lucas had definitely made sure to tell them we'd be arriving in a cop car, but as a pair of criminals, you could never be too sure at the sight of those blinking lights. Through the rearview, I could see their hands hovering by their backs. No doubt they had a gun or two stashed in their pants, concealed in the dark. Lucas stuck his hands out of the door the moment he opened it, signaling to them that he wasn't a threat. Unafraid, he stepped out of the car to greet them.

"Stay here," he told me as he passed by my window. "These guys are a bit delicate."

Of course, I didn't. I got out immediately, much to his exasperation, shutting the door behind me. The two men stopped the moment they saw me and started speaking in hushed tones. Once again, their hands reached behind their backs. Lucas calmed them down in French.

"These are the guys who're going to help you get on the cargo ship," he said, adding, annoyed, "And because you didn't listen to me and got out of the car, they almost shot ya. Thought you were a mole or something. Guys like these are always on edge, you see."

"Lucky for them, they didn't try me," I mumbled, watching their hands fall back to their sides. "Not really in the mood for any crap right now."

Lucas laughed loudly to cover up my voice and draw attention back to himself. He spoke to the men, moving to the rear of the cop car. With a few swift clicks he opened the trunk. While they stood on either side of Lucas, busy eyeing the contents with a kind of ravenous greed, I sidled up next to them.

Wow. Weapons. Some Sect grade, some not. Killing machines coated in silver. And Lucas was selling them.

"What?" he said after catching my side glance. "Honey, you knew I was trouble when you married me."

He turned to Mustache Guy and flicked his head toward the trunk. The two men nodded to each other and began lifting up the handles of the duffel bag Lucas had stuffed them in for ease of transport.

"This is the price of your trip," Lucas said, closing the hood of the cop car. "Nothing's for free."

"So what's *your* price?"

His smile spread into an innocent grin I knew was anything but. With a long finger, he tapped his cheek.

My incredulous laugh made Lucas's friends turn their heads for a moment before going back to their business stuffing the duffel bag into the back of their pickup. "You've got to be kidding me."

"It's a pretty cheap price. Notice I'm not tapping anywhere else."

"You do and you'll lose a finger."

"Vicious." Lucas folded his arms and leaned against the car. "I guess that's to be expected after that whole ordeal with your sister. Or is it something else?" He tilted his head to the side. "My incredibly handsome face not to your liking? Or—" I fidgeted beneath his studious gaze. "There's someone else?" Somehow the sight of me rolling my eyes made him snap his fingers in triumph. "That's it, isn't it?"

"It's none of your business," I spat back, but the bite in my bark faded quickly. Seeing June, knowing she was alive, didn't mean Rhys was too. Saul would have saved her because she was useful. But not Rhys. My sister was alive and evil. And Rhys, who was relatively good, was still dead.

In situations like these, he'd be a cool head, a helping hand. He'd try to understand. He'd give me courage, even if he was terrified himself. At least that was the Rhys I chose to remember. The one who guided me along this hellish path not knowing he would never make it to the end of it.

He'd made terrible choices under terrible circumstances. Nothing could absolve or excuse him from his actions. I knew that. But how could anyone live a life so cruel and short?

Lucas must have realized that the time for teasing was over, because he didn't say anything else. Soon the men called us over. No, not us—me.

Lucas confirmed it. "They're going to take you into town."

They looked like they'd sooner cook me than give me a ride. "What about you?" I asked quickly.

Lucas scrunched his nose in confusion. "I thought you hated me."

"I don't *hate* you!"

"Well, make up your mind, woman." Lucas winked and slapped the top of the car. "Don't worry. We have an agreement. They look a little mean, but they'll keep to it." Reaching into the passenger bench, he took out my backpack and handed it to me. "Wait, don't forget this." My floppy fisherman's hat. Lucas fitted it over my head. "Do what you need to do," he said, patting the top of the hat down. "Remember that number I gave you on the way here. Don't hesitate to call if you need help. Jin and our crew—if we can get to you, we'll do what we can."

"Thanks." I slung the bag over my shoulder.

Lucas shut the door and, after a slight hesitation, placed his hand gently on my arm. "You'll be okay, Maia. You'll sort it out with your sister. Just don't do anything rash." He looked at my blister. "Or rather, don't do anything I wouldn't do."

I smirked. "Well, I'm not a criminal, so that shouldn't be too hard."

Lucas laughed and patted me hard on the back. "Full a' jokes, this one."

With a cute, lopsided grin, he shook his head, mumbling my words again in amusement. Then, after getting back inside his stolen car, he drove off down the road.


I didn't know the names of Lucas's "colleagues" and they didn't tell me. I rode into Dunkirk in the back of their pickup truck, lying beneath a burlap sack. Again. It wasn't until we got to the cargo ship that I realized the ship was theirs—or their gang's, rather. I'd heard of this before. Too many ships on the market and depressing prices gave traffickers an easy way to buy off aging ships and stuff them full of migrants, refugees, and whoever else needed a place on board—for a price. Lucas had already paid mine. But there were no people on board, aside from the criminal crew. This one was filled with weapons, like the ones Lucas had given them. Weapons that could find their way to the hands of people like the ones who'd helped Saul take over Oslo. Guess that was the problem with relying on a sweet but morally ambiguous handsome dude. You felt icky and grateful in equal measure.

But these were desperate times. The ship was to cross the Atlantic to Pointe-à-Pitre in nine days. That meant nine days in this smelly, cramped cubicle of a room until I reached Guadeloupe. Then I'd have to find my own way to the temple and hopefully the answers within.

Nine days on a narrow, rickety, flat bed screwed into the rusted wall was not a luxury trip. I felt like a Dickensian orphan eating the stale bread loafs they gave me once a day. I still had the food I'd taken from Dawson, but when I wasn't eating, I was staring at the piles of dirty clothes and boxes thinking about the mess I was in. Either that, or I was thinking about the heroes I'd placed upon a pedestal—Natalya, Belle, June—knocked off one by one, mired in the dirt with the rest of us. After what had happened with June, I was afraid to sleep for days, fearing my mind wasn't strong enough to keep Natalya's murdering whispers out of my head.

June was right. None of this was fair. Despite her now mangled sense of morality, she was right about a lot of things. She wanted our parents back. So did I. And at the core of her madness was a fury toward those bullshit cosmic forces that had allowed all the tragedy in our lives to happen, forces that decided who got screwed and who didn't, and when, not caring about the consequences.

*Who twists fate?* Who *controls fate?* Who *decides who lives and dies and suffers?*

Good question. Who was it twisting us so?

I thought of others on the long voyage across the Atlantic. I rarely came out of my room, which really wasn't all that different from how I used to live before I turned Effigy, but this time there was no Wi-Fi to keep me sane. So I asked questions. The same questions I'd been asking since I woke in Mr. Dawson's cabin and ones I never considered. Like the other girls, Lake and Chae Rin. Would they be drawn out of their hiding places because of what June had done in France? It wouldn't take much effort for June to ambush either one of them. And if she did, what would she do? Maim them?

Kill them?

No, I didn't want to let myself think of it. I couldn't let myself imagine Chae Rin or Lake hurt and suffering. June used to love the Effigies when she was a kid. But now, if they stood in her way and she had a chance to fool them just long enough to take them down, she would. She'd do it with a song in her heart. All to see her family again.

Everything was so wrong. I couldn't stand it.

As the rickety cargo ship rocked back and forth, I hoped to god my friends would find me first.

# 11

I DIDN'T LEAVE MY ROOM FOR NINE DAYS. THE crew spent most of their time above deck. Traveling alone made me nervous, especially without my powers to rely on. I kept my weapons near just in case anyone tried something, but the rocky voyage eventually came to an end without me needing to use them. One last inoculation load left. I emptied it into my neck before leaving the ship. Smelling the fresh sea air for the first time in days, I stepped out onto the docks at Pointe-à-Pitre and figured out my next move.

It was a hot morning when I arrived. Beads of perspiration already dotted my forehead, some slipping down my nose. The backpack felt like an unneeded weight; shifting it around only awkwardly slid my shirt across an already damp back. Still, I gripped the straps and took a look around. White gates separated the port and the ships from the narrow road. On the other side, people of different shades, mostly on the browner side, hung out chatting next to a row of parked cars. Across the road, two boys rode on their bikes down the sidewalk past a graffitied, boarded-up shack and a long row of two-tiered buildings painted half in aging yellow and maroon. It was too familiar.

Reminded me of those times I visited Kingston with my family. June always loved running around in the humid, sweaty airports with our luggage. But then she was like that everywhere we went. *She* was the confident traveler.

I gripped the strap of my backpack tighter because I realized I didn't have to think of June in the past tense anymore. She was alive—and killing.

Shaking my head, I continued down the sidewalk, following where the boys had ridden. My legs burned from the fatigue of nonuse. I mimicked a few people catching a taxi on the sidewalk to get one myself. Ugh, French again. The man probably asked me where to and I told him "food," because I couldn't put it any more simply. Probably pegging me as a tourist, he shrugged and drove anyway. The taxi traveled through the commercial district of the city where tall palm trees separated the two directions of traffic. The buildings had that worn-out feel that was definitely nostalgic—along with the soda brand names painted on the side of white-plastered walls. "Fisi Cola," one said. "Flan" peanut butter spread. My stomach growled in response.

Every time I looked up, I could see the taxi driver's eyes staring at me before flitting back to the road. Quickly, I touched the side of my face. Almost smooth but for the slight indents of crusted skin; still, a big, splashy mess of boiled flesh wasn't going to stop people from recognizing me anymore. I tied the bandana around my face just as he entered a narrow, one-way street and stopped. Thankfully, I hadn't used the money Dawson had given me. The driver accepted the euros and dropped me off onto the sidewalk. It was a squished-in area, rows of run-down housing with tiers built like Legos stacked on top of the other, each tier closed off with metal, gated terraces that people could step out onto. The rust and graffiti crawling up some of the buildings strangely worked in tangent with the vibrant colors of the walls: purple, blue, orange, and maroon alternating with white. And *pink*—outside that building, two people sat in white plastic chairs chatting. The soda they took out of their bags told me this was the place I needed to go to eat something better than stale bread and cereal bars.

Unlike in France, I didn't feel like I stuck out so much here, except maybe for the bandana. But I still had to be careful. It'd been over a week since I'd seen June; there was no telling what else "Maia Finley" had done in the meantime. Luckily, some people looked, but nobody bothered me. My hair was enough of a shield from the gazes.

This time I bought stuff legally: some food, a charger for my burner, and a map of the area. The guy at the counter was nice, kept joking with me even after he realized I couldn't really understand him. He was pointing to his face. Oh, he was wondering about the bandana.

"I'm sick," I said.

He nodded as if he thought everything I said and did was the pinnacle of hilarity. As he rung up my map, I tapped it against the table. "Basse-Terre?" I opened the page so he knew what I was talking about. "How do I get to Basse-Terre?"

"There are ferry services," answered the younger man stocking cigarette packs behind the counter. Thank god, someone I could communicate with.

"How much are they?"

"Twenty-four euros. I can tell you where."

To my everlasting relief, he took out a marker and drew all over the map I'd just bought. It was beyond satisfying to be around nice, *regular* folks after nine days of cloistering up with murderers and traffickers. I sized up the store. Little kids were running around. Pregnant mothers with strollers. And to think I'd slunk into town on a cargo ship meant to sell weapons.

Weapons that could end up in their communities.

The ship's trafficking gang wouldn't have come unless they already had buyers lined up. Desperate times, yeah. I had no other way of getting here. But I was still an Effigy, sworn to protect people. I couldn't just forget that.

I figured out what to do pretty quickly. I'd kept off my burner phone to save energy the entire trip across the ocean. I asked the woman in her plastic chair how to call the police by repeating the word. After she showed me, I walked down to the edge of the sidewalk, checking behind my back to make sure nobody in this claustrophobic closet of buildings would hear me.

"Hello? Police?" I kept my voice low. If I did this just right, I could make this work in my favor too. "There's a cargo of weapons that just came into town half an hour ago." I gave the location of the dock, as much info as I could about the ship, but the more I talked, the more they asked me—in English—for further details, including who I was.

That was what I was waiting for.

"My name is—" I paused. Okay, I hoped this worked. "Sibyl Langley. Sibyl Samantha Langley. Please help."

I clicked off the phone before they could ask more questions.

If Sibyl was somewhere on this planet manning Team Rebel Alliance, she'd have her feelers out for me for sure, especially knowing what the other me had been up to on the news. If it somehow got to her ears that "Sibyl Langley" was actually in Guadeloupe, she'd investigate. But the message was not just for her. It was for Uncle Nathan, working under her employ.

Samantha. The name of my mother.

The idea was to leave bread crumbs for the right people. If I couldn't find them, maybe they could find *me*. And I got a weapons bust out of the deal. But agents would come here looking for Sibyl, too. A dangerous plan indeed.

I'd have to go back toward the port without a taxi to save my money for a ferry. Look at me, the consummate traveler. A short, incredulous chuckle climbed up my throat as I continued following the directions down sidewalks, past the palm trees and the cars under them. Ten minutes of walking, of tired legs drenched in sweat. In the past few months, I'd been on almost every continent in the world. June was the one who wanted to backpack through Europe one day. But then, as I was well aware, we didn't get to choose our fate. June knew it too.

*It's not fair!* June's words echoed in my thoughts. And because I was thinking of June, I wasn't watching where I was going. The man and woman I almost bumped into stood out from the other pedestrians in their black suits and ties. I'd seen enough of them to know they were Sect agents.

Panic forced my body to react before I had a chance to think. With one smooth movement, I ducked between buildings just as the two lowered their shades and began opening the doors of their van.

"Okay, keep your eyes out, then," I heard the woman say, maybe into the earpiece I noticed. "Report the second you see her or any of the other Effigies."

What? Whom did they mean by "her"? Was it me? Was it because of the bread crumbs? No. I phoned the police ten minutes ago. I could buy them looking for Sibyl, but no way they would have figured out it was me and get here that fast. They didn't sound like local agents either. If they were here, it was because they already had intel that an Effigy was here—maybe before I'd even gotten here. Someone could have seen me and called it in. Maybe the taxi driver figured it out. But what if . . . ?

What if . . . ?

After the Sect van drove off, I slipped out from behind the building.

June?

I was fully paranoid now. Sweaty, tired, and paranoid.

But I also wasn't alone in Guadeloupe. I felt it in my bones.

This was going to be tricky.

People stared on the ferry even with my face covered by the bandana and floppy hat, but it was always the same story. They'd look away after a few seconds. The "No, it couldn't be her" syndrome. People were least likely to believe someone famous was sitting among them, even with regular celebrities who weren't wanted terrorists. When the ferry dropped us off at the island docks, most of the passengers traveled toward the beach, or toward the little town, its white buildings with red roofs scattered along the coast. My target was the temple beyond the rolling green hills. I followed the map carefully. Pastor Charles warned me the greenery beyond the village was a Dead Zone, and the little skull and crossbones marked on the map made that abundantly clear. Leave it to me to go *toward* the human remains.

At the perimeter of trees, a tall yellow sign on a yellow stake protruded from the ground. I didn't need to understand the scribble; the pitch-black drawing of a beast with its jaws wide open sent the message loud and clear. I suppose it was cheaper than a state-of-the-art antiphantom fence. Even with the patrols I'd hidden from earlier driving around in their open Jeeps, it was like playing Russian roulette with people's lives. Then again, they would have been largely correct in assuming that few people would be stupid enough to venture into a Dead Zone. You could hear the phantoms' cries from here, deep and hypnotic, like singing whales in the deep ocean. No telling how many were in there.

There were no patrols around. I could be in bed illegally streaming television on my laptop like everyone else right about now.

With a heavy sigh, I entered the forest, swallowed up by trees. No phantoms yet. The forest was deceptively peaceful. I'd already been following a dirt trail for about ten minutes before I came to a spring, a waterfall cascading down the green hill into the rippling pool.

If it weren't for the ripples, perhaps I wouldn't have noticed the dead body being pushed toward the perimeter of stones at my feet.

Throwing my bandana and hat to the ground, I reached into my backpack and took out the gun I'd grabbed from Dawson. Just in case. I jumped into the water and began dragging the body out, only to feel something wrap around my legs. Oh crap.

It yanked me under the water, the familiar pressure battering my body. No time to think. I couldn't see, so I pointed the gun down to wherever I thought the tentacle was coming from and shot like mad. Even underwater, I could hear it scream. It shook, desperately trying to hold on to me, but after another shot, it receded down into the depths. I swam up, grabbed the dead body, and waded ashore.

The carcass I dragged out onto the bed of rocks belonged to a man, a tourist judging by the cheesy blue shirt he wore, which looked straight out of a gift shop: I ♥ GUADELOUPE! The body wasn't decomposed. He hadn't been dead long, maybe not even a day. Strange. Phantoms mimicked the forms of beasts in all shapes and sizes, but the one I'd just faced didn't seem the type to leave a body intact during an attack. The only way that person wouldn't have been torn apart by that phantom is—

—if they were already dead.

Setting the gun down, I checked his body for wounds, stopping when I felt a groove in his chest. Tearing the shirt revealed a gaping stab wound there—straight through the heart.

A *human* killed this guy. Why?

My mind buzzed with flashes of the hooded figure just as the water began bubbling again. June? But wouldn't she have just burned him? Guess there was no time to investigate further. Grabbing my gun, backpack, and bandana, I left the poor guy and ran in the other direction. As I ran deeper into the forest, kicking away raccoons and mosquitoes, haunting footsteps rattled the ground beneath my feet. Tropical leaves swayed above the treetops, likely because a monster was moving through them. That woman Yulia and her traveling Deoscali sect really came here every few months? And if what Pastor Charles said was true, then she was due back soon. Maybe I'd bump into her here. It'd be a great opportunity to ask her how the hell she managed to get through a mess of phantoms with no tech. I picked up the pace, following my map to the temple.

If that figure I saw before was June, and June really did kill that guy, then what was her plan? Had she devolved so far that she was just murdering indiscriminately now, like a damn phantom? My left hand tightened around the strap of my backpack as the other clutched the gun. Sweat dripped down my soaked neck as the sun blared overhead. I was almost out into a clearing.

The joints in my legs went rigid as steel, but they kept working, this time faster. They had to because something was tracking me, a black shadow slipping through the trees behind me. I broke into a full-on run, swinging my arms, my wet clothes dragging me down. A few steps and a phantom's jaw burst out of the trees, not behind me but beside. I couldn't get a good look at it until after I shot my gun, my back hitting the soil. It was on all fours, a shadow jaguar twice my height with black bones protruding through rotted flesh and forming a row of razors down its back. Its drooling teeth came fast and vicious, snapping until I shot out its eye with a blast of blue energy. The trees behind me were rustling. More were coming. I jumped to my feet and fled while the phantom was distracted. One phantom chased me. Two more like it followed.

More swiveled out from their hiding places, breaking the ground as they landed behind me. The force propelled me forward, but I stayed on my feet, running for dear life, shooting behind me. I leapt down the steps that led to a bridge stretching over the valley. The terrible crash of wood exploding under the rampaging phantom who'd jumped after me and landed behind me sent a flock of birds screeching into the air. The entire bridge almost collapsed, but I jumped just in time and held on to the stake in the ground on the other end. The phantom roared as it fell into the valley, my gun along with it. I still had my other stuff. I pulled myself up and kept running through the trees, throwing a smoke bomb to ward off the other phantoms that began gnarling toward me, but it could do only so much. More beasts on all fours barreled toward me. A smoky swarm of black phantom bees like the ones I'd faced in New York swept down from the skies. But I could see an opening in the distance and beyond it—a narrow clearing. The temple. I just had to make it there.

Suddenly, the head of a phantom broke through the soil right underneath me, launching my body and gear into the clearing in opposite directions. The sound of my shoulder cracking rattled my head as I crashed against the ground. *Get up!* I rolled onto my back, my nerves screeching.

Magic. The magic in me erupted, overriding the inhibitor still strong in my system. My hands were on fire before my feet could steady themselves on the soil. I was ready to attack. Ready to set the entire forest on fire to save my own life.

But the phantoms didn't come.

I could see them, their blank eyes bright as moons peeking through the trees. None of them dared to follow. Because of me? No, phantoms weren't afraid to come after Effigies. If anything, phantoms craved Effigy blood. And yet the smoky swarm changed directions and flew back into the Dead Zone, which welcomed them.

Apparently this place didn't.

I could feel a spiritual pulse in the soil feeding the flames crackling in my palms. As the magic in me swelled, my muscles relaxed and my breathing settled. Even after all the fleeing and terror, I was able to catch my breath quickly, but only because the air filled my lungs without the opposition of panic. Peace permeated the clearing. All around me . . .

Calm.

It was the same sensation. Though not quite as powerful out here as what I'd felt in Pastor Charles's chamber or the cellar where we found Castor's secret volume, the calm here was unmistakable.

Behind me stood the temple, magnificent as a monument, though after more than a hundred years, nature had begun to overrun the structure: Vines stretched down the roof, draping the gray stone walls. Twisting tree roots grew over the marble platform upon which the temple was built, tree leaves rustling with the air. The temple itself didn't look too large from the outside, but its presence commanded respect nonetheless, as if it'd been standing for a thousand years. Limestone stretched across the bottom half of the exterior, smooth and continuous behind tracks of green moss, but the top of the temple looked as though it was pieced together hastily by slabs of stone, leaving an uneven roof that traced out a cityscape in the clear blue sky.

My body was no longer in fight-or-flight mode, but my senses were still on alert. I fetched my gear, keeping my eyes on the forest, noting the creatures, natural and supernatural, prowling just beyond the trees. The platform left room in the center for a wide stone staircase that led to the entrance. The stone was crumbling, so I stepped carefully, eventually walking through a pair of marble columns that held up a little pyramid-shaped roof, like an umbrella that shaded the stone door tucked inside. More vines dangled down the entrance's triangular roof, but the moss growing on the lintel—the wide slab of stone stretching vertically to form the bottom of the triangle—couldn't obscure the design I saw etched there.

The lintel's design was more than just extravagance. It told a story, carved in stone meant to be read from left to right. Etched into the structure were a series of bodies, each figure passing off an object to the other. I couldn't see what the first girl passed to the second. Her features were exaggerated—wide nose, round lips, and hair that billowed behind her like a nimbus cloud. Fierce eyes burned as she passed a swirling light to the second woman, duller in design, her plain hair and simple dress flat in the stone. Then the next pair: The second woman handed the light to a tall man—looked like one of those American frontiersmen with the high boots and frock coat. His nose was bulbous, his hands large as he reached out for it. Keeping with the pattern, he was the giver of the final pair, handing the light—this time as small as a pebble—to a short woman in flowing robes. But the four weren't alone; carvings of phantoms enveloped and separated each pair. If this slab told the story of the temple's creation, then it was hard to see how phantoms would have bothered them. The ones chasing me wouldn't even go near this place.

The mystery had puzzled Pastor Charles too; how had they managed to build this place in the center of a Dead Zone?

I was here to gather information, so I drew out the phone in my jeans pocket and took pictures. This was the kind of weird shit I'd have to give to Sibyl whenever I found her.

My gear was slipping off my shoulders, so I pulled it back up. Harry's little backpack had seen more adventure than it'd need in a lifetime.

But the adventure wasn't over.

After one last look behind me, I went up the stairs and into the temple.

• • •

A dark tunnel on the other side of the entrance. How cozy—especially the horseshoe arch ceiling above that looked less like horseshoes and more like a row of bones, rib cages maybe. Whale bones? *Phantom* bones? I shuddered and absently pulled up the backpack as it was slipping down my back. Could have been limestone or something. Honestly, who knew how they'd been able to put this place together. Beneath the arched roof was a row of mirrors bordered by the same brick I saw outside. Several Maias stared at me with bloodshot, sleep-deprived eyes, the purple scars on their right cheeks almost faded down to whispers on the flesh. I looked away. I didn't need to see so many Maias. Two was more than enough.

The deeper into the temple I ventured, the more my power seemed to swell. Good for protection, bad for evading detection. It limited the time I could spend gathering info in this place. I just hoped there wouldn't be a swarm of Guadeloupe's finest waiting for me outside once I left. The last time that happened, it didn't end well for anyone.

Midway through the long hall was a statue of the last girl from the lintel. Slight, and with a bun at the top of her head, she sat in a throne of howling phantoms, dressed in flowing robes. An odd fashion choice. I leaned in, inspecting it, but as it was, her hollow eyes seemed to be inspecting me right back. It was always the same with statues. There was always something about the eyes that unsettled me.

The plaque at the statue's platform:

EMILIA FARLOW: LEADER OF THE DEOSCALI AND TEMPLE DIRECTOR,

WITH THE AID OF LOUISA ALTO

What? Was this tiny, pug-like girl really Emilia? The robes she wore certainly looked like the kind of cult-y stuff you'd see Scales wear, like the ones at Pastor Charles's services in London. If this was Emilia, then who was Louisa?

There were more words written below the names.

AS THE SERVANT GAVE TO THE TEACHER, THE TEACHER GAVE TO

THE TRAVELER. AS THE TEACHER GAVE TO THE TRAVELER,

THE TRAVELER GAVE TO ME.

It must have been in reference to the story told through the lintel's design outside. The servant . . . the teacher . . .

Emilia. Emilia Farlow was a teacher. She was studying to be one, ended up passing on her crazy phantom teachings instead. But then, that couldn't be right. According to the plaque, *this* girl was Emilia, the "me" of the equation. How could Emilia be two of the four figures on the lintel? I had to be wrong.

And the servant—

"Marian?" I whispered. I tried to remember. Belle, Lake, Chae Rin, and I scried together in Prague. Belle said something about Emilia needing to find Castor after the disaster in York. Thomas Castor, who traveled around the world finding Effigies and learning about the phantoms for the Sect. The servant, Marian. The traveler, Thomas.

"Emilia Farlow . . ." I leaned in, noting her wide, square jaw and scowl, the bun at the top of her head thick and unruly, even as stone. "What are you trying to tell me?"

I took more pictures and passed through the doors at the end of the hall.

"Wait!" I yelled. A figure had just disappeared through a wooden door on the other end of the pentagon-shaped room. Right before the entrance shut, I caught a glimpse of a charcoal coat fluttering in the breeze. My nerves stung with the same panic I'd felt in town listening to those Sect agents warn each other of a recently spotted Effigy. I was right. I wasn't alone.

June?

I ran around the fountain at the center of the room boxed in by four torches—a long, lizard-like, petrified phantom spilling water from its gaping jaws. Nice touch. Creepy. More importantly, the torches were lit. Could have been June. She was after me, right? She found me in France; she could have found me here, too.

My paranoia wouldn't let me believe otherwise, which was why I expected to find her beyond the door, but the figure was gone. The open air greeted me instead, a rush of power and—

Spirits—yes, spirits. I couldn't see them, but I could feel them. They were swirling around me in this palpable energy, an energy I'd felt once before. I didn't remember much from dying, but I remembered this feeling. Those white lights taking my soul away. It was the same as Prague and Pastor Charles's chamber—no, more potent. Because I knew what it was like now to be them, even if it was just a shade of a memory. Spirits. Souls.

I shuddered so deeply, my muscles were still seized up for a moment afterward. My magic. Life and death. Fate. All of it burst from the same spring, the same well of energy—

I shook my head. If I couldn't block out the feel of those spirits, I wouldn't get anything done. Finding June was paramount.

I breathed, tried to not feel the spirits, instead focusing on the energy, the magic swelling inside me. The power. I'd stepped into a courtyard blessed by the heat of the sun above. Stone steps led down from each wall enclosing the yard, and the walls each had their own shadowy entrance for June to escape through, except there was no way she would have been fast enough to just vanish like that. She certainly didn't cross over the grass, unshorn and forest-wild except in the center area where the wooden gazebo stood.

Within the gazebo was something else I'd seen before in Prague— that flat concrete plaque, like a gravestone. Half buried in the grass, shielded from the sun by the roof of the gazebo. This one had already been moved once. I could tell because it was a little skewed over the soil. After wading through the grass, I set down my backpack and read the inscription.

AND AMONG THE SHADOWS, YOU WILL FIND THEM. FOR ONLY IN CALM CAN YOU HEAR THEM SPEAK.

The spirits, maybe. Except I hadn't heard anything. And having been a spirit myself, I distinctly remembered the lack of a mouth.

I grabbed the handle and lifted the plaque, pushing it aside. Not too difficult with the power surging in me. If I didn't leave quick, I'd be found out for sure. The shallow dirt pit underneath was empty but for a few shards of stone scattered across the concrete.

Stone shards—like the stone of Saul's ring and the shards in Alice's cigar box, wherever the hell that was now. The boxes were the same make, same wood and embroidery. I picked them up—same weight, feel. Except the stone that granted wishes was pure white but for the black streaks sometimes tingeing its color after it'd been fed by the death of others. *This* stone was tinted in deep blue, sparkling like energy.

"Life," I whispered, though I didn't know why. But it fit. That had to be why I felt protected here, why the phantoms couldn't come near this place. If Saul's stone was powered by death, why couldn't there be another powered by death's merciful opposite?

This had to be the secret something buried beneath Pastor Charles's chambers, though he probably didn't know it. If I went back to the museum in Prague, I'd find these blue shards in the cellar where we'd found the secret volume.

I took pictures of the shards; then, after putting them and the plaque back in their place, I took more pictures of the area. That's when I noticed, for the first time, the symbols carved along the walls. My eyes had glazed over them earlier, mistaking them for simple design, but the harder I looked, the more I realized that each symbol scrawled all along the stone perimeter of the courtyard was separate and distinct. I snapped furiously, trying to find the symbol Natalya had drawn—the symbol of the flame—but I couldn't find it. The others mapped an indecipherable language, one I couldn't crack alone.

*Just take everything to Sibyl,* I reminded myself. *They'll know what to do with it.*

Suddenly, I was jolted out of my thoughts by a woman's blood-curdling scream ricocheting off the walls from behind the shadowy entrance across the courtyard. I whipped around, nearly dropping my burner phone.

"June?" I called out, panicked. "June, is that you?"

My legs pumped as hard as they could toward the sound, every awful outcome playing out in my wild thoughts. Up the stairs and through the shadowy entrance brought me into a dark corridor, unlit torches hanging on the walls.

I shivered. A sudden chill slid from beneath the wooden door. Flakes of frost drifted past my leg. And the knob. The knob was cold. Ice cold.

My fingers clasped the metal but didn't turn right away because they were shaking—shaking in fear.

The girl on the other side of the door wasn't June.

Slowly my hand twisted the knob. Pushed open the door.

The chill rushed out so quickly my throat closed as I inhaled the frigid air. Ice crawled up the stone walls, coating the windowpane above, through which sunlight filtered inside the room in haunting beams. It was fitting, perhaps, that this Effigy didn't stand in the light. Kneeling in front of an altar upon which rested a stone coffin, she'd been holding her head, wincing in pain. But her shoulders relaxed once she heard my gasp. Her arms fell to her sides. Her long red coat swiveled as she turned.

Belle.

A walking corpse. That's what came to mind when I saw her. Not because she was malnourished, like June, or even because of the nosebleed she wiped away without much thought. It was because of the dead eyes that didn't blink even as they saw me standing before them.

"So you *are* alive" was all she had to say.

Trap and release. I called for the temple's energy to enter my body, and so it did in a frantic rush. Terror pumped it through my veins and out of my hands in the form of a scythe. I held it ready.

Belle wasn't going to kill me twice.

# 12

BELLE GAZED DOWN AT MY SCYTHE, THEN AT THE fury in my eyes. None of them seemed to interest her. My hands could have dented the smooth pole of my weapon, but no matter how tightly I gripped it, I was too scared to move toward her. I hated her. I wanted her to suffer for what she did to me. But did I want her dead? Could I even kill her if I tried?

Belle turned away, looking up into the light. She didn't seem angry or unhinged like I'd originally imagined she might be. She simply looked tired. Worn out from the inside.

"You . . . ," I said through gritted teeth at her silence. "You fucking *killed* me."

Belle winced again, bringing a hand back to her forehead.

"Hey!" I barked, and lifted my scythe higher. "Are you listening to me? You *killed* me, but you won't even listen to me?"

"I wondered who I would bump into first." Belle didn't look at me. Her eyes were still closed, forehead furrowed as she rubbed it. "You, or the other you burning cities."

The other me. June. My scythe lowered absently. "How did you know that wasn't me?"

"You're not the murdering type."

"Not like you."

"Or Aidan," Belle added, her gaze locking on me once more so suddenly I nearly jumped back. "But we received our punishments. We're both dead."

Tears sprung from my eyes as I remembered the bright light Rhys had vanished in, but I blinked them back. I couldn't show any sign of weakness.

"Is that how you're justifying what you did?" My confidence wasn't nearly as fierce as I tried to make it sound. She terrified me now. Every movement of hers made my throat close and my knees buckle in fear. I hated it. I hated it all.

"It's the same as you. We all have sins to answer for. That's why I'm here." Belle turned around and looked up at the ceiling again. I was too scared to take my eyes off her, like she'd summon her sword and try to stab me again the second my guard was down, but curiosity got the better of me. I looked up.

The symbols. Each one carved into the walls. The flame. The phantom. And the swirls of energy joining together. They were positioned in a triangular pattern around the window.

"How did you f-find this place?" I asked, cursing myself for stuttering. *Calm down, you idiot.* It was like I was meeting her again for the first time at La Charte Hotel. Except instead of making a fool of myself before my favorite celebrity, I was cowering before my attempted killer. The reality of it all was almost too awful to bear.

"I scryed it." Belle's blond hair spilled over her fingers as she gripped her head again. "I've been scrying. Intensely. In Pastor Charles's church. And here too. Searching through the horrible memories of strangers until the memories I saw just now appeared. I saw a girl build this place with the villagers and the British men lent to her by Castor."

"The traveler."

"He had found a tiny girl, Louisa, on the streets of Portugal, the first Effigy of ice and water he'd discovered."

"Louisa?" I whispered, because the name was familiar.

"She said she would come with him, but only after he helped her build a monument here as a favor for couriering to him precious information before she fell ill and died. Back when she was in her own body. Back when she was Emilia Farlow."

Back when she was Emilia Farlow. Emilia had taken over Louisa's body.

*With the aid of Louisa Alto . . .*

The statue in the temple. The pug-like girl in the robes. So the plaque was correct—that *was* Emilia. Wasn't it Pastor Charles who'd asked how a woman who was already dead could oversee the construction of a temple? Well, it was certainly possible for an Effigy.

Emilia was both the second and the fourth figures of the riddle. Emilia had given Castor precious information, and in turn, Castor had given her, as Louisa, the resources to build a haven for followers of her new doctrine. A chain of giving as told by the lintel outside.

"This temple wasn't the girl's objective, but Emilia's," Belle said, as if anticipating my suspicions. "Even after all my scrying, I couldn't learn everything. But I did learn *something*. The phantoms were Emilia's obsession after the destruction of York. These symbols, her creation, her mission. One given to her by the Fire Effigy, Marian."

My body tensed. "Marian?"

"It was while I was in Pastor Charles's church that I had the vision." Belle shook her head, trying to remember. Maybe that was why she didn't just kill me where I stood. Why she was bothering to tell me at all. She was trying to make sense of it too. "Marian asked Emilia to bury 'his body.' Alice's father."

"Alice . . . ," I whispered, picturing the girl's ice-blond hair and cruel grin.

"'Everything may depend on it,' Marian told her. 'It could be the key to everything.' And so they dragged his dead body out from his secret study and buried him in the backyard of his estate, placing a stone placard in case they would need to visit him again. When I went to York, I saw his remains myself."

"I'm not surprised you'd be fascinated by dead bodies," I mumbled spitefully.

Belle smirked. "Emilia certainly is. Why else would she let me see such a memory? Why am I dreaming of the burial grounds of men? And not just Alice's father." Belle gestured back at the stone coffin upon the raised altar. "Thomas Castor's bones lie here."

I couldn't believe how casually she'd told me that Thomas Castor, the Sect pioneer whose writings were at the center of our mysteries, was just a dusted corpse a mere few feet away from us. My eyes fixed on the stone, but I was too scared to take a step toward it.

"Dreaming of the dead. I see now what Natalya must have gone through. After I ran from Dover, I tried to carry on. Tried to grasp what she had tried to. But there wasn't much I understood except this: Emilia and Castor both had missions. One wanted to understand the world and the other wanted to protect it. I thought I could reclaim my own desire to do both. But . . ." She looked at me. "No matter what I do or where I go, I just can't seem to."

I pulled my scythe closer to me. She looked nothing like the girl I'd once admired. Why had I fought so hard to be like them— Belle, Natalya? Why had I looked up to them so, for all those years? Because even when June was alive, their strength made me forget my own weakness. And after June died, I needed people who could fill up the pit she'd left, and for a moment I thought I had. Belle, Lake, and Chae Rin. The team I belonged to. Simply gone.

The step she took toward me forced me back into fighting mode. "Hey! Don't come any closer," I yelled.

But Belle didn't seem interested in fighting me. She wasn't even looking at me.

"So, what now? You don't care about anything, so you're going to finish me off?" I asked, wanting badly to run and stand my ground in the same breath. "That's the goal, right?"

"My goals are different now that I know that Natalya died for nothing." She stopped. "Murdered by a friend for a corrupt organization." The derisive smirk she flashed was the only sign she was even still alive.

"I know that I screwed up by lying to you about how Natalya died. I shouldn't have let my personal feelings for Aidan get in the way of doing right by her. And you."

Her face tensed; she pressed her lips together, her chest rising in a sharp inhale.

"I'm sorry," I said, and I meant it. "But you—you didn't have to *kill* me."

Belle let herself relax. "This isn't about you anymore. It's bigger than that."

The end of everything.

She continued forward again. This time I extended my scythe, my hand shaking as it held its position. As her heels clicked against the marble floor, the memory of Pastor Charles's words echoed like alarm bells. *If you can't reason with Belle, you may have to—*

"Don't come any closer!" I yelled, but before I could move, Belle grabbed my scythe and with a show of dangerous force broke off the blade. I stumbled back with a gasp as the rest of my scythe dissipated, and for a moment fear completely took over. I keenly felt the scars papering over the stab wound in my chest courtesy of her rage, felt them burn and scream as she drew near. My head was spinning. Fear. Pure fear. The memory of falling off the Dover cliffs. "Don't . . . come any closer. . . ."

But Belle walked past me. My knees shook. My hands clutched my T-shirt. And she just walked past me out of the room.

*Move, move, move,* I ordered myself, but I was too scared. Move. I didn't for several minutes. I couldn't until my breaths no longer tumbled clumsily down my throat like little grenades. When I could inhale again, when I could stand again, I ran back down the dark corridor into the courtyard.

"What exactly are you planning to do now!" I yelled as I stepped through the threshold.

And stopped short.

Belle had already reached the gazebo, but she wasn't the one who answered me. That was when I realized that her coat wasn't the one I'd seen disappearing through the door. Hers was red.

*His* was charcoal.

The figured who'd quickly escaped into the courtyard only to disappear into thin air. He now stood on the other side of the clearing at the top of the staircase, his hood down.

"She's not planning anything, Maia," Saul said, his gray coat billowing. "It's me. As it always has been, *poupée*."

# 13

I WANTED TO BURN HIM ALIVE. THE MAN WHO'D ruined cities, who'd killed Rhys. The man who'd resurrected my sister only to turn her into a murderer. I wanted him *dead*.

My hands crackled with power. "Belle, watch out!" I raised them, ready, but Belle kept walking across the courtyard. Saul's presence didn't alarm her. Didn't so much as bother her. *"Belle!"*

A serene smile, just barely noticeable, played on Saul's lips as he wordlessly met my anger, his gaze from deep-sea blue eyes searching my face. He'd called me *poupée*. Only Alice did that. But Alice's blood-lust wouldn't usually allow her to be this careful and calm. So who was this? Nick Hudson or the girl sharing his headspace?

The gears in Saul's metal hand whirred as his mechanical fingers stretched and clenched. It took me a moment to realize Saul's eyes weren't on me anymore. "You scried, didn't you? Did you find some clue as to how to read the code?"

I clenched the fire in my fist, letting the smoke slip past my knuckles. "What the hell are—"

"No." It was Belle who answered. But that couldn't be right.

Saul started down the staircase, gazing around the courtyard at the symbols carved painstakingly into the crumbling stone walls. "The volume's filled with these. Like I just told Blackwell in Greenland, I don't know what they mean. I dropped you off here for an assessment."

"That's none of my concern," Belle said. "You and Blackwell can sort it out."

Saul's face darkened with a little grin, quietly wicked. "It was your concern the minute you decided to work with us."

The fire extinguished into smoke as my hands fell to my sides, fingers still curled as I grappled with the silence that followed.

"Oh well." Saul dusted himself off. "I'm sure they'll manage to figure it out regardless. But really, what a waste of time this was."

Belle. Saul. Working together. And since Saul was helping Blackwell, that meant she was now in that faction too. "No. That can't be right," I said, my voice trembling as I stared at the back of Belle's head. "You can't be so broken that you'd work with"—my lips curled into a snarl as I shifted back to him—"that psycho."

"Am I the psycho? But it was Belle who was kind enough to go back to my father's estate when I asked her to and bring me this." Calmly, Saul slipped out of his coat a pretty silver jar just small enough to fit into his pocket. "Alice's father's remains."

His ashes. I stifled a gag, staring back at Belle in disbelief.

"Marian did say it could be the key to everything, didn't she? Alice never bothered with him after killing him in the first place. These ashes are a nice little keepsake regardless, courtesy of your friend."

Belle was all in. Saul—Alice or Nick, it didn't matter—he was an insane murderer, working with other villains like Blackwell to maim and destroy, and Belle was now in bed with all of them.

It was disgusting. It was beneath her, even after everything she'd done. This? *This? This* is what Belle was now?

Well, I shouldn't have been surprised. Belle had told me once already in that Paris alleyway. There are no heroes. I should have believed her then.

"The end of everything, right?" I said, but only after managing to pry my teeth apart. "The end of the Sect?"

"The end of one thing is just the beginning of another," Saul answered in Belle's place, turning his terrible ring around his flesh finger. "It's the end goal: to make something new."

"That's why you're manipulating my sister to get to me."

Pebbles crumbled from the staircase, tumbling down the side of the steps as he descended to the courtyard. "I told you in Morocco that I'd give you a sign."

And I didn't miss it. I jumped off the edge of the platform, landing easily on the grass. "Hey, Belle!" I shouted "Do you know this bastard resurrected my sister and sent her on a murder mission promising her she'd see our parents again?" Belle barely flinched. Her apathy made me want to burn down the temple. "Hey! *Listen to me!* Do you realize that whatever he promised you is probably a lie too? He doesn't give a shit about either of you! You're not going to see Natalya again."

"I already know that." Belle reached into her coat pocket. "And Saul didn't promise me anything." She turned to me. "Except that if I go along with Blackwell's plan, the Sect would crumble."

My jaw felt locked into place. I spoke carefully. "I'm obviously not a fan of the Sect either. But it is as corrupt as it is now *because* of what Blackwell and Saul did. Natalya's death, all the traitors, the assassinations, the cities being attacked. It was all part of the same plan. So, out with the old, in with the new, but do you honestly think that what *they* have in mind is anything to look forward to?"

"As long as it changes." Weariness aged Belle's face, curdling her in seconds as she glanced up at me. "I'm tired of fighting. Aren't you?"

My mouth opened, but I couldn't speak. I knew too well that the first word out of my mouth would affirm her assumption.

"Tell me, why should I continue to fight on? Duty?" She spat the word like poison. "Natalya lived for duty and still ended up dying for nothing. We fight and die and yet nothing changes. We're driven beyond madness and yet *still* nothing changes. That's the world we Effigies live in."

"So, what?" I raged back. "You have a tragic past, and that gives you the excuse to kill people? To kill me? To work with genocidal monsters?" I thought of the charred bodies of my parents in the ground. I thought of my sister, now alive and making charred bodies of her own. "You think you're the only one who's ever felt pain? People suffer in life, but that doesn't give them the excuse to hurt others. It *doesn't*, Belle."

How could she not understand this? She, June, Natalya—how could these girls, once so envied and admired, not fundamentally understand what came so naturally to someone like me, insecure, ridiculous Maia Finley? I couldn't fathom it.

Belle lifted a phone out of her coat pocket, staring at it with narrowed eyes. "The world needs to change," she said simply, her voice trembling. "I don't care about what Natalya would have wanted. I don't care about your feelings either," she added, another dagger in the back. "I don't care how angry you are, or what I did to you. All I want is the Sect destroyed. And I will help *anyone* who will make that happen. The world needs to *change*."

Belle looked deathly serious. Blackwell's brave new world. Saul, June, and Belle, a host of Sect agents, and public opinion on his side. How many others wanted to see it too?

"It's a world I don't belong in anymore," she continued. "A world

I don't want to stay in." And I knew what she was really telling me. I held my breath. "But I won't disappear until the Sect does—along with everyone else standing in my way."

She dialed a number on her phone. I didn't have even a moment to figure out whom she was calling before she began speaking. "My name is Belle Rousseau," she said. "I am here with Maia Finley at the Deoscali Temple on Basse-Terre. There's a dead tourist outside. Please come and arrest us."

*"What the hell?!"* I'd just managed to scream it before I felt the hairs on my neck stand on end.

Saul was behind me.

"It's time." He made sure to use his good hand, the one I hadn't cut off in France, when he almost too gently grabbed my wrist. "Maia. Let's go see your sister."

"Screw off!" I pulled my wrist out of his grasp and swung for his face, but he dodged. My scythe was out. I had to kill him. I had to kill him *now* or he'd do something else to June, I just knew it. The tip of the blade tore his coat but missed the flesh. He flipped back— landing on a bed of flames. He hadn't anticipated my attack. It was the first time I'd seen him this shocked, but he merely disappeared again, reappearing this time atop the gazebo. With his feet balanced on the wooden tip of the roof, he squatted low, staring at me.

"You know where you need to go next. Don't worry, you won't languish long; he'll come for you at the right time." He'd said it while facing me, but I knew he was talking to Belle. But Belle didn't respond to the man she'd once attacked in the name of justice.

"You killed that guy, didn't you?" I brushed the curls out of my wild eyes as I accused her. "That tourist in the forest. More of the 'make the world hate the Effigies' campaign, right? And that guy was, what? Wrong place, wrong time?"

Belle's silence spoke truth to my fears. She was completely gone. Shattered forever.

"You're wrong, Belle." I dug the blade of my scythe deep in the ground. Belle was already at the other side of the courtyard, starting up the staircase Saul had descended. "The world needs to change, but not like this. I don't care what you think. You're *wrong*."

"The Sect is evil," Belle said. "My family is dead and my friends are traitors." The word "traitor" squeezed down my throat like a rock. "What's right and what's wrong doesn't matter anymore."

Saul came for me again, and this time it was his metal hand that gripped my throat, pushing me down hard against the ground. The back of my head buzzed hot from the contact. Both my hands squeezed the metal and started tugging.

"I need you, Maia," he told me in a voice so tender it could have been from a lover. He squeezed my throat tighter. "Come with me."

"Just—" I struggled to get the words out of my closing windpipe. "Use your r-ring." I saw it shimmering on his finger. "Bring her back. . . ."

"Marian?" Saul laughed. "No. The extraction of her information has to be done delicately, you see. If I simply brought her back to life, she'd never tell me. Never. She knows what Alice is capable of. . . ."

A curious second passed during which Saul's eyes lost focus. As he relieved the pressure on my throat, I kicked him back. He rolled on the ground, halting in a crouch, and lifted his head, his glare menacing. "You're going to come with me now, Maia," he said in a quiet voice. "You're going to come with me without a fight because you know I have your sister and she trusts in me."

How *dare* he use my twin as a damn poker chip!

"You want me passive, huh?" I said, jumping to my feet. "As passive as you are? Acting like Blackwell's lapdog."

Saul flinched.

"June told me that Blackwell was planning on using that stone for himself eventually. Didn't you tell me again and again that you had this grand plan to reshape the world? You didn't need Jessie for that. Or Vasily. There were so many times you could have grabbed me by yourself, *for* yourself. I damn near thought you forgot about me after France. You've devoted more time to doing Blackwell's bidding, helping *him* set up *his* new world order. What exactly are you getting out of that? Or"—I paused, tilting my head—"or is Blackwell manipulating you with promises like you're manipulating my sister and Belle? Did he promise you his wish-stone leftovers?" I couldn't help but laugh at the pitiful thought as Saul remained deathly silent.

"For a bad-ass supervillain, that seems pretty pathetic—"

Saul disappeared, and suddenly I could feel his arms wrapped around me from behind, my back against his chest. His ring glinted beneath the stinging sun as he brought his flesh hand tenderly against my forehead.

"We're going now," he said, closing his eyes.

Trap and release. The phrase Lake had imprinted into my mind while teaching me how to control my power. She didn't know how it worked—just that there was a force all around us that we could bring into ourselves and transform into our element to manipulate at will. This spiritual energy was the force she spoke of. Concentrated here, but existing all over the world. Drawing the power into himself, Saul was creating a field, bending the laws of physics to force the two of us through space.

I had to think fast. "Nick, stop this!" That moment of distraction wasn't a fluke. I could use it. "Nick Hudson!"

Like on the Brooklyn Bridge. His eyes snapped open, but we'd already begun to disappear, the two of us. I could feel the energy around me being sucked into a void, taking my body with it. I kicked him off me, but he landed on desert sand, and so did I. I rolled smoothly onto my feet. Raging winds tore through the sand, whipping it across our faces. Saul looked around in shock. Wherever he'd meant to take me, this wasn't the place.

What was this? The Sahara? It was possible. There was nothing but sand in every direction, nothing but sand as far as my eyes could see, but even as a mistake, Saul would have taken me somewhere familiar to him.

"Look familiar?"

Saul returned my goad with a silent glare.

Weeks ago, we'd tracked a signal here, a signal we'd thought was his, but it had belonged to one of the Silent Children of Project X19. An engineered Effigy. We'd only been able to track him once his body started to degrade along with whatever tech was masking his frequency. That kid somehow had the ability to travel through a Dead Zone unharmed. But Saul—Saul still needed his ring. The death energy inside it shone obsidian black as he lifted his hand.

My scythe materialized just as he closed his hand into a fist, and four phantoms streamed out of the ground. I slashed at one's black skull splitting into rows of teeth as it launched for me on Saul's command. Flipping around, I slit the neck of another and dove to the ground to avoid being struck by a long, thick reptilian torso. I spread out my arms and set their black, rotted flesh on fire, but as they screamed, Saul appeared behind me, grabbing my scythe with his metal hand and breaking it.

"Don't call me that name anymore." He shook as my scythe demate-rialized, its dust floating past his face with the sand. "It's irrelevant. I'm Saul."

Like he'd told me once in Morocco. Nick or Alice—it didn't matter anymore. But I wondered if that were true. Both had a wish to reshape the world. They were working together.

No, not these two. They were only *trying* to. I knew firsthand what it was like to have your body taken over. Even in the name of the same goal, it was a relationship built off dominance—a partnership of oppressor and oppressed. I could use that to my advantage. Exploit Nick's trauma and break him first.

"You're Saul. Is that what Alice wants you to think, Nick? Is that how she controls you?" I laughed. "Look at you. She's even got you talking like her, calling me *poupée*. Disgusting."

Saul went for my neck, and when we reappeared again, we were back in the courtyard by the gazebo. I materialized my scythe and sliced down before my knees even touched the grass. It split his shirt all the way to the bottom, tearing some of the flesh on his torso, but it wasn't the death blow I'd expected. As my blade drove into the grass, he tore off the rest of his shirt and flung it with his coat to the ground next to—next to Harry's backpack. I'd set it aside when I'd moved the plaque. The inoculation device.

He disappeared and reappeared behind me, wrapping his arms around me so tightly I could feel myself being crushed against his bare flesh. A blunt attack from the back of my head sent a shock wave through my skull as I hit his forehead, but he released me. I dove for the bag. I grabbed the inoculation device first, then the knife—and when he blocked the former, I plunged the latter into his leg, the steel blade going in deep. As he cried out in pain, I turned around, thinking Belle might come to his aid, fighting with the enemy against me. But she was already gone, probably outside the temple, waiting for the police to arrive. A sin of omission was just as bad as the commission.

Saul smacked the bloody knife from my hand as I turned back around.

"You're Nick Hudson," I said through gritted teeth as he grabbed my hand. "Born in 1847."

We disappeared, but the next time my back hit the ground, a frigid chill ravaged my body. Snow. Fields of snow. It stuck to my legs, my shirt. As I stood up, it tumbled down my hair and slid inside my nails. The sudden change in the air density made it hard to inhale, but it was the magnificent aurora borealis, streaking the dark sky gold, violet, and green, that stole the rest of my breath.

Saul groaned, clearly dizzy, as he brought himself up to his wobbling feet and caught his breath. He looked around. "Greenland ..."

Far off in the distance was a facility that looked military—or Sect. A high fence blocked the flat, multiwinged building from the snowfields.

Greenland. According to Saul, that's where we were.

Greenland ...

The Fisk-Hoffman facility suddenly entered my mind. But this couldn't be it. . . . That house of horrors was supposed to have burned to the ground. . . .

I shielded my eyes from the lights streaming down from the watch-towers erected at each corner of the plot of land. The lights had been swinging back and forth, looking for intruders. But now they were trained on us.

Sirens began wailing over the frigid air. Panicked, I looked back at Saul, who'd begun waving his hands. He wanted to get caught.

No, this was where he'd wanted to take me in the first place.

I worked fast, remembering all the information I'd gained over the months from Sibyl's interrogations, Agent Chafik's debrief in Morocco. From the pictures and memories. "Nick, why are you doing this? Why are you letting Alice control you? Do you think this is what Marian would have wanted?"

He lowered his arms. Darkness swept over his features. "I'm doing this for Marian."

Alice would never say that. Nick was surfacing, his resistance crumbling. *Good, good, keep going,* I told myself. Out of the two, Nick was the one I could break. "Does she know that? Marian was . . ." I crawled back into the memory I'd seen in Prague, the fire burning the York estate as the phantoms barreled from the skies. "Marian was a servant." I remembered the white of her apron, remembered the way the simple fabric lay against my body. "But you? Nick Hudson? The son of a railway mogul? It's a surprise you ever noticed her."

"I noticed her." It was Nick now. I was sure of it. Saul would never allow his enemy to see his wide eyes glistening wet even while hidden behind a wall of murderous fury. "I loved her—" He stumbled back, doubled over. "No . . . stop . . . stop, you idiot. She's trying to—" Nick gripped his head before suddenly looking up, armed with a sharp smirk. "You think this is gonna work? Nick is mine," Alice said. "I own him. He never loved that mud wench. A *negro maid.*"

She said the last two words with such spite, my hands clenched into fists, ready to find Alice's jaw. The wildness in her eyes made me shudder. She was having fun. But when she mentioned Marian, the whimsy playing across her lips was undermined by the sting of jealousy in her tone.

"Sounds like you did, Nick." The screeching of metal in the distance. The gates of the military facility were opening and Range Rovers were piling out one by one. Running across the snow, I grabbed Saul's shoulders and shook him. "You loved Marian. You loved her. You heard Alice. How could the son of a wealthy British businessman fall in love with a black maid? But that's exactly what you did. Did your brother, Louis, know before he died?"

"Yes," Nick whispered before shaking his head, trying to block me out.

I checked behind my shoulders. Crap, more of them were coming. "Did you go to him for help?" The words rushed out of my mouth as the panic rose. "He's buried in Argentina, right?"

The thought of his brother's final resting place made Nick stand up straight, stricken with horror. "Oh god. Oh god, she's . . . Marian—"

"Take us there." I shook him, but he was trembling, his teeth clenched. "Take us to him!"

"No. No!" He grabbed me and we disappeared, but this time my body hit solid tile.

Scientists in lab coats gaped at us, terrified from behind their sleek tablets. The dark room illuminated with the glow of translucent tubes lining the walls, big enough to fit a human being—because they did. Inside each one was a person, male and female, young enough to be college students. Naked but for some simple underwear, they floated inside blue-tinged fluid with their eyes closed, respirators plugging their noses and mouths. Peaceful in sleep.

"What the hell is this?" I could barely believe my eyes. They were incubating *humans*. There had to be forty of them, twenty along each wall, but the R-22 above the metal doors told me this wasn't the only room. Yet the scientists were looking at me as if I were the monster.

But as shocked as I was, it was Saul who looked around the room in pure terror. Eyes bloodshot, he scratched his metal nails down his cheeks.

"No, not this room. Not this room, not this room," he said again and again, the gears in his knuckle joints whirring and jittering in the sockets. "Not this room again."

"Dr. Grunewald. Saul has successfully brought Maia Finley back to the facility," said one scientist after tapping the comm in the wall next to the door.

"Good." A voice came out from the other end crippled with age. Each syllable wheezed lazily from the speaker. "Bring her."

"Oh, *hell* no!" I jumped to my feet and began wielding fire in my hands. "Come near me and get charred extra crispy, got it?"

The scientists weren't warriors, but they also had to have known that security would take care of it once they got here. As they scrambled away from us, I lunged for Saul and dragged him to his feet. He was my only ticket out of here.

"Come on, Nick." I shook him. "Come on. You don't want to be here, do you?"

Nameless bodies reflected in his pupils. "No, no," he answered hurriedly.

"Get us out of here. Take me back. Your brother, Nick. Remember your brother."

Nick was screaming as he rushed forward and crashed onto me, holding on to me desperately as we flew into the air. With one last, final cry, we vanished. '

Nick gasped in pain as his bare back crashed against the gravestone. I slid off onto the grass with the inoculation device miraculously in my hand, almost crushed, with one last injection supply left. Still on my back, I gathered my surroundings. The tall headstones and grave monuments on even plots of land, spaced out by red cobblestone. The mourners at the site now fleeing the area beneath the late-morning sun. It was a familiar scene to be sure. Only after reading the gravestone beside me did I realize I'd been here before:

IN MEMORY OF LOUIS HUDSON, WHO DIED MAY 30, 1883,

AGED 33 YEARS

This was Chacarita, the cemetery where we'd staged our first mission to capture Saul. But while I'd escaped that horrible facility, I was still in danger. Someone was crying, *"Policìa!"* and it didn't take a rocket scientist to figure out the English translation. This place would be swarming soon. There was no use for this inoculation device anymore, but what I could do was jam it in Saul's eye while he was flailing on the ground. Get rid of him, get rid of the threat to June. Show the world who the real terrorist was.

The first strike was to take his ring while he was still writhing around, grasping his head. I grabbed his nonmetal hand and pulled the ring off his finger. Then, throwing it to the red-cobbled ground, I stomped on it as hard as I could. Pitch-black light burst from beneath my shoe, swirled around me, and disappeared into the air. I held the inoculation gun ready.

But as I loomed over him, ignoring the cacophony of Argentinean civilians, the inoculation device shook in my hand. Tears began streaming down his cheeks as he lay flat, staring up at the sky.

"Alice kept coming back here," he said. "She wrote her letter for Marian and eventually buried it here in place of a body. The letter would be Marian's memorial. When visiting my brother's grave, I would also be visiting her . . . Marian." Nick sat up, letting the tears fall. "It was after York. After the phantoms came. Years after. Marian only sailed to Argentina, to our family home, because she was looking for me." I didn't ask him, but this was his confession about what really happened to Marian. He couldn't look at me. Maybe because he was scared he'd see her instead. "Alice was inside me, walking the earth. I was gone for so long. Marian thought Louis would know where to find me. She didn't expect me to be there in the manor. I *was* there, but I—"

He looked at his large hands, the palms drained of blood. "With these hands, Alice . . . with my hands, she—" Nick let out a cry and threw himself forward. Thinking it was an attack, I stumbled back from shock, dropping the device. But Nick's arms found the gravestone instead. He draped himself around it, sobbing. "Marian, I'm sorry! I'm *sorry.*"

He killed her. Marian had died by his hands. The truth was as clear as day.

Watching him cry, I finally realized the real reason he didn't bring back his lover with the wishing stone—though I could only guess. Despite all of his excuses, the truth was that he couldn't bear to face her again. Not after ending her life. And though her murder may not have been Nick's fault, if Marian were alive, she'd see what he had become: a horrible, murdering mess of a man she'd once loved . . . with her true murderer, Alice, always lurking deep within his mind, waiting to strike again. . . .

Saul was shaking. "Something's wrong with me." He gripped his silver hair. "Something's wrong, something's wrong." Fistfuls of hair. He tugged so hard I thought it would rip out. "Something's been wrong all this time." His fingers grazed his forehead, running along to his temple. "I'm . . . not right. . . . Alice . . . did you know about this?"

I'd never seen him lose control like this. It was like his mind had shattered into pieces. He laid his head against his brother's gravestone, sucking in several sloppy breaths.

And then a moment of realization. Slowly, he lifted his head from the stone, his mouth open in a kind of horror that had struck him wordless.

"Blackwell . . . ," he whispered.

"Stop! Maia Finley!"

The police had arrived, rows of them pointing guns at us. I ran a few steps in the other direction to escape before realizing that they had made a perimeter around the area. There was nowhere to go.

Saul. Saul was my only ticket out of here, but as he unraveled himself around the gravestone and stood, a palpable bitterness darkened his expression, cloaking the anguish I knew was still seething. Saul was Nick, certainly. But I'd awakened something in him. I could tell. A fierce, deadly determination different from anything I'd seen before. He wasn't taking me anywhere.

"Hands up!" the police said, knowing to speak English so we'd understand. They inched toward us, their guns trained, but shaking. "Ms. Finley! Saul!"

Realizing that they considered us a pair made me livid. But if I attacked them and escaped, I'd only be proving them right. Slowly, I put my hands up, but Saul kept eerily still. Shadows from his disheveled silver hair cast over a pair of lidded eyes that peered out at the officers with murderous focus that switched to me, quick as a blink. He stepped toward me, but my scythe was out before his foot could hit the ground.

"*Arma!*" a police officer screamed, and guns were clicking.

Saul and I froze, completely surrounded by Buenos Aires's entire armed forces. Neither of us could make a move. Even if he did try it, he had no weapon, no ring to command phantoms. I still had my powers and my scythe, if I could manage to swing it without getting shot down. He couldn't take me. He wouldn't dare, would he?

He didn't try to. "It doesn't matter," he said, though I couldn't tell whom he was talking to—or if he was even talking to anyone at all other than himself. He shook his head again, running his hand through his hair. "It doesn't matter," he repeated. "I have a wish to grant." He looked at me, his expression a cage that could barely contain the wildfire quietly raging in him. "A wish. Not only to have Marian back. Maia, I told you I *am* going to reshape the world. I'll make things as they should have been. I swear it on my brother's grave." He gripped the stone as if to break it. "It's the only penance possible. But whatever I do, I won't do it Alice's way. Or Blackwell's."

"Saul . . . ," I said, but I was wrong. "No. Nick . . ."

I could tell by the pain and malice he couldn't conceal that he'd hated what I'd done to him, hated the mental anguish I'd dragged him through. The memories and feelings he'd suppressed were raw like the flesh wound I'd already given him. If anything, that made Nick more frightening than Saul ever was. "I'll see you again, Maia," he said before disappearing, leaving me at the mercy of the city police.

# 14

"TURN TO THE SIDE," SAID ONE POLICE OFFICER in a heavy Spanish accent as the light flashed. "And to the other side."

My first mug shot. Chae Rin would have been proud. My curly head reached just below the solid black "5 ft. 5" line. I was inoculated and chained, wrists and ankles bound in pairs, and another solid chain stretched from one pair down to the other. They saw what June had done to those police officers in France—what they thought I'd done. They weren't going to take any chances.

They took my phone and locked me in a solid metal room where there was only a table screwed into the ground. The door was so heavy, opening it sounded like a heavy crate being dragged across the floor. Once they seated me at the table, they chained me to both it and the floor and left me alone in there with the cameras in the top corner trained on me, waiting for me to make a move. The metal choker around my neck was their inoculation device, programmed to inject another inhibitor when it sensed my frequency rising above a certain level. A nifty device, probably provided by the Sect. How kind of them.

The last time I was in Argentina I was lauded a hero for taking down Saul. Now I was locked up like the worst of criminals. I felt like freaking Hannibal Lecter in here. I was surprised they didn't muzzle me.

Before leaving, the police told me to hold tight—someone would be in to see me shortly. I didn't know what I was expecting. The worst as always.

But after two hours of letting me stew, it was Brendan Prince who walked through those metal doors. I couldn't believe my eyes. *Brendan.* My mouth hung open, but he didn't seem to notice. Flanked by two Sect agents, he walked in briskly and took a seat at the other end of the table, setting down a thick file with my name on it.

The last I'd seen him, he'd tried and failed to stop his father from blowing up part of a city and killing his brother. The last I'd *heard* of him, he and his father had been captured. I could see the signs of interrogation too. Despite his perfectly coiffed, country-club, dirty-blond hair, his neck was scarred, the sunken crevices beneath his eyes a perpetual shadow. Scars on his hands, too. I could see them across the popping veins, and his left pinky was not completely aligned with the rest of his fingers. He'd condoned torture once too, against Vasily. I wondered if there were others in the Sect who believed that some things needed to be done at any cost.

There were only two sides in the Sect now: the side running and the side chasing. Blackwell's faction was the latter, growing more and more as he swayed agents and public opinion on his "tear down the Sect" agenda. Another one of Blackwell's speeches had played on the television news in the station while I was being brought in. I guess Brendan had seen the light with a little help from advanced interrogation techniques. But then, why wouldn't he eventually, after what the Sect had done to his little brother? No matter how fiercely his father had abused him into obedience, there was no way he'd ever be able to forget the sight of his brother disappearing in a flash of light. I could never forget it. I *would* never forget.

"I can't believe they sent *you* to deal with me." I leaned back in my chair. "I thought they arrested you."

"They did," Brendan said without looking at me, flipping open the brown cover of the folder.

"But they let you go?"

"They had no reason to keep me." He looked up. "I work for the Counter-Sect Task Force now."

"The Counter—what?"

"An interim group created in the wake of Oslo," he told me. I knew it was an agent-eat-agent world out there, but I didn't know they'd managed to organize and name themselves. I must have missed that while I was stuck on a cargo ship with no Wi-Fi. "The head of which is Blackwell."

I scoffed. "Of course."

"Our job is to bring in and interrogate rogue Sect employees, including you."

"If I was ever a Sect employee, why wasn't I paid?" I gave him a sidelong look. "I thought Effigies got paid."

"What this means," he continued, ignoring me, "is that as a member of the CSTF, I'm no longer an agent of the corrupt Sect." The intensity as he spoke those words was unmistakable. It sat on me like a weight. I guess watching his dad kill his brother changed things.

I remained silent as he flipped through the pages in my file. "Multiple cases of arson," he read. "First-degree murder, treason, and terrorism."

"That's quite the rap sheet." The chains jingled as I lifted my hands just enough to place them on the table. That was about as high as they could go anyway. "Good thing none of it's mine."

"You've been photographed in multiple cities in France." He pointed at the grainy satellite photos in the file. All of them were of June, except for one outside the police station. There I was in the backseat of a police car with Lucas driving in the front. "This is you with nineteen-year-old Lucas Macgregor. Believe me, his information wasn't easy to find. He's a trafficker who's been active throughout Europe under different pseudonyms. He's still in the wind, but I'm sure we'll find him soon enough."

I pursed my lips without thinking that it could be taken as a sign of guilt, but it was. Lucas helped me and now he was in danger of being arrested too.

"Brendan, you were there in the Communications center with us." He frowned as I spoke, but I didn't relent. "You saw what happened in Oslo with your own eyes. That girl with Saul—she looked exactly like me, didn't she? I know I wasn't the only one who saw her. But I was several feet away from you. So how do you explain it?"

Brendan noticed the two agents standing at his side shift somewhat uncomfortably and straightened out his back. "Trick of the light."

"Seriously?"

"It was an intense situation. We all saw—"

"—the exact same thing? That's not suspect to you?" My voice was rising dangerously. I could tell the other agents were on alert by how they slowly slipped their hands out of their pockets.

"Maia—"

"I'm not a killer or a terrorist. And that wasn't me. I'm being framed by my—" I stopped. Would he believe me? While he was the former director of the Sect's European Division in Sibyl's place, he would have had my personnel file. He'd have known my family was dead. I couldn't very well tell him I was being framed by my good-turned-evil twin, but that's exactly what was happening. "You can't seriously believe that I'd do something like this. But you do, don't you?" I shook my head. "Just like you believe I hurt your mother."

His eyes narrowed. "You were spotted in Natalya's apartment where my mother was shot and almost killed."

"I was there, but I didn't do that."

"So it was just a coincidence that you were there at the same time." Brendan's laugh was frighteningly cold. "That's a lot of coincidences piling up around you, Maia. Like bodies."

The chain rattled around my bound hands. "I was trying to save her. I—wait a minute." I rewound his words in my head. "You said *almost* killed. So . . . so she's okay? Naomi's alive?"

I was relieved to see him nod his head. Naomi Rhys was one of the few people in the Sect on our side. "Where is she?"

Brendan gave a curious glance to the camera over my left shoulder, a quick one to the bodyguard over his, then sucked in a breath to steady himself. "I don't know," he said, and I wondered if he was telling the truth. "I'm sure she would have been moved to a secure location."

"Okay . . . ," I said. "So, what now?"

"Now you give up the locations of the other girls. Belle Rousseau has already turned herself in to the police in Guadeloupe and is currently in the custody of the CSTF."

Yeah, because of that ridiculous stunt she pulled trying to get me caught too. What did Belle even gain from giving herself over to Blackwell's men?

"But we know there are two more Effigies out there," Brendan continued. "Maia, I want you to tell me where to find Victoria Soyinka and Chae Rin Kim."

So they hadn't been found yet. Another wave of relief washed over me like a balm. "No clue where they are. And if I did, I wouldn't tell you."

"You sure?" Brendan took a phone out of his pocket. My burner phone. "This is yours, isn't it? What'll I find if I go through this, you think? Logged calls to the girls?"

"Go ahead and look," I said confidently. A bunch of bizarre temple symbols and a call to Pastor Charles weren't going to give him any usable information. "But I doubt it'll help because I haven't called them. I haven't called them because I don't know where they are or how to reach them."

"You're lying."

"No, *you're* lying." I tilted my head. "You said the Sect, or I guess, the ICS-*whatever* just let you go, but they didn't. Did they?"

Brendan's face went rigid. "What are you talking about?"

"Well, I mean, they wouldn't just let you go for free. You gave them something in exchange." He struggled not to flinch as I searched his face. "Information. On what?" I leaned in. "Or whom?"

There he was; the Brendan who always looked so uncomfortable while trying to save face in front of peers, superiors and subordinates alike.

"Sibyl?" I asked, leaning forward. "Or your dad. Maybe both."

Brendan didn't respond. I watched him nervously as he sifted through the file without saying a word.

"I'm telling you, I didn't do a damn thing," I insisted. "Why won't you believe me?"

"Because, Maia"—Brendan stopped and flipped the file around—"people are dying."

I looked down at the open file, and there in front of my eyes was the corpse of Baldric Haas. The Council member whose family had protected the secret volume since Castor had written it. The only Council member I knew who, with Naomi, stood against Blackwell's plot to tear down the Sect. He was dead. One gunshot to the head. I pressed my lips together, wanting to throw up.

"He was found murdered in a one-room apartment in Bangladesh," Brendan said simply.

I glared at him. "And you think I teleported to Bangladesh to murder him with the gun I don't have?"

"The Haas family are friends of my family," Brendan said, and I could see the tension in his face as he fought to control himself. "You need to tell me what's going on."

"I don't know what's going on." Hot, angry tears wet my eyes, but I wouldn't let them fall. "And you're disgusting for even suggesting I could do this. You want to know what's going on? Don't make me laugh! You're just doing what's easy. Following someone's orders like a sniveling *coward*."

Silence.

"Agents," he said after clearing his throat. "Can you leave us?"

The agents hesitated, giving each other a quick, silent glance before leaving the two of us alone together. The door shut. Uh-oh.

"You gave up your own people to save your ass; now you're shucking and jiving for Blackwell," I spat hurriedly because he was on his feet and coming closer. The dark circles under his eyes told me that one aspect of Brendan hadn't changed; he still wasn't afraid to get dirty in an interrogation room—like the good old days. "You know what Blackwell's been doing? You know why he's been slowly and steadily turning the world against the Sect, having Vasily free Saul, whose terrorists activities are, by the way, all part of the Big Plan? You know why he had Senator Abrams and your dad take the fall for *his* idea of frying Oslo? You know why he needs the only people who can stop him in jail cells like this? You really think you're making things right by all those people who died—"

He grabbed me by my collar and lifted me to my feet. My chains rattled, my neck groaned and burned as he forced me to look up at him.

"I should have known you wouldn't have had the stones to stand up to them," I said as a matter of simple fact. "No matter how screwed up Aidan was, he still tried to do the right thing. He *died* trying to do the right thing. You're not even half the man he was."

My chair skidded to the wall as Brendan pushed me onto the floor. He leaned in close until he was almost completely on top of me, his legs tangled up in mine, his left hand on the other side of my head. A second of pure terror flashed as I watched him look up at the cameras, as if considering if he could really go through with whatever it was he wanted to do to me. Apparently he could. He put his lips close to my ear and spoke in hurried, hushed tones.

"Blackwell has control over Minerva," he whispered.

"Wha—"

"Don't talk," he hissed. Footsteps outside. "He had the code changed by hackers. It's in his sole possession now. No one knows except a few in his inner circle. Everyone on the Council has fallen in place. He'll use special agents to secretly assassinate the rest. My mother . . . my mother is . . ."

Buenos Aires police officers burst through the doors and began yelling at Brendan in Spanish. "Yes, I know, I know," he answered in English as he got up, leaving me on the ground. "I lost my head. This prisoner tried to kill my mother, after all. I'm sorry."

But the meaningful look he gave me before turning his back spoke a different truth. "We'll begin the process of transporting the criminal to the task force headquarters in upstate New York."

"New York . . ." For the first time in a while, my lungs filled with a gentle, needed brush of warmth. Who knew my impending incarceration could be so oddly comforting. But after traveling the world, I was going back home.

The agents who had flanked Brendan dragged me up to my feet and plunked me down onto the cold metal seat once more.

"She'll be held here until preparations are ready. Make sure her inoculations proceed as scheduled."

"There's press outside the police station," said one agent. "They want a statement."

"Yeah . . ." Brendan ran his hands through his hair, and I could see the jagged lines of scabbed flesh on his hands. "We need to let them know that we have Maia Finley in custody. And that in a few hours we'll be transporting her from the Buenos Aires police station to our headquarters."

"You sure we need to be that specific?" The agent peered at Brendan through his shades as he brushed past him. "There'll be press from all over the world waiting for us once we get back to HQ."

But Brendan stood firm. "They need to know their world is a little safer with her off the streets. I'll give the press conference now. Oh, and, Maia."

I jumped at the sound of my name, drawing my chained hands on the table closer to my body.

"You're right about one thing," he said. "I'm probably not half the man my brother was. But I'm *not* a coward. I am and always have been devoted to the protection of humanity . . . from all those who seek to rule over its fate."

The doors slammed shut and I was alone in the room with my bruises. Tiny red dots blinked on the cameras screwed into the ceiling corners. We were being recorded. That was why Brendan needed to find an excuse, no matter how brutal, to get close enough to tell me what I needed to know.

Blackwell had Minerva. I could still hear Brendan's voice in my head, dripping with dread when he'd whispered feverishly in my ears. Having sole control of a satellite particle weapon didn't sound necessary for a man who wanted to replace the Sect with a more benevolent peacekeeping structure.

It was the bold move of a man who wanted power as an end in itself.

This was getting bad. Like, apocalyptic bad. I had to get out of here. I started jerking my chains, trying to break them loose, but I was still weak from the inoculation. They rattled uselessly, keeping me locked in place. *Ugh*, if Brendan wasn't really with the CSTF, then he should have at least given me the key to escape out of these stupid cuffs.

I waited for three more hours, hearing the police's footsteps rushing back and forth outside. When the door opened again, Brendan and a few more agents reentered, one of the agents carrying a silver briefcase I'd seen before. Another inoculation. The agent opened the case in front of me and took out the pen, but Brendan took it from him.

"I'll do it," he said, and jammed it in my neck. A familiar whir and release of gas fizzed into the air as I felt a warm liquid pump into my veins.

"It's time," he told me, and to the agents: "Get her up."

I avoided the glares of the officers as the agents dragged me, bound and chained, through the halls. A row of Argentinean police followed in front and behind, guns drawn in case I breathed the wrong way. Then into the glaring lights of cameras. I couldn't make out individual faces because there were just so many reporters shouting things at me in different languages, shoving microphones in my face. And it wasn't just the press—civilians waved around signs written in Spanish, but I could tell by their angry voices that it wasn't anything complimentary. A protector turned terrorist. A disgrace to humanity. Tears stung my eyes as the reality of their hatred seared me from the inside out.

After getting me through the crowd, the agents shoved me inside the back of a van, one in a long procession of vans and blaring police cars that would take me out of the city to the airport, where I'd then be extradited to America. Two large men in shades sat on either side of me, one of whom tightened my chains, locking the ones around my feet into a pair of hooks jutting out of the floor of the van. From the passenger seat, Brendan coordinated with the other vehicles behind and in front of us, flinching when food and trash started pelting the windows.

"I want this area cleared," Brendan ordered into his walkie-talkie before adding, "Not very popular, are you, Maia?"

It wasn't too long ago that fans would line up to shove fan letters through my car window. That little girl in London. She'd asked me to go to her convention, and I never even gave her a response. What must she think of me now? How many of those civilians pelting the van used to admire me too, only to see what they thought were my "true colors"? The pain of seeing a hero fall. A pain I knew too well.

"None of it is my fault," I whispered, tasting a tear on my lips. I started to move my chained hands up to wipe it away, but the agents' hands were already on their guns, ready. I kept them on my lap.

Brendan scanned the streets through the windshield, watching officers haul people away from the row of cars. "That's what everyone says once they're caught."

If he wasn't really with them, he wasn't going to just let them lock me up in another prison, was he? Was it a trick? Or the whisper in my ear—was that the trick? Brendan's eyes were so cold and I was so worn that I just couldn't tell anymore. Trust was like glass. Dawson was right. I felt like I was staring through broken mirrors trying to make sense of reality and all I could see were shattered reflections.

In the distance, a little jet flew toward us overhead, red paint streaking the name of an airline news station on the side. The noisy propeller added to the pandemonium of vicious insults and cries from the public. Worst of all were the kids clinging to their parents, staring into my tinted windows and imagining what kind of monster could be inside.

"All I ever wanted was to be good like them," I said. June. My parents. The Effigies. "Strong."

Brendan squinted his eyes as he stared up at the afternoon sun for a few seconds before turning to the crowds on the sidewalk. "You may still yet," he said.

I didn't know what he meant until I noticed something falling from the sky. No, not something—some*one*. A figure tumbling out of the jet above, rocketing toward us from the clouds.

"What the hell?" The agent driving looked up through the windshield after stopping at a set of traffic lights. "Does he have a death wish?"

But it wasn't a "he" at all. I could see her long black ponytail flapping behind her in the wind, her dark, lanky legs stretching out through a pair of jean capris. As she fell fast through the air, it looked like a force field distorted the air around her, blowing the clouds out of her path, sending flocks of white birds thrashing in all directions. The details of her face were still a blur when a cannonball of pure wind launched down to earth, crushing the street to the left of our van, then to the right. They were precision strikes. Not one bystander was close enough to be hurt, but as the ground began caving in, I realized that was the goal.

I also realized who it was.

I barely dared to hope, but her face was clearer now. Civilians still on the sidewalks fled inside buildings. The agents next to me held on to the back bench as the van tipped back with the crumbling street, but my eyes were wide, my chest swelling as I peered out the windshield. "Oh my god. La—"

A massive, invisible pressure pummeled into the street, again and again like a hammer until our section collapsed, taking my van and a few others with it. We didn't fall too far, just low enough to be rendered helpless as she landed in a crouch on the van at the edge of the crater she'd made.

"Lake!" I cried, struggling to sit up in the van. "Lake! Oh my god, yes! Thank *god*."

I could see her through the front windshield, standing above us atop the van on the other side of the broken road. After giving us a little salute, she lifted the crumbling earth and concrete falling on top of our vans out of the depression, depositing it onto the street to ensure our safety. This was a rescue mission, after all, and Lake wasn't out for blood. Pushing her hands forward, she tore off the roof of our van.

"Lake!" I yelled, knowing this time she could hear me. "And Chae Rin?"

"No, it's just me." Her eyes were brimming with tears, but she wiped them before they could fall. "Hang tight!" she said with a decisive nod.

Around her wrist was a curious mechanical band with several indents all along the sides. I didn't have time to ask her what it was. Lake may not have been out for blood, but the Argentinian police and the CSTF were another story. A blast exploded out of the roof of the van Lake stood upon. The bullets pierced the metal so suddenly they almost caught her, but she reacted fast, jumping down, sliding onto the truck and into the crater. One of the agents sitting next to me made for his gun, but I cracked him hard against the forehead with my own, tugging with all my strength against my chains until—until they *burst apart*. I hadn't even realized that the adrenaline pumping through me had invigorated my power as well. But that shouldn't have been possible. Brendan had given me an injection.

Wait. *Brendan* gave me the injection. Just as he let the cavalry know exactly where we'd be heading.

He turned around in the front seat right when Lake jumped onto the hood of our van. I swung my fist into the other agent sitting next to me, knocking him unconscious before breaking my legs free with a grunt.

"Agent Prince," said the driver, his knuckles pale as he gripped the steering wheel. "What is th—"

One whack to the base of his neck and he was out. Brendan wrung out his hand before looking up at Lake through the shattered windshield.

I'd thought they were in on this rescue mission together, but Lake blinked at the sight of him, shocked to see him helping her. "Aidan's cutie older brother? Weren't you in prison?"

"My mother," he said all in one frantic breath. "She's with Langley, isn't she? It's what she told me when she came to visit me in my cell. It's why I—" He sucked in a breath. "Is she okay?"

Lake nodded. "Yeah. As okay as she can be."

At the sound of her words, his shoulders slumped and his head lowered as if all his muscles had relaxed at the same time. He took a moment, breathing deeply.

"Good," he said finally, and tossed me a phone—my burner phone. "Go," he told us. "Go *now*. Stop Blackwell's madness." Then, lifting his walkie-talkie to his mouth, he clicked the device on. "The subjects are escaping!" he yelled into the crackling static.

Agents and police crowded around the crater and aimed their guns at us, apparently not caring that agents were still inside. Lake blasted the bullets with a ring of wind that blew out of her body.

"Put this on." Lake tossed me a bracelet like the one she had on her right wrist. "To activate it, press the red button."

Shoving my phone back into my pocket, I blinked, staring at the bracelet in my hand. "What is this thing?"

"Just do it!" As I started fumbling it on like a watch, Lake turned to

Brendan. "Glad you're not one of the bad guys, Prince," she said. "We'll tell your mum you said hi." With a flirty wink, she launched the two of us out of the hole. I could feel my body flipping forward through the wind, arching in the sky from the same force that blew some of the vans back into each other, pushing them down the street. We landed on our feet in the middle of the street and closed ranks, our backs facing each other as the agents who surrounded us pointed antiphantom weapons in our direction.

I lifted my arms, ready to fight. "They really want us to go down, don't they?"

Lake scoffed. "Well, after what your sister did in France . . ."

Surprised, I shifted my head to the side. "You know it was her?"

"Well, duh, who else could—"

"Maia Finley and Victoria Soyinka. Come with us quietly!"

Lake put her hands on her hips and looked at them in disgust. "You all do know you're working for a megalomaniac, don't you? We're not the ones you should be scared of!"

"Last warning!" someone cried way in the back.

Lake shook her head. "Oh hell," she said as the guns started clicking. "Maia, bracelet! Red button!"

We clicked it on at the same time. It was like the electromagnetic armor, the EMA, used to protect cars and planes, only it burst out of the metal band in the shape of a body-length shield. I crouched behind it, staring in shock as the bullets and antiphantom energy beams dissipated on contact.

"Dot's latest design. Ugh—" Lake grunted as the force of the attack pushed her back.

"Dot's with you guys too?"

"We're heading there now. It's time you come in from the cold, prodigal girl. Hold on!"

Wrapping her arms around my waist, she clicked off her device and launched the two of us into the air. The tornado of wind she created was enough to knock the agents and officers off their feet, but I kept my shield up to catch persistent attacks. As we flew higher into the sky, I scanned the streets, cringing at the force of energy blasts against our electromagnetic shield, flinching from the narrow misses from bullets. Seemed like every cop and agent in the city was firing at us from the streets below, taking cover behind the open doors of their parked vans and police vehicles.

Eventually we left them behind. I was too busy scanning the streets for more of them to notice the soldier standing on the roof of a high-rise down the street. And by the time I looked up, she already had a rocket launcher aimed at us. A soldier in a navy blue armored body-suit, her head obscured by a robot-sleek white helmet. The uniform of Project X19's Silent Children. But because this Silent Child wanted us to know who she was before she killed us, she clicked off her helmet, letting her red tresses tumble down her neck.

Oh no.

"You really thought you were going to get away clean," Jessie Stone said in her Australian accent, chuckling with the excitement of impending bloodshed.

"Lake," I shouted, "watch out!"

Jessie fired a single bullet, but not at us—above us. The bullet detonated just as it flew overhead, the force from the explosion sending Lake tumbling out of the sky.

"Yes!" Vasily's psychotic partner stood and pumped her first. "*Steee-rike*, bitches!"

I slipped out of Lake's grasp as we fell, and though I caught Lake's hand, she was too busy trying to use what concentration she had left to slow our fall. It worked, but barely. We crashed on top of a civilian car, the people outside scrambling out of the street and into a shelter like the others. Lake almost fell off the car. I pulled her back up, but I could see the hole in her blue blouse the explosion had made—and the burns on her back.

"Lake? Oh god." I touched the torn flesh, feeling the sheen of warm blood against my fingers.

Lake groaned. "It's not . . . as bad as it . . . probably looks. . . ." She was still conscious, still moving, or struggling to. But could she fly us out of here?

She would have to because another soldier was coming straight for us, striding powerfully down the street, paying no attention to the fleeing civilians. This soldier had no reason to reveal his face to us, though I could tell he was a man by his strong, chiseled build. Unlike Jessie, he didn't taunt us. He didn't speak at all—and that made him all the more menacing.

"Lake!" I shook her, and though she groaned and got up to her knees in response, I could see the pupils of her eyes disappear as they rolled to the back of her head. I shook her again. "Come on, we gotta go." The police and agents we'd escaped would get here soon too.

The soldier hopped onto the trunk of the car just in front of us, then onto the roof. He carried no guns. Instead, he pulled out two knives from the holsters strapped to his legs. With a click, a hazy blue electrical charge zipped down the blades, two blazing, serrated edges made from energy alone. I'd seen this before. Where had I seen this before? They were Sect weapons.

They were—

He jumped off the roof. Sliding Lake back, I summoned my scythe and blocked his wrists with the pole as he brought the knives down over my head. The force of his attack pushed me down, denting the car just enough to make me shake on my feet, but I couldn't be distracted.

This guy was trained and he was trying to take me down.

My scythe was too big and I was too slow. He kicked my stomach, and I launched back off the car, but not before grabbing Lake's leg and pulling her down with me. We both tumbled to the pavement. The soldier jumped down again, but I was on my feet before he could start attacking. I just barely dodged his attacks before sending out waves of fire to push him away. He fell back, but only for a moment. Running along the perimeter of the flames I'd made, he rushed headlong through the fire and drove his knife into my arm, the second aiming for my neck, but I blocked it with my other arm and kneed him in the stomach. Blood gushed out of my biceps as he pulled out the knife. My mind went blank in this brutal fight for survival. It wasn't like with Saul. It wasn't a matter of revenge. I had to kill him. Because if I didn't kill him, he'd kill me.

I screamed. I didn't mean to. I barely even noticed as a pillar of fire exploded out of my throat, hitting him point-blank. Grunting, he stumbled back and, after fumbling for the button at the base of his helmet, threw his burning mask to the ground.

His black hair tumbled over his forehead, sweat dripping down his sharp jawbones. A pair of wild chestnut eyes blazed hot as the fires at his feet. His chest rose and fell as he inhaled the impossible breaths as quickly as he could—impossible because he shouldn't have been alive, impossible because I'd watched him die. But ghosts were illusions in my world. Life and death a hair's wisp from each other, separated by a single thread of a twisted fate that brought Aidan Rhys to the streets of Buenos Aires, ready to murder me.

I fell back, too numb to feel the ground beneath me. The world fell silent. I stared at him, shaking my head as Rhys wiped the blood from his lips and gripped his knife, ready to strike again.

"Rhys," I whispered, maybe too quietly, because he didn't speak.

He didn't even look as if he recognized me. "Aidan? Aidan!" I cried. *"Aidan!"*

Rhys flipped his knives around and stalked toward me. *Fight, you idiot. He'll kill you. Fight!* I was furious at myself, but completely paralyzed. *Fight!* He raised his arms. *Fight!*

A powerful gust blew Rhys in the other direction, propelling him through the brick walls of a bank on the other side of the street. Lake limped toward me, one arm wrapped around her stomach.

"We gotta go," she said, helping me to my feet. "Now."

"Jessie's still up there." I wasn't even sure how I'd managed to string the words together. My eyes weren't on Jessie at all but on Rhys, moving in the rubble of brick.

Without answering, Lake took my hand and launched us both up in the air with a boost that blew cars off the street. I was right. Jessie was waiting, but Lake was ready this time. With a mangled cry, she let out a torrent so powerful it knocked Jessie off her feet, her projectile gun flying off in the other direction. With the blood gushing from Lake's back, she didn't wait to see what had become of the soldier. She kept flying, higher and higher, away from the city until the chaos of the streets below faded into the background.

Lake went as far as she could before setting us down on the rolling fields next to the highway. We both collapsed to the ground at the same time. But I was the only one who let out a frustrated scream so loud a flock of birds took to the skies.

June, Belle, Rhys. People I cared about were now enemies. Saul had taken June and Rhys out of the fires of Minerva, lifted them from the gates of hell for the sole purpose of murdering me. Escaping death only to be turned into demons.

Did Brendan know his brother was alive? Did he know what had become of him? His uniform was the same as the rest of the Silent

Children's, the kids from Rhys's elite cohort of fellow trainees at the Sect's ill-fated Fisk-Hoffman training facility. After the fire that took the facility, kids like Jessie had been spirited away and experimented on while Rhys was taken home safely to his prestigious family. But they finally got him. Saul must have taken him there. Had they injected nanotech in him, too? Twisted his mind, put him under control like they'd tried to do to me? Whatever they'd done to him, it'd destroyed the Rhys I knew.

But who *was* the Rhys I knew?

A rich kid. An abused child. A loyal soldier turned murderer. I thought he'd died without ever having the chance to make up for his sins. And now that he was alive, he was being used to commit more. He didn't deserve this. I knew that in my heart. There was no trace of him in those soulless eyes. If I hadn't seen him breathe, I would have thought that it was Jessie animating his corpse.

This world really was terrible. I let my head fall into my hands.

"Don't worry, Maia." Lake pushed herself onto her knees. "I don't know what those psychos did to Aidan, but we'll get him back. Your sister too."

Lifting my head out of my hands, I looked at her through swollen eyes. "If only it were that simple."

Lake cocked her head to the side. There was no point in lying to spare her. Keeping my expression as controlled as possible, I told her about Belle—how she'd stabbed me on the White Cliffs of Dover. How I'd found her scrying at the temple with Saul—*for* Saul. How she'd turned herself in to Blackwell's CSTF for unknown reasons. By the time I was done, Lake's lips had already pressed together, stretching out into a thin line.

"No." She shook her head. "No way. You are not trying to tell me that the strongest Effigy out of *all* of us went to the *dark side*." When

I didn't answer, she let out a frustrated yell. "This is—this is just—really—*really*—bloody—*perfect*."

"You're telling me."

Lake worked the idea around in her head, and I could see it go like a merry-go-round behind her eyes. "No way." She was shaking her head again, her hand against her forehead. "No way . . . not Belle . . . but she . . ."

The cold, hard truth of a team shattered, of a leader fallen. Silence.

*"Why?"* I hated seeing Lake utterly devastated and confused at the same time. It was like watching myself crumble all over again. "How *could* she? Was it because of what that Surgeon guy did to her in the Hole? The torture must have messed up her brain, right? I mean, what else could it be?"

I couldn't tell her about my lies. I simply sucked in a shaky breath. "Everything's just so messed up."

"That's a really polite way of saying we're almost totally screwed." Lake took a moment to calm herself. "But even so . . . there's still hope. There *has* to be. Hell, I'm *saying* there is. And that's that." She grabbed my hands. "We'll find a way," she reassured me, gripping so hard I could feel my knuckles shift and roll. Maybe she was reassuring herself, too. "No matter how bad it gets, just don't give up hope, okay? Got it?"

Don't give up.

I stared at Lake, fire and fear burning hot in her eyes. Then, wordlessly, I gave her a hug. Lake was taken aback but giggled and squeezed tight, ruffling my hair.

Not all my friends were new enemies. The world may have been against us, but at least I wasn't alone anymore. After the days of hell I'd been through, after what I'd witnessed, seeing the smile of a friend was the sweet bit of relief I needed. For the first time in what felt like centuries, I could breathe again.

Heroes and villains. Where was the line between them? I understood how someone could crumble beneath crushing forces that wouldn't stop their assault until they'd taken everything good from her. But there had to be a way out of the darkness. I had to find it.

"What do we do now?" I asked.

"Now we regroup with the others." Lake winced, stretching out her damaged back. "Damn it, that better heal within the week or else we're screwed. Blackwell's going to unveil some big project at the UN Assembly in eight days."

"Brendan told me Blackwell's got sole control of Minerva."

Lake looked horrified. "That satellite weapon?" After I nodded, she sighed. "Another complication."

I drew my legs in, barely flinching as the grass prickled against my skin. "You said we gotta regroup with the others. You mean Sibyl, Chae Rin . . . and Uncle Nathan, right?"

Lake nodded. "And there's a whole bunch of others at the base."

The thought of seeing my uncle almost made me want to cry again, but I'd done enough of that already. "You're not going to fly us all the way to La Resistance HQ, are you?"

"Oh god, no. Even I have my limits," she said. "My back is screwed, and you've put on a few pounds since I last saw you. Not to mention I really have to go to the loo. So no way."

My laugh came out more like a strangled cry, and before I knew it, tears were legitimately falling down my face. Strange, I didn't think I still had the energy to laugh, or hell, even the emotional capability. Yet here I was. "Sorry," I said, rubbing my face. "I'm just relieved. I didn't even know whether you guys were dead or alive, and I—"

I thought of Belle stabbing me through the chest, leaving me at the mercy of Saul. And of my sister burning men alive, Rhys brutally tearing through my flesh. I fell silent.

"I can tell you've got a lot to say," Lake said. "You can let me know what happened when we're on the jet. It's waiting for us a few miles from here. I can take us there, after I catch my breath. Once we meet up with Sibyl, we can figure out how to take down Saul and Blackwell for good. We have to do it now before things get worse. And believe me—they can get worse."

Lake was right. Whether it was taking down the bad guys or saving my friends-turned-enemies, it was now or never. And after everything I'd been through, no matter how tempting it was to fall apart, I couldn't let myself break, I couldn't run away, and I couldn't wait for others to be a hero *for* me.

Lake and I got to our feet at the same time, scanning the rolling fields. It didn't matter how shattered we were. We were still Effigies. Where other heroes had fallen, we would stand—I would stand. And save the others.

"The jet," I said. "Where is it taking us? Where exactly are Sibyl and the others?"

"Where it all began," Lake answered solemnly. Her ponytail whipped behind her, delicate in the gentle breeze. "Seattle."

# PART TWO

*Links in a chain.*
*A dangerous game.*

# 15

THE HISTORY OF SEATTLE WAS THE HISTORY
of human misery made manifest. A seven-day war against all manner of beasts, an onslaught against a population unprepared for the
devastation. Hundreds of people had died on the first day during the
poorly planned evacuations, more still as shelters protected with their
comparatively basic technology became too filled up with terrified
bodies to accommodate everyone. There were those who'd died on
the streets and those who died in the shelters as the buildings collapsed over their heads. It was just a matter of who died first and who
died last.

Hubris. The Cold War arms race between the Soviet Union and
the United States had led to a proliferation of antiphantom technology
the world had never seen before, technology born from experiments on
the cutting edge of science—and on the razor's edge of legality. No one
considered there could be a flaw in their systems. No one considered
the cost of relying upon the work of man. At least, that was what we'd
been told. A glitch. A freak mistake that spawned several decades more
of heightened antiphantom research and development.

Decades the world spent totally unaware that the Seattle Siege had not been caused by human error, but by human malice.

The grainy footage fizzled black-and-white on the tablet Cheryl'd given me. She was in the passenger seat of the SUV Sibyl had sent to pick us up from the jet. Seattle was a no-fly zone, not that we could land in the middle of a phantom-overrun city anyway. We'd have to go another way—a shadowy entrance by Mount Rainier, a platform that lowered into an underground tunnel designed to take us to the secret facility that had become Sibyl's base of operations.

I sat next to Lake, who, like me, had been given a change of clothes on the jet. She was still in pain from the wound on her back, but the rest and medical attention was speeding up her natural healing process.

The lights lining the tunnel flitted by my window as we traveled under the earth. "No one's ever seen this footage before?"

Inside the Seattle control center, men—and only men—sat behind rows of clunky computers that looked more like radios stretched out on torture racks. Behind wide screens, needles flitted from one direction to the next. Little rectangular buttons, perfectly spaced, stretched from one side of the metal plate to the others, and beneath them were knobs their hands spun around to control the frequency of the antiphantom device that was supposed to keep them all safe: Seattle's Space Needle, at the base of which the center operated. The busy workers stopped their knob-spinning and button-pushing once the explosives that rolled underneath the door detonated. After the first round of chaos, a group of agents in black ski masks and combat clothes burst into the control center with machine guns—and murdered everyone.

"Get rid of them all," one of the agents said. "Then report back to Blackwell. Take the video footage and bring in the cleanup crew." He paused for a moment before standing up straight. "Speaking of cleanup."

The door shut quietly behind him. And the young man who walked into the frame looked several decades ago exactly as he looked now.

"Saul." The cameras didn't catch his face clearly. I recognized it nonetheless. But unlike the others, who wore uniforms, he was dressed almost in rags—a white shirt that clung to his frail body, beige corduroy pants that looked too long for him. His hair was disheveled, his eyes slightly unfocused. Saul had once admitted that he was the one who'd caused the Seattle Siege. I'd always imagined Saul waltzing into the city with that triumphant, horrible grin I knew too well, but the Saul in the video could barely focus. He was mumbling something. That was when the footage ended.

I lowered the tablet onto my lap. "Uncle Nathan managed to swipe this footage?"

"Yeah, with a bit of help."

It was Redman who'd answered from the driver's seat. After being knocked out by Belle on Dover's cliffs, he'd managed to find his way here without being caught, avoiding the fishing ship Sibyl had sent to pick us up. I'd worried Belle might have killed him, or left him to be picked up by the French Coast Guard she'd tipped off, but apparently she'd just disappeared after she'd killed me. Shortly after I boarded the jet, I'd updated the group on Belle's recent exploits, and Redman had seemed relieved that she was "out of the picture"; but as I'd warned him then, even though she was currently in CSTF custody, there was no telling for how long—or what her exact game plan was.

"That footage was stolen and in Sect custody all these years," Redman continued. "Probably only top-level officials knew about it. Like the Council."

"Or at least the members of the Council on board with the plan," Cheryl clarified, her Cockney accent unmasked. She must have ditched her posh voice after going on the run. There really wasn't any use for it anymore. "The plan was to destroy Seattle using Saul and a Sect strike team."

"A strike team." Black fatigues and concealed faces. Like the ones who'd attacked Naomi in Natalya's Madrid apartment. "Why would the Sect need a strike team?"

"For secret missions." Cheryl rested her arm on the window ledge with a sigh. "On paper the Sect's main mission is to fight phantoms. Most agents are trained for that purpose. But other agents are trained to take care of other problems. Informers, for example, deal with potential liabilities within the Sect."

Like Rhys. Once given the mission from unknown officials in the Sect, Aidan had perfectly stalked Natalya, gathering information on her activities until finally poisoning her, dooming himself to a hell built of his own guilt and misery.

"So the Sect destroyed Seattle?" Lake shot me a weary glance. "Talk about dark."

"Indeed." Cheryl adjusted her tiny rectangular glasses. "This footage confirms certain members of the Sect—topmost officials— were working with Saul for decades. Half of those Council members have been there since the sixties. Senators, presidents, billionaires, military. All with insane resources. Only one of them would need to be in on it."

"Surely not Blackwell, though," I said. "Dude's what, in his forties at the most? The Seattle Siege was 1968. If he was even born then, he'd have to have been pulling the strings in his diapers."

"Trust me, Maia, we've been doing a lot of research and intelligence gathering while you've been traveling the world." Cheryl flitted through pictures on her phone. "Blackwell wouldn't have been involved, but his father, Bartholomäus Blackwell the fifth, was."

Turning, she lifted her phone for me to see the picture of three men in the middle of one of those high-class political gatherings, but I recognized only one: Blackwell. Not our evil Blackwell, but apparently his equally evil father. Long black curls, a sturdy frame, pin-sharp eyes. They all looked the same, the Blackwell men, with only minor differences in the width of their noses, the shape of their heavy jaws, and the breadth of their chins to convince me that they weren't the same person. The pompous air was the same, though, powerfully passed on through the bloodline as if part of the genetic package.

It would make sense that he'd be there. It was his English manor, his spiraling, kingly staircase in the background. That statue of the woman in robes, her hand clutching a white pearl high above her head, stood exactly where I'd first seen it: in the center of the reception room. What wasn't there was that acrylic painting. Yes, that painting. For whatever reason, my mind slid back to it, remembering its golden-rimmed frame. The painting Blackwell had stood by the night of his dinner party as he made his dubious speech about his family's centuries-long loyalty to the Sect. I remembered it well: the medieval knight standing atop corpses. The tip of his sword aimed at the eye socket of a pleading skeleton. It was nowhere to be seen in Blackwell V's mansion. Must have been his son's personal purchase.

Next to him was a short young man with a bad seventies haircut, his robust cheeks stretched with a grin. His tie lay almost perpendicular to his chest, flat on his bulbous gut rolling over his belt. He looked familiar. The third man too, but in a different way. The second guy, I was sure I'd seen before. But the third . . . it was a feeling. The cut of his jaw, high cheekbones, dark brown eyes, and black hair. Tall, slender but masculine, his handsome features kissed with a delicate touch even in his old age.

"Rhys," I whispered, because I could see the boy ghosting the man's features.

"Griffith Rhys." Cheryl tapped the screen with her long, painted nail. "Former leader of the OSS, the precursor to the Central Intelligence Agency. Naomi Rhys's grandfather. With Blackwell the fifth and a young Mayor soon-to-be Senator Abrams."

"Rhys's great-grandfather." Lake leaned in, took the phone from Cheryl, and whistled. "Talk about your silver foxes."

Rhys and his great-grandfather really did look alike. I shook my head. Rhys had mentioned that he came from a Sect family, but he didn't even know his mother was a member of the Council. He had no idea what stock he came from.

"There's another picture." Lake flipped to the next one. This time it was Senator Abrams and Blackwell V in golf shirts at some resort, or maybe a country club, their dark hair slightly grayed due to the passage of time. A young caddy had been captured by the photo but not by design; standing next to the golf cart behind them, he stared straight at the camera with an intensity that swallowed its focus even with half his body obscured by Abrams's gut. It was Blackwell. Our Blackwell. I knew immediately. His black hair, though short, still curled upward in loops, too wild for his baseball cap.

Lake squinted, pulling her face closer to the phone screen. "Is that who I think it is?"

"Yup," I said. "Blackwell."

Teenager Blackwell. Senator Abrams and the Blackwells really did have a history.

I handed the phone back to Cheryl, shifting in my seat. The two images unsettled the hell out of me. Too many ghosts gathered in one place. Or ghouls. "Senator Abrams resigned recently," I reminded them. "I don't think he had any idea what Blackwell was planning."

"But Griffith must have." Cheryl turned back around and waved out the window. "The tunnel we're riding through? The facility we're going to? Griffith was involved in building it. An entire secret facility built on the resources of the American government without anyone's knowledge."

The tunnel lights flashed through my window, reflecting off the whites of my wide eyes. "Seriously?"

"Your uncle hacked the footage from the base. If it was stored here, he must have known about it. Must have been in on it. This is a plan that's been decades in the making. And since Blackwell the fifth died in 2006, I can only assume that our Blackwell inherited his father's will."

Even if this was a plan set in motion by his father, I doubted Blackwell was simply following a plan laid out by his daddy. I remembered the look in his eyes as Director Prince Senior dressed him down in the London facility briefing room. What had he called him? Ah, right: a spoiled little boy with nothing to offer.

*Like father, like son, I suppose.* That's what Prince had said.

Blackwell could have torn him apart right there, but he'd kept himself under control. Now, a few weeks later, Prince was in jail and Blackwell was on his way to placing himself at the very top of a new world order. He'd played everything perfectly. Like father, like son indeed.

The tunnel opened up into a wide area—looked like it was supposed to be used for parking. The white lines painted on the concrete hadn't faded even after all these decades, probably because there hadn't been too many vehicles driving over them through the years. But if this were an underground parking lot, there should have been an elevator taking us up to the building. Maybe it was supposed to be there. Maybe remnants of it still remained, buried beneath the rubble. The exit would have been infinitely easier to reach if half the section of the tunnel on the other side of the parking lot weren't in ruins.

Redman parked our SUV near a booth, supposedly a little station where someone could monitor the APD system. "We don't know when the tunnel collapsed," Cheryl said, unbuckling her seat belt. "The path is completely blocked."

"Not to mention the APD is totally wrecked there," added Lake, and she groaned while opening the door. "Sibyl had us block the area off with that fiber cable they set up there, but there are still phantoms on the other side. Not even Chae Rin could move all this mess back without causing a bigger cave-in."

I shut the van door behind me, stretching out the sweater they'd given me. It was needlessly itchy, of all the clothes they could have picked up for an already agitated Effigy on the run. "By the way, what's going on with Chae Rin right now? Have you heard from her yet? You mentioned on the jet that she'd been sent to Guadeloupe, right?"

"Right. To look for you," Redman said. "That call you made to the police about the trafficking ship."

Bread crumbs. It was a smart plan after all. "So where is she now? Still there? Or on her way back?"

Cheryl hedged a bit before answering. "Well, to be honest, that we don't know." And when she noted the look on my face, she added, "I didn't want to worry you before I was sure, but I got a text from Communications not too long ago."

Lake and I exchanged worried glances. "What do you mean?" I asked slowly. "She's all right, isn't she?"

"Remember, for a long time, we couldn't find you," Cheryl said. "We figured it was because you were inoculating yourself to block your cylithium frequency. But then your signal suddenly exploded in Basse-Terre. Along with Belle's. Before going dead again. Chae Rin had to keep her frequency hidden too, so we couldn't track her, but we *could* talk to her—at first. Her comm-link must have been damaged somehow, because after a while we stopped hearing from her."

Lake, hearing this for the first time, listened with an anxious scowl. "It went dead?"

"Not quite," Cheryl answered. "We can communicate from our end, but we can't hear her. We don't know what happened to her after that or if she even reached the city. I'd been waiting for word from Communications that the problem had been fixed, but unfortunately . . ." She trailed off.

Belle had called the police herself before I disappeared with Saul. But Brendan had told me that only Belle had been taken into CSTF custody. My stomach lurched. What if Chae Rin had reached the city? What if she'd found Belle looking for me?

"How can you lose track of her?" The thought of her just disappearing off the grid chilled my blood.

Cheryl bristled at my accusatory tone. "We couldn't have anticipated a glitch like that would happen. Your uncle's been tracking her family's phone activity at their business and residence. We know she called from inside the city, probably from a pay phone, and told them what was going on. But nothing after that. It's not like we have a landline she could call."

"We haven't seen her in a while." Lake shook her head on the other side of the car. "This is bad."

"I know." Cheryl nodded. "But don't worry. We've got people in the area looking for her. Still, we can't worry about that now. Chae Rin's tough. She can survive out there. Besides, my orders were to bring the two of you to HQ, and that's what I'm going to do. We need to be careful from here on out." After she and Redman nodded to each other, they walked to the trunk and pulled out two Sect-grade antiphantom guns each. Cheryl slid one down her back under her belt while Redman went to the station. Both slapped on the same metal bracelet Lake had given me in Argentina.

Lake pointed at the ladder stretching up the side of the back wall several feet behind the booth, its metal bars leading up to a hatch. "We're going up there. Believe me, the fun part is over."

Redman clicked some buttons, and after a symphony of gears unfastened, the hatch opened.

"Lake." Cheryl gestured toward the hatch.

"I know, I know." Lake looked at me. "Effigies first." She squirmed for a second or two, but she already knew what she had to do. She climbed up and I followed with Cheryl and Redman close behind. Lake had just touched topside when I heard her grunting from a collision of force—her wind against a burst of black smoke. Phantoms.

Lake ran forward, making room for me to climb up. Loud footsteps behind me galloped fast. I whipped around just in time to see the phantom's eight black eyes first, blazing white orbs in two rows on his black-skull head. Pincers. This one had pincers and a sharp, toothy jaw like some rotted nightmare crab, sharp enough to cut my body in half with one swipe. Black smoke sizzled off rotted flesh as it jumped forward. I didn't bother wasting time with my scythe—I set it on fire just as Lake waved her arms to the side and launched it into an already half-destroyed building.

The building.

Oh my god.

All the buildings were in ruin. All of them.

There weren't any more phantoms in the vicinity, so I had time to take it in: the skies covered in ash and pollution, probably from the waste some companies had been illegally dumping at the city's former municipal garbage site. Or maybe it was smoke from the ashes of bodies that had lived here. Either way this was a city that hadn't seen the sun in years.

Lake pulled me back so Cheryl and Redman could surface. There were still cars in the street, some demolished, some intact. Broken lamps, shattered windows. The buildings were rusted down to a russet shade, half of a high-rise toppled across the street; when it'd fallen, it'd clearly taken a convenience store with it. I could see old toiletries in the rubble.

It was like this as far as the eye could see. Not a soul in the city, not a sound to be heard but for the wailing of monsters in the distance. A city for ghosts silent with memories of devastation.

"There's another entryway into the facility a few blocks down Jackson Street at an old train station." Cheryl reached behind her back and brought out her gun. "It's not ideal, but we'll have to make a run for it."

I'd thought I'd be able to take a break from running for my life once Sibyl's crew found me, but I guess this was just an activity I had to get used to. Steeling ourselves, we ran down the torn streets, but no matter how fast we were, we couldn't escape the phantoms. Slithering serpents burst out of the ground and through the window of an old bakery, but Lake redirected them into the sky with a grunt. Cheryl and Redman were firing their guns at phantoms I didn't even see before they burst into smoke. I was setting on fire anything that moved without even checking to see what it was first. These bracelet things were put to good use—the electromagnetic field from the shield exploded a horde of phantom smoke swarming around us like bees. Finally we reached the train station, its gray roof half in shambles, its clock tower toppled and broken, lying in pieces over the train tracks and the neighboring highway. Our feet squeaked against the marble floors of the empty halls, echoing across the high ceiling. In the waiting room, I maneuvered around the broken chandelier smashed against the floor in a pile of rubble left over from the classic European interior.

There was a secret room behind the ticket hall, an elevator that shuddered open only when Redman input the right code into the keypad screwed into the wall.

A monstrous growl shook the ceiling.

Just beneath it, a mammoth phantom appeared from the very atmosphere, rotted limbs manifesting from within a haze of black smoke. Its skull jaw stretched out from the blazing ash, snapping its teeth. Like an apocalyptic steed of death, it stomped its hooves, smashing the broken chandelier on the ground. Its spiked tail whipped in the air as it charged for us.

"Hurry!" Lake screamed. We rushed inside, the elevator doors shutting just before the phantom crashed headlong into it. I jumped back, landing hard on the floor. The dent the phantom had made could have punctured me through if I hadn't, but the structure held for now. There was another keypad at the base of the hatch. It opened, and we began scrambling down the ladder. I was last.

"Hurry up!" I yelled after another crash against steel. The phantom rammed into the door again and again. It wouldn't stop until the door was destroyed, and it was only a matter of time before it got its wish. "Come on!"

One more crash. The door flew across the room, and the phantom lunged, its snapping jaw screeching from the assault of my flames the last image I saw before the hatch closed and locked us into darkness.

"There's EMA down here," said Cheryl beneath me. "We'll be okay."

"Goody," I managed to snark while panting. They really had to do this each time they went in and out of the facility? Couldn't they have found a nice house on a beach somewhere to carry out their super-secret operations?

But this was Seattle now. The fear, destruction, and chaos was all that remained of a once great city. It was a tragedy no one wanted to see repeated, a tragedy that shouldn't have occurred in the first place.

And with Saul, Blackwell, and the others causing mayhem on the world's stage, a tragedy that could happen again.

# 16

UNLIKE THE APOCALYPTIC RUIN OF A CITY
above us, the area below the hatch looked at least partially maintained;
it was the kind of sleek metal facility I was used to from the Sect.
Cheryl and Redman led Lake and me through the halls until a set of
doors opened.

Control center. Not a big space, certainly not as decked out in technology as your typical Sect facility. It was just three stations of computers, one at the front and two at the sides. Couldn't miss the huge
flat-screen screwed into the front-most wall, though.

As for the crew manning the warship, they were all there. Sibyl
Langley was in one of her pin-straight fitted white suits, her arms
folded over her chest. She was hunched over the shoulders of a man at
the front terminal, clicking away at his computer.

"Uncle Nathan!"

He swiveled around so fast, he nearly fell off his chair. Uncle
Nathan looked tired and unkempt, a light beard growing around his
thinning cheeks. His sunken eyes were bloodshot, maybe from hours
of staring at a glowing screen, but more likely from the nights he'd

spent not knowing where I was. That ecstasy of relief bringing life
to his sallow skin as he watched me run toward him was the same as
when I'd come back home half a year ago, after a night of wandering
the streets, listless, lonely, and missing my parents and sister, his bear
hug as warm as the one he'd given me in Toronto. After what we'd
been through, we both needed to be around family.

"Thank god you're alive." Uncle Nathan's stubble scratched my
forehead. "And I'm really, *really* getting tired of having to say that."

"I'm getting tired of hearing it." I beamed at him.

"We got your message in Guatemala. Or wait, Guadeloupe?" Pete,
as always, was rubbing the back of his hairy brown neck as he thought,
swinging around in his chair from his terminal at the left side of the room.

"Guadeloupe," I said. "Good to see you're alive and well and . . .
cleared of all charges. . . ."

I trailed off because I wasn't prepared to see Lake run up to him
and sit on his lap, planting a kiss on his nearly bald head while throwing her arms around him. I couldn't see Pete's flush beneath his ebony
skin, but the fluster was all in his wide eyes and awkward grin as he
pushed Lake away with an embarrassed series of chuckles.

"Okay . . ." I blinked. "When did this happen?"

"Oh, you know, danger and all that." She shrugged, shooing away
the question with a flippant wave of her hand. "Plus, he's not evil like
we originally thought."

"Yeah, that's right." I snapped my fingers and pointed at him, nodding as the memory flitted back in. "You totally *didn't* try to have me
brainwashed."

"What? Brainwashed?" Pete sat up straight so fast, Lake almost
tumbled off his lap. "Yeah, no, that was *not* me." He couldn't have made
it any more obvious with his rapid, adamant hand waving. "Mellie.
Had no idea she was on the other side. If I had, I wouldn't have—"

"She knows." With an annoyed sigh, Sibyl turned around. Rather than looking relieved to see me alive, she sized me up, ending the quick examination with a sturdy nod. She was ready to put me to work. "We've been trying to track you since we lost you in Dover. After you sent in that tip in Guadeloupe, I was going to order some agents to go down there, but you were gone by then. Meanwhile"—Sibyl grabbed a controller off the closest terminal and pointed it at the screen—"your sister's been doing some damage in your name."

The flat-screen changed to concurrent footages of June, her dark curls flying as she left the port towns all along the Spanish coast in flames. Uncle Nathan's hand gripped my shoulder, almost as if he didn't want me falling to the ground. He didn't have to worry. Though the footage was a death blow to the heart, I stayed sturdy on my feet. Determined.

"We can't track her," said Pete after gently pushing Lake off his legs. "Of course, part of that is because there's, like, ten of us here."

Pete was right. Aside from him, Uncle Nathan, Cheryl, and Redman, there were just a handful of others operating the terminal. I'd seen a couple of them before at the London facility. Agents loyal to Sibyl. I thought Howard and his wife, Eveline, would be here too. Last I'd seen them, they'd been on their way to Oslo. What if they went and didn't make it out?

As I wrung my hands together, Pete continued. "The other side of it is the tech," he said, sliding a hand over his closely shaved black hair. "Whatever nanotechnology she's got in her must be like the other Silent Children—undetectable until it's degraded. And judging by our autopsy of the one you guys found in the Sahara Desert, that could happen soon. If you remember, that guy was dying long before you found him because his body couldn't handle the artificial cylithium from the tech network."

"What does that mean?" I stepped forward, staring from Sibyl to

Lake, searching their eyes for answers. "You're saying June's going to end up like him? Hey, answer me!" I barked because Pete didn't answer quickly enough.

"It's looking that way." Uncle Nathan answered behind me, his voice solemn. I hadn't even considered what the news of an evil June resurrected from the dead would do to him. He seemed to shrivel a little as he said it, lowering his head as if weighed down by the memory of what she used to be. "I didn't even think—it was possible at first. But I knew it wasn't you. And I knew it couldn't be anyone else. Bringing someone back from the dead would be nothing for Saul and that ring of his. But between reawakening and having her body tampered with . . ." He held on to his chair to keep himself steady, but I could see his arms shaking. "What she must have gone through. I can't imagine being brought back from the dead only to have someone force me to kill."

As Uncle Nathan fell silent, I considered telling him what June had told me: that there was no mind-control system set up in her head the way there had been in mine, the way there had been in the other scientifically engineered soldiers like Jessie. June was doing this of her own free will. Though the kill chip in her brain would make a powerful defense in court, it didn't change what she herself had confessed. It was as if being alive again, the possibility of getting her parents back, and her newfound ability to *finally* affect her own life and fate superseded her concern over the threat of being returned to rotted flesh if she didn't follow Blackwell's orders.

But what warps a human being? Just like Natalya had gone mad in death, wasn't it possible that June had too? It was obvious in that jail cell that she hadn't been brought back as herself—that she hadn't been brought back *right*. I'd been dead only a couple of minutes. June had been dead for more than a year.

And now, with the engineered cylithium in her system, June was in danger of death anyway. Saul had brought back June only to let her die again.

No. I wouldn't let it happen. I had to save her before it came to that. But she shouldn't have had to suffer in the first place. This shouldn't have been her fate.

"It's my fault," I told him. "Saul brought her back to mess with me, to manipulate me into giving up information I don't know."

"About the stone," Sibyl said. "At the end of the day, it comes down to that. Because it's with the stone that Blackwell will consolidate his paramilitary force."

She clicked the remote. Project X19 appeared at the top of the screen, blinking in bright blue with the phases laid out below.

*Phase I: Research*

*Phase II: Silent Children Program*

*Phase III: Minerva*

*Phase IV: Consolidation*

Sibyl folded her arms, peering up at the screen through narrowed eyes. "Research on the kind of technology that went into creating the Silent Children would have started in the sixties after the siege."

"I told you before in Toronto," Uncle Nathan said. "Remember?"

"There's a lot of things about Toronto I'd rather not remember," Lake grumbled. I was sure most of that had to do with her former girl group completely embarrassing her in front of millions.

Uncle Nathan did that thing where he was very clearly suppressing an eye roll. "Well, like I told you then, some defense agencies were working on a black project that eventually got axed."

Sibyl brought up a picture of a man half mummified by age; though a thin sheet of long white locks dangled past his shoulders, the crown of his head was bald, a sheen of light shimmering across the pale, veined skin.

"That guy right there," Uncle Nathan said. "Dr. Grunewald."

"Oh yes, I remember hearing his name a couple of times in the past." Lake squinted while studying his picture, as if counting every liver spot. "Okay, so what's his grand, Freudian, supervillain backstory then? He looks like he has one."

Uncle Nathan laughed. "Hate to burst your bubble, but it's nothing special that a project like this would require researchers. He was said to be working on nanotech years ago at a Scandinavian university before he fell off the grid—probably when he was recruited for this. His work is clearly being used to simulate Effigy's parapsychic matter manipulation, generation, and degeneration. You said one of the Silent Children mentioned his name, right?"

Not only that. I'd heard his voice in the dark room Saul had taken me to—dark but for the wash of blue light emanating from the glowing tubes incubating humans.

I walked up closer to the monitor. "I might know *where* he's working. Saul zapped me there while we were fighting."

I told them about our struggle, about the bodies in the pod, about the magnificent lights over the field of snow outside. I faintly heard the door open again behind me, but I was too involved in telling my story to react.

"The Silent Children Program may have started with the Fisk-Hoffman kids they salvaged from the fire," Sibyl said. "But the research would have continued after that."

"In facilities like this one," said a voice behind me. "Hello again, Maia."

Naomi. With her long raven-black hair tied up in a ponytail behind her, she pushed herself into the room on a wheelchair that looked expensive, custom made, but its sleek exterior couldn't distract from the fact that after what she'd suffered, she'd likely be in it for the rest of her life. She confirmed as much when she noticed me staring.

"It's okay," she said. "It's not as bad as losing my life. As long as I'm alive, I can at least see my childre—my *child* again." In that moment her dark brown eyes welled up with tears because, as far as she knew, the boy who'd taken her features almost perfectly was dead. I gave her a sad smile, nodding in understanding. I could tell her Rhys was alive, but I couldn't tell her what he'd become. I'd begged Lake in Argentina to keep quiet about it too. I'd save him first and then give him back to her. It was a promise I made to myself as I watched her stoically blink the tears back.

"This building was to be one such research facility, but it was condemned after a series of debates into the legality of black ops programs. I knew my father was a member of the Council." She strained herself readjusting her position in the wheelchair. It seemed like she could move the upper half of her body though her legs remained still. "He told me about this place once. That he helped oversee its construction before it was condemned and abandoned. It was Sibyl who brought this place back up and running."

"What I could manage," Sibyl said, and I thought of the solid wall of debris in the tunnels. It was a miracle each of them had been able to make it through the phantom-infested zone in one piece.

Lake leaned on the terminal next to Pete. "Was your granddad working with Blackwell?"

"I didn't know until Mr. Finley decrypted footage of the siege from this base." It pained her to even speak, physical and emotional turmoil fused in an awful partnership. "As a former member of the OSS, my grandfather would have been involved with the safety of the country. I never knew him as anything other than upright, but now I see that he must have been living a double life."

And that shamed her. It was clear enough on her face.

"What I did know is that my grandfather hated Blackwell in the end. The man was as pompous and arrogant as his son, so hating him would have been a natural response. He never confessed any wrong-doing to me, not even on his deathbed. But by the time I took his place as a member of the Council, at the end of his life, he told me not to trust the Blackwell family—and never to listen to them."

Keeping the mask on right until the end, just like Rhys. The apple didn't fall far from the tree. We would never know if he was really the good man Naomi remembered, or if it was all a lie. But if he did love his family and wanted to protect them, then I understood why he'd stay silent. Looking at Naomi, I thought of her sons, her husband—the legacy Griffith would have passed on to him had he been outed as complicit in one of the worst domestic terrorist operations in history.

"It doesn't matter now," Sibyl said while Naomi turned away from the group. "If what Maia said is true, we're way past the research stage. Those tubes you saw, Maia. Those people. Imagine an army of Effigies, perfectly controlled to obey the whims of their master."

I did, and immediately felt sick. My fingers curled against my legs, scraping against the jeans material. Lake and I glanced at each other, and when I saw her body stiffen I knew she was thinking what I was. Nobody understood just how dangerous Effigies were except other Effigies. And maybe their victims.

"Consolidating his power after firing Minerva would take various stages. First"—Sibyl clicked the remote—"dissolving the Sect." The words appeared on-screen. "Engineering consent from the masses in the form of inciting widespread panic."

"June." Uncle Nathan breathed her name, and I could see his hands clenched into fists.

"Creating a new global organization to replace the Sect, of which, I'm assuming, he'd be in charge. World leaders have already come out in support of the leadership he's shown. Of course, on the surface, the organization would be democratically voted on with the participation from the United Nations. But behind the scenes—an arsenal of warriors at his command."

"And Minerva," I added. "Brendan told me in Argentina. He has the codes."

Dread—muted yet distinct—signaled Sibyl's shock. "And the final piece would be the stone. A stone that grants wishes is the power to warp fate itself."

A stone that granted wishes with the power of death. A stone that protected life from the hands of the agents of death. Three symbols. Two stones. Unless there was another. . . .

"My god, with a private arsenal like that, nobody would be able to unseat him from power," Naomi said, her face screwed up in worry. "Using the new organization as a front, he'd be able to remake himself as a dictator."

But I was too busy considering what I'd seen at the temple. The shards of blue stone in contrast with Saul's and Blackwell's white stone. Three symbols. Two stones. Unless there was another. . . .

"Maia!"

I jumped at the sudden shriek bursting from the open door. Dot Nguyen's tiny frame sped across the room.

"I heard you were here," she said, her black hair in tatters across her face as usual. She brushed her bangs up out of her eyes. "Good, good. Tell me what you found in Guatemala. Hey, move." She pushed Uncle Nathan, who went spinning to the side with his rolling chair.

"Hello, Dot," I said slowly, watching my uncle grab for the terminal. "And it was Guadeloupe."

"Right, right." Dot was clicking at the computer Uncle Nathan was sitting at. It was only when she looked up and saw the metal band on my wrist that she smiled. "Oh good, you got my new thingy.

Tell me what you found in Guatemala. It was a temple, right?"

My phone! Suddenly remembering all the pictures I'd taken, I brought it out. "How did you know I was there?"

"After we got wind of the call you made in Sibyl's name, I started wondering what you were doing all the way down there. That's when I noticed this." Dot cast the screen from her computer onto the large flat-screen in front of us. A map of the world zoomed in on the Guadeloupe area. A hazy splotch of red swirled on the flat-screen, right on the Basse-Terre area, surrounded by a fading yellow. "The red is the Dead Zone in the island. The yellow is where people can live. But this." She tapped her own computer screen, but I saw it on the larger monitor. A dead space of no activity. "Smack in the middle of a Dead Zone. I don't know why I've never noticed this before, but something like this is incredibly rare." Dot stood up. "What did you find there?"

"Calm," I answered, and showed her the pictures on my phone.

"What the hell is this?" Uncle Nathan said after getting up and peering behind me. "Symbols . . ." It took him a second to upload the pictures to his computer screen so we could see it on the bigger monitor.

"Do you have any idea what these mean?" Sibyl asked.

"No clue. At the temple, Belle told me the symbols were Emilia Farlow's creation—one of the first Effigies who eventually founded the Deoscali cult." Naomi squirmed at the sound of Belle's name, but I continued. "It's supposed to be some kind of code. Without it, they can't read Castor's thirteenth volume. And I'm assuming that if that holds all the secrets of the Sect, then it holds the secret to the stones, too."

As Uncle Nathan went back to inspecting the symbols, Lake narrowed her eyes. "Of course, if Belle were here with *us*, we could ask her for more information. But she's too busy being locked up, making us look like heartless criminals." She shook her head in disbelief. It still hadn't sunk in yet. "Since she's with the CSTF, we can't get too close to her without any danger to us. Even if we could, *she's* more of a danger than any ex-Sect agent. We don't even know what she's planning next. We don't know where Chae Rin is, either. . . ."

The room fell to silence.

"Those codes . . ." After a while Uncle Nathan walked past me around the terminal, closer to the monitor, his jaw open slightly as he studied each symbol. "This is all of them, right? You didn't miss any others?"

Whatever was stirring in that huge brain of his was clearly more exciting than news of a newly christened rogue Effigy. "Three more, but I didn't get the chance to snap those."

"Draw them for me. Does anyone have a pen and paper?"

Redman went to grab some, and I drew to the best of my memory the three symbols I'd seen in both the temple in Guadeloupe and the museum in Prague.

"It's polyalphabetic. . . ," Uncle Nathan whispered.

Once again I had no idea what he was talking about. "What?"

"This could be polyalphabetic. Like the Alberti cypher—a method of encryption based on substitution." And when he realized no one in the room knew what he was talking about, he added, "These symbols are a code—*the* code. You said Emilia came up with this? She must have been involved in writing the thirteenth volume."

The lintel on the temple. *As the servant gave to the teacher, the teacher gave to the traveler. As the teacher gave to the traveler, the traveler gave to me.* Castor gave resources to the Ice Effigy to build Emilia's temple. Belle had said it was in exchange for what she'd given him— information. What if he was paying back Emilia, the genius who gave him a perfect method to keep the writings in his secret volume secure?

And if Marian was the servant . . . what could she have possibly given to Emilia?

"Another way of looking at it is that you can compare these symbols to the Greek alphabet," Uncle Nathan said. "If we can figure out what this code says, we might be able to read that volume and cut Blackwell off. Maybe get the stone before he does. Of course, we'd need to get the volume first. Which means we need to find where it is first."

Sibyl gave him a sidelong look. "Do you think that you can crack it?"

Uncle Nathan chuckled nervously. "Well, cryptography *was* my first major." He waited, and when nobody responded, he added, "No, no it wasn't. I was kidding. Applied and computational mathematics was my first—look, never mind." Flustered, he tried his hand at answering the question again. "To answer your question, yes, I'd like to think I can do anything with a bucket of coffee in my system. But, I mean, I hope the punishment isn't death if I don't."

Sibyl, who found nothing funny, least of all when the world was on the brink of disaster, barely offered him a curt nod for his troubles. "Okay, that's your task," she said. "The volume could be anywhere, but the best way to find out where is through interrogating higher-level agents who work closely with him. I have some agents who are already gathering intel. But you, Maia, your task is the same one I gave you after your first mission in Argentina. Scry. Scry to find out what Marian knows."

"Marian . . ." I brushed away the uncomfortable memory of Saul wrapped around his brother's gravestone.

"She must know something that isn't in that volume. Otherwise Saul wouldn't have tried to kidnap you. So scry. If there is something powerful out there, we need to get it before Blackwell or anyone else does and put it into safekeeping."

With a strained smile, I nodded. "Sure," I said even as my shoulders slumped in defeat. I didn't want it to show on my face: the sudden swell of anxiety scraping up my nerves from my fingers through my arms to my neck, the pressure impeding each breath that worked its way in and out of my chest. *Calm down*, I told myself. *Don't worry about Natalya. If it comes to it, you'll beat her.*

I thought of Emilia taking over the body of a homeless girl to build her temple. The temptation to live a second life was hard to pass up for anyone. But what happens to the one who didn't even get to live her first?

"In the meantime," Sibyl continued, snapping me out of my panicked thoughts, "Maia, you and Lake have a mission that needs completing now." She nodded to Uncle Nathan, who pulled up a world map, projecting it onto the flat-screen. The map zoomed closer and closer on the western coast of Canada until it locked on to a red dot blinking over Vancouver, British Columbia. "We intercepted a call that Senator Abrams made a few hours ago to the Counter-Sect Task Force headquarters in upstate New York. Listen."

With a few clicks, Uncle Nathan brought up the audio file.

"I want to speak to Brendan Prince." The voice was familiar—or rather the loud sniff from his inhale. Hairy and messy. I'd had the pleasure of hearing it for the first time at Ely Cathedral, when Blackwell forced me on one knee and bullied me into swearing a phony oath to an organization he'd been secretly planning to destroy. During that awful "inaugural assessment," he'd made it a point to pick on my lack of skill, citing reports just to drive the knife in harder. He was also the first to call me *Ignis Ensis*: the Sword of Fire—not that noble terms mattered much when your bosses were looking for reasons to kill you and start over with a new girl.

So that voice was Senator Abrams all along.

"Sir," said the female voice on the other end of the line, "Agent Prince is in transit from Argentina and has no cell phone reception currently—"

"Brendan Prince!" he snapped, sniffing hard as if something were stuck in his nostrils. "He'll make time for me. I'm Senator Abrams. I know his parents. I have information for him. Information on the Sect. Tell him to meet me in person at my Vancouver estate this Sunday at midnight. Tell him it's urgent. And tell him"—he paused—"tell him I have nothing left to lose."

The call ended.

"Sounds like he wants to squeal," said Lake. "Squeal like a pig."

"Blackwell manipulated him and Prince without either of them aware of what Blackwell was planning," I said. "But even if he was kept out of the loop, as a Council member, Abrams would have realized that something isn't right about this whole anti-Sect thing. Not to mention he knows the Blackwell family and he's been on the Council for years. Imagine the dirt he's privy to."

"Agreed." Pete tilted in his chair. "Perfect opportunity to get back at the man who canned him, I reckon."

"Abrams is a petty man, but he's usually cautious." Naomi's fingers curled around the arms of her wheelchair. "That's why he didn't want to speak over the phone. But he has no idea that the CSTF is just a tool for Blackwell—not that many of the CSTF agents even know that themselves, especially those who joined in the wake of Oslo. They think they're catching the criminals responsible for corrupting the Sect. They want to bring terrorists to justice. But Blackwell will use them to flush out and destroy his enemies, including us—and now Abrams. He's already killed Baldric Haas and Cardinal Donati."

"Cardinal Donati?" I hadn't heard that name before.

"He was never revealed to the public as a member of the Council,"

Naomi said. "His death wouldn't have been big news outside the Catholic community since he died officially as a result of a robbery, but I know better. If he was killed, it was because he stood against the rest. Like . . . like Baldric." She lowered her head, struggling to control herself.

"Abrams is next. Blackwell will send another strike team." Sibyl breathed out a deep sigh. "According to my intel, Abrams recently made his usual restaurant reservation for Sunday, eight o'clock at the Northwest Restaurant a few miles from his estate in Vancouver's Shaughnessy neighborhood. Maia and Lake, you'll intercept him on his way home tomorrow. Find out what he knows, then get him out of the area."

"Just be careful, guys." Uncle Nathan swiveled around in his chair. "You have to be ready for whomever they're sending to whack him. Maia . . . you . . ."

But without the words, he fumbled his way into silence. I could tell it frustrated him. He stared at his feet, his right hand curling into a fist. Fighting, fleeing, killing. This wasn't the reality he wanted for his brother's daughters.

"I'll be okay," I told him, with a smile that was meant to reassure him even though I couldn't quite reassure myself. It wasn't confidence that drove me but an indescribable pulsing urgency propelling me step by step—toward my sister, my family, my friends. To make things right for them. To save them. To end this madness.

"Don't worry, Nathan. They won't be alone." Bending over my uncle's terminal, Sibyl pressed several buttons. Chae Rin's name popped up in solid metallic green on his flat-screen next to the word "comm-link."

"Chae Rin, if you can hear us, wherever you are, we've got Maia. But Belle's gone rogue. We need you in Vancouver with the other two on this mission."

We remained silent as Sibyl told her the details. Chae Rin may not have been able to communicate with us, but if she was out there—if she was still alive—we had to do what we could to bring her back to the fold.

"If you can get there by Sunday at midnight," Sibyl finished. "Chae Rin . . . if you're still out there . . . find your way home."

# 17

FIGHTING OUR WAY THROUGH SEATTLE WAS
somehow worse the second time, the phantoms even fiercer this time
around. But after two days of food and rest at the facility, I was more
than ready for them. We slashed our way back to the tunnels, made it
up to the surface of the land of the living, where a truck was waiting
to smuggle us into Canada. Though her control center was pretty bare
of personnel, Sibyl had a small network of followers ready to help us
get to where we needed to be—some agents she'd worked with, some
she'd saved. Then there were other agents, like Dawson, who trusted
Blackwell's media-driven ascent from symbolic Council representative
to "Savior of Civilization" as little as we did.

With the blessings of conservative politicians and pundits like
Floridian Senator Tracy Ryan, Blackwell's face was on the news in a
near constant twenty-four-hour cycle with continual but unnecessary
updates on the hunt for rogue agents and Effigies and on his plans
to introduce a safer global structure designed for humanity's total
protection.

"*Wanker,*" Lake spat as she clicked off her phone, the darkness replacing a new Blackwell-focused headline. She'd spoken pretty quietly, but nobody would have recognized us anyway as we made our way down Robson Street under the streetlamps speckling light into a dying evening. Lake had changed her hairstyle on the way, donning a short, black bob wig she'd insisted Redman pick up on the way. And while my messy bun wasn't exactly stealthy, we both wore shades to keep our identities veiled. We wouldn't have needed the disguise except that there was somewhere we needed to go before ambushing Abrams. That was why our truck dropped us off a block earlier, waiting close by for our return.

We looked up the graphitized red brick to the plaque at the top of the restaurant, which read DAEGU GRILL. The Kim family restaurant. As expected, the CLOSED sign was still up on the window—the one that wasn't smashed and boarded up. The television on the back wall broadcasted world news to nonexistent patrons. It was a risk being here, being out on a busy street with pedestrians around. Lake had tried calling them on a secure line from the truck, but they weren't answering the phone. If Chae Rin had made it to Vancouver, there was no way she'd be able to keep that a secret from her family.

And her family was right here. Two figures were sweeping what looked like a new round of trash off the floor. Ha Rin, Chae Rin's older sister, maneuvered her petite body around a dented metal trash can stained with garbage on the inside. The man sweeping behind the counter must have been her father. He wasn't much taller than Chae Rin, but stocky in build. He seemed tired, his black eyes blinking from behind a pair of round glasses. He was wiping the sweat off his bald head when we opened the door. The two Kims reacted to the bell's ring like a bomb going off, the shell shock written on their faces. Mr. Kim's broomstick dropped out of his hands. Ha Rin turned around so quickly she almost fell against one of the long, rectangular tables jutting out from the side of the wall. She gripped the bench to keep herself steady while her dad yelled at her in Korean.

"I thought I did lock the door!" she answered back, hurriedly straightening her sweater. "Damn. Who are you—*oh my god, it's you.*"

I put a finger up to my lips and closed the door behind us as she let herself fall into the bench. "It's okay," I said as we approached her, looking around to make sure there were no lingering looks from the street. "We called earlier, but since you didn't pick up, we thought we had to come here. We're just here to see if you—"

"Appa!" Ha Rin pointed at her father, still frozen behind the counter. "Call the police!"

I stopped. "Wait, what?"

Lake threw her head back and groaned. "Oh, you've got to be—no, don't do that, please." She ran to the counter, snatched the phone out of Mr. Kim's hand, and placed it back onto the receiver. "We're not the bad guys. We're just looking for Chae Rin, that's all. We want to know if you've seen her."

"Why?" Ha Rin barked. "So you can drag my sister into your crazy terrorist shit?"

We'd only risked coming here in the first place because we knew Chae Rin had been in contact with her family to tell them what was happening. Wouldn't Chae Rin have told her that we weren't trying to kill everyone?

"I thought your sister called you—hey, stop that!" I stalked over to her and swiped the cell phone out of her hands. "We're not terrorists. We're trying to stop the terrorists. Didn't Chae Rin tell you?"

Ha Rin paled as she pushed herself deeper into the bench until her back was flat against the wall, fear in her eyes. Fear of my face—*June's* face on the news striking terror in the hearts of citizens around the world. "Yeah, she said you were innocent. As if I'd believe her covering for your ass. So who's the girl going around burning cities? Your evil twin?"

I rubbed my forehead, shooting Lake a look. "Well, actually . . ."

"Ha Rin." Chae Rin's father put up a hand to calm his eldest daughter. "It's okay. Stop. I . . . believe them."

But she wasn't convinced. "What are you talking about? Look at this mess!" She gestured around the room with a sweep of her hand. "They're attacking us because of her." Her eyes turned vicious when she looked at me. "This is all because of *her*."

Mr. Kim came out from around the counter, his striped white shirt dirty from the grease and dirt he'd had to clean. "The girl on the news is a killer." He was calm and deliberate in speaking, as if measuring each word. "If they wanted us dead, wouldn't we already be?"

"I'm not a killer!" Lake stuck her hand into the air like an overeager student. "You haven't seen me on the news, have you?"

"Actually, I have." Ha Rin shrugged. "You were leveling a street in Argentina."

"But it was to *save*—ugh." Lake threw her head back in defeat. "You know, I bet when she called you, Chae Rin totally sabotaged me, didn't she? Told you I was a terrorist, *didn't she*? She'd totally do something like that."

"No," Mr. Kim said to his daughter, pushing away the red brick in his path with his loafers. There were a couple of those lying around. Probably the culprits behind the broken window. "She told us to trust them. Even if it sounded insane."

Ha Rin fell silent as her dad walked behind me and took a seat next to her. "We're both worried. Between the restaurant and—"

He pressed his lips shut, a deep guttural breath rumbling from his chest and through his nose as he sighed. He was looking around his ruined business, at the advertisements on the wall, porcelain faces hawking beer in tiny green bottles, the vandalized refrigerator emptied of all refreshments.

"The last I heard from my daughter, she told me she was in Florida *on the run*—" A hint of the baffled expression he'd probably made when his daughter had told him remained sunken in his features. "And looking for you," he added. He stared in a way that made me sit with my back perfectly straight, like I'd be scolded otherwise. Despite their softness, his eyes were sharp and quietly tense like both of his daughters'. "She didn't say exactly where she was. I told her not to call here anymore. That it was too dangerous. We haven't heard anything since then."

"She was going to Guadeloupe," I said. "I was there too, pretty recently."

"Guadeloupe . . . ?" Ha Rin's slight features pinched as she rolled the name around on her tongue, thinking. "Appa, wasn't there a story about Guadeloupe on the news this afternoon?" Ha Rin waved back at the television on the wall to the left of the menu. "A story involving 'rogue agents'?"

"Things like that are always on the news," he said. He was right. It was easy to lose track of all the constant updates pouring through the media.

"They said some traffickers and agents were rounded up near there," Ha Rin said.

"But no news of Chae Rin?" Lake asked, disappointed when Ha Rin shook her head.

"That's actually good," I told them, poking Lake so she'd nod enthusiastically with me. "That's a good sign."

If they were agents that Chae Rin had traveled with, the fact that she wasn't caught with them gave us some hope. But as father and daughter cast forlorn gazes to the table, I wondered if there was any hope possible for this family whose lives had been ruined by Blackwell's plot.

"Sister's missing, business is ruined, reputation dead, and Mom barely holding it together." Ha Rin shot me a miserable glare. "You'll forgive me if I'm supposed to be enthusiastic about anything right now."

The mop she'd left balanced on the side of the bench slid to the ground onto the trash can. Every Effigy knew that when fate called, it wouldn't just be their lives that changed, but the people around them too. It wasn't just our destiny to bear. But the Kims shouldn't have had to shoulder this. Even if I told her it wasn't my fault, what difference would it make to them?

"I'm sorry," I whispered. "I'm really sorry about all this."

"Yeah, yeah." Ha Rin laid her hands on her lap and sat back against her bench. "You know, they keep telling us to go back," she said, looking out the window onto the street. "The stuff they painted on the walls. 'Go back to Japan' or whatever. We're not even *Japanese*. The police won't do anything about it. When we were still a hot news story, reporters pretended to sympathize, but we haven't seen them or their social consciousness since. I get that we're a terrorist family now, but aside from the vandalism, it's really the same shit we've always dealt with." She stared at her phone on the table. "Why do they keep telling us to go 'back'? Like there needs to be a reason we're here in the first place."

It was getting late. We'd have to arrive at our mission spot soon. But a part of me didn't want to leave the Kims here wallowing in misery because I understood, at least somewhat, how it felt for people to look at your family like you were the piece of a puzzle that didn't quite fit.

"Oh, love, believe me, I get it." Lake ran a hand through her black

bob. "Some people believe nonwhite people have to have a good reason for *existing* in stuff." She shook her head. "When I was in Girls
by Day—excuse me, *GBD*—critics were always asking how my non-
whiteness 'added' to the group, as if the only reason I should be allowed
to be around in the first place was if my being African somehow ele-
vated things in some profound way. I'm sure the assholes terrorizing
you out here were just looking for an excuse to unload. But don't worry.
Maia, Chae Rin, and I won't rest until we've put everything right."

Ha Rin didn't look convinced.

"We mean it," I said, turning my gaze from her glare to her pensive,
solemn father. "I'm going to fix things. Just hold on, okay?"

When I was a heroic Effigy, I knew I could inspire a bit of confidence by spouting the right words, even if the words were empty.
These weren't, and yet there was no confidence to be found in either of
the two who sat alone in their broken restaurant.

"If Chae Rin calls again, let her know we came by," I said.

Lake and I left father and daughter clasping their dirtied hands
over the table, protecting each other in place of the heroes who'd failed
them.

At nine o'clock, just as Abrams left the restaurant, he received a call
from Naomi. Sibyl had her call on a secure, untraceable line. Lake and
I heard the conversation through our earpieces.

"Naomi? You've been released from the hospital?" Abrams sounded
stuffed up through the phone. "Where are you?"

Of course, Naomi wouldn't answer that. "Brendan couldn't contact
you on his own. It's not safe. But through me, he wants to say that
there's a change in the meeting place. I'll tell you how to get there."

On Naomi's word, Abrams's driver would take him off the busy highway and through a far less traveled rural route out of the prying eyes of other cars and pedestrians. A dark area shrouded in high trees lit only by the moon and a car's own headlights. The perfect place for an ambush. Lake and I waited on different branches of the same tree by the side of the road, boots secure on the bark.

"We're at the location," I told Sibyl, tapping my earpiece on.

These earpieces weren't as high-tech as the ones we'd used before. I had to keep my fingers pressed just so I could hear Sibyl on the other end. Otherwise, she couldn't hear me either.

"Good," Sibyl said. "We'll keep trying to contact Chae Rin. After you retrieve your intelligence from Abrams, bring him to the meeting point outside the city."

Lake and I replied with "Roger," at the same time before cutting the communication.

We hid in silence, minutes passing by slowly. Through a veil of trees I scanned the road for any sign of light or movement from the black Rolls-Royce our agents had described to us.

"You know, I was thinking of going back to school after all this is done," came Lake to my right. Her branch was thick and sturdy enough that she could safely shift to a sitting position, one leg crossed over the other. She gripped the branch above her to stay balanced.

"School?" I went back to scanning the street. "Like high school?"

"Yeah, I dropped out when I joined Girls by Day. Then I took another two years off to become an Effigy. I mean, they teach you pretty much everything at the facility while you're training, but it's not the same. I'm only seventeen. I can still go back."

"Oh yeah? What about that single you keep promising?"

"No single," Lake said. "I'm quitting music."

That took my attention off the street. I genuinely gasped. "Really?" Before I was an Effigy, I used to make fun of Lake for pursuing such frivolous work. But with her bright personality, I could tell that entertaining people truly made her happy.

"Is it really surprising? Maia, you saw how Chae Rin's own sister treated us. We're pariahs." The sharp, straight edges of Lake's bob slid through her fingers as she took it all in—the ridiculousness of it all. "I can't do music while being a formerly accused terrorist. Even after our names are cleared, that's not exactly a stench that goes away."

"I don't know." I shrugged. "Could be a decent angle. You could switch to a less pop-y, more hard-core sound, paint your nails black, shave your head. . . ."

"*Shave* my *head*? Okay, now you're asking to get hit." Lake groaned. "Who am I kidding? They're not going to accept me back at school either. Even if I survive all of this, I'll be shunned the rest of my life. And my parents—how many more times are they going to have to give interviews trying to convince people of my innocence?"

I understood Lake's fears acutely. I couldn't imagine walking back into Ashford High at this rate. Even if we did manage to somehow stop and expose Blackwell, the clearing of our names depended solely on whether the public chose to believe our innocence or the steady diet of lies they'd been fed by a twenty-four-hour news cycle. My face especially had already become as associated with Saul's terrorism as Saul himself. Who would believe that it wasn't me? I never had much of a life to begin with. But at least my life of solitude was safely anonymous.

I sighed. "Don't give up, Lake," I told her, because it was what I needed to hear too. "On the upside, you've still got tons of Swans supporting you online."

She seemed to perk up at the thought. "Yeah . . . *yeah*. Maybe I could start a blog and—"

"They're coming."

I pushed myself back into the leaves as the black car that fit our agents' description approached us from the left, slow and cautious down the dark, narrow road. Lake scrambled to her feet. I waited until the car was close enough to jump down onto the hood.

"Hi!" I waved at the windshield of the spooked driver.

The brakes were on immediately. I hopped off as the tires started skidding, and before the car could come to a full stop at the side of the road, Lake opened the back driver's-side door and slid into the seat next to Abrams.

"No police." Lake snatched the phone out of his hands before he could call for help. "We're here on Naomi's orders."

The few strands of gray hair left on Senator Abrams's bald head trembled as he scrambled away from her. Lake grabbed him before he could escape through the other side while I knocked out the driver.

"I'm sorry to be kind of blunt," I said, sliding into the passenger seat, "but we gotta make this quick. Whatever you were going to tell Brendan, you need to tell us, and you need to do it fast before Blackwell's strike team shows up to kill your ass."

Abrams's gut rumbled as he shot up straight in his seat. *"What?"* he spluttered, gripping the smooth, leather back of his seat. "Blackwell is—"

"When you called Brendan at the CSTF headquarters, you tipped Blackwell off that you were going to spill something," I said. "Something that could hurt him. Problem is, Blackwell is using the task force to get rid of anyone who might oppose him while he amasses international power and support. If he thinks you know anything that could expose him, you're done."

"But we can help!" Lake's chipper tone didn't do much to calm the panicking rise and fall of Abrams's chest. "Blackwell and some of your friends on the Council have been behind Saul's terrorism from the beginning. Right now I'm pretty sure we're the only ones trying to actually stop them. Tell us what you know. We can get the info to Brendan *after* we get you to safety."

But Abrams was staring at me, his mouth agape in frozen terror. "You . . . you were just in Italy," he said.

"I guess you're not privy to the whole scheme if you're not aware that my doppelgänger is out there making a mess of things." I tapped the digital clock on his dash. Nine thirty in the evening. Our inoculation was wearing off and we'd be on the grid soon. "We don't have all the time in the world."

"No, we don't." Lake leaned over and pulled Abrams's phone out of his jacket pocket. Too terrified to resist, he watched her turn on the recording device. "Okay," she told me.

"Now talk," I said. "What is it that you were going to tell Brendan?"

Abrams hesitated, his gaze switching nervously between the two Effigies in his car before clearing his throat. "If you know that Blackwell is dirty, then you know I had nothing to do with Oslo."

"Aside from giving Prince the go-ahead to fire a death weapon," I reminded him.

"I discussed it with Blackwell first." Abrams quietly slid to the window. "In fact, he was the one who pressed me to do it. I never would have otherwise. But we were in a state of panic, and he convinced me that it was the only option. As the Council representative, he didn't have the codes or authority to do anything himself."

"He's certainly fixed that now." Lake crossed her legs. "According to Brendan, he's got the codes to Minerva. He can use it whenever he wants, and he will."

"I . . . I know." The skin on Abrams's throat trembled as he swallowed, his bulbous Adam's apple scraping up and down. "The Council voted after I resigned. There are three standing with him now: Wang Liu, a highly influential businessmen in China and owner of one of the largest media providers in the world; Betty Briggs, a former US secretary of state; and Judge Antero Nylund, who is serving on the International Criminal Court—all people who can use their power and influence to gather legal and financial support to force Blackwell's post-Sect creation. Naomi is in the wind, and Blackwell recently assassinated Baldric and Cardinal Donati. And I—" Looking at us, he pressed his back flat against the door.

"I don't get it," Lake said. "Why would they all agree to work with Blackwell when, according to Director Prince, Blackwell was just some guy who inherited the job of the Council's mouthpiece from his father?"

Senator Abrams's nostrils contracted as he sniffed in air, coughing a little as he cleared his throat. "There are usually a handful of reasons why powerful men would follow another powerful man into hell," he answered. "No one can amass power without a vision, but some visions are so breathtakingly bold it takes a special fool to see it through. It's easy to become curious—to get swept up in the scheme, especially if you're promised more power out of it, and *especially* if you can claim your spoils while remaining in the shadows."

"It was Blackwell's father who started all this," I told him. "He and a few of the Council members then were behind the Seattle Siege. Did you know that?"

He clenched his teeth. "No, not 'he and a few Council members.' At first it was simply Blackwell and Griffith Rhys."

Rhys's great-grandfather. The man who built the underground bunker in Seattle. Well, he'd hid footage of the control center massacre, so they were clearly partners.

"Cardinal Donati gave me this information shortly before he was killed. We met in secret. Blackwell made it a point to woo the Council members one by one over time, ensuring their loyalty before bringing them into his fold. But even after all my years on the Council, neither Blackwell ever approached me. Maybe they thought it was easier to use me."

He looked bitter about that, too. He sucked in a breath. "Blackwell and Griffith conspired with their associates to cause devastation in order to force the Senate to adopt a secret black project to be backed by America's Defense Advanced Research Projects Agency. It was as if Griffith and Blackwell formed a secret council within our *already* secret council. I was a member then, but believe me, none of us knew. We all treated Seattle as the tragedy it was. In fact, one of the Council members at the time lost his only son in that attack. He never would have allowed that. No, the Council was not involved until after Blackwell died in 2006. He died slowly, so he would have had time to initiate his son before dying, perhaps even groomed him. The Blackwell of today would have brought in the other Council members when and only when it was time."

"What about Griffith?" Lake asked. "Didn't he do the opposite of Blackwell Senior? He never told Naomi anything. Hell, according to her, at the end of his life he told her not to trust *any* Blackwell."

"Griffith was a shell of himself in his later years. Perhaps the guilt caught up to him." Abrams looked evasive as he cleared his throat and shifted in his seat. "But it didn't matter if he repented. He helped develop secret research and development programs for the Sect, and one such endeavor laid the foundation for Blackwell's opus: the Silent Children Program. This is what I wanted to tell Brendan: the creation of scientifically engineered supersoldiers who can mimic the abilities of Effigies."

"Oh, we know about the project," Lake said. "We've run into a couple of those lab rats, and it hasn't been fun."

"Right under my nose." Abrams struggled with the reality of it. "Griffith and Blackwell helped orchestrate one of the greatest

tragedies in American history. Even if the first project they proposed
to the Senate was axed, the incident invigorated nations to fund and
advance cutting-edge antiphantom and Effigy-related research, setting the stage for the development of the tools currently in Blackwell's
control. It was Griffith who created the overall shell of the Silent
Children Program adapted from his initial proposal, bringing in
researchers while coordinating espionage on other development facilities overseas to strengthen their project. I can only imagine how far
their research has advanced by now. And now most of the Council is
with Blackwell."

"People *trusted* you guys with their *lives*." I couldn't stop myself
from snarling at him. "You people *jeered* at me and cajoled me into
swearing an oath to protect humanity, and meanwhile, *you* were the
mess behind the scenes. The *Council*." I let out a bitter laugh. "Acting
as if you had the right to 'manage' the Effigies when you couldn't even
manage your damn selves."

Abrams avoided my eyes as he lowered his head. "That's why I'm
here. To atone. And I can do that only if I confess my sins."

Reaching into his jacket pocket, he pulled out a chip. "The
Fisk-Hoffman facility," he said.

Lake and I exchanged glances. "What about it?" I pressed, trying
not to let anticipation show on my face.

"The facility was world-renowned for forging the best agents out
of the most difficult training. But I knew. I knew about the torture
and assault." Abrams's hand shook as he squeezed the chip. "I helped
keep it hidden until Agent Brighton's serial murders and Irina Volkov's
jump out of a ten-story building into oncoming traffic in Vienna made
that impossible."

Agent Brighton, the man who now tortured for the Sect as the
Surgeon, and Irina Volkov, Vasily's mother and his reason for tearing

down the Sect. Both graduated from the facility as celebrated agents only to end in the darkest of depths.

"But along with Blackwell and Briggs, I fought for it to remain open. Even despite the tragedies, glorious agents could still be forged within those walls." Abrams looked sick with himself as he spoke. "That's what I thought. But I knew nothing of what would come next. There's a tablet in my glove compartment," he told me. "Please hand it to me. I'll show you."

Once I handed him the tablet, he jammed the USB inside. Lake and I leaned in as images of a facility in the snow swiped across the screen with his finger. A facility in the snow . . . The shape and breadth of this one was completely different from the one Saul had taken me to, but it was familiar all the same, right down to the aurora borealis lights streaking the sky in some of the images.

"This was the *original* Fisk-Hoffman facility," Abrams said. "Before the child trainees at the facility killed the trainers and burned down the facility."

"What?" I grabbed the tablet and flipped through the next three images of the facility. What I saw earlier was the "before." This was the "after": a flaming wreckage in the snow.

"You guys told everyone it was an electrical failure," Lake said.

Everyone believed it. Eventually, I started to think that maybe the Council had set the fire on purpose in order to have a secret place to run their Silent Children experiments. "How could kids . . . ? Why would they—"

"Because they were well trained, and they'd had enough of the trauma, enough of the blood, enough of the abuse." Abrams shut his eyes against the haunted memories. "Because he was efficient, we kept Fisk-Hoffman's sadistic son in charge of the facility. He made those kids fight each other until their bodies and minds were broken. Starved them. Tortured them."

It was why Rhys and Vasily had called it the Devil's Hole. A hellish cage operating under the guise of forging the greatest. I shuddered, my lips curling up at the thought. What Rhys must have gone through . . . what he was still going through . . . a never-ending nightmare. . . .

"I don't know when they planned it or how many kids were in on the plan. But when they struck in the dead of night, the aim was total annihilation." Abrams clenched his jaw, sniffing loudly as he breathed in. "They murdered the entire faculty, the doctors, the trainers. Fisk-Hoffman's son last. And to destroy evidence, they burned down the facility. All of it on that little boy's orders. Aidan Prince . . ."

The tablet slipped out of my hands and fell onto the emergency brake. At the sound of his name, my heart jumped up my throat so suddenly I couldn't speak right away. Aidan . . . It was *Rhys's* plan?

Vasily's bloodied lips grinned back at me from deep within my memories. Tortured and broken by the Surgeon in the London facility's underground prison, he still had enough malice to taunt his former friend.

*You remember, don't you, Aidan?*

"No." I shook my head, tears stinging hot in my eyes. "No way. He wouldn't. He couldn't—"

Kill? But he did kill. He killed Natalya. I'd known he was a killer. I just didn't know he'd been one his whole life. I doubled over in my seat as Lake hesitantly took the tablet. After a few seconds, the shivering voice of a young boy roused me once again. I looked up and saw, on the tablet, a video of a raven-haired boy in a lonely little room, sitting across the table from someone I couldn't see, even though I could hear her gentle voice asking him questions.

"Aidan, the fire was an electrical issue, wasn't it? Given that, tell me what happened."

He must have been a preteen here; his thin body, gangly in awkward ways, didn't quite match his head in proportion. He wrapped his arms around himself, but he couldn't keep still. Instead, he was rocking back and forth, his eyes unable to focus anywhere. "I told you," he said in his cracking voice. "We did it. I did it. I had to. I had to protect them."

"You had to protect them *after* the fire started," the female voice said. "So then, Aidan, after the flames woke you up, what did you do?"

These weren't questions. She was *coaching* him.

"I told you I *killed* them!" he shouted, the anguish driving him to his feet, his cheeks stained with tears. "I *had* to. They were going to kill us. They were going to—" He was breathing fast. "Oh god. Oh my god. I'm sorry. I'm *sorry*." For a moment he clutched his head before lowering his hands again, staring at the camera pleadingly. "You can't tell my mother. I'll do anything. Just please don't tell her. . . ."

It was Abrams who shut off the video. "This is why I wanted to speak to Brendan," he said quietly. "To confess to him. To apologize to his parents, whom we'd kept this from. We kept it from everyone. I helped cover everything up to save the Sect's reputation. Aidan was too strong to break, but he kept his mouth shut anyway. He wanted to move on. This all happened after Griffith died. By then I believe, Blackwell had enlisted Briggs alone as the sole Council member to advance what Griffith and his father had started. I didn't know what would become of those children. . . ."

Abrams rubbed his hands up his forehead over the wrinkles. "But it didn't matter. I failed them. Worried about the Sect's brand, I tried to bury the truth of what happened at Fisk-Hoffman. I didn't ask questions when I was told that its plot of land had been sold to the US military. Because I purposely averted my eyes, I never knew Blackwell had rebuilt and upgraded the facility for his own purposes."

"The Silent Children Program," Lake said. "Your Council friends brought back the facility, pretending it was something different entirely." She flipped through the images until their faces showed up: the seven children of Fisk-Hoffman's final cohort dressed in their finely cut maroon blazers, unaware of the tragedies that would befall them. "You know what they're doing with some of those kids, right?"

Their names were written below their images. Philip Anglebart, the dead soldier in the Sahara. Alexander Drywater, the grotesque corpse puppeteered by necromancer Jessie Stone. Talia Nassar and Gabriel Moore, who were still missing. Vasily Volkov, the child turned monster at the hands of an organization that shattered his life. And Aidan Rhys. It was his moniker within the Sect, a sentimental attachment to his mother, a way of distancing himself from his true identity as the youngest Prince. Aliases and lies. Secrets and murder. A boy smashed to pieces. A broken image in a cracked mirror.

"By sweeping them under the rug, you made it all the more easy for Blackwell to grab them and experiment on them." Lake shoved the tablet in his face so he couldn't look away from them. "And there's going to be a lot more where that came from."

"I didn't know," Abrams insisted. "I didn't know about Blackwell's larger plan—"

"But you helped him by refusing to protect these kids." Lake clicked the screen off and dropped the tablet onto the seat. "Did you even check up on any of them to make sure they were okay? Or were you only worried that they'd snitch on you instead? They were bloody *children* and you were busy trying to *brainwash* them."

A shaken Senator Abrams remained very still. "I told you, I want to atone. Blackwell will unveil his plan at the United Nations' special three-day Assembly in New York two days from now. He's been working with his diplomatic contacts outside the Sect, getting them on board. The legal documents have already been drawn to shift power, and a vote will take place to determine who will lead this new 'organization.' Between his Council resources, the favorable media coverage, and all the blackmail and bribes, he has the support he needs. And even if the UN says no . . ." He shut his lips, his breath seeping through his nose in a low, guttural rumble. "One can be quite convincing with a satellite weapon at their disposal," he continued. I imagined that was Blackwell's Plan B. "I want to help you stop him."

"I hope you're ready to testify, then. And if not?" Lake waved his phone. "I've recorded this whole conversation. So one way or another, the truth is going to come out. About all of it."

Abrams remained silent, staring at the glowing screen of his phone. Then he pulled a small photo out of his breast pocket. It was an old one—he was younger in it by a couple of decades, probably. It was a suit-and-tie event, maybe a fund-raiser. He sat at the table with a few people I didn't recognize—but one I did. Blackwell, our Blackwell, in a black suit, college fresh. He flashed a smile that was as comfortable as a family friend, as pompous as a boy saturated in a legacy of wealth. The look in his eyes told the story of a rich boy already enamored with dark thoughts and malicious dreams. But this was a boy who'd never once been given an inkling—by his rich parents, by his family friends, or even by his society—that the fulfillment of those dreams could be anything other than his divine right. He sat surrounded by power, thinking of nothing else.

"I was going to show this to Brendan to help explain it all," Abrams said. "Though, considering his family, I thought he might understand a little. You see, sometimes when you have wealth and power, you begin to believe that it's what you're owed. You're taught to believe that the laws don't apply to you. That you're above the law—or worse—that the laws of men serve you. For many of us in our world, the word of the powerful and the expendability of the rest of humanity is nothing more and nothing less than common sense. But there are material costs. And I understand now more than ever that those costs are too high."

I thought of Rhys weeping, confessing his sins in front of the world as he knelt, disgraced before Saul. An innocent boy had been turned into a killer by every powerful adult who'd failed him. Children becoming monsters. A legendary Effigy murdered and buried. Another driven to madness. Countless people dead and dying from the attacks the Council's maliciousness and negligence had caused. I wanted to spit in this man's face, spit out the venomous fury corroding my insides, let him taste just how corrosive it was. Instead, I got out of the car, pulling the driver into the passenger seat before opening his side door.

"Get in the driver's seat," I ordered. "You're going to drive to the location we give you. You don't deserve it, but I'm still going to save your life." I turned my back to him. "Because *someone* has to be good."

Lake and I took the backseat while he started up the car. "Ms. Finley," he said.

I wasn't in the mood. "What?"

"There's something you need to know about the current Blackwell. Something he's been keeping from everyone."

Maybe I was. "I'm listening," I said, watching him intently.

"Like I said, some men want to see themselves as gods. They feel like the laws of men don't apply to them, but the laws of nature—no man can escape that."

Beside me, Lake raised her eyebrow. "What are you talking about?"

"No matter how much wealth and resources we have, the one rule we can't escape is death. When death comes, poor and rich are the same. Blackwell the fifth died after living with Huntington's for only ten years. The Blackwell of now would have watched his father waste away before dying. That does something to a man."

A degenerative disease. "Why are you telling us this?" I asked him.

Headlights approached us from down the street, headlights that drew close enough to blind us before shutting off, along with the truck they were attached to. We were supposed to meet Sibyl's agents just outside the city. What I didn't expect was for their truck to meet us halfway down the road. This wasn't the plan.

"What's going on?" I leaned over the passenger seat and peered through the window. "Is that Redman and the others?" I clicked my earpiece on. "Sibyl? Did you change the plan? Why are they meeting us here?" Static. "Sibyl? *Sibyl?*"

"Something must be blocking our communications," Lake said, tapping her ears with her finger before letting out a frustrated yell. "These things aren't great, but we only get static when we're underground."

The truck stopped a few feet away from us. The passenger door opened. It wasn't Redman. I had barely noticed the man's black combat uniform and ski mask before the bullet from his gun pierced straight through the windshield. Abrams's hands slid off the steering wheel, his body slumping to the side as blood dripped from the bullet hole in his forehead.

We were next.

# 18

LAKE HIT THE FLOOR. I WORKED QUICKLY, jumping out of the car, opening the passenger door to shield from the bullets.

"Come on." Ducking my head low, I shook my hand, rousing the sleeping power inside me, willing it to come to the surface. "Come *on!*"

A spark. Like starting a car. My arm tingled with what dwindling power I could manage, and my flames slashed the road. I'd meant to hit the truck, but I couldn't reach far enough. Still, the row of fire I made stretched high enough to shield us from the truck's view. It'd have to do for now.

Lake and I dragged Abrams's body and the driver's—still alive, but out cold—to the backseat and slid into the front.

I clenched my teeth. "Lake, you can drive, right?" The keys were still in the ignition.

Gripping the steering wheel, Lake smiled at me. "Nope!"

"*What?* You know how to drive a damn motorcycle!"

"Learning was a passion project!"

Bullets started flying again. Ducking, I pushed the gear into reverse. "Hit the gas!"

Lake did, and we start motoring back, spinning around in a wild circle when she swiveled the steering wheel. The centrifugal force knocked the wind from my chest. For a moment Lake froze, her eyes bulging.

"Let's go!" I shook her shoulder before buckling my seat belt. "Drive!"

After I snapped her out of it, she stepped on the gas again. The wheels turned, but we didn't move. The bullets had stopped too. Confused, I turned around.

And my stomach clenched.

The flames did not burn the tall girl who crawled out of them, step by pincer step, like a spider tiptoeing up a wall. Sweat speckled her bald head from the heat nonetheless, dripping down the shadows of her face. Though she wore the same gear as the other Silent Children, her helmet was nowhere to be found. We had full view of her dark, unhappy eyes, their gaze pinned to the back of our truck as she spread her arms out in front of her. The strain showed in her labored breathing, but she wouldn't have been able to scream even if she wanted to—not with her scarred lips sewn shut with jagged string.

She waved the car to the side, sending us skidding into a tree. The driver's side bore the full brunt of the impact, and by the time a branch broke off and landed atop the roof, Lake was out cold.

"Damn it." I unbuckled my seat belt and got out of the car. A Silent Child. Must have been Talia. She looked just like her photo—aside from the baldness and mutilation. My powers had barely returned, and my only backup was unconscious. But if I could catch her off guard . . .

The flames in front of the truck were beginning to dissipate. Focusing my concentration to a point, I boosted the flames, just as two strike team agents thought it was safe to cross. Their screams caught Talia's attention for a half second, and I made my move, running toward her and slashing flames across her face, but all it did was annoy her. A flame-resistant bad guy. Not exactly the type I wanted to go up against.

But her skin tissue already looked intimately familiar with other forms of torture. It looked slashed, chewed up like an animal's plaything. Shaking my attacks off with ease, she frowned at me and sent me flying back into another tree. Telekinesis.

Two powers? Was that the reason she looked so utterly battered from inside out? Just how long had they tinkered with this girl? How long had they wrecked her to make sure they got the biotech just right? And she could have other tricks up her sleeve too.

Great, just *great*.

"Capture her alive!" one man said. "Kill the other one."

"As *if*." Using the tree trunk to steady me, I got back up to my feet and stared down Talia, who stood with her neck bent at an odd angle in the middle of the street. None of this was her fault. The girl couldn't even speak. With her life twisted by the greedy and powerful, she was left as nothing more than a bloodhound. But I couldn't let them take me or kill my friend.

I wasn't going to lose anyone else.

I mustered every bit of power I had in me. Trap and release. But the effects of the inoculation still buzzed in my system. My power was slow to move, lumbering lazily through my veins. Release. *Release.* Body shaking, blood dripping down my nose, I squeezed my eyes shut and felt the ground move.

Wait, the ground really *was* moving.

Blackwell's strike team screamed as the road quaked and split in two. They say you can always tell when an Effigy had been in a city from the wreckage they left behind. As the truck fell through the fault, bodies jumped out of the way only to land on crumbling asphalt. It was a welcome mess, one that the reckless Chae Rin left joyfully.

Adrenaline burst through my veins at the sight of her running down the street in her corduroy jacket. She looked worse for wear, grease and soot dirtying her pale skin like she hadn't bathed in days. Talia had leapt out of the way, but now she simply looked at Chae Rin, puzzled. Her agitated eyes darted about. The man who'd barked orders slid onto his back, having narrowly missed falling into a crater like many of his fellow agents. Ripping off his skewed ski mask so he could see more easily, he reached for his gun, and when he couldn't find it, called for Talia once more.

"Kill this girl too," he ordered, his voice hoarse. "And secure Maia Finley."

Talia stopped jittering. It was as if she needed orders to keep her mind focused. Chae Rin didn't wait to see what this girl could do. Pushing her hands forward, she lifted a big chunk of the rubble and tossed it at her, but Talia stopped it in midair. Chae Rin looked surprised, but not defeated. They both pushed, a tug of wills forcing the boulder in each other's direction with a force so powerful their shoes skidded against the street as they slid back.

But this was my chance. Lake was starting to stir in the car, but she wouldn't be awake in time to help. While Talia was busy with Chae Rin, I ran forward and launched myself at her, jumping on her back, wrapping my arms around her neck, and squeezing. Talia began to choke, grasping for her throat, but once she dropped her concentration, Chae Rin's boulder broke free from her influence and launched toward us.

It was a split-second decision. I jumped out of the way and let the boulder hit Talia, crushing her chest against the pavement. The sight of her blood splattering out of her mouth drained the adrenaline from my body, snuffing out that frenzied fight-or-flight drive that would have had me doing whatever it took to save myself and my friends. I collapsed onto the street, staring at the light dying from her eyes until it was finally snuffed out.

I thought I'd become desensitized to the presence of corpses. It wasn't even the sight of blood dripping from her eye down her cheek that made the walls feel like they were closing in. It was her mutilated lips, spotted red and purple with bruises from the needle punctures. Dry and cracked, they stilled in the silence of death. In the end, she couldn't even scream. Why? Why had they sewn her mouth shut? To keep her from screaming during the experiments? Or was it of her own will? Now Talia would never be able to tell us.

Chae Rin knocked out the last conscious strike agent before running to my side. "Are you okay? Sibyl told me you guys were up here, but I couldn't get ahold of any of you. Hey!"

She slapped my head because subtlety wasn't her strongpoint. Groggily, I lifted my head. "Chae Rin . . ."

"Chae Rin!" Lake was up. She ran out of Abrams's car, not even bothering to shut the door, and hurtled toward us. "Where the hell have you been? How did you get here? Oh dear, she looks—"

Lake had found Talia and recoiled accordingly.

"Later, kids, we gotta go." But I noticed Chae Rin wouldn't look at the corpse. Her face was tense, her body still high on the adrenaline of battle, though her eyelashes nervously fluttered the one time her gaze strayed to the ruined road upon which Talia lay. "The cops will be here soon. I'm sure we're showing up on everyone's tracker right now." With a rough yank, Chae Rin lifted me off my feet. "You guys have a car?"

"Yeah," I said, tearing my eyes away from Talia's dead body. "Yeah, there's—"

"What the hell?" came a terrified voice from Abrams's car. The driver. He was staring at his employer's dead body. "What?" At the chaos on the streets. *"What?"* Sleeping Beauty was awake and everything was terrible. "What the fu—"

"Okay, that's enough of that," Chae Rin said, stalking toward him in her worn-out sneakers.

We had to take Abrams with us, at least. We didn't need the headline or the frame job. As for the driver—we had no choice but to leave him behind, though Chae Rin could have chosen a gentler method than roughly pulling him out of the car and dropping him onto the street like a sack of potatoes.

"Fancy car," Chae Rin said, impressed as she checked the inside Abrams's Rolls-Royce.

"You really took your time in getting here." I slammed the passenger door. "But I'm glad you did."

"Unfortunately, a well-timed hero moment isn't nearly compensation for the shit I went through to get to you guys. Good thing I could still hear Sibyl over the comm, but forty-eight hours of hitchhiking with a bunch of creepy Effigy superfans wasn't exactly as fun as it would sound to someone like you—" She looked at me. "You know. A creepy Effigy superfan."

"Glad you're back!" Lake tried to wrap her arms around Chae Rin's neck, but Chae Rin made a face and shooed the girl back before starting the engine.

"I have to confess, though." Chae Rin checked the rearview mirror, making sure she wouldn't run over Abrams's driver when she backed up. "I could have gotten here sooner, but I had to make a stop first."

"Your restaurant?" I assumed.

"My house. My mom."

I breathed. She'd told me once about her mother's sufferings, about her guilt over steering clear of her. "What did she say?"

Chae Rin looked at me. "She said she believed in me." For the first time since she arrived, her featured softened, but determination in her eyes burned nonetheless. "Let's not disappoint her."

Chae Rin's gaze lingered on the review mirror. Talia. One of the many children failed by the institution sworn to protect them. But it was a passing moment. Hitting reverse, she backed up, narrowly missing the driver, before speeding down the street.

# 19

I WAS RIGHT. THE STRIKE TEAM HAD BEEN using some device to jam radio frequencies in the area. They had also gotten to Redman and the others first. We found their corpses strewn by two bullet-riddled vans at the rendezvous point. There was nothing we could do for them. Heavyhearted as I was, what scared me most was that I would soon become numb to the sight of dead bodies.

We were finally able to connect with Sibyl on our way out of the city. We told her about the attack, about Abrams's death, about Talia's appearance. As for everything that Abrams told us, I hesitated to repeat it, knowing Naomi was listening on the other end. But I didn't have a choice, and she deserved to know.

"Wait," Chae Rin said. "You're telling me Rhys *burned down* an entire training facility and convinced a bunch of tortured misfits to murder the staff when he was thirteen at the *most*?" With her hands on the steering wheel, she whistled. "That's some *Lord of the Flies* shit. I always thought that whole sexy-cute nerd shit was all a front—"

"Hush. *Up*," Lake said, because unlike Chae Rin, she hadn't forgotten that Naomi was listening.

Nobody spoke for too long, not even Sibyl. But then it was Naomi's slow, soothing voice that came through my earpiece. "I knew that something had happened in that facility. That there was more than he'd told me. I knew he was suffering, even if he could never tell me why."

Lights from the highway lamps passed by my window, illuminating my silent reflection.

"I told you once that a trigger can't pull itself. He led a difficult life, as short—as short as it was." Naomi's voice cracked. I shut my eyes against the sound of the long breath she inhaled. "I just . . . I hope that he's found peace—"

Naomi's words broke off.

"You guys still there?" I said after a moment, keeping my finger pressed against the earpiece.

"Yeah." It was Sibyl who answered. "She left."

From the backseat, Lake gave me a prodding look. Yes, I knew. Rhys was alive. But in the state she was in, telling Naomi that her enemies had saved her youngest son's life only to enslave him to their will would not make her feel better. Rather than giving her more bad news, I'd bring her son back to her myself. That was all I could do right now. For both of them.

"Rhys was locked in a hellhole as a child with no way out. It was either do or die, and he snapped. They all did." I couldn't shake the image of his gangly thirteen-year-old form shaking from the horror of his memories. And now he was out there, hunting us.

"There's definitely a lot of tragic stories on our team," Chae Rin said. "And speaking of tragic, what about Belle? You told me she's gone off the deep end, which doesn't surprise me in the least. So what, is she going to sit in prison, or is she eventually going to come after us?"

"I don't know," I said, my expression dark. "I haven't seen her since

Guadeloupe. Or Saul, for that matter. Who knows what either of them is planning."

Chae Rin let out a bitter laugh, shaking her head. "Just perfect."

She kept her foot on the gas, speeding down the highway to the rendezvous point. Sibyl quickly dispatched Cheryl to meet us so we could get another boost to deaden our powers and help us stay off the grid. We eventually found our way off the official, antiphantom-protected highway and onto an old road through a Dead Zone plain. Abrams's car was one of those fancy, expensive ones equipped with electromagnetic armor. A barely perceptible sheen of light covered the car like an angelic glow, ready for any shadow creature that dared to stray near us. The EMA definitely helped us get through the worst of it. Lake and I still shuddered and winced as phantoms rushed toward our vehicle, jaws snapping, vaporizing once they got too close to Abrams's car. But since it was just like traveling to the Cirque de Minuit in Canada, only with fewer safeguards, I could imagine for Chae Rin it was just like driving to work every morning.

Halfway to our rendezvous point, Abrams's phone rang in Lake's pocket.

"You didn't turn it off?" I stared at it as she took it out of her pocket. "What if they're tracking its GPS or something?"

"They're probably already tracking us," she answered. There was no name on the display. She let the phone ring until it fell to silence once again. Then she listened to the message.

"This is Brendan." His voice was hushed. "I don't have much time. I'm talking on a secure line, but there are cops in the building. I'm at the Vancouver Police Department with a task force unit."

He must have gone to the city earnestly to meet Abrams. "I tried to get here as fast as I could. I knew Blackwell would send a strike team, but I was given Abrams's message too late. They deployed before I could. Maia—"

I perked up in my seat. This message wasn't for Senator Abrams at all.

"Maia, you're there, aren't you? With the others. We saw the wreckage on the road and talked to the witness you left. The police are tracking your signal now. Make sure you disappear off the grid as quickly as you can before they catch up to you. As for the dead girl, they're processing her as we speak. Talia Nassar. I know she was one of the children who trained with my brother in Greenland."

His brother. His brother had fought me just a few blocks away from him in Argentina. Did Brendan know? It didn't sound like he did.

"The good news is," Brendan continued, "I might be able to use Talia's body as evidence that there are illegal experiments going on out there. The bad news is we have to be able to pin it to Blackwell and the others in the Council as evidence of their wrongdoing. Otherwise it could get twisted into more anti-Sect propaganda. And there's something else."

He stopped suddenly. I could hear voices in the background, feet shuffling, then a door softly closing, blocking the voices out. "There's something else," he repeated. "In two days, Blackwell will be in New York to present his plan of a new unified world force. I'll be part of his security detail on Blackwell's personal request. I suppose he wants to show the world that even the son of the shamed Director Prince is on his side. But tomorrow he'll be at Carnegie Hall watching a performance from the Tokyo Philharmonic—the same night June Finley and Vasily are slated to hit the city."

My body numbed at the sound of my sister's name. I could feel Chae Rin and Lake's concern searing the hair off my skin. I couldn't handle it right now.

"Every CSTF team has at least one of the original Sect traitors who knew of and supported Blackwell's plans. In my team, I
pinpointed who they were pretty quickly and managed to tap their
phones. It's how I learned about Minerva. It's how I know Belle's been
conditionally released from Guadeloupe—relocated—though I don't
know where yet."

Belle was on the move. I swallowed carefully. Was this part of her
plan? What was she *doing*?

"But for Blackwell," Brendan continued, "using June and Vasily is
just a ploy to silence his dissenters. Having them attack while he's still
in the city would garner support for his proposals while casting himself
as another unsuspecting citizen endangered by terror. Make sure you
stop them."

I turned back around, pressing against my seat as the message
ended. A swirl of black mist raged outside, the hollow white eyes of
a phantom watching me from the other side of my window before it
came too close to the yellow haze of our electromagnetic armor and
exploded into dust.

June would attack New York tomorrow. If she was determined to
play puppet, then I had to be more determined to save her.

I guess the Finley sisters were going home.

We met up with Cheryl close to the border, dumping the car in some
woods and switching over to the Sect jet, the same that had taken me
out of Argentina, its tracking system manipulated by Uncle Nathan's
hacking to help it stay off the grid as we flew among the clouds.

Chae Rin, Lake, and I sat toward the end of the plane, with Cheryl
sitting in the other row. While they went over the files on Senator
Abrams's tablet, my mind wandered, and I began staring out the window.

I wasn't as scared of flying anymore. I'd had too many experiences with phantoms already to let their undulating forms in the air scare me much any longer. But June was never scared, even when we were children. On the odd occasions we'd fly out of the country, she'd be the first one to push up the blind and stare out the window. Fascinated by monsters. Fearless in the face of the death they could bring . . .

"There's definitely a lot here," Cheryl said. With her legs crossed, she flipped through Abrams's tablet on the table next to a silver briefcase, studying the photos, including the ones he'd shown us. "All this information he was going to give to Brendan, most of it revolves around the tragedies at the facility. He even screen-capped some private e-mail conversations on the facility between him and the other Council members. Like this e-mail chain implicating himself and Briggs in pushing for the facility to remain open."

"And unlike Abrams, Briggs was probably on Blackwell's side by then." Chae Rin sipped her half-empty can of soda in the seat opposite me. "She must have known about how Rhys's training cohort ended up being the trial run for that mess—at least, the kids they could get to. Rhys may not have even realized it, but by burning down the facility, he gave them the exact opportunity they needed. Once it was officially closed and people weren't looking, Briggs and company could just go ahead with their sick plan in secret."

Cheryl nodded. "And they would have perfected it by now."

"Okay." Tearing my eyes away from the window, I pulled myself out of my memories of June and focused on the rest. "So Blackwell's making an appearance tomorrow in New York, where June and Vasily are gonna attack. What exactly is the plan, then?"

"If the Special Assembly's taking place soon in New York," replied Cheryl, "then we need to get Blackwell off the streets before then. It'll buy us some time."

"Time for what?" I asked.

It was Sibyl who answered through the communications system. "Lake, you recorded your conversation with Abrams, didn't you?"

"Yeah." She took out Abrams's phone. "It's all here."

"Along with the material on his tablet, it might be enough to bring to the attorney general," Sibyl said. "I'll do it myself."

Sibyl, come out of hiding? I didn't like the sound of that. "You sure that's wise?"

"I know him personally. I've worked with him concerning legal matters in situations where the Sect and the American military had joint operations. Believe me, not everyone is buying what Blackwell is selling despite his fearmongering tactics and media manipulation. The attorney general's one of the few still vocal in their criticism toward Blackwell's handling of the dissolution of the Sect. He'll want to hear this. We've been building our case using what we've found here. That recording may push them to investigate the American military base operating where Fisk-Hoffman used to stand. In the meantime, you need to incapacitate Blackwell to stall the Assembly."

Chae Rin scrunched her nose, skeptical. "And how do you suggest we do that?"

"Do we have any agents on the ground who can help?" Lake asked.

"We had a couple associates near the state, but they were already among the team who helped you girls in Vancouver. They"—Cheryl paused, sucking in a breath—"they died with Redman."

She fell silent, looking away from the team. No matter how long you were out in the field, the toll a colleague's death took on the soul could never be understated.

"We didn't have that many people helping us in the first place," she continued. "You girls might be on your own."

"I mean, breaking in anywhere just requires a distraction and multiple entrances." Chae Rin leaned back. "We'll sneak in and pull the fire alarm. We'll definitely get through the hall undetected if people are screaming in terror."

My back snapped up straight. "Pull the fire alarm . . . that's it!" I stared at the girls excitedly. I loved those lightbulb moments. Too bad they didn't come often enough. "We pull the *biggest* fire alarm—New York's war siren! It'll get people off the streets and into shelters in time for June's and Vasily's attack, and it'll clear people out of Carnegie Hall. We can grab Blackwell while he's escaping with the rest!"

"Yes . . . ," Sibyl said. "And so long as you obscure your faces, nobody will notice you're not supposed to be there while they're busy evacuating. Good thinking, Maia."

I wanted to pat myself on the back but thought better of it.

"Nathan, you used to work at the city's Municipal Defense Control Center. Do you think you can hack into the system and set off the alarm?"

Uncle Nathan wasn't in the communication link with us, but he was definitely in the room with Sibyl. I could hear his answer in the background. "Yeah, I might be able to manage that. Pulling a false alarm would be much safer and a far less complicated process than taking the entire Needle off-line."

"Good," Sibyl said.

"Dot wanted me to give you these." Cheryl opened the silver briefcase on the table and pulled out a metallic red pen. But pressing the tip sent a silver tube jutting out of the bottom, dripping with a thick silver liquid. "You're inoculated now to avoid tracking, but this'll block the influence of the inhibitor in case you need to snap into action. It looks like a pen, so nobody would glance at it twice. Same with the bracelets you had. There's one for each of you in here."

Lake took it from her. "An anti-anti-Effigy-power . . . power-blocker?

I think I got that wrong." She happily examined it nonetheless. "The pen's really pretty, though."

"Take this, too." Cheryl pulled her gun out of the holster strapped to her side and gave it to me. "In case using your powers is out of the question."

I held it apprehensively, hoping I wouldn't have to use it.

"If anything happens to your communications devices, make sure to call Cheryl and me, or the Seattle HQ, using the numbers I had you memorize at the base," Sibyl said. "Cheryl will meet me in DC with the evidence from Abrams. As for you girls—you know what to do."

The three of us locked eyes and nodded. The mission was a go.

Though it was the same New York, Carnegie Hall was in Manhattan—twelve miles and a bridge away from where I used to live with Uncle Nathan in Brooklyn. Being back in the busy city was an out-of-body experience. The endless yellow cabs, the pizza shops and convenience stores and bakeries and everything else clustered down the blocks with jaywalking pedestrians crowding the street under a starless sky. It was easy to smuggle ourselves into the city and move around undetected because nobody cared enough to notice Effigies were among them. A pair of shades obscuring our eyes and the cabbie asked no questions. I watched the road and remembered bodies littering the streets from Saul's attack, the phantom smashing through cars as it tore its way across the Brooklyn Bridge. With the traces of mayhem erased, the city went on.

But I couldn't. My sister was here in the city. I could sense her presence. I didn't know how, but I felt it in my bones. I felt the handle of Cheryl's gun against my back, too, the weapon concealed under my blouse.

The cab dropped us off a block away. Expensive black cars lined Seventh Avenue. As we drew closer to the hall, we noticed a crowd of people swarming Carnegie Hall's entrance, waving signs mostly in support of the man who'd just had his car door opened for him. Blackwell arriving fashionably late to the performance, camera flashes illuminating the ochre Roman-style brick, the American flag hanging over the arched openings. I saw his thick, long curls first, his ebony body-length coat nearly sweeping the asphalt as his penny loafers clicked against the street.

Brendan got out of the car in front of him in a finely cut black suit, a wire hanging down from his ear as he performed his duty as security detail, scanning the streets for any sign of trouble along with two other men. It was almost scary how easily he blended in to the role of Blackwell's toady. Nobody even seemed to question it. But then he'd once stepped on Sibyl's neck for the opportunity to take her position as director of the European Division. At least now he could use his reputation for being a sycophantic opportunist for the greater good.

The three of us turned our heads as Brendan scanned the streets, keeping step with the other pedestrians walking, oblivious, with us. By the time I turned back around, Blackwell, Brendan, and his team of two had already disappeared through the entrance.

No, it was a team of three. There was another, slighter frame in a black suit between Brendan and the two brawny musclemen flanking him. A woman, maybe. Face obscured by sunglasses. But I couldn't see her clearly before she was swallowed up by the doors.

I tapped my earpiece. "Uncle, you almost ready?"

"Just got inside the system's mainframe," he said. "You'll know when it's time to go in."

"Yeah," I said. "The city'll tell me."

We didn't have too long to wait. After three minutes, the war siren began wailing. It was like the city froze. Hurried footsteps halted against sidewalks; cars screeched to a stop. When I saw the panic dashing the faces of the people around me, I instantly regretted the plan. I knew that fear only too well. The fear of impending chaos, of possible death. I'd gotten used to its unique taste, but for the citizens who'd lived through two phantom attacks only a few months ago, the siren's quick pulses were an impossible blow to be dealt. Still, I needed them off the streets. Even if a phantom wasn't attacking, the damage a fake Effigy could do would be just as devastating.

People got out of their cars and began running down into the subway. It was for the best, I kept telling myself, to bite down the guilt as the girls and I pushed through the crowds dispersing outside Carnegie Hall. We sped through the doors and cut through the lobby against the flow of patrons streaming out the door.

"Do you see Blackwell?" I asked the others. It was hard to see anything with these damn shades on, but the last thing we needed was for people's attention to be on anything other than their own survival.

"No. Damn it." Chae Rin grabbed a staff member by the crook of the arm. "Hey," she said. "Is Bart Blackwell still inside the hall?"

"I—I don't know?" the staffer said, both petrified and baffled by this strange girl barking at her. "Last I saw him, we seated him in the third row of the balcony."

"Show us how to get there."

After getting the terrified girl's directions, we made our way down the halls and up the stairs to the balcony. Below, the orchestra musicians were quickly gathering their instruments and making their way offstage under the guidance of security. And yet in the middle of the empty third row, Blackwell remained, calm despite Brendan's prodding that they escape.

On his right ring finger was the ring that held the stone of wishes.

Of the two rings Sibyl had tried to get to safety back when she was still the director of the European Division, only one of them made it to their secret destination. I may have managed to smash the ring Jessie had retrieved for Saul, but there was always one more ring left—and the Sect was compromised. Who knew when Blackwell had managed to secretly scoop it back into his possession? But here it was.

Would he use it?

I didn't know why he'd chosen to stay, and I didn't care. The smug smile on his face infuriated me. In that passing second, I thought of everyone in the city who'd died the last time New York's Needle went off-line. The woman in the elevator I couldn't save. The people screaming as phantoms tore them apart. All the lives lost just chips in his bid for power.

Brendan's team noticed us by the stairs. Lake and Chae Rin quickly jammed Dot's red pen into their necks, giving them the boost that would revive their powers. But I lifted my gun—and pointed it straight at Blackwell's head.

"You're coming with us," I said, a quiet, murderous rage in my voice.

Brendan and his two fellow CSTF agents lifted their guns, though hesitation was barely hidden behind Brendan's eyes. Blackwell, on the other hand, remained calm in his chair, watching the last remnants of the evacuating musicians and patrons below.

"I'd wondered," he said, "why the city would send out a false Category Three signal when I'd already been assured that the defense system was up and operational."

He didn't look at us as he spoke. He sank deeper in his chair, his legs crossed casually as he tapped his knee almost in rhythm with the siren pulses outside.

"It must eat you up that there are people fleeing in terror around you—and you didn't cause it." I held the gun in place. "It wasn't all part of your grand master plan."

"Maia." Shutting his eyes, Blackwell tilted his head to the side. "What exactly do you think this plan is about?"

"Typical dictator shit." I smirked. "As if you're the first insecure man who wanted to manipulate your way into power just to stroke your fragile ego."

Blackwell wasn't angry. Rather, he looked up, shaking his head as if disappointed I hadn't yet figured it out. "This was never about ego, girls."

"Um, you've got three rings on your fingers and a Rolex." Lake shrugged. "Pretty sure it's a little about ego."

He chuckled quietly, the sides of his shut lips quirking upward. "Yes, well. Maybe it is, a little. But you'll see soon enough that it's more than that. Maia, what I want to do—all I've wanted to do—is to know the secrets of the world."

"The secrets of the world," I repeated almost lifelessly as the temple's courtyard flitted back into my memories.

"And to use the secrets of the world"—Blackwell turned, his dark eyes glinting under the hall's bright lights—"to do the impossible."

A cold breeze slipped past my skin, chilling the air. The tip of a blade breathed snowflakes against my neck. I didn't need to turn around. The frigid air, the shock on Chae Rin's and Lake's faces, and my own terror made everything abundantly clear.

"Put your weapon down," Belle said.

Blackwell's laughter echoed in the empty hall. "Now, this is a sight to behold," he said. "The four Effigies reunited at last."

My gun fell to the floor, clattering down the steps. The team was together again.

# 20

"IF YOU DON'T SURRENDER, I'LL KILL HER."

Belle said it as if it were just a fact. The lack of emotion in her voice startled Lake enough that she pressed a hand to her chest, but it didn't surprise me. I'd already witnessed her decaying eyes in the Deoscali Temple.

When Chae Rin made a move toward us, Belle gripped my neck, the steel of her sword shimmering as it hovered dangerously close to my face.

"Do it now." She squeezed the air out of my throat.

While tears began welling up in Lake's eyes, Chae Rin lowered her hands, her acrid disgust palpable under the harsh lights. Brendan nodded to his two agents, who slipped handcuffs out of their pockets and clasped them around the two Effigies. The sight of them in chains relaxed Belle's grip around my windpipe.

"When did you meet up with Blackwell, huh, Belle?" I hissed, but then I suddenly remembered Saul's command at the temple. *You know where you need to go next.* Ah, yes, to Master Blackwell, the one to deliver the Sect's head on a platter.

"Didn't you hear the news?" Blackwell answered for her. "She's been *flipped.* I had her released into my custody. She's promised to lend us her skills for the time being in exchange for a lighter sentence. I intend to make use of them."

Belle didn't flip for a "lighter sentence." I doubted she'd even flinch at the death penalty.

"You look distraught, girls." Blackwell reveled in stating the obvious. "You need to understand things from my perspective. You see, we're all just struggling to deal with the hand dealt to us by fate. For all my family's wealth and power, within the walls of the Sect we were never respected. What did your father call us once?"

Brendan bristled at the mention of his father, his hands trembling slightly as he placed his gun back into its holster.

Blackwell thought. "Ah, yes. The 'ceremonial crust on the Sect's toe.' It's true that the first Blackwell may have used underhanded means to become part of the organization—to gain a prominent position on the world's stage. Unlike the others, he built his empire from nothing with his own hands. All he wanted was respect among his peers. A seat at the table created by elites to raise themselves above the rest of the powerful. You could say I inherited his entrepreneurial spirit."

"What's that?" One of Blackwell's agents tapped his ear, the coiling wire draping behind it shaking a little at his touch. "Sir," he told Blackwell, "reports are coming in of an attack on Coney Island while tourists are still evacuating."

"Ah." Blackwell looked my way. "That would be the other Miss Finley."

I breathed in too sharply. Belle must have thought I was making a move to escape, because she gripped my throat harder. I swallowed against her hand, wincing from the pain.

"What do you need us to do?" Brendan asked, but Blackwell didn't answer right away. The two men locked eyes, the younger stewing under the taunting grin of the older. Brendan must have known how much Blackwell enjoyed seeing Arthur Prince's son under his thumb. It was a truth written on both of their faces.

"What I need you to do, Brendan," he said, relishing every word, "is to arrest the *Terrae Ensis* and the *Ignis Ensis*. With the war siren blaring, I doubt the press would make their way over here if I call them, right?" He twisted the ring around his finger once, then twice. "Nevertheless, I'll make sure it becomes a headline by the end of the day. Miss Rousseau will bring Maia. We still need her, but she can't be seen. After all, she's in Coney Island right now."

"How could you use my sister?" The words burst out of my mouth, strained but powerful. I didn't care that Belle still had me in her vise grip. "Why can't you leave us alone?"

Blackwell stood. "I wasn't the one who chose you, Maia. It was fate—fate that took your sister, fate that turned you all into warriors. When my ancestor turned himself into an integral member of the British Crown's Imperial Sect, he was fighting against fate. It's fate that drives all of us. But what if we can be free of it? What if you could conquer it?" He leaned forward, and whatever levity had drawn his features seconds before was replaced, in that moment, by an unmistakable intensity. He looked almost bitter when he mentioned the word "fate." Defiant. "What if you could lift yourself above those who control it?"

*Who controls fate?* June's desperate cries echoed in my mind.

"Is this your big villain speech?" Chae Rin raised an eyebrow. "God, spare us. You may think you have this grand, existential reason for causing this mess, but there's nothing interesting or unique about you. Nothing." She gritted her teeth. I could tell she was just itching to break free, and if it weren't for the sword to my throat, she would have. "You're not some visionary. You're a shitty person doing something shitty because you can. Period."

Blackwell tipped his head like he knew he couldn't deny it. "You should listen to your elders when they speak, Miss Kim," he said. "Especially when they speak of the secrets of the world. This game is one where knowledge will control all our fates."

With a jerk of his head, he signaled one of his bodyguards to follow him up the stairs past Belle and me and out the balcony area. Brendan and the other guard reached into their other holsters and brought out smaller, sleek guns—inoculation guns, just like the one Vasily fired at us in Prague. The last time we were hit with one of those, it was like getting dosed with a horse tranquilizer. The two dart guns were trained on Chae Rin and Lake while Belle continued to keep her sword pressed to my neck.

Chae Rin narrowed her eyes at Belle. "You really have sunken so low." She shook her head, not in disbelief but in pure revulsion. "So what, your mommy-slash-bestie-slash-mentor-slash-crush-slash-*whatever* died, and so now nothing matters anymore?"

"Belle, why are you doing this?" Lake said, nervously watching Brendan and the guard. "Natalya being assassinated was a tragedy—"

"Maia knew." It was obvious Belle was trying to keep calm even though her voice wavered. "She knew Natalya was murdered by his brother."

Brendan lowered his dart gun. I shut my eyes, and even still I could feel everyone's shock and judgment crawling up my skin.

"You stabbed me in the chest and watched me fall off a cliff," I replied calmly. "So I think we're more than even. And you realize it was the Sect—no, it was *Blackwell* who murdered Natalya. Aidan was just a pawn. He was wrong, but he was a pawn. The man you're working for and the people on the Council supporting him. *They* ordered her death because she was getting too close to the truth. The Sect—"

"The Sect will disappear!" Belle's shout reverberated through the hall. "It will *disappear*. Blackwell said it himself. Those who control the fate of others—*they* are the ones who are evil. Those with power curse and manipulate the people under them."

I'd felt it too intimately in Ely Cathedral, kneeling before Blackwell and the Sect's codex under the weighty gaze of the Council, helpless despite my power, insignificant despite a legacy of warriors that had come before me.

"Like flies to wanton boys, so are we to the gods." Belle's hand on my throat began to tremble. "They kill us for sport. Not anymore. The Sect will be obsolete. I will support Blackwell until he makes that happen, by whatever means necessary."

"Enough talking," said the guard. "Blackwell's waiting for us outside. Prince, let's finish this."

Brendan raised his dart gun at Lake but didn't fire. In silence, he stared at the smooth barrel. "Natalya. My brother. In the end, I guess fate just wasn't on their side." He shut his eyes. "Let's hope it's on mine."

Switching his aim, he shot the guard.

"Wha—" Belle began, but Chae Rin had broken out of her handcuffs before the guard could even hit the ground. If the dart was powerful enough to daze an Effigy, he wouldn't be up for a while. Lake broke free of her chains, and though Belle threatened me again with the sword, she must have known they weren't going to let her treachery slide. The two girls lifted their hands, ready, but Belle was too fast. She pushed me at the girls to distract them. Then, two swift kicks so vicious and quick I didn't see the impact, but I heard Lake and Chae Rin grunt as they hit the balcony. I gripped the banister, but I'd only just begun pulling myself up when Belle grabbed me by my collar and jumped off the balcony with me, both of us crashing onto the hall's red velvet seats.

She was aiming to escape, to bring me to Blackwell even if she didn't quite know why. She was willing to sacrifice me if it meant her own absolution, but Lake and Chae Rin followed nonetheless. A powerful gust of wind blew Belle clear over several rows, throwing her against the edge of the stage. The ground opened up, splitting through the floor and encasing her in a shell of earth before she could properly land. I pulled out the red metallic pen and jammed it into my neck and within seconds felt my power coursing again within my body.

"Maia, you need to stop your sister," Brendan said from the balcony. "I'll take you there." He disappeared up the stairs and out of the hall.

Landing in the aisle next to me, Lake tugged my sleeve. "Come on," she said. "We can use this chance to grab your sister and keep her locked up until we stop Blackwell, then maybe get her into therapy or something."

"Right." I looked back at the sphere of rock sitting on the damaged floor, caging Belle. "Let's go."

We were halfway to the door when the entire hall began quaking. A torrent of icicles smashed through the stone and sliced through the air. We jumped behind seats to avoid their deadly tips, though one stabbed the seat behind me, narrowly missing my head. Belle was free, her sword newly manifested in her hands.

"Okay, this ends now." Chae Rin jumped out from her seat and into the aisle, facing Belle, who was slowly making her way up the red carpet. "Lake, Maia—you guys go find June."

"You're *mad*." Lake backed away, her fearful eyes on Belle. "You can't take her alone."

"Maybe, maybe not." When Chae Rin turned her head, I could see a smile playing on her lips. "Either way, I've been dying to find out."

The floor was shaking again. Chae Rin steadied herself. "Go!"

We didn't need telling twice. Lake and I made for the door while a flurry of ice covered the walls, the ground, the ceiling. I skidded on a cold patch, but we found the exit and made it to the lobby, where Brendan was waiting, just as another deep rumbling shook the entire structure.

Lake stopped, shielding her head from the dust falling down from the ceiling. "They're going to tear the entire place down!"

Brendan put his hand across her shoulders and gently pushed her forward. "Let's not stick around to watch them do it."

"Blackwell's limo!" I pointed out the door. He'd waited long enough. It was obvious something had gone wrong. It was taking off.

I charged through the doors, fire swirling around my hands as the limo steered off the curb. The pole of my scythe formed in my hand as my feet trampled the empty street to catch up as the limo began to move. In a few seconds, it'd be out of my reach. With the war siren still blaring overhead, I lunged forward, my scythe crashing into the window, the blade hooking into the back of the leather seat. I held on for dear life as the limo swerved and accelerated. Blackwell sat on the left side of the limo, his arms and legs crossed, his head tilted as he gave me an impressed, sidelong look. It was the image of my face on the television screen on the far right that made me lose my grip. My face, and a sea of flames behind me.

No, not my face. *June's* face.

I struggled to keep hold of the scythe, but it slipped from my grasp, and as my concentration shattered to pieces, so did the weapon. I tumbled onto the street while the limo drove off, leaving me behind.

"Maia!"

Lake. She and Brendan ran up to me and lifted me to my feet.

"The police and a local CSTF team are on their way," he said. "They know there are Effigies inside. They can track you—hell, they can hear you."

Carnegie Hall rumbled again from the foundations.

"We need to get to Coney Island," I said, panting.

"I can take you there." He looked at his car. "But traffic is stalled along FDR Drive. Plus, with police on their way, I have to do what I can to keep them off you."

"Don't worry," Lake said. "I'll handle it—or better yet!" Down the street, past Brendan's car, a motorcycle was abandoned in the chaos. Lake nudged me, pointing in its direction. "I'll handle *that*. Hey, if we're gonna go, why not go in style?"

I grinned immediately. "Let's do it."

"Wait!" Brendan grabbed Lake by the crook of her arm. "There's something I need to tell you."

Lake gave him an awkward, apologetic grin. "I'm sorry, I'm seeing someone."

A flush scorched Brendan's forehead in that way I remembered. Ah, simpler times. "That's not—" It was clear he'd only grabbed Lake because she was closer, but he was speaking to both of us. "That isn't what I—wait . . . really?"

Lake's shrug seemed to bother him, but he shook himself back to the task at hand. "There's something I need to tell you both," he said. "You two need to make sure my mother knows that what my brother did wasn't her fault. That his death wasn't her—"

"He's alive," I blurted out.

He really must not have seen him in Argentina. Brendan's next words froze on his tongue, his mouth parted in a silent gasp—or scream. "You . . ." His bottom lip bobbed up and down. "You can't mean . . ."

Under the pulses of the war siren, different sirens called into the night. The police were coming.

"Sorry. This'll have to wait," I said as Lake pulled her arm out of his grasp. "I promise we'll tell you everything."

"By the way, I do find you really handsome, however!" Lake called back as I pulled her across the street to the motorcycle. There was no key in the ignition, but we both knew we wouldn't need one. Lake jumped on first, and I followed. A swell of wind crushed into us from behind, and with a battle cry, Lake took us into the air. We soared above the buildings just as a massive pillar of ice burst out from the ochre brick walls of Carnegie Hall. But although Lake's breath caught in fear for Chae Rin, the wind kept carrying us away. My sense of direction had been battered by the adrenaline. Even though I'd been to Coney Island so many times with my family, I couldn't figure out where to go. I contacted Uncle Nathan through my earpiece. He had his hands full evading the detection of the MDCC but acted as our GPS nonetheless. We headed south, over the Brooklyn Bridge jammed with traffic, and the East River. We kept going until we could see the flames, the smoke rising into the sky from the amusement park.

June was riding the carousel. She sat on a painted horse frozen in a jump, one hand gripping its imperial golden mane, childlike music churning out the melody of a proud march under the war siren's pulses. There were no patrons left; they'd all fled the flames, leaving behind their trash, wallets, game prizes, and junk food. Only the two remained: June riding her royal steed and Vasily, who spun into my view on a chariot, his dart gun pointed up at us.

With one eye closed, he aimed and fired. Lake dodged the first two rounds, but the third scraped one of her hands wrapped around the handle, spooking her enough to lose control of the wind. We plummeted, crashing on the other side of the carousel, my body rolling as if it were nothing more than a fleshy sack with a collection of scattered bones inside.

"Damn it." Lake rubbed her head, her black bob slightly askew.

"Are you okay?" She knelt next to me, immediately turning when we heard a pair of feet clop against the ground.

June. I sat up. She was concerned, staring at my bruised and battered frame, but she didn't step toward me. The carousel sang and rotated behind her as she wrung her hands.

"My god," Lake whispered, staring between the two of us. "You really do look the same. . . ."

"You shouldn't have come here, Lil Sis," June said. I remembered her the last time we saw each other. There was no telling how quickly that would give way to viciousness. "But it's okay. Now that you're here, it'd be easier if we leave together." She stretched out her arm, extending the kind of earnest hand meant to save a drowning man. "Come with me and Vasily."

Smoke billowed from the flaming booths, and inside one I could see a woman's burning body behind a counter. One of those who couldn't escape. I swallowed back the rising avalanche of horror threatening to overtake me. I kept myself calm, even as Vasily began to swing back into view.

"Yes, Maia!" He jumped off the chariot, his short blond ponytail swinging behind him as he sat on the silver platform next to June. "Come with us. It'll be the reunion of the century. And not just with your sister. I'm sure you miss Aidan, too."

My hands twitched at the sound of his name. "Rhys . . ."

The war siren finally stopped. It was only a matter of time before the MDCC got back control over their system. I was now left in the silence of fire crackling into the sky.

"Aidan didn't die in Oslo, Maia," Vasily said. "He survived. Saul saved him."

But I didn't know what to make of his expression. His last words tangled in his mouth and came out with a hint of bitterness that was unmistakable.

"Doesn't seem like you're too happy about that," I said. "I thought you'd love the chance to torture him some more. Last I remember, you seemed to enjoy doing it."

And each time, he would do it with a smile. No matter how many lives he took, how many fingers he cut off, it was Rhys's anger, his torment that seemed to make Vasily the happiest. Each and every time. The boy whose orders had taken him into the depths of hell. But the Vasily who stood before me wasn't the boy who cherished the sight of anguish. He'd turned to stone at the mention of Rhys, his gaze distant.

"Well, he's not really the same Aidan anymore," Vasily told me. "So seeing him in pain doesn't quite have the same thrill it used to, you know?"

The twinkle in his blue eyes was back. "Do you know why Saul saved us, Maia?" He leaned over, his arms balanced on his knees. "It's because our work isn't finished yet. So many lives ruined by the Sect. If we tear the Sect down, think how many lives can be saved in the future."

"You want to save lives?" Lake scrunched her face in disbelief. "You've got to be kidding me."

"Of course I do, contrary to what you might think. I'm not a monster—" He paused. "Okay, I'm a little bit of a monster." His thin lips slid into his catlike grin. "But all I've ever done was for the greater good."

"I seriously doubt that," I said, remembering the ecstasy on his face as he cut off a man's finger to take the ring of wishes.

"We're not doing anything wrong," he insisted as I spotted another body in the tent.

"Um, you're *killing* people." Lake squeezed her hands into fists. "You *just* killed people."

June turned toward the fires she'd made, staring for a moment at the burning corpse of a teddy bear near a food stand before lowering her head, shuffling uncomfortably on her feet. But Vasily wouldn't be deterred.

"We're revolutionizing the world." He stood, brushing a few strands of blond hair from his sweaty forehead with fingers stained with blood. "Bodies are expected."

Vasily had said it as if it were the simplest truth in the world. As if his only truth were the inevitability of death.

I studied his face, the leftover scars from his torture at the hands of the Surgeon still evident on his skin, overlaid atop the older ones he'd born in his youth. But the scars I couldn't see—years of torturous training and abuse, a mother dead by her own hands—they were the ones that had torn apart something deeper than the flesh.

"Trust is glass," I whispered, remembering Dawson's words.

June narrowed her eyes. "What?"

The Sect as an organization wasn't evil in and of itself. The aim of protecting humanity wasn't wrong. But the people at the top, the ones with the power to affect lives—Blackwell, Abrams, and others on the Council, Fisk-Hoffman and his son, so many adults with power and means—had used it to manipulate and destroy those beneath them for their own gain. These fires burning through the amusement park were a hell of their creation. And it was a hell that had long been Vasily's reality.

"I'm sorry, Vasily." I never thought I'd hear the words spring from my lips, but there they were nonetheless, a bridge between us. "I'm sorry for what happened to you in the Devil's Hole. I'm sorry for what happened to Aidan, to Jessie. To all of you."

Vasily's jaw clamped down hard, his body rigid. He watched me coolly through slit eyes, but the slight quiver of his head told a different story. "Funny, I didn't ask for an apology," he said, so quietly I almost couldn't hear his voice beyond the sound of crackling flames. "Or pity."

"But I do pity you," I said, and it was true. "You, Aidan, and the rest. None of you should have had to go through what you did. You were *children*. So I'm sorry. I am truly sorry."

Vasily went deathly still, his eyes darting to the ground, the pupils unfocused and faded as he searched for the meaning of my words.

"But I'm taking my sister back."

I charged at him, our bodies crashing onto the moving carousel and crumpling together inside one of the chariots. Before he could figure out what was happening, I punched his face, blood splattering from his mouth.

I could hear the snap of June's fingers, then a gust of wind followed by her scream. I looked back to see June's body flying sideways, but I shouldn't have. Vasily's head-butt almost split my forehead in two. He grabbed me and threw me against a camel, my back cracking against its hard wooden hide. For half a second I thought of bringing out my scythe, but this wasn't Saul. This was the remnants of an abused child, not some supernatural foe. He deserved a trial, not an execution.

But that was easier said than done. Vasily slipped a knife out of his back pocket and narrowly missed jamming it into my waist. Thankfully, I evaded the blow, jumping onto the camel's back, holding on to the pole to keep myself steady. He made to grab my leg, dodging my kick by leaping onto the head of a roaring lion.

We stared each other down, our animals bobbing up and down as the carousel turned and turned. An explosion by the roller coaster split the air, followed by another gust of wind and more screams. Lake and June were still fighting. This time I kept my eyes on Vasily.

When he reached behind his back, I thought I'd be dodging another dart, but it was a real gun he pulled out and a real bullet he shot into my arm. Screaming, I collapsed against the center pole.

"I will take you back to Blackwell." He jumped off the lion. "Even if

I have to take you piece by piece." Leaning over, he grabbed me by my shirt collar, drawing his face so close to mine his nose slid up the sweat on my cheek. "You're sorry, are you?" I felt his breath on my ear and the barrel of his gun on my left temple. "You're sorry I watched my mother dive headlong out of our high-rise apartment? Tell me, do you think that's more or less painful than lowering the burned corpses of your family into the ground?"

I let out a gasp that was more like a cry, terrible memories flooding back into me. Vasily pressed his gun against the side of my head and cocked it. "*Never* feel sorry for me."

"Vasily! *Stop doing that to my sister.*"

June. She leapt onto the carousel and, with an enraged cry, pulled him off me. While he was still in the air, she snapped her fingers. The fire exploded in his face. He landed near the motorcycle, thrashing and rolling. While he screamed, June grabbed my hand and we ran.

"We have to go," she said, panting. "Now."

I was barely keeping up. "Wait!"

"Come on!"

I stopped, pulling myself out of her grip when I saw Lake by the death-drop ride, struggling to crawl away from a patch of flames. I didn't even hesitate. After putting out the flames, I ran to her, helping her up.

"Maia?" June called. "Maia, come with *me!*"

My good arm around Lake's waist for support, I looked up, my breaths short and harsh, sweat dripping down my forehead. June stared at us as we crouched by one of the many fires she'd made.

"Come with me," June said again, confused as she stared at the two of us. "*Me*, Maia. I'm your sister, not *her.*"

I heard the wings of a chopper overhead. I thought it was Blackwell's reinforcements until I saw the local news logo splashed on the side. Reporters. I could see their cameras, the man speaking frantically into his microphone as he peered at the mess below from the safety of his news helicopter. The two Effigies, a burning man, and a doppelgänger—all packaged in minute-to-minute updates for viewers at home.

June clenched her teeth as she looked up at the helicopter. Two Finleys. The jig was up. Hurriedly, she extended her hand to me once more. "Come with me, Lil Sis." I could tell she was straining to keep herself calm. "What's wrong with you? What's *wrong* with you?" Her elbows rose in frustration, but she let out the tension with a sigh, her lips trembling. "Please, Maia," she said. "We can save our family. Next time we come here, it'll be with Mom and Dad again. Like it was before."

It was all that I wanted. Everyone together again.

Truthfully, there were moments in the dead of night when I would lie awake and wonder if my best years were behind me. If things would never be as good as they were when I was a child cocooned within my family. I'd felt like this even before my family died. It was like every year I got older, the more sullen I became, until somehow I found myself on a school bus ignoring a child being bullied even as he sat right next to me. I couldn't face the world. I hated living in my skin. I wanted our days back. Our trips to Coney Island. I wanted to turn back time so badly, my body shuddered and burned from my own desperation.

But this . . . this burning wasteland. This was wrong. I had to be strong enough to face it. To face June. Things couldn't be what they were. They would never be again.

"No, June." Hot tears slid down my cheeks, passing like time into oblivion. "No."

June let out a shuddering gasp, her chest shaking as she stared at me. The sound of the chopper's wings drew nearer. The news helicopter had gotten too close. June's head snapped up, her tearful eyes suddenly narrowed to slits. I knew what she was going to do. I got up just as she raised her hand and tackled her to the ground, my hands wrapped around her throat before I even realized I was kneeling over her. Taking in a sharp breath, I released my hands. Neither of us moved. Our brown eyes locked us in place. It was like looking into a filthy mirror. I couldn't tell what it was that had dirtied either of us.

Vasily's kick to the head sent me tumbling to the ground. His face—half his face was burned flesh. He was too weak to try me again, but my sister was another story. He still had his eyes to see, to glare at my sister as he yanked her to her feet, and when she looked as if she was about to fight back, he silenced her quickly. "Don't even try it. Looks like you forgot about that kill chip in your head, huh?"

She seized up, paralyzed.

"You little witch." Grabbing her collar, he glared at her menacingly despite the pain, his hand raised as if he wanted to slap her. "I need treatment. I'm taking you back with me to Grunewald before you can do any more damage on your own. And you better not try anything on the way there. Remember, one word from him, and you can be killed anywhere in the world."

She was boiling, but she said nothing. She'd already died once. She didn't seem too eager to die again. He pulled her toward the motorcycle we'd crashed near the carousel. It was upright, its motor rumbling. While we were talking, he must have gotten it running. He jumped on, pulling her in front of him.

"Wait!" My head was still spinning. I tried to reach for June, but she was already riding away. "Stop!"

Then they were gone.

"Maia, the fire," Lake said. "The park . . ."

Just like in the French police station, June could start fires, but she couldn't stop them. I could.

Blood dripped from my bullet wound, which I knew wouldn't heal until I could pull it out. I couldn't see the damage from here. I needed a higher vantage point. I peered around the burning amusement park, stopping when I saw the Ferris wheel.

"Lake," I said. "Can you get me up there?"

She nodded. She didn't bother getting up from the ground. Instead, she sat, crossing her legs, shutting her eyes, stretching out her arms in a meditative pose at her sides. The wind began gathering at my feet, gusts flapping the flags perched on long, solid poles. A boost of wind and I began flying, up into the sky. The helicopter backed off to keep from being swept up, but it caught everything. I was sure, in that moment, that I was on every television news station in the world. That millions of eyes were watching as my feet touched the top of the still Ferris wheel. I blocked them out. I blocked everything out but the air seeping in and out of my lungs.

The flames were truly spread out all over the park. As I surveyed the damage, the memory of the elevator woman, the one I couldn't save, mocked me. Her screams echoed in my mind just as they'd echoed down the shoot that swallowed her. The bodies left behind in that hotel. The flames I couldn't banish.

I lifted my arms. As I breathed, the fire breathed. As I exhaled, the fire flickered back, pushed by an invisible force. Trap, release. Inhale, exhale. My teeth locked, a single dribble of blood spilling from my eye as the power extended out of me like vines sprouting over the earth. One last exhale and the fires blew out, the smoke streaming into the sky. The flames were gone.

I stared up at the moon, my small grin trembling. Then everything went dark, my foot slipping off the Ferris wheel just as I lost consciousness.

# 21

WHEN I WOKE UP AGAIN, IT WAS STILL DARK, and I was crumpled up in the backseat of a car—new, by the fresh smell of it. Lake was in the backseat with me. I couldn't see who was driving, not until my vision cleared. Brendan. Maybe he was the one who'd taken care of my newly bandaged wound. The red and blue lights from outside blanketed his sharp features, from his pointed nose to the sharp cut of his jaw.

"She's up," Lake told him before nudging my feet with her hip. "Hey, how're you feeling?"

"Like I got hit by a truck." I groaned as I pulled myself into a sitting position. "And then it backed up and hit me again."

"Sorry. That's the inoculation dart," said Brendan, and he patted his leg where his jacket covered his holsters. "It's just procedure."

The plan was to scratch my head with a clammy hand now that I could feel it. But moving my hands only jerked my wrists against the metal cuffs biting into them. "What the hell is this?" I lifted my wrists so Brendan could see the mistake someone had clearly made. Except Lake was bound too. The cuffs jingled as she shook her arms to show me. "What's going on?"

"We've been arrested!" Lake said cheerfully.

"What?" The red and blue lights. We were in a black van, the same kind as the one that'd transported me from the police station in Buenos Aires. "You've got to be kidding me."

Brendan apologized as I slumped against the seat. "With the massive police force that descended on you at the amusement park, it was the only way I could get you out of the city in one piece. I had to really play some mind tricks to get them to let me transport you myself."

"Transport us where?" I looked at Lake. There was no trace of her earlier grin anywhere on her face.

"Upstate," Brendan answered. "To the Counter-Sect Task Force headquarters. Chae Rin's already been captured."

The fight at Carnegie Hall. Belle must have gotten the best of her.

"Where is Belle?" I asked quickly. "And that guy—they both saw you help us."

"Rufus . . ." Brendan shook his head. "I got called in to regroup with the rest of my unit at the police station for a joint operation to stop the 'Maia' in Coney Island. Carnegie Hall's outside structure was mostly intact, but the inside hall was almost rubble by the time I got back there. I couldn't find him."

"Oh." Lake lowered her eyes.

"Well, granted," Brendan continued after thinking about it, "he was one of the guys who ambushed you in the tunnels outside London. Probably killed off some other agents."

"*Oh,*" Lake said, perking up immediately. "Then screw him."

Well, that was one way of putting it. A terrible beat pounded inside my skull. Guess I was still in recovery mode. "What about Belle?"

"Belle was already gone by the time I got there. So far she hasn't told anyone. Otherwise I'd be the one in cuffs."

Maybe the part of her that was good was still in there somewhere.

Or maybe Brendan simply wasn't relevant to her endgame. I'd won-dered if Belle cared about anything anymore except seeing the Sect fall. "She'll stay by Blackwell's side," I said. "She'll see him through the Assembly meeting, right up until that document gets signed. Sibyl wanted us to stall Blackwell until then."

"I don't know if that's possible anymore," Brendan said. "Look behind us."

I twisted my back and peered out the window. An entire fleet of vans followed behind us on the highway, their own lights flashing.

"We may not be able to get to Blackwell, but we *can* get to Chae Rin," Lake said.

"That's the plan." Brendan slowed as we approached a toll, but I could see his eyes peeking at us through the rearview mirror. "You three need to escape. If Belle really is with Blackwell, then I imagine only the three of you working together can stop her."

"Stop her." Lake's nervous chuckles petered out into silence. "Sounds simple."

"One problem at a time," I said, before shutting up and putting on my disgruntled prisoner face for the tollbooth officer.

Brendan drove all the way up to a building in the middle of a field, a converted, flat-roofed manufacturing plant. Two rows of windows stretched along the white plaster, cars parked at the back. There were already news reporters waiting for us, crowding the area with Effigy-haters and fans with their usual signs and slogans.

"Maia," Brendan said as he drove up the long driveway. "I seem to recall you telling me that my brother is alive."

My back stiffened, but I nodded. "Yeah," I confessed, and my heart gave a painful jolt as I remembered the shadows under his eyes haunting his features, dark as the ghosts made by his hands. "I saw him down in Argentina. He must have visited that new Greenland facility, because whatever they put in Jessie, my sister, and the rest, they put in him, too."

Brendan gripped the steering wheel tighter, his shoulders rising as he struggled to keep himself calm. "Where is he?"

"I don't know."

"I'll find him," he whispered, more as a promise to himself than to me.

The reporters rushed at us the second Brendan and another agent from a different car pulled us out of the van and marched us through the front doors.

"Who is the other Maia Finley we saw on the news—"

"Isn't it true you have a sister?"

"Maia, who was the other girl you were battling on Coney Island—"

"Yes, that was my sister," I said, and though Brendan tried to signal me to hush up, I couldn't. It was time to *say* something. "I've been trying to stop her. But it's *not her fault*," I added fast. "She was brainwashed under Blackwell's orders."

The reporters' furor only seemed to intensify.

"What do you mean?"

"Prince, can you corroborate—"

"Shut up," Brendan hissed in my ear as he pushed me through the doors.

"It's true. They need to know—"

"There's nothing to back up what you're saying except for a bunch of confusing news footage," he whispered low enough so only I could hear. "All of this can easily be manipulated into a narrative that works *against* you."

He was right. There were too many ways to interpret what they'd picked up with their microphones and cameras. The truth wouldn't get out that easily.

We walked in silence through the metal detector and down the twisting metal halls. Then, for the second time since I'd met him, Brendan threw me into a cold cell.

"Here we are again," he said as I found my spot against the back of the cold wall. "Hey, gently with that one," he added to the agent handling Lake. I guess despite being rejected, he still had a soft spot for her.

I gazed up at him. "You seemed a lot meaner when you locked me up in one of these last time."

"I don't need to be rough with you now that I know what side you're on," he answered, coded words I understood immediately.

"Blackwell's personally sent over reinforcements," said one of the agents. "Just in case. They're on their way."

Personal reinforcements? Maybe Belle had come after all. I suppressed a shudder.

"Make sure they know Kim is on the third floor," Brendan said. "Also, I heard there was an issue with our security system."

The agent seemed confused. "I haven't—"

"After I finish my paperwork, I'll be paying a visit to the security office to make sure everything's running smoothly."

He was talking to us.

The agent shrugged. "Whatever you want."

Once Brendan stepped out of my cell, a buzzer sounded, and the automatic door slid shut, locking with a loud series of clicks. *Just wait*, his eyes seemed to tell me. I did. The walls were soundproof, and my earpieces were gone; maybe they'd been confiscated when I was captured, or maybe they'd fallen out during my battle with Vasily. Either way, I couldn't talk to anyone. So I retreated into my own mind. I listened to my breathing. I felt the rise and fall of my chest. I meditated.

I scried.

I didn't know when next I'd be able to. I had to take my shot, at least for a few quick minutes. I knew Lake would come get me when it was time to break out. But I would have to be careful. Very careful.

I knew who awaited me.

Perfect calm, Belle had told me once before. It was the difference between waltzing through an open door and being dragged in through a tiny window. Repressing my fears, I lifted myself out of the cell and into the white stream deep within my subconscious.

"I've been meaning to ask you, Maia, since your last trip to this realm."

Natalya stood in front of her red door, curious, but perhaps no less murderous. My legs quivered. Here she was again: my potential executioner. I sucked in a breath, trying to bring down my spiking fear.

"You saw it at the moment of your death, didn't you? Because I see through your eyes, I saw it too."

The water rested still against my ankles. "Saw what?"

"The truth of all things."

The light. The light that had taken my spirit out of my body. The streams of life and death twisting across the universe, giving spirits unto new life, making matter from death.

"Yeah," I whispered. "Everything is connected."

Natalya looked up at the golden ridge of the door shut against her memories. "Like links in a chain."

"Like the law of thermodynamics. Everything has to come from something—or someone."

"Even wishes." Natalya placed a hand against the red surface. "Even fate."

"Fate?" I repeated, staring at my reflection in the crystal waters.

"What's a wish except the desire to twist fate?" Natalya's fingernails scratched down her door.

It could only be fate that changed life into death and back again. Fate that brought one Effigy's mind and power to the next—the next link in a chain. If fate really was a palpable force in the world . . . if it had a spiritual presence that could be harnessed like capturing souls in a bottle . . . in a stone . . .

"Let me see Marian," I said. "I need to know—no, I *want* to know what she does."

"She is the first of us," Natalya answered. "The first Effigy of Fire. You'll have to walk in all of our shoes before you get to her. I told you once before. You'll have to see all our most difficult memories."

"I don't have *time* for that." The water splashed as I stomped my feet. "If you really see through my eyes, then you know what Blackwell's up to. He has the thirteenth Castor volume. He has Belle—she's already scried Emilia Farlow's memories. How long do you think it'll be before she finds out how to read that code? Hell, they may have cracked it already without her."

"It does you no good to worry about Belle after what she's become," said Natalya. "She's weak. A disappointment."

Natalya's curt words wrung out of me a feeling of indignation I didn't know I still could have on Belle's behalf. "You're her mentor," I reminded her in disbelief. "She's broken because of you."

"None of that is on my shoulders."

"Isn't it?" My voice rose higher, grew louder—and as I thought of Belle's sword through my chest, so did my anger. "How can you say it's *not*? She worshipped you. She *loved* you. After finding out what the Sect did to you, she just completely lost her reason for living."

Natalya whipped around. "And like I said." For a moment, I thought her face had turned as unyielding as her unsympathetic words, but as she shook her head, I caught the glimmer of humanity, back for just a moment behind those brown eyes. "Why is that on my shoulders? I didn't ask for any of that. I didn't tell her I was perfect or worthy of such emotions. I didn't ask her to live or to die for me. You tell me, Maia. Isn't it unfair to expect me to bear such things?"

There was a hint of accusation in her voice that forced me back a step. Mentor. Idol. Hero. It was all well and good when you were the fan, but it was only when you looked from the other side of the glass that you could feel just how heavy those words were. A weight Natalya had been forced to bear since childhood.

I couldn't respond.

"Belle was already sick when I found her and took her to the Sect," Natalya said. "Abused and unloved as a child. Traumatized by her early days as an Effigy. Because she followed and looked up to me, she was never able to find her own self, never able to discover her own worth apart from the value she thought I had given her." She looked up to the sky. "There was a moment I wondered if meeting all of you would change that. But in the end, none of us could fix what was already deeply broken inside her."

"But you still tried," I said. "You must have seen some worth in that. Otherwise, why help Belle at all? Why train her? Why guide her?"

Natalya lowered her head and thought, her downcast eyes shaded by a veil of dark lashes. For a moment she seemed almost like the Natalya that could still empathize. "Being broken is different from being empty," she whispered. "I wondered to myself, all those years ago: by filling someone else with meaning, could I also . . . ?"

As Natalya's words dissipated, I broke the silence. "Emptiness. You mean yours?"

But Natalya would not answer.

All Belle wanted back then as a young Effigy was for someone to help her find her own strength. Isn't that what we all needed now and again?

But Natalya . . . what is it that she wanted to find through mentoring Belle? Or did she simply want to *feel* in the first place?

How easy it was to become lost.

"God help me, but I choose to believe that Belle still has a chance," I said, gripping the edge of my shirt. "I have to."

"Belle . . ." Natalya tilted her head, eyelashes fluttering shut. "A chance . . . perhaps . . ."

"But regardless," I continued. "If Blackwell or even Saul gets his hands on that stone they're looking for—a stone that can twist fate . . ." I shook my head. "It's an atomic bomb in either of their hands. I have to get to it before they do. Forget about Belle for now. You've got to help me with this."

Natalya thought for too long. Then slowly, slyly, she opened her eyes once more. "Okay, Maia. You'll see Marian through me. The memory of her I saw that night." Her door creaked open without the aid of her touch. "Come inside, Maia. . . ."

Come inside, said the spider to the fly. Despite our little heart-to-heart, Natalya was nevertheless an enemy. She could still strike if I let my guard down. I kept my wits about me and my eyes watchful as I passed by her through the entrance.

The air was sticky sweet and far too hot, even with the sun sinking behind the clouds. The windows were open in the living room, but there was no breeze for relief. If not for the green-and-red-speckled geckos climbing up the rose-colored wallpaper, it would have looked like any Victorian home. A grand piano by the window next to a bookshelf lined with musty first editions. A fireplace crackled beneath a brass mantel with urns, candelabras, and a glass decanter spread out across the surface. The wide-framed, yellow-stained portrait above the fireplace was of a family. A husband and wife with two young boys, both dark haired and pleasant to the eyes in their frock coats and pants. They were seated on one side of their mother, her thin, bright hair rolled up and pinned behind her neck. Their father was standing on the other side, his mustache drooping past his chin like the leaves of a weeping willow.

In front of the fireplace was a woman in a simple beige dress that looked homespun. She was nervous. Her dark hands played with the edges of her long sleeves, dirtied and worn. Her black hair was tied up in a bun above her head, her face oily from the heat but beautiful nonetheless, her full, dark lips moving as if whispering a mantra I couldn't hear. Balanced on her lap was a cigar box—*the* cigar box. Alice's cigar box.

She was watching the door with a pair of chestnut-brown eyes sharp like daggers. It was only when the door behind me clicked that she stopped mumbling.

"Master Louis?" But when the door creaked open, she set the cigar box on the couch and stood up. She was speechless at first. But then her eyes welled up with tears. "Master Nicholas. You're alive."

I turned. It was Saul. Saul in his former life of Nick Hudson. Tall and sweepingly handsome, his hair carefully cut in its original brown. Perhaps it'd only gone silver with age. But he looked just the same. The same beautiful man no matter the era. They hesitated as they saw each other, neither of them daring to speak, daring to move. Until . . .

"Marian," Nick whispered.

And then suddenly they were across the room in each other's arms, weeping.

"Oh, Nick," she said, lifting her face out of his neck. "I came here, to your family's home in Argentina, to see if your brother knew where you were. Where have you been? You disappeared after the tragedy in York. After the phantom beasts came. But that was five years ago."

Nick didn't look sure himself. "Five years . . . I believe I've been . . . wandering the world. . . ."

"Wandering the world?" Marian watched him press a hand against his head as he grimaced, trying to remember.

"I feel like I've been asleep for a hundred years," he said. Seeing her worried expression, he softened his with a smile. "Like one of the old stories I used to tell you when we were children."

But Marian was too upset to return it. "You disappeared without a trace. Louis is out right now. When he comes back, I'm sure he'll rejoice."

"What have you . . . ?" Nick winced from the pain in his head. "Marian, where have you been all this time?"

"Fighting. Fighting the monsters the best I could. Trying to *atone* the best I could." Marian straightened up and stepped back. Then, without another word, she sparked a flame in her hands. The fire of an Effigy.

Nick stared at it in terror. "The *occult*! Marian . . . are you a witch?"

"Master Nicholas, I've been wanting to tell you," she said, banishing the flame as easily as she'd summoned it. "I've been wanting to tell you about my sin. About *our* sin: Miss Abigail, Miss Emilia, Miss Patricia, and . . . Miss Alice."

Something wicked flickered behind the pupils of Nick's blank eyes. "Alice . . ."

"What we did. Oh, Nick!" She dropped every pretense of formality and rushed forward. Grabbing hold of his suspenders, she looked into his eyes earnestly. "I couldn't tell anyone. What Miss Alice's father told me. The terrible stone in his possession. How we . . . how we stole it. How we did awful things. We thought it was a game. A horrid game." Her fingers shook as they linked around his suspenders. "A dangerous game."

"A dangerous game. Links in a chain," Nick said. "Links in a chain . . . ," he whispered again, shutting his eyes.

"How did you know that phrase?" The sound of it seemed to startle her. "Did someone already—"

"I don't know." He shook his head. "I don't know what's wrong with me."

"Never mind. I'll tell you everything." Marian looked to the window. Day was turning to dusk. "There's more I need to confess."

She walked over to the couch, picked up the cigar box, and gave it to him. He frowned, confused, when he opened the lid and found shards of white stone inside.

"Marian . . ." The stone glittered in his eyes. "What . . . ?"

"Like I said, there's so much I need to tell you. Alice's story. The terrible secret Master Vogel told me. The rest of the stone. Why I had to bury his body, keep it safe. Everything. *Everything.* I don't know where even to start. However, before I tell you, you must promise me something. Promise me that after you understand everything, you'll come with me."

Nick's head was clearly still aching. He winced from the pain of it. "Come with you where?"

"Egbaland. I have to go back to Egbaland." Gently, she touched Nicholas's collar, smoothing it. "I have to go back for Tinubu's treasure."

"My love, you're not . . . you're not making any sense."

"Then, Nick, I'll tell you everything." Marian let go of his collar, readying herself. "I'll confess everything to you. Nick?"

Nick yelled, dropping the cigar box. Grimacing again, he held his head, clenching his teeth from the pain. But before Marian could check to see if he was okay, he opened his eyes once more, his breathing steady. Suddenly, to Marian's surprise, he cupped her face and gazed into her eyes. Then, without warning, he kissed her. It was a long, full, dark kiss, one that made them bend into each other as if their bodies were returning to the same whole. Marian gasped for breath after he released her lips, but he didn't let her go. Not yet.

"Confess," he whispered. "Like how you murdered Alice that day in York?"

Marian narrowed her eyes, her thin frame frozen in shock. "What . . . ? How do you—"

"Or how you stole Nicholas's love from her?"

"Nicholas?" Marian was truly fearful now. "Nicholas . . ."

"But now I have him. I have him forever." Each step he walked toward her, she stepped back until her legs buckled against the piano bench. "I suppose you could say it's your final punishment."

"Who are you?" Marian couldn't fathom what was happening. Perhaps because she didn't fully understand yet—about the Effigy line. About the endless cycle that started with the dangerous game they'd played all those years ago.

It was a secret Alice wouldn't tell her. "I told you I would change the world," Alice said, grabbing the cheeks of her terrified servant. "And I told you that you won't stop me."

Then Alice snapped Marian's neck.

The shock of her death, the sound of her body crashing against the piano keys, wrenched a violent shudder out of me. In a sadistic play to punish the flesh she'd taken, Alice receded back into Nick's consciousness, allowing him control, allowing him to see his lover dead on the piano in front of him. Nick's desperate howls curdled my blood.

It was a shocking sight, terrifying. Marian's death reverberated down my spine as if my own neck had been the one to snap so viciously. But my moment of confusion, my moment of weakness, was Natalya's chance. Once again she was in front of me, her hands gripping my head as if inspired by the violence Alice had just done. My fear spiked, the shock and terror wringing tears from my eyes. I had to wake up. I *had* to wake up!

*Wake up, damn it!* I ordered myself as Nicholas buried his face in Marian's chest, cursing the woman locked inside his head. *Please! Wake up!*


"Wake up!" I shouted, nearly jumping out of my skin when I saw Lake kneeling in front of me, shaking. The sirens were blaring. My cell door was open. All the cell doors were open.

Brendan.

Lake pulled me to my feet. "Time to go, love."

# 22

BECAUSE I WAS STILL HALF IN A DAZE, LAKE had to pull me out of the cell and through the hall of freed, weapon-less former agents. Some recognized us, but their own survival mattered more. They let us be while we ran, eventually separating from the pack by dashing into the stairwell to climb up to the third floor. A security guard burst through the stairwell door and started shooting at us, but we ducked flat onto the stairs, dodging his fire.

"Better suit up." Lake pulled out her power-boosting device. Nobody had thought to confiscate what looked like regular red pens from our pockets, so we had a way to fight. As she gave herself the shot, I followed suit, jamming the device in my neck as Lake breathed out a torrent of wind that knocked the man back, his gun clattering uselessly against the floor. I kicked it away before we entered the third floor. A row of open cells just like ours, agents wrestling down two security guards who'd been quickly disarmed.

"Chae Rin has to be in one of these cells," I said. Lake and I took opposite walls, avoiding the agents trampling their way out of the hall. One door. The next. The next. Then—

"Oh my god," I breathed. It wasn't Chae Rin.

It was Director Prince. Aidan's father. Unlike the agents he'd probably commanded once upon a time, he sat in a long brown shirt and pants, the same prisoner uniform the others had been given, his once intimidating frame shrunken. He looked like he hadn't eaten in days, and I could tell by the untouched plate of food gathering flies in the corner of the room that it was possible he hadn't. A light blond beard had grown on his once cleanly shaven face, his hair as dirty as the creases in his aged face. His eyes barely flitted to me when I called his name, but when he saw me, they widened, his thin lips parting, struggling for breath.

"You," he said, his voice weak from lack of use. "It's you."

"Come on, sir," I said, the word "sir" slipping out of my mouth by accident, as if I were trying to remind myself that this frail, defeated man used to lead the North American Division of the Sect. "The door's open. You can go!"

But when Director Prince moved his hands, he could only stare at them quivering in the air. "I killed my son," he said, his Adam's apple bobbing after swallowing. "My boy . . . I don't deserve freedom."

Rhys had wondered once if his father was involved in his order to kill Natalya. If he'd known about his torture in Fisk-Hoffman. But this was a man shattered by guilt. When I asked him those questions, he only confirmed my suspicions.

"I turned a blind eye to all his suffering," he confessed. "I *caused* his suffering with my own hands." He stared at them, at the veins highlighting his skin, at his pale knuckles. Perhaps it was the memory of their contact against young flesh that sent a shudder through him. "I was so wrapped up in my disciplinary role that I forgot to protect the very thing that should have mattered most to me." The veins in his eyes were distinct, his pupils dimmed. "And now my boy is dead."

"He isn't." I strode toward him and, ignoring his startled gasp, slung his arm over my shoulder and helped him to his feet. "Let's go. When you see him, you can apologize yourself."

"Maia!" Lake cried from the opposite side of the hall.

I pulled Arthur out of the cell just as Lake pulled out a battered Chae Rin. One of her eyes was swollen shut, her other half open. She could walk, but only with a limp, her left arm useless. It hadn't been too long since her fight with Belle. She was most likely already healing, but until she was all right, we'd have to drag her along with us.

"Oh man . . ." Chae Rin groaned. "Am I missing my teeth?"

"Nope," Lake said after checking. "All accounted for."

"I'm sorry." She coughed out blood. "I got her good, but . . . she was too strong."

"It's okay." Lake wrapped Chae Rin's arm around her neck to support her. "Next time we'll do it together."

The four of us walked past the unconscious security guards and followed the rest of the agents into the stairwell. We met a new round of guards at the foot of the steps. But before they could fire, three agents charged into the stairwell, knocking out the guards with the butts of the guns they must have stolen. They looked up at us.

"Howard?" I couldn't believe it. "Eveline?"

My heart soared at the sight of them. They were alive—and there was nothing I needed more right now than a familiar friendly face. A little bit of black fuzz coated his once-bald head, but I recognized the big man and his slight wife. Her bright green eyes lit up at the sight of us.

"You girls are here too?" she said, and clenched her fists in celebration. "Great. Great. Come with us. We're busting out of here."

"I told you before." Howard clucked his tongue, disapproving and serious as ever. "We can't just run out the front door."

"We have three Effigies," Eveline said. "That's exactly what the hell we're going to do."

The distraction caused by the mass exodus was the cover we needed to weave through without much difficulty.

"I thought you two died in Oslo," Lake said, pulling Chae Rin back up when she stumbled.

"No," Howard said. "We didn't make it there in time to die. But they found out we helped you in London."

"I'm so sorry," I said, grunting because Director Prince was hardly cooperating. Every once in a while he mumbled Rhys's name in despair. He should have thought about it before firing a death weapon on his son. "I never meant to drag you two into any of this."

"It's okay," Eveline said. "We've got you three. Now we can"—she stopped—"escape. . . ."

We'd stepped into a silent lobby—covered in corpses. Corpses of the agents who'd tried to get out were strewn about the floor.

Corpses that had begun to move.

"Jessie," I hissed. There she stood in her full-bodied uniform at the other end of the room by the entrance. With her arms lifted, her fingers jerked and twitched like a puppeteer, except the field of corpses moved without strings—at least not strings I could see. Everything is connected. Life and death alike, the streams of light that carried souls flying around the world. What if she could manipulate those individual pathways to move the bodies that the souls had left behind? Either way, it didn't matter for us. Now all we had to do was figure out how to get rid of them.

Eveline and Howard did the obvious—they opened fire with the guns they'd stolen from security guards, which was about as useful as shooting a piece of rotted meat. Lake managed to fling some out of the way, sweeping her hand across the air, but some of the corpses were faster than the others. One had already jumped on Eveline. As she kicked it away, I placed Arthur down by the wall.

"Stand back!" I cried.

Howard gripped the corpse with both his arms, yanking it off his wife and throwing it to the ground right as I lifted my arms—I set that one on fire first. Then the entire field of corpses. Facing the flames, Jessie put her helmet on quickly and stumbled back against the wall, exhausted. The moment her concentration broke, the corpses fell to the ground as lifeless flesh. I crushed my hands into fists, sending the blaze higher.

"Maia, stop!" It was Brendan. He'd come in from the side door to find the entire lobby burning. But I couldn't stop. I wouldn't stop until the bodies were useless ash, even if it meant we had to find another exit out of—

A single shot shattered my thoughts.

I didn't know where it'd come from or where it'd fired. Not until I saw Howard's eyes roll to the back of his head, Eveline's shrieks cutting the air in two as he fell dead to the ground. Lake clung to Chae Rin, the both of them in shock. I sank to my knees, watching the blood drip down his forehead from the bullet hole. This couldn't be happening. This wasn't real!

In despair, I banished the flames to find the murderer. A soldier stepped through the wall of smoke, his gun still hot from the shot he'd fired. It must have been difficult to breathe. Maybe that was why he lifted off his helmet and revealed himself, his face unobscured, as beautiful and frightening as an angel of death.

"Rhys . . ." I breathed, a spring of relief and horror swelling up inside me.

Rhys lowered his gun, his black hair matted against his forehead from the heat. No emotion crossed his face, no hint telling me that he could even comprehend whom he'd just killed. His former partner lay dead at his feet, the man's wife holding him and screaming, half crazed. Without emotion, without guilt, and without a soul, all he could do was point his gun at her, too.

"Aidan, stop!" Brendan approached carefully from the wall, his gun out, trained on his brother. "Aidan." His voice broke. "You . . . This isn't you. . . ."

Rhys's dead eyes ascertained the figure of his brother, but he said nothing in return. Behind him, Jessie's laughter cackled in the air, her white helmet still on as she dashed out from the other end of the wall of smoke.

"Good work, honey," Jessie said, running her hand through Rhys's hair as if he were just another one of her dead playthings. "Now kill this screaming bitch too for extra points."

Eveline stopped screaming, her body trembling, but she kept her face buried in her husband's neck.

"Aidan, you have to stop this." Brendan's eyes welled up with tears. "Snap out of it, little brother."

"He's right." I got back to my feet. Even with her face covered, I could tell Jessie was glaring at me, but I didn't care. "I know, Rhys—*Aidan*. I know what happened at Fisk-Hoffman. I know you set the fire. . . . You did what you had to in order to protect yourself and your friends—"

"Shut up!" Jessie snapped, her voice muffled inside her helmet. "How dare you talk as if you know? You don't know a damn *thing*. Aidan's better now. He's with us." She stroked his face. "Like he should have been from the beginning."

"No!" I spread my arms out wide. "This isn't where you belong. Look at us! It's me. Your friends. Your colleagues. Your brother—your *father*." I stepped to the side so that Rhys could see him clearly. The boy's eyes widened just slightly, but it was as if his muscles wouldn't move unless someone commanded it. "Don't let these people hurt you more than they already have," I said. "Come back. Please come back."

Those were the same words he'd spoken to me that night at Blackwell's estate, after my mind and will had fallen to pieces. But the plea wasn't just mine.

"Come back to us, brother." Brendan lowered his gun. "Come on, man . . ."

"Oh, for god's sake, I told you to kill them, not have a damn intervention." Jessie snatched Rhys's gun out of his hands, clicking the button behind her ear to take off her helmet. "I guess if you want someone in the ground, you've got to do it yourself."

Jessie had just lifted off her helmet when Eveline's bullet caught her between the eyes. The redheaded girl's lips parted in an awkward shape as she fell back into the smoke, dead. But Rhys's attention wasn't on Eveline, her shaking body, or the tears staining her face. It shifted from us to Director Prince, helpless against the wall. Father and son stared at each other, each as bewildered as the other.

"Aidan," Director Prince whispered. Only once.

Rhys cocked his head to the side, studied the once broad and bold man, now decaying from the inside. The man who'd raised him. The man who brutalized him into subservience. The man who'd left him in the care of monsters.

Rhys aimed his gun at his father's head.

"No!" I don't know why I did it. My body had already flung on top of him as the gun fired into my gut, my arms already wrapped around his neck while I fell into him. I'd already started running before I could stop myself. There must have been a hundred different ways to stop him. A hundred different strategies to keep the bullet from flying. I chose the easiest, stupidest one. Lake screamed, leaping over corpses to get to me. Brendan and Chae Rin were calling my name. But my eyes stayed on Rhys as he gazed down at me, confusion twisting his features as he gripped me tight and hugged me to his chest.

"It's all right," I told him, even though I wasn't sure it was. The bottom half of my shirt was already stained with blood. "It's all right...."

An eternity in the white realm of dead Effigies awaited me. An eternity standing in front of that door, slowly going mad. I wasn't okay. I didn't want to go. But for his sake, for *his* sake, I kept repeating the words. The lie: "It's all right...."

He struggled with the words at first. But soon a light emerged from behind his eyes, his breaths laboring out of his mouth.

"Why...?" It sounded like a breath, but the longer he repeated it, the louder it became until I heard the word, soft but clear, powered by anguish. *"Why?"*

It was a good question. But I was already well aware of the answer. "I can't let you kill your father. No more tragedies, Aidan." I smiled at him. "No more..."

Howard, dead on the ground, his wife cradling his head. The corpses. Me dying in his arms, my blood oozing over his hands. His gaze darted here and there, taking everything in, the gears in his head turning, the veins reddening in his eyes until it was too much. His scream thundered through the lobby, so loudly I almost didn't hear the quiet footsteps approach me from behind. It wasn't Lake or Brendan. It wasn't Chae Rin or Arthur or even Eveline who knelt down next to me and brushed the curls out of my eyes.

Saul studied me with an expression so solemn, I knew right away that it couldn't have been anyone other than Nick in control of his body.

"I've had time to think," he told me, his voice distant as I started losing consciousness in Rhys's arms. "Come with me."

I felt my body vanishing before everything went black.

# 23

"MAKE SURE SHE'S STABILIZED."

"Bring her to the operating room."

Sounds came and went as I slipped in and out of consciousness. Shoes clomping along the floor, a monitor beeping too quickly. Even with my eyes closed, I could tell I was flying down a stretch of hallway. My heart erratically pounding in my chest. Men and women chattering out terms I couldn't recognize.

The withered voice of an old man.

"Do what you can to save the subject before you bring her to me."

A door closing. They put me under.


*Am I dead?*

No . . . no, I was definitely not dead. I'd been shot, yes. I knew that much. But I could tell by the bandages around my stomach that they'd taken the bullet out—whoever *they* were. I was alive and breathing. Alive and in a bed.

A bed I was chained to.

Once I felt the steel against my wrists, panic began to set in. The adrenaline cut through whatever fatigue had sunk deep into my bones, and I pried my eyes apart.

Months ago, when I'd woken up in that recovery room in France, it was Rhys who'd remained by my side. The room was brighter. I'd felt his warmth as he touched me.

Now my body chilled at the sight of Saul sitting at the foot of my bed. Frigid and stiff as this tiny, lifeless gray room. He sat with his back to me, his body hunched over, propped up by his elbows upon his knees. He didn't look at me as he spoke. "After twenty-three hours, she finally awakens."

He stood. My wrists were cuffed to the bed, but my ankles weren't. I drew my knees in to get as far from him as possible. When I tried to twist my body, it wasn't the straps but the sharp pain in my stomach that stopped me. Stitches. Wincing, I watched him move to the wall, his hands clasped behind his back. His face hidden from me.

Even coughing was painful. "Where am I?" I asked in a voice that scraped my throat.

"You've been here before, Maia," he told me. "We saw the Northern Lights together."

Northern Lights. I yanked my bound wrists, grunting from the pain of the cuffs biting into bone. The snowy fields. The lights from the military facility watchtower.

"Greenland." I jerked my body again, but to no avail. "The Greenland facility."

"I told you, I've had time to think. I was gone because I had to remember. I had to make sense of things." Saul finally turned. "To make sense of my own mind."

He was so calm as he stared at me, his face partially obscured by the shadows that lived along the edges of this dimly lit room.

"Oh?" I shook my arms again. They must have inoculated me. My powers were completely dead. "And what did you figure out while you were on your little spiritual quest?"

"Are you curious?"

"I'm curious about what the hell your deal is." I had to bite the inside of my cheek to calm my terror-stricken pulse. "Like why you'd agree to work with Blackwell and murder innocents."

"Would you believe that it was all Alice's idea?"

"No," I answered flatly. "You said yourself once that you and Alice had the same goal: the stone. Then again, you two can't seem to make up your mind as to whether you're working together or trying to get rid of each other."

Saul chuckled in a low voice. "That might be true," he said. "Alice has lived inside my head for a century. Sometimes it feels like we've become contentious lovers. But that can't be right," he added, staring up at the light dangling from the ceiling. "Since she killed my lover."

This was not the same man wailing about Marian over his brother's grave. He showed the perfect serenity of a corpse, his expression still as he slowly approached me.

By scrying into Natalya's memories, I'd seen how Marian had died. Their last moments together, her lifeless body crashing onto the piano keys, still freshly imprinted on my thoughts. But I kept silent.

"I want to see her again, you know." Saul's tone was as casual as his gate. He slipped his hands inside his pockets, his faded blue eyes bright in the darkness. "That was my single driving thought as I slept through the decades . . . as Alice made her home in my skin and traveled the world under a new name: Saul, the first king."

He stopped at the foot of my bed. "She was the daughter of an explorer, after all. That occultist. Benjamin Vogel." He uttered the name as if for the first time in centuries. "The pleasure Alice had felt holding the ashes of her father in her hands," he said, and I remembered with a shudder that vial Saul had slipped out of his coat. "She truly hated that man. And yet respected him all the same. In life, she'd always wanted to travel like him . . . to be released from the weakness of her body, the burden of a society that caged her. When she took me over, she had the freedom. The time. That was what she'd wished for, unlike the others. To be unbound by time and space."

Suddenly, a deep shiver pulsed through his body. He grabbed on to the bed, his fingers curled into the white sheet. Though I'd already moved them away, my legs reacted as if to the touch of his hand against vulnerable skin.

"These were the memories, the feelings Alice kept locked from me for decades," he said. "Memories I had to fight to recall."

As he winced, I realized that though his gaze remained locked on my helpless form, he wasn't looking at me at all—nor anything in this reality. Alice. It must have been Alice he saw as he carefully unfurled the scroll of those memories.

"She'd watched, for more than a century, the mayhem of the phantoms," he said. "Experimented with the rings she'd crafted from the shards of stone she took from Marian. Learned, like her father, of the mysterious, unseen forces in this world. After a century of observing, of witnessing how she'd changed the course of human history with her game, she began to believe that perhaps she too could become one of those unseen forces, reshaping humanity for all eternity. An enchantress. A goddess. Well, it's not surprising, is it? She told you she liked games."

I remembered too well. Saul straightened, began moving up the bed toward me. "She had no need for any more stone. She had already achieved her goal of godhood. But she didn't count on one thing. Humanity adapted to the mayhem she'd caused. Technology developed. Researchers. Scientists. Military. She wanted to shape the world, and she did. That's how they found her."

"*Found* her?" He was getting too close. My mouth tasted sour as I swallowed. "What do you mean? Who's 'they'?"

Saul's human hand twitched as it rose. "Neither of us knew. Not me, nor Alice. It was how they wanted it. They wanted us to think we were driven *solely* by our own wishes." He touched the back of his neck with his metal hand. "Wanted us to lose time . . . and forget where we'd been."

"What do you *mean*?" I demanded, coughing again. "What are you—"

"But I do want it," Saul continued, his eyes wide, his words quicker, breathless. "*I* want it. For myself. I *need* it. I need the stone." This time he sounded desperate. He was hovering above me now. "The volume is here in this facility."

My chest jerked as I sucked in a harsh breath. Castor's thirteenth volume. Here . . .

"Blackwell's people have already cracked the code," Saul said, and I recoiled at the thought. No matter what we did, we were always too many steps behind. "But I don't need the secrets of the Sect," he told me. "I need the power to change fate. And for that I need you."

"No way," I spat. "It's not going to happen. I'm not telling you crap."

As I watched Saul's hand reach for my face, I sank back into the bed, anticipating a strike. But it was a caress he gave me instead, slow, starting from my head down the side of my left cheek. Somehow, that felt worse.

"Unfortunately, your silence is just one of the problems I have," Saul said, gazing down at me. "There's no use in you giving up such a secret if I can't use it for myself. It's all meaningless if that idiot Blackwell were to reap the benefits alone, don't you agree?"

What? Why wouldn't Saul be able to take it from him?

Saul leaned in close, his breath light on my ear. "But like I said, I've done some thinking. And that problem? I've already figured out a way around it." I could feel his grin twisting into a wicked smile. "Don't think any more about Alice. It's you and I who will have to work together, Maia."

The door opened, and Saul shot up straight. A much shorter man walked through the door, flanked by medical assistants. His glasses hung from the collar of his closed lab coat. He looked old enough to need a respirator, his liver spots sunken red into wrinkled, pale skin, his head bald but for the few wisps of white hair stretching down the chicken skin of his neck. When he saw the two of us, he slipped some kind of recording device out of his breast pocket.

"What are you doing here, 01?" His voice was raspy, low, as if the sound was trapped deep in his chest. It felt too big for his frail, withering body. He said, "01" again, and somehow I could tell that he was referring to Saul. "Step away from my subject."

When Saul hesitated, the man lifted the device to his lips and spoke his command into it again. If it were some kind of microphone, it didn't work properly. Instead of a magnified voice, static enveloped his words—like interference. I'd heard it before, in Blackwell's mansion. It was the sound that'd played through Jessie's phone right before I—

Right before I was mind controlled.

But although Saul's hands twitched, he didn't check out like I had. He looked very much in control of his faculties as he stepped away from me.

But then Jessie had said theirs was a newer, more efficient system.

I clenched my jaw, my body numb as I finally understood why Saul had placed his needs behind that of Blackwell's.

So this was Dr. Grunewald.

He had a businesslike air to him. He lifted his chin as he stood by the side of my bed. "We're ready for the experiment," Grunewald said, his right eye twitching weirdly as he passed Saul and inspected me like merchandise. I wasn't flesh and blood to him. Or maybe that was all I was. "She seems in good condition now for us to prod her mind for Marian's secrets." He nodded to the technicians. "Take Subject 13 to room five-A and get her prepared for the proceedings."

Subject *13*? "I have a name, you ass. Hey! Get away from me!" I bit at his fingers as they drew too close to my lips. "Hey, stop it!" There were too many of them grabbing me, uncuffing me, lifting me off the bed and onto a metal table they'd wheeled in. I tried to bite one's shoulder only for someone else to elbow me in the face. And while I groaned in pain, Saul stood in the shadows lining the wall, the very opposite of the menacing mastermind I once thought he was. A puppet Effigy. Obedient to his master.

I was laughing. It felt like I was choking on blood, but I laughed nonetheless. All this time. *All this time.* The terrorist attacks, the fear, the hatred. The nightmares of Saul's promise of chaos. And it turned out he was more powerless than I was.

The gears in Saul's metal hand turned as he watched them man-handle me, strapping my arms, legs, and chest to the cold table. I could hear it over their din.

"Did Grunewald give you that too after I sliced off your hand?" I asked Saul once I was completely fastened. "Look at you. *Look* at you!" I gritted my teeth as I turned my head to look at him. "From Alice's puppet to Blackwell's. The sorry, pathetic tale of Nick Hudson—*ugh!*"

One of the assistants placed a thick gray tape over my mouth. Saul watched me calmly as I struggled.

"I didn't remember until I brought you back here," he said, his breathing even. "It was like I kept forgetting. Or maybe I didn't want to remember how this all began. How Alice told them everything—about the phantoms, the rings she'd made. The power of the stone. That was when Blackwell hatched his plan. And when he died, he simply transferred my ownership over to his son to carry on his will." Saul chuckled, placing his hand on the glass. "Like I'm a slave."

It was all the same to me. Saul, Blackwell, Grunewald, whoever. I wasn't giving any of them a damn thing. They were all *trash*.

"Maia," Saul said. "I told you in Argentina. I swore upon my brother's grave. You remember, don't you? The promise I made?"

I did. I remembered his burning intensity as the police trained their guns on him. Atoning for Marian. Reshaping the world—his own way. As Nick Hudson. I could see it in his eyes . . . the will to defy the ones who'd enslaved him through the long, brutal years.

"Enough of this," Grunewald said. "We're wasting time. Take her to the room."

"Wait, Doctor." Saul stepped forward hesitantly before they could begin wheeling me out the room.

Grunewald truly looked at Saul with the same level of dehumanization evident in his refusal to call him by name. Instead, he was 01. The first subject, maybe. The first lab rat.

"I have a proposal," Saul said. "I want to be prepared for cross-spectrographic coupling."

"For what?" Perhaps it was his indignation over being addressed by a lackey, but Grunewald's pitch rose into his curved nose as he spoke. "We have no need of you."

"You remember, don't you, Maia?" Saul said quietly. "Back in New York? The moment between you and me . . . between Marian and me?"

The kiss. At that time, Alice was in control, but the contact between the two of us awakened both lovers. It was a shock of power that burst open every door in my subconscious.

"Marian will react to me," Saul told Grunewald. "She's done it before. It's our connection."

"And if your brain waves are in sync, you'll be able to cross the threshold into her subconsciousness . . . scry into her mind as she does." Grunewald thought. "Of course, the process would leave you vulnerable too. You'd be susceptible to each other."

"I have nothing else left to hide," Saul said. "Once I know what Marian does, I will be the one to relay the information to you. Her silence won't matter anymore."

My jaw tightened. He was right. And if he succeeded, there wouldn't be anything I could do to keep Marian's secret safe.

"It's an interesting idea." After a while, Grunewald nodded to the assistants waiting in the back. "Prepare the two Effigies for the experiment." And when he noticed me fight and scream against the tape around my mouth, he added, "And don't take her to room five-A. Take her to room six-B."

"But, sir," said one of the technicians, "that room is opposite—"

"I know full damn well, you fool," Grunewald snapped. Another lackey to put in his place. Grunewald seemed to relish it. "Take her. She needs to know what the stakes are."

Saul flashed me the smallest of smiles as the technicians wheeled me out of my room. Saul and I, working together. I guess I was about to find out how.

# 24

IT WAS AS IF I'D BEEN BURIED. THE METAL straps dug into my skin, the table hard against my back. I was helpless in this frigid, dark room.

After wheeling me inside, the technicians prepped for the new experiment, but I was as rabid as ever even while strapped onto my table. Having managed to chew through the tape, I spat in Grunewald's face.

Grunewald sighed impatiently, wiping my saliva from his face. "You'd do well to quiet down, or this experiment may be more painful for you than it needs to be." Grunewald's voice was low and menacing, his threat unmistakable. "You're not the first Effigy I've experimented on. I found others after 01. How else do you think I came to replicate your skill set?"

Horror crept in as I began to contemplate the vicious reality of being an Effigy in captivity, prodded, electrocuted, experimented on, bloodied, maybe even dissected, waiting months or more for merciful death. Is that what Saul had gone through too? How many other Effigies had they spirited away since they set their plan in motion?

He went over to the counter, swiveling between busy technicians, and reappeared with a needle. "Stay away!" I cried as he reached for me. I was thrashing on the table, fighting so hard, so desperately, the straps began to loosen.

"You need to settle down, 13," Grunewald said as I spat again, this time missing his face. "You should really think about cooperating with me."

He turned and motioned to one of the technicians, who nodded and moved to the side wall of the room. I almost couldn't see the shaded window through the mass of bodies hooking up equipment. But when the technician turned a switch, the dark tint gave way to clear glass. Soundproof glass.

I could tell because I couldn't hear Rhys screaming.

I could see him through the window in the room next to me, out of his uniform and into a now-torn shirt and a pair of loose-fitting pants, trapped like a lab rat as a man I'd seen before cut into his bare chest. Blood stained his torso like paint and dripped from the Surgeon's scalpel.

"Rhys!" I fought against my straps. "Rhys! Stop it!" I pleaded. Rhys started convulsing. "Stop it! Leave him alone!"

"Settle down," Grunewald said. "And I may tell the Surgeon to take a break."

Squeezing my lips shut, I kept still against the metal table, seething as he injected me with something that relaxed my muscles. Grunewald kept his word at least, telling the Surgeon to hold off over the intercom. Rhys's torn flesh didn't seem to bother him either way. Indeed, when this man peered at me, it was as if he were peeling apart my skin with his gaze, following the neurological network spreading down my body.

None of us mattered to him.

"What is wrong with you?" I whispered after Grunewald took off the rest of the tape on my mouth, confident I wouldn't spit at him again. "Why are you doing this? Do you understand what your research is being used for?"

He walked behind me. I wasn't sure what he was doing until I suddenly felt a pair of electrodes against my temples. "A world of science is a world of men," he said simply as he taped them on. "Everything can be explained through observation and analysis. Except you. You Effigies and your phantom friends. Magic beasts. Creatures of legend." He brushed my hair off my forehead, sticking on more electrodes in its place. "What makes you little girls so special, hmm? What makes you defy the rules of men? I simply want to know. Science is the pursuit of knowledge, after all." Grunewald leaned in. "And I want to know everything."

There was a sharp edge to his voice when he mentioned us "little girls," us Effigies. I could tell by the way this man spoke to me, by the way he barked orders at his assistants, by the way he treated me like a slab of meat on a table, that he loved his power almost as much as he resented me having more. How much pleasure did it give this feeble man to see Saul and me powerless under his control?

"Like Blackwell," I whispered. "You're all the same."

"It takes men with vision to change the world, after all," he answered.

Or those with no regard for the humanity of others.

The lights in Rhys's rooms went off. I couldn't see him anymore as the technicians continued to prep Saul and me. As in Morocco, I felt like a helpless frog waiting to be dissected, hooks and cables stretching out from computers, connecting me to Saul on the table next to me. Cold white electrodes stuck to my forehead like tape. My body was too weak to fight from the drugs Grunewald had pumped into my veins, my magic deadened from whatever they'd given me while I was unconscious.

It was almost time. After all these months, soon I'd learn Marian's secret. It wasn't that I didn't want to know. But what would they do with the information once I came to and they forced Saul to tell them?

What would they do with me?

"Adjust their cylithium levels," Grunewald ordered.

"Starting electrical coupling," said a technician. "Inducing the meditative state."

Saul was still conscious enough to grab hold of my hand, and though I didn't have the power to reject his touch, I knew it wasn't for me anyway. Saul squeezed my hand as if it were Marian's, a tender touch wrapped in a desperate grip. It wasn't the cylithium, the electrical pulse surging between us, or the cables hooking us together—it was his touch. Like the kiss that had torn me out of my own mind.

It was like before. My body twitched as scenes of Effigies streamed through my visions, so many they blurred into one another. Flashing faces leading to the first. Marian. She was awakening. But it wasn't just her. I saw other visions I shouldn't have. Too many to count . . .

"Ah, but Madam Tinubu, my dear. I have something more valuable than money." A white man who looked as if Blackwell had time-warped to the Victorian era tipped his frock hat before stretching out his large hand, closed, to an African woman. The woman sat in a wooden chair inside a thatch-roofed palace of earthen walls and a brilliant clay floor. Servants wrapped in plain brown fabric fanned her with a palm leaf as she listened to the British trader, her arms folded on the floral-patterned fabric tied around her body beneath them. When Blackwell opened his palm, she leaned over slightly to see what he was offering her.

It was a light blue stone, the size and shape of an eye. Alluring.

Dangerous. Powerful. I recognized it immediately. Shards of it were still locked in the Deoscali Temple, protecting the temple from the dangers of the phantoms outside, turning it into a haven—a land of pure calm.

"You can see it too, can't you?" The man had the grin of a snake oil salesman, but I could tell by the shrewd glint of her eye the woman knew what his narrow mind couldn't conceive. The power in this stone. He'd stolen it, thinking it a precious jewel for his collection. After having it appraised in Britain, he knew it was not monetarily worth more than the amount of slaves he was asking for. He thought he was tricking her, dazzling her with its azure sheen.

But she felt it. There was something special about this stone—something special he couldn't see. If he could, then the greedy fool wouldn't have given it to her.

I knew all this because Marian knew. Because from within my consciousness Marian was telling me, narrating a fuller picture based on what she knew in that moment, what she'd discovered years afterward, and what she inferred through her own musings. I couldn't hear her voice. I wasn't seeing through her eyes. Instead, I could feel her words blanketing me. It wasn't the scrying experience I was used to. This experiment could only induce mechanically what came naturally to an Effigy—scientific guestimation that was throwing my brain waves—and the process itself—slightly out of whack. But maybe it was more than that. Marian's presence was all around me. She needed me to know. . . .

"I was gifted this little treasure by the famed Castor and Vogel of Britain. This stone would be worth a hundred slaves, wouldn't it?"

It was then that the woman took the stone and nodded to one of her servants. Soon, a child, small and frail, was dragging her little body out the palace doors with so many others, following Blackwell to his ship. I knew right way.

*Marian . . .*

It wasn't my voice, but Saul's—no, Nick's. There he was behind me in his ragged clothes, his pale silver hair dangling down while he hunched over, watching the little girl with a pained expression as she disappeared through the doors with a row of others sold to Blackwell. Saul and I were watching together . . . witnessing together. . . .

A flash. The scenes changed too quickly. Marian was a child in one moment and a young adult in the next. They were inside an estate that smelled of ashes. Outside, the distant cries of phantoms shook the town of York's very foundations. Bending over a table in a drawing room, Marian furiously scribbled symbols onto a piece of paper for a young woman with plain brown hair. Flame, shadow, and three lights.

"Where did you say . . . ? What did you say happened to Alice?" The brown-haired woman could hardly catch her breath, her wide green eyes refusing to settle on any one image.

"Miss Alice is dead." Marian didn't bother to explain further. She drew as if she was running out of time, because she was. The town was.

She shoved the paper into the terrified young woman's hands. "Miss Emilia, you need to find Master Castor," she said, her maid's dress dirty from soot. "He'll understand if I give him these. They're his symbols—the ones he made with Master Vogel. You need to tell him what we did. When he sees these symbols, he'll be able to understand in full."

Emilia unfurled the note. The three symbols: one that looked like fire. Another, a frightening monster. And finally, three swirls of light. She stared from the note in her hand to the open cigar box on the table. Shards of stone were strewn about inside, though some were on the table, on the floor, as if Marian had sloppily swiped the pieces inside. "The stone is broken? But how . . . how did it break?"

A flash. The scene had changed.

"'Tinker, tailor, soldier, sailor.'" Four teenage girls sat and sang the divination in a circle on the floor of a bedroom, passing a white stone between them while the servant Marian watched from behind the door. "'Rich-man, poor-man, beggar-man, thief. What will I be?'" The blonde turned her head to the door. "Marian, come join us."

*Alice* . . .

As if something pulled me back, I suddenly returned to the former memory. Marian and the symbols in Emilia's hand. Emilia was the shaken one. Marian, knowing full well the mayhem besieging the town, swallowed her own terror in an effort to remain determined. It was a wonder how the former servant could focus so clearly on her goal when she'd just killed someone, but she had to do what she could.

"First we need to bury Master Vogel's body," Marian said. "In case the phantoms destroy this estate, we cannot let his body become lost to the rubble. And then, Miss Emilia, please find Master Castor."

Emilia stared fearfully at the three symbols in her hand. "What do you expect me to do with this? What are you going to do? Why won't you come with me?"

Marian gripped her arms. "Because I have to find Nick."

*Nick* . . . It was Marian's voice echoing. *Nick* . . .

*But she couldn't find me.* Saul again. Though I didn't turn to the source, I could feel him behind me. *The moment Alice died at Marian's hand is when her soul found my body. They made the wish at the same time, holding the same stone. And so I became cursed.* . . .

He became an Effigy.

Flash. Bodies were strewn about a control center, machines blinking with no one to man them. The setting had switched, but where was I? Computers—I wasn't in the nineteenth century anymore. I'd jumped forward. A Sect strike force with their guns smoking. I'd seen this scene. This was Seattle.

We weren't in Marian's memories anymore. These were Saul's. Saul walked in through the door as if half in a dream, his eyelids heavy as he stepped over dead bodies.

"You know what to do," one of the strike force agents said. "We're counting on you."

Another gunshot fired at the front of the room, and a dying wail. They were leaving no survivors.

"You sure that little stone's gonna be enough to control the phantoms?" another agent asked, flicking his head toward the gleaming ring around Saul's finger.

"Well, we'll find out soon enough. The operation starts now. Everyone evacuate!"

But as the war siren began blaring, I was ripped out of the memory and into a drawing room where Alice sat at a desk, her Rapunzel hair spun over the chair like gold. I'd seen this memory of Marian's before. The old musty curtains still against a set of windows next to the desk, the shadows flickering across a bust of a man's head, which was placed near the crackling fireplace. Alice had been resting her head atop a pile of books, but once she heard Marian enter, she smiled, her pale blue eyes glinting with a childlike sort of mischief that felt somehow innocent and wicked all at once. "Ah, Marian, you came." Her lips twisted into a conspiratorial smile. "Good. I have something to show you."

Marian approached with hesitant steps across the polished floor until she noticed the only book open on the desk. She read the title scrawled in capital letters on the exposed page. *"Tempe Restored..."*

"Yes, you remember that one, don't you, *poupée*?" Alice tapped the hard cover. "I read you that masque when we were children, along with all the other stories. When you were still learning English. *'Twas I, whose power none can withstand, who opened both her heart and hand.*" She recited the words from memory. "Do you remember, Marian?"

"Yes, I remember. Circe, the evil sorceress." Marian's eyes slid to Alice's right hand. That she was clutching something in it was only half her concern. Alice must not have noticed that the red bruises on her arm had not been fully covered by the lace of her long sleeve.

"Not just a sorceress, Marian, a goddess." With her other hand, Alice pulled the book toward her and began flipping through its pages. "A goddess of witchcraft, an enchantress. A conqueror who turned lover and enemy alike into horrid beasts of all kinds as a point of personal pleasure. But this masque would have us all believe that such a conqueror could be quelled by a god of love and Jove—the all father." She shook her head, incredulous at the thought, squeezing her right hand even tighter. "Preposterous."

"Miss Alice, your arm . . ." Marian pointed, and it was when Alice lifted her right arm that Marian could see the blood dripping from within her hand. "What—" Marian stepped back. "What is that?"

"Oh, this?" Alice's grip only needed to release slightly for me to see the white stone against her palm. "It's what I wanted to show you."

*Links in a chain* . . . Marian's voice. *A dangerous game* . . .

Another flash, and I felt a force so powerful it knocked the wind from my lungs. I hurdled back into a dark room. Saul lay flat on a silver surgical table much like this one, strapped and screaming, electrodes sending torturous shocks through his system. Another Blackwell loomed over him, but it wasn't just him. Grunewald. The light from the overhanging lamp highlighted the lines on his shriveled face. And that man in a gray suit—Griffith Rhys. Naomi's grandfather.

Once again I'd crossed over into Saul's mind. This must have been Alice's memory, not Nick's, because Saul was shrieking and cursing, promising to tear them apart from the inside.

"Dear me." Grunewald laughed. "Where was this feistiness when you were ambushed and drugged? You might have gotten away and avoided all this."

As Grunewald turned and walked over to the clunky computers at the side of the room, Blackwell scratched the stubble growing on his sharp chin. "Don't pay *her* any mind. With some 'persuasion,' this personality has already told us enough. A stone that grants wishes . . ." He lingered on the last word. "Such a thing exists? Griffith." The handsome man responded to his name. "Do you know what the original aims of the Sect were? I mean, the early organization that would inevitably become the Sect?"

"Of course." Griffith gave him a sidelong look. "It was created during the height of the British Crown's obsession with the occult. As always, the aim was imperialism. But why are you asking me this?"

"They didn't know a stone like this existed. It's not written anywhere in Castor's volumes. And according to him"—he gestured toward Saul—"there's more of it out there. The 'rest of the stone,' he said. . . ." Blackwell looked down on the shrieking body of Saul and grinned. "The Sect lost its way when it started protecting humanity. What if we could bring it back to its imperial aims?"

He leaned in just as Saul's body fell limp. "We need to find the stone, don't we?" he whispered into Saul's ear. "Imagine what we could do with that kind of power. If all goes well, Saul, you'll help me reshape the world."

"Re . . . shape the world . . ." Saul gasped, sputtering out loud. Blackwell's words. Not Alice's. Not Nick's. At least not yet. "Marian . . ."

*Marian . . . Marian . . .*

Nick repeated the words again and again, louder each time, so loud I shut my eyes and covered my ears until it stopped suddenly—like the sound had been sucked out of the room, like the air was a flickering flame that had been snuffed out. I opened my eyes.

A field. I was in a field, a beautiful, grand English estate in the background. I could see Saul on the other side of it, but he wasn't watching me. He was watching them—the two young teens sitting in the grass. A handsome, well-dressed young boy passed a doll into the servant's hands. Confused, she could only give him a nervous smile.

"It's your birthday, isn't it, Marian?" he asked.

Saul repeated the innocent question almost as if in a daze. He repeated it until he was hunched over, his fingers grasping his head, his words blending into a bloodcurdling scream that tore across every corner of my mind. My heart was pounding. I could feel it—his rage, his despair. And then I heard it. Just for a second, I heard Alice's conspiratorial whisper:

*Give it to me. This ungrateful wench. The thing she wanted most. Give it to me and let me keep it for eternity. . . .*

The scene before me blurred to black as the blood thundered against my skull as terrible as his guttural yell. Power was surging in me, rumbling awake from its dormant state, so fiercely my eyes snapped open.

"Adjust the frequency levels!" Grunewald ordered in a panic. "*Stabilize* them!"

But it was too late. I hadn't felt this since the alliance between Natalya and me at Blackwell's estate. It wasn't just my power but Saul's, the strength of two Effigies blazing through our nervous systems, passing through our hands clasped in a vise grip. An uncontrollable power that sent a shock wave from our bodies, burning the electrodes and the wires attached to us. Grunewald and the doctors were blown off their feet against the walls. Above us, the windows shattered.

The alarms went off. Saul hopped off his table, staring at his own hands as if he'd never seen them before. He touched the back of his neck, lightly rubbing the skin.

"I'm free." He clenched his metal hand into a fist. "I'm *free*."

Our combined power must have short-circuited Saul's chip. It was clearly what he'd wanted from the beginning. I could tell from the satisfied smirk on his face. He approached Grunewald, relishing each emancipated step.

"01." Grunewald's voice was weak, his eyes unfocused. "*Subject 01*," he tried again, struggling to keep his head lifted against the wall. "Wh-what are you doing?"

Saul slipped the device out of Grunewald's pocket and stared at it quizzically. "You're such a tiny man," he told Grunewald, flipping it over to inspect the back. "You must have relished it so much when you got to use it. A tiny, pathetic man."

With only his metal hand, Saul stabbed Grunewald through the heart.

As blood dribbled from the old man's mouth, I tried to feel some sense of horror, but I felt only numbness. Saul pulled his hand out of Grunewald's chest and shook off some of the blood, then turned to me. I lifted myself off the table, raising my hands to fight as Saul walked toward me, but he didn't seem to care. He wasn't even looking at me as he walked out the door.

The memories were still a blur. Words, dates, faces all a tangled mess. I didn't have time to unravel the pieces and I didn't have time to wonder where Saul was going. Rhys. I had to get him out of here. With the windows smashed, I could get to him. I scrambled up and jumped through the opening, landing on broken glass. Rhys was breathing on the table, bloodied but still awake. The Surgeon must have looked up at the wrong time—a shard of glass stuck out from between his eyes, his body limp on the ground next to his cart of torture tools. Grimacing at the sight of his dead body, I ran around the table.

"Rhys." I shook his shoulders gently as he grimaced. "Rhys!"

I drew my hands across his chin, the light stubble on his face prickling my fingers as they passed. His lips were cracked, his pallor dull and gray. He managed to sit up on his own, but he was worn from the inside out, his wounds still fresh.

"Are you okay?" I asked. The blast had shorted out Saul's chip and practically all the other tech in the area. It could have worked for Rhys too, couldn't it?

With lidded eyes, he stared at me, and for a second I didn't think he even knew who I was. But when his lips stretched into a sweet smile, it was like every shadow cast over him had dissipated at once. My chest swelled, singing relief as he gave me a tired nod.

"It's not like . . . I haven't been tortured before," he said, his voice as rough as his breathing. He wore the brave face of a boy who wanted to prove he was himself again, but he couldn't hide his grimaces when he twitched from the pain.

He was so used to pain. A spring of tears welled up in my eyes, and without thinking, I wrapped my arms around him and buried my face in his neck, gripping him so tightly I could feel the air escape from his mouth.

"You're back." My fingers tangled in his shirt and squeezed. I could feel his hands trembling across my shoulder blades. "You're back. Thank god."

"Ow," he whispered, and that's when I remembered he was injured. I released him immediately, checking his body.

"I'm sorry," I said quickly. Some of his blood had gotten onto my shirt.

"Trust me, I'm"—he laughed and shook his head—"I'm *not* complaining."

He touched my arm, his thumb sliding across the fabric. My body flushed, an odd addition to the fight-or-flight panic that still had me rigid. There was too much we wanted to say to each other, but the alarms were still blaring, and we were still in the middle of an enemy base. Escaping came first.

"Come on." I slung his arm around my neck. "Let's get the hell out of here."

But the moment we stumbled into the hallway, we froze in shock. The red light in the corner of the room flashed over the dead bodies of security personnel strewn about the floor. I swallowed the urge to retch. The handiwork of a vicious, powerful Effigy they would never be able to see coming.

"Saul has escaped," cried the voice over the intercom. "All units, all units!"

Saul could have easily disappeared from here. This bloody show was his payback. I figured that was the only reason he'd stay behind. But the whispering from a half-conscious guard lying bloody in the corner told me otherwise. "The program . . . He's heading . . . he's . . ." It was all the man could manage before convulsing into silence.

"Come on." Tearing my eyes away from the dying man, I pulled Rhys through the hall. "We can get out more easily with everyone's attention on Saul."

We stumbled down hallways, stepping over dead bodies along the way. I'd seen too many in my lifetime. But I would never get used to it.

"I never thought that I would come back here," Rhys said after a while, as the alarm blared. "It's the same. Death. Blood. Nothing's changed."

"I know," I whispered, and held him closer to me. "I know what happened here. What they made you do. What they turned your friends into."

"There's more," he said, his left eye closing suddenly as he grunted from a sudden shock of pain. "Soldiers. Not like me. They only controlled me, enhanced my abilities. But these guys . . ." He shook his head. "These guys are like Jessie and the others."

"Fake Effigies." The bodies incubating in the tubes. "I've seen them."

"So have I." His skin turned a shade of fear as he looked at me. "The people here, they've been developing a special suit—the Omega Suit, they call it. It stimulates cell regeneration and speeds up the healing process. I was wearing it too. Kinda helps when a girl's breathing fire in your face," he added, giving me a little smile that made me flustered. But that moment of levity didn't last. "On top of having psychic abilities, they'll be able to heal themselves like an Effigy and live well past the age of a regular human. Blackwell's planning on mass producing them, but, Maia . . . there are already at least a hundred in here."

A mass army bred for destruction. "One problem at a time," I told him, and walked faster. If I stopped moving, my knees would cave in.

"Wait!" Rhys stopped, holding me in place. "There was something else."

"Rhys, what is it?" The alarm seemed to only grow more aggressive. "We need to get the hell out of here!"

"Wait, wait, let me think, let me *think*!" He pushed off me, clasping a hand to his forehead. "I was in another room on the top floor with Grunewald—and Saul. It was just before he was sent to Guadeloupe to find something."

"Find something . . . the key to the code . . . ," I said.

"They were looking at some hieroglyphics or something on a screen. And there was a book. They were trying to read it."

I understood immediately. "I almost forgot! Saul told me not too long ago that Castor's secret volume is here. Hey!" I added, because Rhys was wincing again from the pain. Cupping his head, I searched his eyes. "You need to hold it together. We have to get that book."

Saul may not have known what they'd meant, but Grunewald's people must have been doing what Nathan was trying to do—crack the code themselves without a key. If I stole it back, we could get in front of Blackwell.

"Show me where it is," I told Rhys. It was difficult to sneak through the halls with Rhys still leaning on me, but we managed to evade security personnel and enter an elevator unseen. Most were chasing after Saul elsewhere in the facility. That's why the elevator doors opened into an empty hallway. Rhys took me to a room at the end of the hall that needed a code to enter.

"I think this is it," he said, tapping the key into the pad. Because he'd only seen others enter it, it took him a few tries to remember the exact sequence of numbers and letters, but eventually the doors slid apart.

Emilia's code flashed along a screen that spanned the entire circular room. We were enveloped in them. Chairs were overturned by the terminals, computers left on and running, notebooks, pens, and a couple of cell phones left strewn about the floor. The personnel must have heard the alarm and left in a hurry. Nobody wanted to take a chance while Saul was on a rampage. We went around the entire conference table and began searching the room, but we couldn't find the book anywhere. Saul must have already taken it.

"Here." Rhys limped over to where a blinking flash drive jutted out from the side of a flat-screen. He yanked it out, passing it to me. "They scanned and encoded it onto this thing."

"I thought I'd find you here."

The metal doors shut behind Vasily, back from Coney Island, his long blond hair only partially obscuring the ruined mess of his face. "I can't let you take that, Aidan."

"Vasily," I whispered, surprised to feel Rhys's gentle touch pushing me from him. Without my aid, he stepped forward, the blood still fresh on his shirt.

"You're back, aren't you?" Vasily searched him. "Yes . . . yes, you're back. Completely. I'm glad to see you again, Aidan . . . excited." It was obvious. His expression radiated a twisted sort of joy, like he'd just been given a new weapon to test out on someone's torso. "To be honest, I couldn't stand to see you walking these halls, mindless as a drone. Not when there's still so much we need to talk about."

Neither boy spoke as the alarm shook the facility. They didn't have to. Years of shared torment were written down their bodies in the language of scars. Evil memories screamed from behind their eyes, memories born from this place that used to be their hell.

"It's just like before, isn't it, Aidan?" Vasily shut his eyes, breathing in the chaos outside. "The alarms. The panic. The bodies. The pain. It's almost too much to handle. Do you remember, Aidan?" He opened his eyes again. They were glistening. "Do you?"

"Yeah," Rhys whispered, his fingers twitching closed.

"It doesn't matter what they build here." With a shaky hand, Vasily touched the boils on his face. "Doesn't matter who's in charge or what they do. This place is still the Devil's Hole."

Rhys remained silent. Being in this place with Rhys seemed to loosen whatever strings were still holding Vasily together. It was like too much of the past was flooding into him at once.

"I told you I wanted us to go back." Vasily reached behind his back. "But now that you're here, I can't let you leave."

He pulled out a knife. Its smooth silver blade was already stained with blood. I lifted my fists, power crackling, ready to rush forward, but Rhys stretched out his arm, blocking my path. "Stay out of it," he whispered to me. "Don't get involved."

I stared at him, dumbfounded. *"What?"*

But Rhys didn't tell me again.

"Aidan," he said, trailing a finger gently on the sharp edge. "I was with you when you killed Fisk-Hoffman's son. It was in that messy office of his. I remember it so clearly. The light disappearing from his eyes in those last few seconds."

I didn't realize I'd drawn such a sharp breath, however quiet it was. Rhys's head twitched toward me, but for just a moment. He kept his eyes on Vasily.

"Do you remember what he told you? Before you stabbed him with his own knife?"

"Only one of us is leaving here alive," Rhys said.

Vasily lifted his knife, grinning like the Cheshire cat. "Let's make this quick."

# 25

IT WOULDN'T BE A FAIR FIGHT. RHYS WAS STILL recovering from the Surgeon's wicked hands, but as he'd told me himself, he'd been tortured before. He was acclimatized to pain, taught to power through it. So when Vasily jumped onto the center table and launched himself at Rhys, Rhys ran to meet him, blocking the swing of his knife the way he'd been taught. Vasily tried again, charging for Rhys. Ducking Rhys's swing, Vasily shoved him against the table, pinning him there with his hips before bringing the knife down over his head. Rhys caught his wrist, his back bending under the force of Vasily's attack.

This was insane. Drawing out my power, I let the flames erupt from me, transforming them into the scythe in my hands.

"No!" Rhys knocked the knife out of Vasily's grip and cracked his forehead against his, pushing him back. "I said stay the hell out of it!"

"Why?" I cried as Rhys flipped back onto a table, his bloodstains spreading across his shirt as he found footing. Vasily followed him up and started swinging. I felt useless watching Rhys dodge Vasily's kicks while blood sprayed out of his mouth from his injuries. But I was too scared to argue again, to break his concentration. I knew something was happening in this room that went beyond logic or strategy, something deeper at work in this place where boys had been forged into demons. If this was Rhys's fight, then I had to believe in him. But that didn't mean I had to be a helpless bystander.

I found one of the cell phones lying on the ground. My in-ear communications device was long gone, but I could still contact help. To memorize Sibyl's number, I'd used a jingle from that stupid car commercial that always got stuck in my head growing up.

I dialed, and I heard someone pick up. "Sibyl? *Sibyl!*" I yelled into the receiver.

"Maia?" Sibyl answered. "What—"

I didn't know who'd yelled, Rhys or Vasily. I looked up quickly to see both boys on the table panting and spitting blood.

"I have the secret volume," I said, feeling around for the thin drive in my pocket just to make sure it was still there. "It's digitized. I'm at the Greenland base—track me. Saul's free, and he's going nuts. We need to get the *hell* out of here."

"We'll send the jet to your location. If you can, send the digitized file to Nathan at the number I gave you."

"What about the others?" I blurted out. "What about—Rhys!"

Vasily had taken Rhys and thrown him so hard that his body rolled like a rag doll on the solid marble floor, crashing against the emergency exit.

"Maia?" Sibyl said on the other end of the line. Vasily had picked up his knife and was already halfway across the room, dashing toward Rhys still writhing in pain on the ground. I dropped the phone just as Vasily dragged Rhys up from his collar and kicked him through the exit. A rush of cold air entered the room, slamming the door closed after them.

*"Maia!"* yelled Sibyl, still on the other end.

Stooping down to the floor, I grabbed the phone quickly. "The jet! Come *now.*"

Clicking it off, I stuffed it into my back pocket and ran for the emergency door. It opened to a small, square platform joining to a bridge that stretched over a deep chasm, connecting to the wing of another building. Halfway over the bridge, Rhys was trying to hold off the swings of Vasily's knife, but it was like his former "friend" was toying with him. It was clear Rhys was too worn, too injured to continue this battle for long. I had to do something.

"Rhys!" A snowy wind whipped my hair as I stepped onto the bridge, holding on to the railing. I held my breath, trying not to look down at the fifty-foot drop below. "Rhys!"

"Stay . . ." Rhys inhaled sharply, his hand shaky on the railing. "Stay back . . ."

It sounded like he'd inhaled his own blood because he started coughing over the railing, droplets falling down the chasm, charioted by the wind. Vasily grabbed his neck and held his head there, sliding the knife back into his pants. He wanted to use his hands. Bone shattering bone. It was a more intimate death.

Vasily's laughter broke me. Fury exploded through my arms as fire enveloped my hands. "That's enough!" I cried, running down the bridge to get to them.

"I said, *stay back!*"

I stopped in my tracks a few feet away as Rhys kicked Vasily's shin, elbowing him in the face once the boy lost his grip on his neck. "This isn't your fight."

"What the hell does that even mean?" Snowflakes drifted past my face, the wind chilling the tears budding at the corners of my eyes. "Why are you doing this?"

"Because I'm *his* responsibility. I'm the one monster he helped create." Vasily wiped the blood from his grin. It smeared his cheek up to his rigid cheekbone. "I was too timid to survive in this hellhole. Do you remember, Aidan? The first year was the worst. I was just a boy with no mother, no father. I had nothing. I was shy. I kept to myself. And when the torture was too terrible to bear, I decided that joining my mother was the only option I had left. But *you* . . ." With two quick steps, Vasily was on Rhys. Gripping his collar, he shoved Rhys's back against the railing. "You, the wealthy son from one of the Sect's prestigious families. It was like you already had that brutal instinct in you. Was it your father who taught you?"

Rhys's eyes darted to the metallic mesh flooring, his resultant shiver, rather than a side effect of the cold, seemed to emanate from deep within him. As if in confirmation, Vasily smirked.

"He did, didn't he? Your father taught you how to be cruel. But you were the one who taught me."

It was then that Vasily straightened up. He was very still as he considered the broken boy in his grip, his fingers loosening around Rhys's collar as his mutilated face stiffened.

"You were the one who taught me." His bottom lip was trembling. Years of torment passed between them in the silence of the wind. "You let go first. And then after you let go, you told me it was okay. You taught me brutality was the only way to survive. So I did. I *did* survive. I've survived for years because of what you taught me. Do you understand now, Aidan?"

It was like they both did in that moment. Like they both realized that the evil that took place in the Fisk-Hoffman facility was not a bloody strike from the hands of the adults alone. That evil was a cancer—a cancer that had metastasized, infecting everyone within its walls, a condition of cruelty that passed from adult to child, from child to orphan and back again. It was an evil Rhys had already learned before touching the snowfields of Greenland. A legacy of abuse that flourished in the Devil's Hole. A legacy he passed on to Vasily in the name of survival. A legacy that twisted both boys' souls forever.

Vasily punched Rhys in the stomach.

"Rhys!" I cried, but the moment Rhys lifted his hand to stop me, Vasily punched him in the face. Again. And again.

"You taught me, Aidan." He threw Rhys down the bridge, the metal mesh quivering dangerously. "What was that game we used to play? If you had to kill him, where would you start?" He stalked down the bridge until he was leaning over Rhys. "The jugular?" With his hand, he chopped Rhys in the neck. "Or would you go for one of the major arteries?" He punched Rhys in the chest, barely flinching when Rhys's blood splattered across his face. "You taught me how to survive. You taught me how to kill. Do you understand, Aidan? You ruined me." He slammed Rhys's body against the railing.

"Rhys! Rhys, don't give up!" I said it because Rhys looked as if every accusation Vasily hurled at him struck harder than his blows. He looked tired, worn. Too many bodies broken, too many lives twisted at his hand. "Don't let him kill you!"

Rhys's head twitched toward me, one of his eyes half closed from the swelling, still sparkling with life as he looked at me. Vasily grabbed his chin and forced Rhys's gaze back on him. Years of bottled-up rage had finally exploded. Past taunts, threats, and torment had given way to burning anger Vasily finally allowed his former friend to see in its purest form. And now that the bottle was open, both boys knew it would never be closed again.

"You thought you were protecting me," Vasily said. "But you ruined me. You *ruined* me," he repeated, like he himself was surprised by the realization. "You ruined me . . . like they ruined my mother." The thought of his mother wrung tears out of his eyes. It was like Vasily could see in Rhys's face the faces of all those he'd killed since Rhys first taught him to blur the lines of morality. "You recovered. You went home to your big brother, your powerful father, your loving mother. You cleaned yourself up and buried your past. But I couldn't. I didn't have anyone to go back to. Nobody but ghosts."

"Vasily." Rhys was struggling against his own tears, coughing blood. "I'm sorry." The words were hollowed out with pain. "I'm *sorry.*"

Vasily shook his head, his teeth clenched as he held Rhys in place. "Why?" he said. "Why couldn't you have just let me kill myself back when I had the strength to do it?"

"I'm sorry."

"*Stop telling me you're sorry!*" He punched Rhys with both hands. "I don't need your pity. I don't need *your* pity!" His blazing, tear-filled eyes were on me. "I don't need *anyone's* pity. What I need is the Sect gone. And for everyone who made me suffer"—Vasily gripped Rhys's neck—"to suffer in kind."

As the blood dripped from the corner of Rhys's left eye, I started charging toward them, but Rhys's hand was already on the handle of Vasily's forgotten knife.

"She told me not to let you kill me," Rhys said. "I can't die." And he plunged the knife into Vasily's lower back.

Vasily cried out in pain, stumbling back. Rhys was gasping for air, his chest heaving as he rested against the railing.

"Vasily," he rasped. "Vasily! Oh god!"

Vasily's hand was gripping the handle plunged into his back, but he didn't have the strength to take it out.

"I'm sorry," Rhys said. "I couldn't let you kill me. There's too many people—" Rhys looked at me before shaking his head. "I'm sorry. I'm sorry for everything. I'm sorry."

"I said stop." Vasily's arms dropped to his sides, his body hunched forward. "Stop." He looked up, his eyes flashing. "Stop telling me you're *sorry!*"

Vasily charged at him. With every last bit of strength he had, Rhys dodged Vasily's hands and pushed him away, but the force took Vasily over the railing. I didn't know whether Vasily grabbed for Rhys or Rhys grabbed for him first, but somehow the two boys were tangled up in each other, hurtling over the side of the bridge. Rhys caught the railing in time with his hand, gripping Vasily tight with the other.

"Rhys!" I ran up to them. "Hold on!"

"Hold on," he told Vasily below him. "Hold on, Vasily, I got you!"

But the knife was still in Vasily's back, the blood oozing from the wound and the strain of battle. Neither boy had the strength to hold on.

And yet Vasily Volkov was smiling.

I thought it was the wind stinging my eyes, blurring my vision, but he was smiling. Not that familiar, wicked, Cheshire grin either. It was a true smile. As the snowflakes drifted past his hair, a wave of relief washed over him. The promise of absolution.

I gripped Rhys's arm. And that precise moment, Vasily let go.

"Vasily!" Rhys's scream echoed down the chasm as Vasily's body disappeared into the snow-flurried wind.

I tugged Rhys back over the railing onto the metal grates, catching him as he collapsed to the ground. I thought it was from exhaustion. But when my knees hit the mesh hard, he crumpled into my arms, and I realized that he was sobbing.

"I only wanted to save them." The back of his head brushed against my chin as he lay still, his legs sprawled out over the floor. "I only wanted to save them. I tried to help. But I—"

He was crying. Like the thirteen-year-old Aidan crying in front of the cameras for the Sect officials trying to coax him into forgetting. But he couldn't forget. He would never forget.

"Natalya too. *Howard*. Oh god. I don't deserve to live." He shook his head. "I don't deserve to live."

"But you *have* to live," I whispered. Wrapping my arms around his chest, I rested my cheek against his head. "You have to live and make up for all of it. Even if it takes the rest of your life. You have to live on."

# 26

RHYS SOBBED IN MY ARMS UNTIL HE FELL unconscious.

I knew we couldn't linger there, but Rhys wouldn't wake, so I carried him on my back and tried to find a way out of this hellhole. I waited for the elevator to open, only to find a group of dead guards crumpled and mutilated on the floor. Saul's work. But there was someone left alive—a short, heavyset woman in a lab coat. She was holding a silver briefcase, shivering in the corner, a bloody corpse at her feet.

"Are you okay?" I asked. With Rhys's weight on my back, I couldn't bend down to check on her. She could barely even twitch her head.

"He asked me where they were. After he killed the guards. He left me alive so I could show him. He just . . . walked out of the elevator. . . . He just . . ."

The red veins in her green eyes bulged. Just how long had she been in this elevator? Her black bun was messy and spilling over its binds. The door closed behind us, but the elevator remained still, waiting for our command.

"Where is he?" I asked.

"The basement." Without so much as blinking, she lifted her head to look at me. "The enhanced soldiers of Project X19. As the head of his new organization, Blackwell was planning on using them as his own personal army. Saul's going to free them."

The soldiers. Rhys said there was a hundred of them, but why would he free them unless it was . . .

Unless it was to . . .

"Oh god." Remembering the look of satisfaction as Saul slipped the device out of Grunewald's pocket, I quickly turned to the woman. "Those fake Effigies. Like the Silent Children? They have chips or something embedded at the back of their necks to control them, right?" If I closed my eyes and concentrated, I could still feel the buzz humming beneath my skin where they'd once tried to enslave me. When the woman nodded, I continued to press. "How does it work? How do they get their orders?"

"They're triggered by voice command. Even after freeing them, it'll take up to twenty-four hours for the drugs to wear off and their bodies to be operational, but after that . . ." She shook her head, clutching her briefcase to her chest. "Grunewald was working on the technology—a device that converts the commands into a specific frequency that's picked up by the microchip implant. The original plan was that once the tech is perfect, the soldiers will respond only to Blackwell's commands. Eventually there would be legions of them, all under his control. The soldiers we have now aren't perfect, but they've already been conditioned to respond to the vocal commands of whoever is in control of Grunewald's device. That means . . ."

That meant Blackwell's army was now in Saul's hands. It was a chilling thought, one that left me speechless for almost too long. But I knew I couldn't stand around, and I knew I couldn't take Saul on alone. I had to escape. Regroup with the other girls.

"What's your name?" I asked her.

"H-Hilda . . . Dr. Hilda Feldman." She shifted her feet, blood staining her wing tips. Bloodied and terrified. Good. She deserved it for
contributing to this nightmare.

"Hilda, tell me how to get out of this facility," I said, setting aside
my disgust. "I need to get to the nearest hospital." And when she hesitated, I added, "Or you can stay here and wait for Saul to finish the job.
Your choice."

Hilda staggered to her feet and, with her briefcase in one hand,
began pushing buttons in the elevator. Finally. With Rhys on my back,
I followed her through the bloodied halls to a hangar. From up here on
the side railing, I could see the row of military Jeeps below. Some were
missing, and the hangar door was already open—I supposed we weren't
the only ones who'd cut and run. Hilda almost tripped running down
the steps as the alarms continued to blare.

"There's nobody out for miles," Hilda said as she got into the
driver's seat, dumping her briefcase behind her.

I laid Rhys out in the backseat. "I guess you can't very well call the
cops to come over when you've got a basement full of secret supersoldiers, can you?"

Hilda flinched at my words, twitching again when I slid into the
passenger seat and shut the door. "I . . . I'm not—"

"Save it for the interrogation," I said. "Drive—"

Before I even got the word out, a gunshot pierced the night, the
bullet hitting the steering wheel between Hilda's fingers.

We both looked up at the same time, but only I called out the name
of the girl who stood behind the railing above us, her gun smoking.

*"June?"* I lifted myself out of my seat to see her more clearly.

"Saul's not done with you yet, Maia!" June called, the gun steady in
her hands.

But June wasn't aiming for me. No matter how twisted she was, she wasn't willing to shoot me in the head—at least not yet. But the longer she remained with monsters, the more comfortable she looked playing the part of one. Her goal was to bring me to Saul, who hadn't yet been able to excavate Marian's secrets from within me. My sister was still a puppet.

"Wait," I said as Hilda took off. "Wait!"

Luckily for me, Hilda wasn't stupid enough to listen to me. I swerved and fell back onto the seat as she floored it for the open hangar, ducking her head each time we heard June's gunshots missing their target. As we left the hangar and drove out into the open field of snow, I looked back at the receding image of my sister, disappearing into the darkness.

"I'm sorry, sis," I whispered. Shaking my head, I looked up at the night sky, blinking back tears under the heavenly scrawl of the Northern Lights.

It took a little more than an hour to reach the snowy town of Nuuk. Rushing straight into their busy hospital was a dumb, risky move for an Effigy on the run. But they had a conscience. It didn't matter to them that the Effigy they'd all seen on TV had carried the broken, dying body of a boy into their emergency room. What mattered was that she was begging them to save him.

I watched them haul Rhys into surgery, and then I sat down in the waiting room. Hilda was with me, but only because I threatened her before getting here.

"You dare try to run away, and when Saul eventually finds me and asks me how I got out, I'll point him right in your direction, Dr. *Feldman*."

I was sure it didn't hurt that she could see the fire burning from the tips of my fingers. I probably could have been nicer to her. After all, it was because of that strange injection she'd given Rhys on the way that he had a chance at recovering.

"It speeds up antibody production and, to some extent, cell regeneration," she'd told me after plunging the needle into Rhys's heart. "Because our enhanced subjects still aren't complete, they're physically vulnerable to the effects of the cylithium in their system, so they require constant maintenance. I was on my way to deliver these to them when . . . when Saul attacked."

Rhys's body had immediately relaxed after that, his desperate gasps for air easing into normal breathing. I could only hope that whatever she'd given him would help him get back on his feet. If not . . .

I sighed. Hilda sat next to me in the empty waiting room for three hours in silence, agitated but too scared to even make a move for the bathroom. Which was how I wanted it.

There was a television screen on the side wall playing the news. It was all in Dutch, but images were worth a thousand words: namely, the image of Blackwell's broad form sweeping out of his limo and into the United Nations building while a crowd gathered around him. A group of official-looking men and women had arrived too, in their expensive black cars, dignitaries, ministers, press, and security trickling into the tall building in Manhattan as the flags of nations billowed in the gentle breeze. The Assembly had begun.

I wondered if they knew that Blackwell had an arsenal of weapons at his disposal ready to threaten them if they turned down his great plan: the creation of a united world force with Blackwell at the helm. Except the soldiers he was planning on using for his own personal paramilitary force were now in Saul's hands. Even though he still had control over Minerva, it was a big blow to him. But nobody was any safer with those soldiers in Saul's control.

What was Saul planning to do? Didn't he want the rest of the stone? Yes, since the beginning, it was all he'd asked for. Even if he was under control, at least part of that was his will. The will to reshape the world. To change fate. Only now he would do it his way. Whatever he was after, it was bigger than just Marian, the girl whose death he wanted to atone for.

I attempted to sort through what I could remember of Marian's memories in my head. The three symbols she'd given to Emilia, symbols I'd seen many times before. Her conversations with a very disturbed Alice. Strangely enough, what struck me most was that I now knew where she came from. The same place as that Tinubu woman. An African country, perhaps. Egbaland.

*I have to go back to Egbaland.* . . . I remembered her voice, desperate as she pleaded with Nick. *I have to go back for Tinubu's treasure.* . . .

Egbaland. Tinubu. Marian must have lived there as a child as one of Tinubu's slaves. And as a slave, she'd met with the first of the Blackwells. She'd gone with him along with so many other slaves Tinubu had traded for a treasure . . . Tinubu's treasure. . . .

"Sit down," I said once Hilda finally gathered the courage to stand. She probably thought I was too distracted by the television. "You're not going anywhere until my team gets here. You have a lot to answer for."

Biting her lip, Hilda slowly sat back in her chair. "I'm not what you think," she said. "I didn't work exclusively on the enhanced soldiers. I was primarily in the biomedical division."

I glared at her. "Doesn't really matter which division you worked for when every division worked for Team Evil."

"I was largely working on medical research," she insisted.

"Oh yeah? What research?"

"Stem cell research for the purposes of neuro-regeneration and neural tissue engineering. It was a special project. His personal project."

She folded her arms across her chest because she knew she'd said too much. When I leaned over, she turned from me, but she didn't dare move.

"Whose personal project?"

*"Maia!"*

Because I thought it was the doctor, I jumped to my feet the moment I heard my name. It didn't register until I saw them run up to me that it was Brendan's voice. And he wasn't alone. I let out a relieved laugh seeing Lake and Chae Rin brush past him and reach me first. Lake threw her arms around me, wailing immediately.

"This is a hospital," Chae Rin hissed as Lake sobbed on my shoulder. She was looking stronger after her fight with Belle, healthier. They were all wrapped in warm winter parkas, which I could have used right about then. With our car heater broken, I'd managed to survive the drive here only by generating flames in my hands.

"Oh my god, we thought Saul had killed you!" Lake said when she could manage it. Clasping a hand to her chest, she stepped back. "Then Sibyl told us where you were—we got here as soon as we could."

"Maia." Brendan walked up to me and grabbed both my shoulders. "Is my brother . . . ? Is Aidan here?"

"He's been in surgery," I answered him. "I've been waiting here for hours, but they've given me no updates. He fought Vasily. Vasily didn't make it, but . . . it was . . . pretty brutal."

"Oh god," he whispered, lowering his head.

"Sibyl told us you have the secret volume." Cheryl had just walked into the hallway after talking to some staff members.

"I used that woman's phone to send the digital file to my uncle on the way to the hospital," I told her. I'd been able to reach him too. Good old nerdy Uncle Nathan had cracked the key. He was probably halfway through the volume by now. Needless to say, Hilda didn't get her phone back.

"Good. We need to regroup. Authorities already know you're here, so if we're going to sneak you out, we'll have to do it in plain sight. As far as the hospital staff knows, you Effigies are in Brendan's custody, and I'm his partner." Cheryl flashed a fake badge. I turned to Brendan, but right now he didn't seem to care much about the conversation. He walked over to the seat, entwining his fingers together and waited for news on his brother. "We talked to the local police as well," Cheryl continued. "They think they're letting us transfer you to the CSTF headquarters in New York. Uh . . . again. But we'll actually be heading to Seattle to meet Nathan."

I didn't much like the idea of having to fight my way through all those phantoms, but until we could properly clear our names, where else could they take us that we wouldn't still be hunted?

"Wait a second." Chae Rin brushed past us to where Hilda was sitting perfectly still, hoping nobody would notice her. Probably waiting for her chance to ditch. That chance had just gone up in flames. "Who the hell is this?"

"She worked in the Greenland facility," I told them, and immediately their eyes were trained on her like a gun. "Though she says she wasn't on Project X19. She worked on a different project."

"But you'll still be an important witness when we bring Blackwell in front of the International Criminal Court," Cheryl said. "Sibyl's talking to the United States attorney general as we speak about searching the Greenland facility."

"It won't do any good," Hilda said, and I knew she was right. "Saul's already taken it over. Most of us are . . . dead." She let out a puff of breath meant to be a laugh as she lost focus, slipping into her own memories. "And he has control of them—the soldiers we developed."

"It's true," I said, hating that I had to break the news because of the resultant looks of sheer terror on everyone's faces. "I have no idea what he even wants to do with them. But he has them. He wants the stone, too." I remembered the way he twitched and shook as he thought of the stone in his hands even while he was still under Grunewald's control.

"But if we had the stone . . . ," Lake said. "I mean, if it's really that powerful, we could use it for ourselves, right? We could fix this mess. Stop Saul and Blackwell."

"We don't know how it works," said Cheryl. "It could be dangerous."

"No, she's right." A stone that could grant wishes. The endless possibilities that came with the power to conquer fate. It was a power that didn't have to be used only by the malicious and the power hungry. "What if we used it?" I asked them. "If we had that stone, we could stop Saul. We could use it as a weapon against those soldiers."

Cheryl frowned. "Maia . . ."

"Well, do you have a better idea?" I yelled a little too loudly, spooking the nurses at the other end of the hall. "We're up against an entire fleet of Effigies with no conscience. Not to mention my sister's still out there, Saul's still out there, and *oh yeah*, Belle's still working for Blackwell. How do you suppose we stop them?"

The stone. The stone was the key.

And yet . . .

*I have to go back to Egbaland. . . .*

"I'm with her." Lake nodded quickly. "Personally, I don't like our odds."

Cheryl let silence stretch between us before speaking again. "And what will it cost to use it?"

The cost. I almost forgot. Even the shard of stone in Saul's ring required a sacrifice of death. If there really was more of it out there, and we reached it—who would have to die before we could use it?

And yet . . .

Egbaland . . . the secret Vogel had told her . . .

"Either way, we still need to get it before he does." Chae Rin lowered her voice as a few doctors walked past. "Maybe we could destroy it."

"I guess we'll have to consider it after we get to Nathan," said Cheryl.

"Wait." I grabbed Cheryl's arm before she could turn.

"What is it?"

There was something important that I was missing. In that jail cell and in the facility with Saul. Both times, Marian had been trying to tell me something important. During Grunewald's experiment, too many of her memories had flooded into my head at once, mixed with Saul's sorrowful journey into enslavement. But something was niggling at me. I couldn't ignore it.

The other stone. The stone that had protected Tinubu's people from danger, transforming her land into a place of pure calm.

Shards that were now buried in the Deoscali Temple.

"We have to go back to Basse-Terre," I said. "And this time, we're all going."

"What?" Cheryl wasn't the only one who'd said it, but she protested the loudest. "That's almost half a day's travel. We need to rendezvous with Nathan—"

"We can talk to them on the way." I was desperate. "Please. I know it sounds insane, but the Assembly's supposed to go on for three days, right? We have time! There's something there I need." I turned to Chae Rin and Lake. "It's about Marian's memories. I need to show you both. We all need to go there."

Everyone looked at one another wearily. Cheryl and Brendan may not have been convinced, but the other Effigies, even without me needing to say any more—they believed me. Once again, they stood by me.

"Let's do it, then," said Chae Rin. "Let's go to Basse-Terre."

Cheryl and Brendan exchanged weary looks, but ultimately agreed.

"I'll stay here and wait for my brother to wake up." Brendan stood and pulled some cuffs out of his jacket pocket. "After I transport you to the city jail for aiding and abetting a terrorist Effigy," he said to Hilda as he pulled her arms behind her back and locked her in the steel.

"Call me the minute you hear anything," I told him.

He nodded. With one last look down the halls where they had wheeled Rhys's body, I followed the others out of the hospital.

# 27

NEW YORK. A CORRESPONDENT STOOD OUTSIDE
a tall tower blanketed in windows, far enough away from the crowds
for her voice to be picked up by her microphone. The wind blew her
blond curls about her face as the flags of nations flapped behind her.

"Yes, Pat, now that a few hours have passed since the start of the
Assembly here at the UN Headquarters in New York, we have several
big updates to report. First, the Assembly has agreed to the organiza-
tional restructuring of the Sect, which would include a redistribution
of the powers of authority to international sovereign states. Now,
there were some who wondered if this would mean suspending the
Greenwich Accords, signed after World War One, which forbid the
Sect, as an organization, to interfere with the parliamentary affairs of
countries. The answer to that question is no. The document was signed
originally to ensure the Sect wouldn't use their arsenal and authority
to interfere in world politics. This still must be an important feature
of the new system. However, in this case, it will be the world's govern-
ments controlling the antiphantom security of the world as one."

The gray-haired news anchor appeared in a split screen next to her.

"But, Margaret, does this mean that we can say that the Sect has effectively been dissolved?"

"Essentially, yes. The Sect is a large organization, and they estimate it'll take another year to finalize its reorganization. In the meantime, antiphantom operations have been left to individual military forces. However, this is only going to be temporary. Because of the limited resources of certain countries and differential military might, the Assembly still believes that a separate, large-scale, intercountry coalition needs to be formed to take on the burden of protecting humanity from the phantoms. It seems that they're seriously considering the proposal Blackwell the sixth, former representative of the High Council, just submitted an hour ago."

"Now, this proposal isn't just a dissolution of the Sect, is it?" asked Pat.

"No, Patrick. Blackwell has unveiled what he calls the Oslo Agreement, inspired by the treaty previously signed in Greenwich. He seems to have the full support of the former High Council and several high-ranking officials of the Inter-Parliamentary Union, all of whom are at the Assembly. These documents propose a united world force composed of a special military unit specifically enhanced for battling phantoms."

"Enhanced? Enhanced in what way?"

"I'm not sure about that, Pat," said the correspondent. "But I am hearing rumors that soldiers from various military forces who join this antiphantom worldwide task force will have the opportunity to sign up for a special enhancement program. Right now I believe the Assembly has put forward nominations for leader of the united military force, and from what I can tell, Blackwell himself seems to be a logical and favored candidate."

"Let's play the clip," the host said, and sure enough, the station played a thirty-second clip of Blackwell standing on a stage in front of a podium, green marble tiles framing the screen behind him.

"The weakness in both the ideology and the organization of the Sect has allowed terrorism to grow unhindered within the organization," Blackwell said. "However, through its exposure, it's given us a way for humanity to move forward, away from the archaic systems of the past." He stretched out his hands, his arms hovering beside the microphones on the podium he stood behind. "The United Earth Specialized Forces will revolutionize the way humanity will deal with the phantoms for centuries to come. If you were to elect me as the leader of these forces, as long as I hold office, I would always do my utmost to prioritize the safety of the citizens of this globe, just as you all have placed the citizens of your country before all else."

"Ugh, enough of this," Cheryl said. By the time Pat brought several paid pundits on set to speculate and overanalyze for what would probably be the next hour, Cheryl knew to turn off the streaming feed.

"Sibyl's still in Washington, isn't she?" asked Chae Rin, slumping back into her seat as Cheryl shut her laptop. "You sure we shouldn't be there with her for backup or something?"

The winter parkas were stuffed in one of the seats behind us. Inside the jet, there was no need for them. The roar of the jet's engine was a soothing lull in the background, but we were all still on edge. "Sibyl has her job," said Cheryl. "The bureaucratic knots are making her crazy, but she'll be in New York as soon as she can. Hopefully with the information you've gathered, she'll be able to stall the debates and expose Blackwell."

"Yeah, but will she be able to stop him if he uses the aces up his sleeve?" Chae Rin lay her head against the wall. She still had her corduroy jacket on, though she didn't seem to notice how often she tugged at the rope strings of her hood. "Or am I the only one who remembers the dude has a death weapon? Even if they don't let him get his way, how many people is he going to take out in the interim?"

"Not to mention Saul's still out there with control of the fake Effigies." Lake groaned. "This is awful."

Awful was an understatement. Part of me wondered if I had sent us all in the wrong direction. But if we were in New York, we'd be as helpless as we were in London when we watched Prince fire Minerva on Oslo. Going back to the temple felt right. I couldn't place my finger on why I hadn't been able to relax since the thought popped into my mind at the hospital.

Cheryl took out her phone and began to dial. "We're already en route to Guadeloupe. Let's concentrate on what we need to do." The ringing stopped. Someone had picked up. "Nathan? Nathan, do we have you?"

"Yep." Uncle Nathan's voice came through the speaker.

The four of us were gathered around the same table in the jet, snacks from the Nuuk hospital vending machine strewn about the surface. Because we all felt like we hadn't slept in days, we'd waited a few hours before contacting him. Aside from giving us time to rest, it had the added bonus effect of giving Uncle Nathan more time to translate Castor's volume.

"Honestly, the fact that the researchers in Greenland were able to digitize the volume is pretty incredible. But what I've read?" He whistled. "If even half of this is true, then good lord."

"Have you finished reading everything?" I asked him, sitting next to Lake, who'd just picked a stray pretzel off the table.

"Not everything. But . . . a lot. Castor's extremely wordy, even in code. I've transcribed the bits I believe are most important."

I thought of Marian's body crashing against the piano keys, dead at her lover's hands. The mystery that murdered her and Natalya, that twisted the lives of countless others, was now within our grasp. "Read us what you have," I said. "Start from the beginning."

## *"London, 1870*

"*The first volume of my chronicles, I imagine, is the most important one I shall write, though I pray that the wrong people shall never lay eyes upon it. For years I have wondered if perhaps it would be better off never written. Too many men have desires to learn the secrets of the world. But too few men understand the dangers that are to be found in those unseen places. Benjamin and I were once such foolish men, convinced of our own brilliance as we traveled the world with dreams of the glory that would be bestowed upon us by Her Majesty the Queen. The lesson we learned was learned too late. The evil our hubris wrought upon the world cannot be undone. There is no atonement possible for the part we played in bringing about disaster. Benjamin already died the day those nightmares fell from the sky as a plague upon our lands. All I can do is document our descent into the depths of hell, document our efforts to restore the world we savaged. Document in hopes that one day our misdeeds might be corrected.*

"*I write this volume in part thanks to Miss Emilia Farlow, whose brilliant and sometimes strange mind concocted the code with which I write this work. It was a code she spent several weeks developing, a code inspired by the three symbols Benjamin and I had once crafted during those days at sea. Perhaps this is her penance. It was she who told me of the dangerous game those girls played, she who showed me my own three symbols so that I may believe in their story. But although I shared with her but some of the mysteries I had learned from my encounters with "them," I did not tell her about their existence. No soul, not even the Council, knows of the source of the power that created the phantom beasts. This story I tell is one that must be told before the others, even if few eyes shall ever lay upon it. The final story, I hope, has yet to be written."*

"So this isn't the thirteenth volume." I leaned over, propping myself up against the table. "It's the first."

"Volume zero," Lake chimed in, crunching her pretzels. "What I don't get is why the queen of England would be interested in two blokes traveling around looking for—what did he call them?"

"The secrets of the world," I whispered. The unseen forces.

"Uh, wait, yeah. I think he mentions it early on." I could hear Uncle Nathan flipping through pages. "See, because there's so much content here and a lot of it, like I mentioned, is kind of superfluous, I broke everything down into categories and indicated page references."

"He's got lots of little tabs in there." That was Pete in the background. Lake perked up. "Yellow ones, long ones, red ones—the book isn't even that big."

"Hi, honey!" Lake waved at the phone, much to Chae Rin's and Cheryl's annoyance. "It's been so long!"

"It's been, like, three days...," I muttered, scoffing at them both.

"That Lake?" asked Pete at the same time I spoke, burying my voice. "How've you been, Vicky? How was the trip?"

"To Greenland? Great, all things considered." Lake popped another pretzel in her mouth. "It's such a lovely place. Once we can come out of hiding, we should totally go—"

*"To answer your question,"* Uncle Nathan interrupted rather loudly. Lake covered her mouth with her fingers and piped down. "The Sect actually started out as a council, much like the Council we have now. Seven families. It used to be passed down, but I think eventually, as

the Sect became more worldwide, they started opening up to a more democratic selection process. The only families here that seem to have been kept on the roster are the Haas family and—"

"The Rhys family," I finished for him. Naomi had told us in Madrid. I'd asked her once about the Seven Secret Houses and she'd told me that it was just a moniker they'd kept to continue to conceal the identities of the Council. But for the Haas and Rhys families, their service to the Sect had truly been since the Sect's inception—and even before that, if what Castor was saying was true. I would have asked Naomi if she weren't resting. Maybe that was for the best. She'd already made the step toward coming to terms with her sons' "death." I wasn't sure if her heart could take news about Rhys until I was sure he was going to be okay.

"According to Castor, he gave this volume to the Haas family so that they'd protect the secrets inside for as long as they were able," Uncle Nathan continued. "He knew the family. They trusted each other. The Rhys family stayed on, as the creation of the Council was their idea. Back then the Council wasn't interested in protecting the world—there were no phantoms to protect the world *from*. They were considered some of the greatest minds in England with the biggest resources. They were commissioned by the British Crown to study and retrieve supernatural artifacts. It's not too hard to believe considering the frenzied interest in the occult at that time. The Brits planned on using these objects as part of their arsenal to aid in their imperial endeavors."

"Not unlike Blackwell." Chae Rin rolled her eyes. "So glad we've evolved since the days of colonialism, eh?"

"Yeah, actually, Blackwell was mentioned here." Uncle Nathan was flipping through pages. "Blackwell the first."

"Blackwell told us at Carnegie Hall that he was a self-made man." I paused. "Um, our Blackwell said that about Blackwell the first."

"Ugh, why the hell do they all have the *same damn name?*" Groaning, Chae Rin bit off some of a chocolate bar.

"Blackwell the first *was* a self-made man—and a pompous man with a chip on his shoulder. Always jealous of the wealth others were born into. Castor seems to hate him. He made his fortune off real estate, speculating, and fur trading. Officially. What he didn't advertise is that he sold slaves on the side, even after abolition."

So he traded slaves—like the slaves he traded Tinubu for the stone he'd given her, the stone he'd stolen, thinking he was taking her for a fool. Marian was among them. Little did he know that somehow that stone was responsible for sparing her people from the onslaught of the phantoms.

"Because of his illegal activities, he was looked down on by many members of the Council. No matter how badly he wanted to be included, he wasn't intelligent enough or grand enough to make the cut of their exclusive club. But they gladly strung him along, using his money, resources, and networks for their expensive travels nonetheless. Couldn't have sat well with him."

A generational grudge. The Blackwells were never given a seat at the table. So somewhere along the line, they decided to build their own table and set fire to everything else.

"What about the symbols?" I asked him. "While I was scrying, I saw Marian scribble down three symbols she handed to Emilia to give to Castor. I thought Emilia was the one who created the secret code he used for the volume, but when she saw those three symbols, she didn't look like she even recognized them. So Castor and this Benjamin guy created them originally?"

"Just those three," Uncle Nathan said. "Those three symbols were the ones Castor and Benjamin created to represent how they found the stone. Remember what he wrote in the very first pages of the book

I read to you: Castor thinks Emilia was inspired by those particular symbols to make her cipher, but other than that, Emilia had nothing to do with them."

Castor also said it took several weeks for Emilia to come up with her code. Marian only knew the three symbols Benjamin and Castor had created. She wrote them down for Emilia to give to Castor, certain that upon seeing it, he'd come to understand, fully, what had happened. More specifically, he'd come to realize that the fall of York was connected to their explorations. If Marian knew those three symbols, then at least one of the men must have taught them to her at one point. But why would either explorer even bother to share information with a servant?

"So what do the symbols mean?" Lake folded her arms. "And it better be good because I've been waiting a long damn time to hear this."

"Uh . . ." Uncle Nathan laughed. "Well, I don't know if it'll make sense at first. Just wait a minute. Let me get there. I'll have to skip some of the minute details of his observational data."

Uncle Nathan flipped through his notes and paused. "Honestly," he said. "This is where things get a little . . . strange."

"Strange?" Cheryl adjusted the phone on the table. "What do you mean?"

"What I mean is, how willing are you to suspend disbelief?"

Chae Rin snorted. "I mean, we already live in a world with phantoms, magic stones, and superpowered girls. Weird supernatural shit being real is kind of a given at this point, don't you think?"

Uncle Nathan hesitated. "Okay, true," he said. "Well, don't say I didn't warn you."

*"For ten years we had been hearing of these lands during our explorations, sometimes whispered in village taverns as foolish tales. There were, as we'd*

*learned, lands that seemed rich with heaven's blessings, lands where navigation instruments ceased to function. We'd read about them in the travels of other explorers—those, for example, who had traveled to the Caribbean islands. Places of the purest calm. Though each tale we heard differed in miniscule ways, each incarnation held what we deduced was a morsel of truth that painted a broader narrative—the narrative of mystic lands yet undiscovered.*

*"The goal we had been entrusted with by the British Crown had necessitated that we become men driven not by science but mystery, framing our explorations around tales and legend. Unlike Benjamin, the method of combining the sciences of cartography and astronomy with the inexact speculations born from interest in the occult had always left me somewhat uneasy. However, it was within the uncertainty born of the uneasy marriage of magic and science that Benjamin thrived. There were limits to where science could take mankind. Benjamin had always told me as such. The limit was that of the human mind. The endless possibilities of the supernatural, the unseen forces of the world, went beyond the confines of the particularities of science, rules, and methods that we had become prisoners within. If we were going to discover the undiscoverable, we would need to accept the unacceptable. We would need to be able to suspend our disbelief, to rethink the world around us, and to use the rules of science only insofar as they would allow us to reach the place where these rules no longer mattered. New rules emerged in those spaces that existed beyond the confines of our imagination. And beyond these confines, we would find them. The beings that dwell within those lands.*

*"Each legend wrote that we would find them only in the time of our death, because it was they who controlled life and death. Indeed, they had existed in different mythologies and in different tales. The Three, the ones who plan out the life spans of man, they were the ones who controlled men's fates.*

*"During our investigations, we learned of a Scottish man who'd*

indicated the same, a man who'd died as a child and come back to life speaking mysteries. After many weeks, we tracked him to a tavern in Turkey. Now old and wretched, he said to us this: 'Only those who have died, if their desire to see them is strong enough, can cross the gate into their godly domain.'

"The old man had never seen them, only learned of their existence in the short time he had died. Death is not perfect, he told us. Over thousands of years, there had been small numbers of men like him who had died and returned with cosmic secrets. Now decrepit and fearful, he warned us of our ambitions. He told us the penalty would be too great. Only misfortune would follow. For a time, I listened to him.

"It was Benjamin who convinced me not to be deterred from the path we had already set out for ourselves, a path that could lead us to glory and knowledge beyond our wildest dreams. Now that we knew of their existence, we could desire to be in their presence. But if we could only see them through the eyes of death, then to find those three, the only choice left open to us was to die.

"Through the blackest of channels, Benjamin secured the drug made from the azalea plant and several other compounds. The purpose was to induce death for but a few moments. To give ourselves eyes of death to see the mysteries we could then bring back with us into life. However, our first attempt in the Americas was unsuccessful. It corroborated the tale we heard once in Greece and was confirmed by the Scottish man: that these beings do not dwell in one place, but many. And that wherever their three bodies reside, the land is bound to become blessed for years to come, even after their departure.

"It was the tenth of March, 1856, when we deduced the pattern. Ten years of documenting, of planning, of tracking the natural patterns and rhythms through new technology that we finally predicted the current dwelling place of those beings. The key was the pattern of the eclipse, where the flames of the sun become obscured by the moon, casting darkness upon the earth. *After a fortnight, we found them in the lands passed over by the eclipse's shadow.*

*"We found them.*

*"What I will describe next is a mystery I would not have believed if it were not for seeing it with my own eyes. Death eyes, Benjamin called them. We separated from our crew, isolating ourselves to bear the risk upon our own shoulders. After taking the poison, with our strong desire to see them carrying us to unconsciousness, our souls left our bodies and crossed over into their realm.*

*"So little from that time do I remember. Time passed differently. Eons and decades and seconds became one. I was adrift in streams of glorious light that saturated the world. This incredible, mysterious substance in the realm of the dead. And within the realm of the dead: they who live in their own domain, their presence a gathering point of potent energy that can only be relieved—only* gradually *be relieved—upon their dispersal. It is the reason they are constantly roaming, the reason why the lands remain blessed for years after they abandon it.*

*"It was the energy, the light that carried me through the gates of heaven into their haven. And the Three I found there.*

*"Death.*

*"Life.*

*"And the greatest among them: fate.*

*"Three beings. Three goddesses controlling the time of men.*

*"They see all, they told us. All life. All humanity. Through their eyes and through their eyes alone do they see all. By the words they utter, we so live. By the words they utter, we so die. Since we had found them in their place of dwelling, they could not just let us go. They asked us our wish, though they warned us it may not be as we desired. 'Let me see what you see,' Benjamin had asked them. 'Give me your power. Give me the gift of fate.'*

*"And so fate gave us her eye so that we would see.*

"*Man's hubris had piqued their curiosity. The stone can grant wishes, they told us. But what would we do with the power of fate? How would we change the fates of mankind? They desired to observe us, to see for themselves the actions of mankind. But they warned us as such: The pathways of life, death, and fate are one. To manipulate the course of fate comes at a sacrificial cost. Benjamin told them he understood.*

"*He did not.*

"*They must have known themselves, the goddesses. It was because of that another eye was given. Another gift: the gift of life. To protect us from the consequences of our follies, the benevolent goddess said. Perhaps she had seen a future we could not.*

"*They told us that no matter how perfectly mankind mastered the tools of discovery, we would not find them again. Except in one instance. I shall never utter the gruesome secret they told us here, not in word nor in code. I did not know until many years afterward that Benjamin had already confided in the least likely of listeners. Perhaps in despair. Perhaps in jest. Before he died, he'd given that servant the knowledge that no other besides us holds.*

"*When we awoke again in our bodies, we were each holding a stone. Blue and white. Life and fate. The eyes of the goddesses that they themselves had given us. Proof that what we had seen, though existing beyond our imagination, had not existed beyond our reality. We had aims to bring the stones back to the British Crown. Our crew was enraged. They did not understand. They had not seen what we had seen, and to them the stones were nothing but useless jewels in our hands. The Crown would never accept it, they told us. It was an opinion shared by Blackwell, who met us on our way back to Britain. However, the tawdry man must have seen some worth in them—monetary, of course. Until his death, Benjamin had thought that he had lost the stone of life. It was only upon Blackwell's death-bed that he confessed he had stolen it, appraised it. It was a jewel, after all, and a pretty one. At the very least, it was worthy of his collection. He did not tell me to whom he had given it.*

*"However, it was after losing the stone of life that Benjamin became paranoid. What if the power of fate he had in his hands was taken from him? And so rather than bring it before the Council, he took the stone of fate to his estate and began his experiments. The stone required a sacrifice, but what sacrifice could twist the power of fate? Years passed, and he became obsessed with learning its secret, obsessed with the goddesses. I returned from a later travel to find sculptures of those three in his estate. Three sets of three goddesses, produced by a French sculptor, commissioned by Benjamin. One set in the dining room, one in the parlor, and the one in the courtyard he gave to me. It was a good-natured gesture he'd called a symbol of our friendship. I suspect, rather, that it was an attempt to assuage my fear for his sanity.*

*"Three sets of three, always the same three:* fātum. *Fate. His hunger. His thirst. The obsession drove him to the edge of madness, but alas, the ones who suffered most were those closest to him—his wife and little daughter, battered for years at his hands. They never could quite conceal their bruises, despite their efforts. And despite* my *best efforts, I couldn't stop my friend from his futile pursuits, even after he'd killed his wife. The symbols we created to represent the connection: the flame of the sun, the shadows of the eclipse, and the fates. He had drawn them again and again in his study, pages of them, questions with no answers. It was not until Emilia told me their story that I realized it was not Benjamin who would discover the secret of stone or the sacrifice that would awaken it.*

*"It was his daughter. It was Alice."*

"Okay, wait." I buried my head in my hands, running my fingers through my hair, bringing them around until they were covering my mouth. "Just wait."

"Goddesses," Cheryl said, sitting back in her chair. "Goddesses of fate." The thought seemed to terrify her. Humanity had long believed that we weren't alone on this planet with only those creatures we could *see*. Every culture seemed to believe that there were godlike beings that could control the fates of men. Well, I guess they were right. But Castor's tale was a truth that none of us had expected. I didn't know how to feel. I didn't know what else I could do except take it for what it was.

"Goddesses? Like those statues we saw in Prague." Lake swallowed her pretzel and looked at the empty, torn package as if her appetite had suddenly been snatched away. "Castor said Vogel gave him one set, and Castor gave the Haas family the secret volume. Maybe they got the statues out of the deal too?" Lake thought about it. "Well, I wouldn't want to keep a keepsake from my loony, wife-murdering friend either."

It could have been more than that. The statues of the goddesses were a symbol of their exploration. A symbol of the moment their lives turned upside down forever. A symbol of that which had driven his friend to insanity.

"Blackwell had them too." I remembered them strewn about his estate. The original Blackwell might have purchased them—unless he stole them too.

Chae Rin, who'd been confident in her ability to suspend disbelief, looked pale, but she remained as calm as she could, tapping her nails against the table as if the continuous rhythm kept her sane. "So . . ." She paused. "Castor claims that he and Benjamin copped a couple of eyes from the fates. Do we believe him?"

A part of me didn't want to. But there were too many aspects of his tale that made sense. Lands of perfect calm, blessed by the presence of the goddesses. I'd felt it myself in Pastor Charles's chamber, in the museum in Prague, and most recently in the temple—which had shards of that blue stone, the stone Blackwell had stolen and given to

Tinubu. The stone of life. The *Eye* of Life protecting man from the consequences of a future we could not possibly have foreseen ourselves.

"Hey, guys." Dot could be heard now through the speaker. "For a few pages, Castor goes on to detail exactly where he'd found lands of calm in the past. Pete and I cross-checked with cylithium-rich areas, and sure enough, they correspond. Basse-Terre was on the list."

"You're saying that cylithium is connected to the goddesses?" I asked.

"Castor mentioned something somewhere else in the volume," Uncle Nathan said. "Some theory he came up with and added to the secret volume after years of researching how and why the phantoms materialized around the world. Remember he said that wherever the goddesses were, a mysterious energy would converge, and to keep the balance, they'd have to leave. It would take years afterward for that pool of energy to disperse. Castor believed that before the phantoms came, those were the same places of calm 'blessed by the heavens,' or however he put it. Why? Because the presence of the goddesses can still be felt there." He reread the portions about the lands of calm, the constant roaming of the goddesses. "Castor came to believe that some physical form of that energy existed in the realm of the living too, as something we could feel."

"Cylithium," Dot interjected, and I couldn't miss the excitement in her voice. "Cylithium might be the physical form of the energy that we can actual feel. With the rest beyond the veil. Imagine."

"Castor theorized that phantoms were born out of that otherworldly energy," Nathan continued, "and that if the energy exists everywhere, then technically so could phantoms. But that also would mean that most phantoms would appear in those places still rich from the goddesses's presence. And as we know, phantoms do tend to pop up most in cylithium-heavy areas. It adds up."

That was why humanity needed antiphantom devices to block frequencies and carve out safe areas to live in, why we gathered in cylithium-deficit areas—areas where that metaphysical energy Castor spoke of was in balance. Of course, that was also why phantoms could appear in those areas *anyway* the moment our APDs stopped working. The phantoms came from that energy. Inside the cellar in Prague, inside Pastor Charles's chamber and the Deoscali Temple, the air had been so cylithium-rich that it felt like phantoms would sprout from nowhere.

Those places of calm left vacant by the goddesses, saturated in the white streams of fate, death, and life—before the phantoms came, before Castor and Vogel found those beings, those places of calm they'd found in their travels were *actually* calm. Now they were the perfect breeding ground for phantoms. How ironic.

"But the Deoscali Temple was protected," Dot said. "A pure spot in the middle of a Dead Zone."

"Because the life stone was there," I told them. "The presence of a goddess is *still* there protecting that place. If not, it would have been overrun by phantoms." A chill ran through me as I remembered just barely escaping them. "Castor must have gotten the stone back."

"Castor mentions a protected place in the first volume," said Uncle Nathan. "In one spot, he talks about encountering a woman named Madam Tinubu, a slave trader and businesswoman in Western Africa at the time."

"Yeah, I read it in Blackwell's study during his gala or whatever." He'd circled phrases and written words in the text itself. He must have been researching Castor's and Benjamin's travels. "He said there was a treasure buried beneath the lands keeping her safe. It must have been the eye. The first Blackwell bargained it to her for slaves, thinking he was getting the better end of the deal."

"Castor realized she had it, too, once he learned who'd given it to her," Uncle Nathan said. "He doesn't mention what exactly it was in the first volume—he just refers to it as her 'treasure.' But he does write that he had to get it back, he had to find one of her servants, who he suspected was a Wind Effigy. He never did, but she suggested another offer instead. Basically, he had to pay out of his ass, and even then she would only give him part of the stone. Gotta keep your people safe."

Shrewd businesswoman indeed. The shards of blue stone appeared clearly in my mind's eye, scattered in the cigar box. "Guys," I said. "I've got something to tell you."

I finally decided to recount what I'd seen there, what I'd seen in death. The brilliant light that ushered my spirit across the world.

Lake crumpled a wrapper in her hands. "I knew you were hurt bad, but you were . . ." She looked at me. "You were dead? Actually *dead*?"

"For a few seconds. Probably more—but I'm okay now!" I added with a tiny pang of guilt when I saw the distress hollow out her face.

"White streams of fate," Dot said. "The unseen, the supernatural. Cylithium, the substance where phantoms spring from, the source of an Effigy's power. What if it's just a physical manifestation we can feel of what we can't see? Is this the source of magic . . . ?"

"Okay, well, whatever. Shit exists in the world and we can't explain everything or change any of it." Chae Rin shrugged, opening another package of pretzels. "What I want to know is, how do we find what we need to stop Blackwell, stop Saul, and end the chaos for good?"

"You mean what Saul said? The 'rest of the stone'?" Lake shook her head. "I dunno. Castor says the stone is some goddess's eye. Benjamin took the whole thing with him. So where's the rest of it?"

"Marian." I thought back to the memories I'd seen in Greenland.

"Marian smashed the stone. Like she couldn't risk it being used anymore. Some of the pieces are gone, and some were in that cigar box Natalya found. But she said to Nick before she died that Vogel had told her how to find the 'rest of the stone.'"

The current stone of fate was broken. The biggest wishes couldn't be wished for with just a tiny shard. Saul said so himself. He needed something more. Something like the original stone. Something like the original Eye of Fate.

And then it hit me.

I sat up straight, my hands lowering to the table. "The other eye."

*"Ew,"* Lake said with a grimace. "Just, ew."

Perhaps, loosely, that was what Marian had meant all along. Vogel had told her how to find the goddesses again, which made Marian the key to finding fate's other eye, a whole new stone powerful enough to cause whatever damage Saul or Blackwell longed for. From what I'd scried of her memories, Marian didn't have the chance to tell Nick about the goddesses. She was killed by Alice before she could reveal everything. But Nick did know that Marian was the key to his goal. Which meant *I* was the key to his goal.

It was just a matter of time before he'd make a play for me again.

"The other Eye of Fate." Dot ruminated over the very concept. "It must be powerful. Powerful enough to change the course of mankind. Well, the first eye was powerful enough to create the Effigies and the phantoms, at any rate."

"Wait, seriously?" Lake squeezed an unopen package in her hand. "How do you figure?"

"What else could have created this mess?" Dot said.

She was right. Marian had said it many times. Emilia. The dangerous game they played. Their sin. I saw it myself through Marian's memories. I saw the stone being passed around the hands of the young girls. Castor had said that it was not Benjamin Vogel who'd discovered the stone's secret of sacrifice; it was Alice.

"Marian is the only one who knows how to get back to the goddesses," I said. "If we find them, maybe we could ask their help."

Or their mercy.

"But to do that, Maia," Cheryl said, snapping herself out of her stupor, "you have to do what Sibyl has been telling you to do from the first."

I nodded. "I have to scry to find Marian. And the place we're going is the one place I know I can reach her."

# 28

CHERYL REMAINED BEHIND WITH THE PILOT
of the jet, and that was fine. This was a journey for us Effigies. With
the dangers in the Basse-Terre forest, we didn't have time to carry
anyone extra, and we didn't bother to hide our powers. If the world's
forces came for us, we'd take them on. Lake, Chae Rin, and I blasted
through the phantoms that barreled for us down the forest and over
the bridge until we reached the clearing and the temple to be found
within.

"Holy shit," Chae Rin whispered as its moss-covered stone loomed
before us.

"Yeah." I led them up the steps. The structure was built in the
nineteenth century thanks to Castor's resources and the direction
of Emilia from within the body of the girl who'd succeeded her. But
somehow it looked more ancient in the dark. The moon cast an ominous light onto the crevices and cracks of the walls and a shadow
down from the lintel.

The servant. The teacher. The traveler. Just three of the main play-
ers in a game that started long ago. Passing their confessions from one

to the other. To Emilia-as-Louisa, the final receiver of the four, he gave not only the resources that would help them build their temple, but the one resource that would help them protect it. Paying Emilia back, he'd given her some of the pieces of the stone he'd managed to buy from Tinubu. The story of their giving was memorialized in the temple, on the statue of Louisa in the center of the long hallway and its bone-vaulted ceiling.

"What is that?" Frowning, Chae Rin lifted her head and listened. "Do you hear drumbeats?"

Yes. The drumming only got louder once we reached the center room and slipped beyond the fountain, its crystal phantom centerpiece spilling water into the clear pool. I was almost afraid to lead the girls through the arched entrance and into the courtyard, but the moment I stepped into the open air, the sight before me left me speechless, breathless. Men and women in black robes chanted along the broken stone walls, their candles flickering flames that smoked up into the sky. Up one of the short flights of stairs on a stone platform, the drummer sat cross-legged in front of the shadowy entrances leading to other, unseen parts of the temple. The drumming stopped the moment he noticed our presence.

Inside the gazebo stood an old woman, her head bowed in prayer. I spotted Harry's backpack against the gazebo railing; I'd dropped *that* during my fight with Saul. It'd been stashed to the side along with Saul's ruined coat and shirt. Forgotten casualties of our battle.

"Continue playing," the old woman ordered. When the silence persisted, she turned and saw us. "Effigies," she said. And then I noticed what she wore around her neck.

The stone. She had a shard of stone locked in a tear-shaped pendant. It must have been how she could reach this place without being torn apart by phantoms.

I could feel the souls slithering past. The power here was unmistakable, undeniable. And I wasn't the only one who could feel it. Lake and Chae Rin trembled next to me.

"Scales." Steeling herself, Chae Rin refocused on the Deoscali chanters, walking down the steps to the courtyard. "Haven't seen too many of you in person. Wow. You're just as freaky as I imagined."

"The Sword of Earth." The old woman called to Chae Rin in a deep, German-accented voice. Her robes were a different sort—silver, to match her hair, still long and flowing down her back. "The Sword of Fire. The Sword of Wind." She stood, turning to us. "These are the names the Sect had given you, yes? What is it that you're doing among us?"

I decided to show her instead. The plaque was just where I remembered it, centered in the patch of grass inside the gazebo. No one protested as the girls crowded around me.

"Like in Prague," Chae Rin said, kneeling down. "'And among the shadows, you will find them. For only in calm can you hear them speak.'" She moved the plaque. There it was buried. The blue shards of stone given by a goddess. Chae Rin looked up at the old woman, who'd made room for us in the gazebo. "Who are you? Did you know about this?"

"I know only what the teacher has passed on to us," she answered simply. "The original teachings we take with us as we travel through the world."

The original teachings. Like Pastor Charles. "You're Yulia, aren't you?" I asked, my question answered with a gentle nod. "Tell me, what does Emilia's teaching say about the stone of life? About the goddesses?"

Maybe it was the age lines sunken into her pale skin, or the flowing robes, but Yulia really did look, at first, to be the all-knowing fortune-teller type. And yet when I mentioned the goddesses, she narrowed her eyes. "I do not know of what you speak," she said. Well, if Emilia didn't know all of Castor's secrets, then neither would she. "What I do know is that this stone is a gift of life—a treasure given to Farlow; I know not from where." She lifted the pendant, letting the stone dangle upon her fingers. "That where this stone lies, calm follows. And only within calm can you hear the spirits speak."

Not just the spirits, if what Castor said was true. But it was the spirits I needed now. Marian's memories held the key.

"What are you going to do, Maia?" Lake asked, dusting off her knees as she stood.

Scry. Learn Marian's secret. Find out where to meet the goddesses. *Goddesses.*

The weight of the truth was almost stifling. *Goddesses.* I thought of the word again and felt my throat constricting. Me? Maia Finley. Was I really going to do this?

As I looked up into the night sky, I felt so small, so tiny in the face of the terrible cosmic forces I now knew existed. It wasn't Maia Finley against Saul anymore, or against Blackwell or against supersoldiers.

Now I was to face *gods.*

How could I? How could I stand up to gods when a year ago I couldn't even stand up to a bully on a school bus?

Could I really do this?

Shutting my eyes, I sucked in a breath. Something had to be done. I had to try.

Guess it was time to do this.

"I'm going to do what I've been told to do from the beginning," I said. "I'm going to scry. I'm going to find Marian." I scanned the crumbling walls and the robed ritualists holding their candles in front of them. "And apparently, I'm going to have an audience while doing it."

"We're going to have an audience." Chae Rin sat down on the grass in front of the plaque. "This story involves all of us. Whatever we can find out can only help, right?"

"Um . . ." Lake scratched the back of her neck. "To be quite honest, I'm not really good at—" Chae Rin grabbed her pants leg and yanked her down.

"Watch, everyone," Yulia said. "Watch this demonstration of the teachings of Farlow. The communion with the spirits. The power of the Effigies."

I sat down last, the three of us positioning ourselves around the open pit where the shards of stone were. As I stared deep into its depths, the stone seemed to stare back at me, drawing me in, calling me into the well of history it held within it: eons of souls born and reborn, of civilizations rising and crumbling. Everything the goddess had seen. As in Prague, no words passed between the three of us. As fate compelled us, we closed our eyes and reached for each other. I gripped Chae Rin's hand first, then Lake's. Though we weren't complete, the three of us connected, spirits whispering to us secrets of the past. . . .

I closed my eyes to a sudden rush, dragging me backward out of the gazebo, out of the courtyard, spirited by the energy through my consciousness, through the white stream that would take me to the other Effigies. But the power here was momentous. Like in Prague, like with Saul, I was hardly scrying. I was *flying* . . . flying straight to Marian—

"Not this time."

It took all of Natalya's strength to stop me. Through her will alone, her door slammed shut the moment it opened. I cried out in pain as my back crashed against the surface, lifting my head just in time to see Zhar-Ptitsa lodging itself into the wood inches from my head. I stared at my terrified reflection in the blade, breathing hard as Natalya spoke, her hand still on the hilt.

"It must have been wonderful, wasn't it?" Her words were as sharp and deadly as her blade. "All those times you passed through this door without having to see my face. Flying through each gate all on the strength of some borrowed power. But you won't avoid my blade this time."

*Don't be scared*, I commanded myself, my chest tightening. *Don't be scared.*

"What do you *want?*" I demanded, flinching when she yanked out her sword. My anger boiled as seconds passed without Natalya's answer. "I *said*, what do you *want?* This whole time, you wanted me to solve this mystery, to stop the same people who ordered your death. I'm on the way to doing that." My back slid up and down the door as my breaths quickened.

"Do you know why I named my sword Zhar-Ptitsa?" She studied its edge. "The firebird of legend, a Holy Grail at the end of a difficult quest. The grail I chased after—peace. Rest. In the end, I was never able to find it."

"Natalya, I can avenge you," I said. "I can give you and your parents some peace!"

"I can never find peace as long as the cycle of Effigies continues. As long as I'm trapped in this place that never changes. As for my *parents.*" Natalya pointed her sword at my throat. "My parents lost their only daughter. The only thing that can give them peace"—she touched the tip against the bottom of my chin—"is for their daughter to live again."

To see a loved one again. I used to think that all that pain and loneliness would disappear if I could just see June once more. A dream that had quickly turned to nightmare the moment it came true. I loved June. I'd missed her to the point of madness. But Saul had used the power of fate to bring her back, and that power had required the murder of innocents. What would Natalya's parents think if they knew what their daughter's rebirth had cost? If they saw her living again in someone else's flesh?

"Some men think the rules don't apply to them." Senator Abrams's words. With trembling hands, I boosted myself off the door, mindful of the tip of Natalya's blade still pressed against my skin. "They think they can sacrifice whomever they want for the sake of their own wish. But don't you see, Natalya? That's why this whole mess started. That's why you were murdered—because of the selfishness of others. Because of their disregard for human life."

Natalya pressed the sword further against my chin, the blade stinging my flesh. "Don't think you can move me with an empty sermon." A trickle of my blood slid down the flat steel surface.

"Not a sermon. Just facts," I said. "You have shit to work through, you work through it. You don't use up other people like toilet paper for your own selfish desire."

"But isn't that what you've done, Maia?" Natalya's grin dripped with malice. "Imagine the pressure Belle felt under the crushing weight of your hero fantasies all the while battling her own demons."

I sucked in my lips as the bitter taste of guilt slid down my throat.

"With no regard to her feelings, you placed her on a pedestal so that you could face demons of your own. Knowing that she was struggling, you lied to her to protect your love. And now that she's completely broken, you blame her for falling. Tell me, Maia: Who is more selfish out of the two of us?"

I said nothing, because in that moment her words sounded like the truth to me. She would know. Just as she told me the last time we'd faced each other: What I'd done to Belle was almost precisely what Belle had done to her, once upon a time.

*Because she followed and looked up to me, she was never able to find her own self, never able to discover her own worth apart from the value she thought I had given her. . . .*

Broken Effigies worshipping other broken Effigies. Scarred teens looking for meaning. For worth.

What was I worth?

As Natalya's words rushed back, I thought of the last day I saw June alive—alive as she was before the fire. I thought of her scolding me on the staircase, her indictment of my inaction crushing what little self-esteem I'd had. That night I'd wandered around the neighborhood with no regard to my own safety because the walls of my home had felt like they were caving in on me. I'd left my family to die.

Natalya laughed as a tear fell off the tips of my lashes. "Look at you, cowering and helpless. I asked you before, Maia, if you've changed. I already know you haven't."

Maybe she was right. I didn't know what it was about that last fight with June. I'd always been able to keep my insecurities to myself by keeping *to* myself, but that day on the bus, it was like my cowardice had been stripped bare for all to see. Like they finally all knew who I was. Maia Finley, the lesser twin. The one who couldn't save them, who couldn't save anyone. The one who made bad decisions at the worst of times. The wrong sister had been given the power of the Effigies. I'd thought it that night at La Charte Hotel, and I'd thought it a thousand times afterward. The wrong sister.

But as an Effigy, I saved lives. As an Effigy I witnessed the suffering of others, just as I suffered myself. Yet I survived. I hadn't noticed it until now, the sturdiness of my legs, which had traveled around the world battling monsters born from the worst nightmares. The death and misery. Standing on my own, I withstood it all, no matter the pain.

My family's death. June. I was strong enough now—no, I'd *been* strong enough for longer than I'd realized to bear that pain, to bear the fires that took their lives, to deal with the aftermath of my sister's rebirth.

And if I was strong enough to face one fear, then I was strong enough to face another.

I looked at Natalya.

"Because of my duty," Natalya said, meeting my eyes, "I never lived life, even when I *was* alive. I am owed a second chance." She gripped the handle of her sword tighter. "Since you don't deserve your life, allow me to take it from you."

Natalya drew back her hand and thrust the sword toward my neck.

I caught it and broke it.

With the strength I once only acknowledged in others, I broke it, and watched the shattered body of Zhar-Ptista falling like feathers to the white stream below. Natalya's eyes widened.

"If nothing in here ever changes," I told her, raising my head slowly until I could see the shock in her eyes, "then I'll change it. And if you can't find peace . . ." I stretched my left arm to the side, fire enveloping it until I could see the tips of a blade forming, feel a hilt in my hands. The fire dissipated. "Then I'll be the one to give it to you."

I swung my scythe at Natalya, the Effigy ducking back and flipping out of the way before the steel could touch her face.

I looked at my weapon. A scythe. I knew Effigies could summon weapons unique to them. The Sect had thus called us the Four Swords. But my weapon was a symbol of death. When I looked at the obsidian black, there were times I wondered what it said about me. But death and life were part of the same river flowing across the world, linked by fate. As I ran toward Natalya, as we fought along the white stream, slashing and weaving, it wasn't death I wanted to give her, for she was already dead. It was a chance at a new life.

There was only one way she would live again.

Natalya flew from my kick, landing in the shallow stream. She'd just barely begun to move when I drove my scythe into the ground next to her head. The white waters slipped between her cheek and the shining blade, peacefully flowing as it had for more than a century.

"I'm going to Marian," I told Natalya. "I'm going to discover her secret. I'm going to use it to find the goddesses. I'm going to take the Eye of Fate. And I'm going to save us both. I have to."

Natalya said nothing. She only stared, silently furious and trembling, as I took back my scythe and walked toward the red door. It opened of its own accord, Natalya's memories waiting within. I stepped through the threshold, looking back at her just before the door closed. "Natalya," I said. "I'm sorry for what happened to you."

The door shut against the Effigy's silent anguish.

# 29

I'D SEEN SO MANY OF NATALYA'S MEMORIES, BUT not this one. She was on some Russian talk show with what looked to be her parents. They'd traded in their wrinkles and tears for fresh faces and bright smiles as they sat on either side of their long-limbed daughter, who couldn't have been out of her teens. Natalya's black hair was longer, just past her chin, but still tidy with starkly cut bangs and edges. Her father in his buttoned vest and a fully grown goatee had his hand on his daughter's shoulder, shaking it a little as he talked with the excitable host sitting in the couch next to theirs. Throughout the interview, Natalya's mother never let go of her hand, squeezing it so tightly I thought she'd snap it off the next time the host made her laugh. But Natalya had the stiff expression of a dutiful child too filial to interrupt her parents while they were talking, let alone *gushing* about her, even if it meant losing a limb in the process.

"Your daughter is only eighteen, and yet look at what she's accomplished," said the brown-haired host, and though she spoke in Russian, I could understand her words perfectly. Holding her fingers up, she counted her accomplishments one by one. "You've been an Effigy for seven years. You've killed hundreds of phantoms. Trained new Effigies, including the newest, Belle Rousseau, who is becoming a little legend in her own right. You've been given countless awards for your service, even a nomination for a Noble Peace Prize. Just recently, you saved a small town in Laos and rescued a United States Army outpost on the brink of destruction."

"She's phenomenal," said Mrs. Filipova in her plain blue dress, her fair bangs shifting a little as she gripped her daughter's hand even tighter. Natalya winced but said nothing. "Because of her, we were able to buy a new house, start our lives again. She truly saved us."

"A savior." The host nodded. "And no doubt a legend who will be remembered for years to come. But what I think most of us want to know about the Matryoshka Princess goes beyond such spectacular deeds. Isn't that right?"

Off set, the audience cheered.

"What you want to know?" Natalya's father's smile shrank a little as he looked at his wife. "As in?"

"Oh, personal things. Like, little Natalya, what do you do in your personal time?" the host asked. "Do you have any friends?"

Her parents looked as stumped as she did.

"N-no . . . not especially," Natalya answered in a dulled voice.

"Well, you must have a boyfriend. Is there anyone special at the Sect? An agent, perhaps?"

Natalya's cheeks did not flush as her mother's had. "There's no one," she answered with a shrug.

"What music do you listen to? Who are your favorite celebrities?"

Natalya's eyes drifted to the audience waiting in anticipation. "I don't know."

Natalya's parents started laughing nervously. "Forgive her. She's shy," her father said, watching the audience's confused reaction. "She doesn't speak often. She's very much about her work."

"Your work, ah, I see." The host nodded, crossing her legs. "Of course, it's true your work now is important. But what about afterward?"

Natalya frowned. "Afterward?"

"After your duties are finished. Surely you have dreams for the future."

As Natalya's body laxed, as her shoulders slumped, as her lips sagged into an unconscious frown, I suddenly understood why this was one of her most difficult memories. For a time she stared unfocused into the distance as if all of the battles of her past raged before her in black and white, clip after clip, bloodied monsters and dead comrades. Then she looked at her mother, smiling nervously. She looked at her father, wordlessly prodding her to speak. She looked at the host and at the audience.

And then she looked at herself. A faceless soldier. One in a long line of soldiers destined for death.

"I have no future," she said simply.

Silence.

"What she means is that she has no future plans," her father said quickly as Natalya silently lowered her head. "She's so busy with work these days she's not worried about anything other than now."

"Yes, yes," her mother chimed in, grinning wide as she brought her daughter's hand up to her lips and kissed it. "She doesn't need dreams for the future. She's already living her dream now! Being an Effigy is the greatest dream she could have ever wished for. Even if she were ever to come to hate it all, she has to keep working no matter what. She can't stop now."

The last line was not directed at the host. The strain in Mrs. Filipova's eyes as she watched her daughter told me so. "She can't stop now," but not because of duty. Not because of humanity. But because of the interviews. The advertisements. The invitations to balls and dinners. The money. The life they could now lead.

She kissed Natalya's hand one more time. "She can't stop now."

Ah, yes. I understood just then. This must have been the moment Natalya's soul died.

She'd survived the Seven-Year Rule, but only in flesh.

There were more girls. More doors. Unlike Natalya, they didn't try to stop me. They'd already been dead long enough to see the futility in fighting. "Ah, another girl," one said. "It doesn't matter to me," said another. "Do what you wish." And so I saw them.

I saw Aya Nasef weeping in a graveyard, her black *hijab* billowing in the dusty air, because although she could protect her town in Sinai from countless phantoms attacks, she couldn't keep her only child from succumbing to sickness.

I saw Mary Lou Russell of Jasper, Texas. I saw the angry crowd of white faces marching behind her with their guns and torches. She didn't need a torch. She burned down each church with merely a flick of her hand, monstrous laughter trailing behind her as the crowd laid claim to the land they believed belonged to them. Burning crosses cast a halo upon her blond curls, the celebrity face her country had come to love as the first Effigy born in America. The media wouldn't speak, at first, of the havoc she'd wreaked or the Sect strike team commissioned to take her out. Not until the body count was too high.

I saw Roselyn Alvarez from Mexico City, looking up at another high-rise toppling over as the phantoms tore through Seattle. I saw her scared and confused, fleeing with the rest of the civilians to avoid the debris when the building crashed into another and crumbled onto the street, crushing cars. I saw the phantoms raging, snatching people up in their jaws. Roselyn fought. She fought when she couldn't run anymore and ran when she couldn't fight anymore. The terror. The smoke-laden air. Ashes that were once men. The death of children she couldn't get to in time. It was the apocalypse, she thought. This was the end of days.

For what felt like seconds and years I walked through their memories, one by one, careful not to let my own mind weaken at the sight of their tragedies lest their consciousness cross over into mine. Step by step I watched as if in a dream until the final door appeared.

Marian did not speak to me. The girl, short and beautiful, had seen everything already. Not a strand of her thick woolen hair, tied in a bun at the top of her head, moved with the gentle breeze. Her soft brown eyes watched me approach, her arms at her sides, small hands lightly touching the simple beige dress Alice had killed her in. She said nothing until I was standing in front of her.

"It's time you see," Marian said. "I will help you understand everything." She stepped aside. "Please. Give Nicholas his peace."

The door creaked open.


Two men argued in the foyer of a grand estate while a quiet little girl in a sack-shaped dress waited nervously in the corner underneath the winding mahogany staircase.

"This is a gift for your daughter," the dark-haired man said. Blackwell. He gestured toward the girl he'd bartered from the African woman in Egbaland. "It's her tenth birthday, isn't it?"

"You must be *mad*. I can't accept a slave—my *god*, man." The blond-haired man stared at Blackwell in disgust.

"Not a slave. A servant. You should be grateful I brought a companion for that strange little girl of yours, Benjamin."

Benjamin did not take well to the little shudder he gave, even if it was done in jest.

"They're about the same age too, I reckon. You can say it's from you. Or do you already have a present for your Alice?" When Benjamin looked away, he laughed. "Ah, I thought as much. A little point of advice, Ben. I know it hasn't been too long since you returned from your previous trip for the Crown. Although we know the results were . . . less than satisfying."

Benjamin bristled but covered his indignation by adjusting his smoking jacket over his puffed-out chest.

"But the longer you bury yourself in your . . . occultic interests," Blackwell continued, "the longer it'll take for your daughter to come visit you when you're too old to wipe your own backside."

"Lucky for you, Bart, much like the Council, I have no interest in your insights," answered Benjamin coolly.

A shadow passed over Blackwell's eyes for just a moment before his grin returned, more strained than before. He turned to the girl. "Come now, girl, you're in luck. You could have ended up in some plantation in the Americas."

Benjamin eyed the little girl warily as she picked up her feet and silently walked to his side. "Why are you giving me this girl, Blackwell?"

Blackwell could barely hide his smirk behind his ringed fingers. "I guess you could say this is your commission. After your contribution, you deserve part of the spoils, I suppose."

"What?"

"Ah, nothing, good chap. I'll be off, then." He dusted his jacket. "And don't worry. I'll make sure my son comes to the little birthday party your wife is throwing tomorrow."

With a tip of his hat, he was gone.

As Benjamin looked down at the little girl and as the little girl looked up at him, neither of them could have possibly imagined the future awaiting them. He introduced her to his daughter anyway, who roused from her sleep, her blond hair falling over her pure white nightgown.

"Happy birthday, my sweet Alice," Benjamin said. "I have a new servant for you."

"A servant?" Alice rubbed the cobwebs from her eyes. "Father, why is her skin so dark?"

"She's from a faraway land," he told her. "From one of the lands of my adventures I've told you about. Do you remember?"

"A faraway land . . ." Alice looked at the frightened girl in wonder, as if she were a living doll made from clay just for her. "Oh, Father, how I wish I could go on adventures too. I wish I could travel the land like you and Uncle Thomas."

Benjamin laughed. "My dear, perhaps one day your husband can take you on a little trip outside York. But you'll have to wait until then."

Because Benjamin had turned to the new servant, he didn't notice that his daughter's grin had disappeared entirely, replaced by a bitter scowl. Her expression lightened, however, when he gestured for the quiet girl to come closer to the bed. She gripped her eggshell cover with excitement, the moonlight slipping in through the sliver of space between the heavy curtains.

"You can name her if you wish, Alice."

Alice looked delighted. "Then, Father, I will name her after one of my favorite stories."

"Stories?" Benjamin laughed. "Mine? Or those books of knights and dragons you're always dreaming of these days?"

Pushing off her bedsheets, Alice leaned over to inspect her new doll, cocking her head this way and that. "Yes," she said finally. "You will be my maid Marian."

Because Marian could not quite understand their words, she only blinked, her little hands clasped and trembling against her chest. She was afraid.

•  •  •

It was one month later. The child Alice had brought her favorite servant, Marian, to her bedroom so that Alice could read to her. The books her father had given her were strewn about her bed—plays and masques, legends and fairy tales. Stories written from a thousand cultures over a thousand years. Since she was born, her father had been buying them one by one from every land he had visited. I couldn't possibly know this myself. But as I watched the two girls sit atop Alice's bed, one in a frilly white dress, the other in a dreary servant's uniform, it was Marian who whispered it to me from the recesses of my consciousness. Marian who guided me through these details, through her secrets, as I scried the tale of her past.

"Do you know what my favorite stories are, *poupée?*" Flipping back her blond braid, Alice slid over one book bound in leather. "This book of masques. Masques are plays that used to be performed in court for kings and queens. There are many masques in here, some written by Ben Johnson. But my favorite"—she flipped through the book—"is this one." And she tapped the page. "*Tempe Restored.* Do you know the enchantress Circe, Marian? Did they teach you of her in your silly little jungle?"

Marian looked confused. A month wasn't enough to learn the girl's tongue, and they hadn't taught her any language other than her own in Tinubu's magnificent thatch-roofed palace.

Alice tilted her head almost whimsically as she flipped through the pages of the masque. "An enchantress who had the power to love and destroy in equal measure. Oh, Marian, she could do anything! Raise the dead and turn men into beasts. Pull down the heavens."

Alice could see that she was losing her servant, so she sighed impatiently. "Surely your people would have taught you this one?"

She reached over and brought a large text that Marian seemed to immediately recognize. The Bible.

"Of course, with all the missionaries fuddling their way through those lands, I'm sure you would have come across this at least once. I don't care much for most of it, to be honest. But one day I will read you two of my favorite stories from the book. The story of Moses and the plagues of Egypt." She flipped to the end. "And maybe the final story of John? I was so intrigued when Mr. Caldwell spoke of it in church several months ago. Or how about this?"

She dug another book out from a pile. "A book of alchemy. My father is interested in alchemy, you see, and he once told me of a physician named Paracelsus who tried to understand the elements of nature. His work was published centuries ago, but I still find it fun to read. Here, let me—"

Marian pushed the books away and began to tear up. It was so sudden that Alice was shocked when the girl began crying, though that shock quickly turned to annoyance when her pleas for her to stop went unanswered. She couldn't fathom that the little girl was homesick, that she was frustrated in a strange land with a strange girl whose words she couldn't understand.

And because Alice couldn't fathom this, she slapped Marian silent.

"You should learn to love stories, Marian," Alice told her with a hint of a warning in her voice as Marian held her stinging cheek in surprise. "Your name is from a story. A story of maidens and knights. But perhaps I should have named you after a knight? Like Sir Gawain, or the Green Knight. Or Sir Lancelot of the Round Table."

The armored man carrying a sword as high as his broad chest seemed to stare up at her from the surface of the book's hard cover. As if in a trance, Marian brought the book over to herself, holding it in her hands.

"Ah, you like that one?" Alice plucked it out of the servant's grip and brushed the cover. "Yes, the story of King Arthur. It's a romance. In fact, it is a story of a fraternity of knights. You know knights, don't you, Marian? Knights have been the most noble of England's soldiers for centuries. There were knights all over Europe once upon a time. They're protectors, you know. They protect their lands, their people. In the romance tales, they fight dragons and witches and monsters of all kinds. And even when they die, there are other knights to fight in their place. They were like links in a chain, overlapping, never ending, one force replacing the other. Why, Marian? Because protecting others is their noble call, of course. Don't let these stories fool you, though. They were written by men. Do you want to know a secret?" She leaned in and whispered into Marian's ear: "The real truth is, only girls can be knights. Never believe otherwise."

It was a truth Alice had decided for herself. A truth Marian had come to believe.

Alice flipped through the pages and read a few lines, pleased that Marian was enraptured with at least the pictures penciled in to enhance the tale. "You know, Marian," Alice said after a while. "Wouldn't it be far better to be a knight or an enchantress than an explorer's daughter?"

Marian, confused as ever, did not answer.

Later that night, Alice snuck into her father's study. Marian was to be the lookout. He was always there these days, locked in with his research. Alice had heard him several days ago talking to Uncle Thomas about a white stone. She was only curious. That was all. She wanted to see. However, Marian was caught by Mr. Vogel and told to go back to the servants' quarters. The next morning she saw the deep violet swelling around Alice's right eye.


Two years later, when spring came and the flowers began to bloom once more, Alice's mother, Mrs. Alexandra Vogel, held a garden party for her and her husband's friends. Marian watched her spread powder over herself and her daughter's bruises, letting the long sleeves and high frilled collars of their dresses cover the rest.

"Best face forward," she told her daughter, who shifted uncomfortably on her feet. "We are women of society, after all."

There were many people Marian had only seen in passing sitting at the tables set up around the estate's garden. She would always hide behind doors when she saw them waltz into the estate because she could no longer take their peculiar stares, their tawdry questions, their hurtful comments about her skin, lips, and hair. All the women were chatting and gossiping in their long lace dresses and beautiful bonnets. The men were socializing with a smoke or two floating into the air as they puffed into their pipes. Marian didn't want to be there. She couldn't take their stares and their whispers. Her maid uniform was old and didn't fit anymore now that she'd grown since coming to the estate. Her hands were tired from carrying around trays of food. And the man who'd brought her to these lands—Blackwell—was here as well, standing awkwardly just outside a ring of men by the rosebushes. She'd made up her mind to avoid him, but he didn't seem interested in her, at any rate. He was too busy being hurt over his ignored presence.

Alice and her friends played away from the adults by the hedges. Four of them. Marian had met them before, so she knew their names. The plain one with flat, lifeless brown hair was Emilia. The pretty one with charcoal hair held in a bun at the top of her head like Marian was Patricia. She had pale skin, her face plump like the rest of her body. There was a tiny, frail girl, sickly in appearance, with a face shaped like the beak of an eagle. Abigail. Marian had never seen hair like hers. Red like fire, it twisted down in two braids over her chest. The girl was coughing. She was always coughing whenever Marian saw her.

They were passing around a rock in a circle, chanting like a coven of witches, the kind that cast spells in the stories Alice had read to her: "'Tinker, tailor, soldier, sailor, rich-man, poor-man, beggar-man, thief. What will I be? Lady, baby, gypsy, queen.'"

Not too far away, the boys were playing—well, playing wasn't quite the word. Two burly boys were shoving a mousy boy between them, ruffing up his light brown hair as he cried for them to stop. Louis Hudson. He was a little younger than the rest. There was another boy, though, who tried to stop them. Chestnut-brown hair and the upright look of a young gentleman in the making. Nicholas, Louis's brother, both of them sons of a railway businessman. Marian had seen him in the estate before but had never spoken to him. Alice would never allow it.

"This is boring," Alice said suddenly, and in a burst of haughtiness, threw the rock at Louis's head. The burly boys cheered when it hit its target. "I want to tell stories."

"Knights and witches and dragons again?" Emilia groaned. "Why don't I tell you a story instead, a story about the *real* world? Last week my older brother gave me a science book on animals."

"I'm not interested in science." Alice folded her arms. "I'm interested in magic."

"Magic doesn't exist," Emilia said simply.

"Father says it does. Father says magic and science are more intertwined than we think."

"They are not." Emilia lowered her book to her lap. "You can only understand the nature of the world through experimentation and critical observation. Science and magic do not blend."

Alice and Emilia were always far above the others when it came to their intelligence. The debate to follow was just one of many to come.

"Centuries ago there were men who disagreed," said Alice. "The physician Paracelsus for example. He learned of the elements of nature and deduced that each was governed by beings of magic. Earth, water, wind, and fire." She counted them off with her fingers. "Gnome, undine, sylph, and salamander—" Alice paused. "And a fifth, ether. The substance of stars and souls. Well, I don't know if there's a magic creature for that one."

"All of that sounds preposterous." Emilia snorted, a sound that made Alice's fingers clench in anger. "But what else can you expect from medieval science? The scientists of today are learning about the world through more logical means."

"Whether it's Darwin or Paracelsus, magic or science, or a blend of the two, they were all just doing the same thing." Alice pointed at Emilia's book. "Trying to understand the nature of the world."

"I scarcely believe that."

Alice didn't look like she appreciated being challenged. Abigail and Patricia tensed at the sight of their friend's rising temper. They'd seen it before, and they knew what could happen if it reached its peak.

"If I were a magic witch," Abigail said to ease the tension, "I would make myself well." She coughed into her hands again. "I would make myself stronger than anyone."

"Well, if it's a matter of magic, yes," said Alice. "But according to Patricia's science books, if you die of sickness, it will only be because you weren't meant to survive with the rest of us. But then, I suppose that's the way of the world, isn't it?"

"Alice!" Patricia touched Abigail's hand. The sick girl had sucked in her lips and fallen silent, clearly upset. "Please don't say such things."

"That is what some scientists are saying these days," Emilia said without emotion, flipping her pages with little interest in anything else.

"Still, I understand," Alice said. "It's not very easy being a frail little girl. All men want power. All men want to be strong, stronger than anyone. Why not us?"

The girls didn't know how to respond.

"Nick, what do you think?" Alice couldn't wait to bring the boy into their conversation, though he was too busy separating the two burly boys who'd just begun to fight with each other. Louis cowered behind him. Nicholas was the same age as the girls, a mere twelve, if Marian remembered correctly.

"I don't know much about those things, Alice. Magic or science. None of it quite interests me," he said with a shrug.

Alice trailed her hand down her long blond tresses. "Well, then, what are the things that interest you?"

Nicholas blushed and looked away, surprised when he saw for the first time Marian standing in her servant's garb, holding a plate of food. As the burly boys began jeering at her, Marian blocked her ears and served them. Even the girls giggled behind their hands, commenting on the "strangeness" of her features. It was only Nicholas who remained quiet and took the food with thanks. Once the boys went over to the tables for tea, Alice leaned in to the other girls.

"Do you want to see my father's stone again?" Her eyes glinted with mischief. "Our divination game would be more fun if we used that pretty little jewel again instead of a regular old rock. Don't you agree?"

They had been playing with it ever since Alice had found its hiding place in her father's study. But Marian knew that the cost of getting caught, for Alice, was too high.

"Please, Miss Alice, do not!" Marian's words were broken and strained in odd places, but after two years, she could manage them well enough. "If your father catches you again . . ."

Alice seemed to understand. The makeup had only covered the bruises, after all. But it couldn't erase the pain. "Quiet." She stood, her anger flaring as she noticed the suddenly curious glances from the other girls. "I said quiet! Who asked you to speak?"

Once again, Marian was frightened. She ran into the house, not knowing Nicholas, who'd watched their exchange from afar, was now watching her escape from the garden.

The cost of defying Mr. Vogel, the cost of disturbing him as he researched endlessly in his study, was too high. It was only two years later when Marian saw, through the cracks of the door, the dead body of Alexandra Vogel in his arms in the middle of the night. The fight was brutal and her death was sudden. One strike of the head against the corner of his desk. Alice had witnessed everything. Marian could see her crouched in the corner of the dark room, her arms wrapped around her knees, which she'd pulled up to her chest. Tears soaked her nightgown as her father babbled meaningless things to himself, his wife's back bent over his arms, her long, fair hair sweeping the floor like a broom. His stupor didn't last. Soon his anger turned on his daughter. Marian had witnessed every terrible strike, helpless and afraid from behind the door.

"You will never speak of this. Do you hear me? Never!" He struck her again and again, and once she was lying on the ground, half dead, he began to pace. "I have to get rid of the body. But how? The stone!" He clasped his hand to his head. "The stone. I could use the stone. I could grant a wish and bring her back. But how do I activate its power? How? *How?*" He screamed in rage, walking over to the other side of the room. Marian could no longer see him, but she could hear his fists pounding against the bookshelves. He did not notice, as she did, as Alice did once she lifted up her head—he'd left the stone on the table.

Within the white depths of the marble-shaped stone had suddenly grown a prominent black spot. This was the night Alice learned of the mystery of the stone. On this night, the last morsel of innocence in her died, replaced by a taste for cruelty learned at her father's hand.


Two years passed. Alexandra Vogel's body became bones in the ground underneath her precious garden, her countenance immortalized in the portraits hanging in the foyer. Alice and Marian were girls of sixteen. Marian stood by the door of Alice's bedroom as she and her three friends sat on the bed, passing around the white stone, divining their destinies with that silly song as they had for years. They were still dressed in black because they had just returned from a funeral. Two of the schoolchildren Alice used to look after had suddenly drowned in a lake. But then, many mysterious deaths had begun to follow wherever Alice walked. Marian never asked.

"You don't want to play with us, *poupée?*" Alice said to Marian, keeping the stone in her hands once they'd passed it to her. To the other girls' relief, Marian shook her head.

Over the years, Alice had always treated her . . . *relatively* well, letting her play with her friends despite their protests, reading to her the stories of knights and dragons she loved so much. But death followed her still. The knowledge of it made Marian shiver as if left in the cold.

It was Emilia who'd asked about the black swirls within the stone.

"I was experimenting. This is a stone of wishes, you see." Alice had answered so simply, she'd left everyone dumbstruck.

"Alice, what do you mean?" Patricia sounded afraid. "A stone of wishes?"

"Yes." These days Alice's voice carried a note of whimsy that always made her seem as if she were singing an unsettling melody. Unconsciously, she pulled down her black, frilled sleeves over her healing bruises. "I discovered the secret. It took me many years, but I believe we can wish for anything now."

The four girls did not know what to say. Alice's humming twirled joyfully into their silence as they watched her turn the stone over and over in her hands.

"Even if that were true," said Emilia, "what would we possibly wish for?"

"Abigail." Alice closed her hand over the white orb. "Didn't you once say you wished to be stronger? Stronger than anyone?"

Abigail coughed into her hand. Somehow she was slighter now than she was four years ago. "Well, I suppose so, Alice, but—"

Alice put up a finger to silence her. Then, putting the stone to her mouth, she began to whisper like a sorceress into a crystal ball. "I wish for Abigail to be stronger than anyone for as long as her little soul shall live."

Marian backed up against the door, that familiar mischief in Alice's blue eyes terrifying her. But nothing happened. Abigail, Patricia, and Emilia exchanged glances.

"How stupid," Emilia said in a huff. "Alice, when will you be done with such childish things?"

But Abigail wasn't coughing any longer. The frail girl placed a hand against her chest, feeling the wind pass through her throat unencumbered for the first time since her birth. Nobody knew why she had descended from Alice's bed just then. Perhaps Abigail didn't know herself. But something within her must have told her to grip the wooden frame. Bending her knees, she began lifting it.

Emilia and Patricia screamed, holding on to the bedcovers to keep from tumbling off the other end. Marian screamed, pressing her back against the door. All screamed but Alice. She was studying the stone carefully in the wake of Abigail's newfound strength. She looked at the books in her shelf by the window, the tales and legends she'd read a thousand times each. Then she lifted her frilled sleeves, each bruise in different stages of healing.

"Why not us?" Alice whispered.

She hopped off the bed and ran out the door, leaving the other girls to quake in her bedroom. Marian did not see her again that day. That night, in the servants' quarters, she woke up sweating because she was too hot. Too hot. *Too hot.*

Her hands were on fire.

The four terrified girls met in the woods as Alice had instructed. Once she was sure they had not been followed, she explained to them what she had done.

She'd spent the whole night thinking of what to wish for—more specifically, she'd spent the whole night figuring out what she wanted to be. She'd thought of all the stories she loved. King Arthur and Circe the enchantress. A fraternity of knights. A coven of witches. Alchemy. Paracelsus. As she rewrote the story of her future in her own mind, she realized she wanted to be everything. But she didn't want to be everything alone. And so she gave herself a gift and shared that gift with her precious friends and her favorite servant.

"Wouldn't you rather be more than just a frail girl?" Alice said.

But Marian was terrified. She had almost been discovered by the other servants. If she hadn't calmed herself, she might have burned down the entire estate. The other girls had similar misgivings, the result of their newfound witchcraft causing them terror in their estates. Abigail had caused an earthquake that no one in her family could explain. Her servants were still tidying the broken vases and fallen portraits. Patricia had only meant to open her window when she was enveloped in a torrent of wind that hurdled her across the room and launched her out of the window—a fall she survived quite easily. Emilia had frozen the pond by her home with just a mere touch of her fingers. Why? they asked. How, Alice?

"I told you, the stone grants wishes. I wrote our tale and made it true. Gnome." She pointed at Abigail. "Sylph." Then at Patricia. "Undine." Emilia. "And little salamander."

Marian stepped back in fear as Alice aimed her wicked grin at her. It was wrong. She was a demon now, turned so by the twisted imagination of a strange girl.

"And what about you, Alice?" Emilia asked. Out of the girls she was the only one tempered enough to ask the question. "What 'gift' have you given to yourself?"

Alice looked up at the sky, the gentle breeze swaying her golden locks. "All you must know, dear Emilia, is that I will never be bound again. Not by Father. Not by anyone."

Ether, the fifth element. Different, grander than the other four. Indestructible and everlasting. The books Alice had read told her that the element governed the gravitational pull of heavenly bodies, the transmission of light and sound. It was the substance of heavens and earth, without which no other element could exist. She'd read of magicians using it, manipulating it, traveling through it, unbound by space and time.

Unbound. Like her father. Not the explorer's daughter, but the explorer at last.

If she'd known the full of extent of what that substance truly was, she would have wished for more. Regardless, she now possessed exactly what she'd always wanted. She had designs to take the stone and travel the world with her newfound magic.

However, there were, as she realized, certain people she would have rather not left behind. Her friends, for example, and her favorite servant, Marian. Marian never used her powers. They made her feel wrong—changed. But as the months passed, the other girls came to love their newfound witchcraft, using it to play tricks on the townspeople. Blowing the bonnet off their teacher's head with a mere breath. Crafting the visage of a bully in a sculpture of ice, his head on a weasel's body. It was their little game. A dangerous game.

"Kid?" Chae Rin's voice echoed in my head. But how was I hearing her? "Maia!"

"Chae Rin?" I turned and found myself on top of a winding staircase in the hallway of a manor I didn't recognize. Oak banisters descended from the second floor with little statues of angels holding up the lights at the end of the staircase. A lavish red carpet lined with golden trims veiled the steps and spread out across the hallway. I watched with Chae Rin as a man in a black vest halfway down the stairs clutched one of the railings and mocked the girl on the second floor.

Abigail. Her expression darkened.

"What is this?" I asked, unable to look away from the scene. "Why am I seeing this?"

"I've been seeing some of yours too," Chae Rin said. "Bits and pieces. Can't you feel us?"

For a split second I could. I could feel their hands clutching mine as we sat in the gazebo, paralyzed with power. I could feel the spirits flowing around us, through us, connecting us.

Bathed in the light from the stained glass window behind her, Abigail had moved toward the grand piano tucked into the corner.

"Uncle," she said too calmly. "What you did to my mother . . . those nights you hurt her while my father was away." Hatred flashed across her face. "I will never forgive you."

With her monstrous strength, she moved the piano.

"I'd always wondered why I was stronger than the rest of you," Chae Rin whispered, stunned, as Abigail's uncle gasped, too terrified to move. By the time the piano was crashing down the stairs, it was too late.

The scene flashed as I heard his muffled screams.

Patricia's memory was of a gentler sort, fitting for the gentle girl. Lake and I watched, relieved somewhat to see Patricia walking through the woods with her sick little brother. It was autumn, and the leaves had fallen onto the ground in shades of gold and red.

"Miles, do you want to see something pretty? But remember, you musn't ever tell." She held a finger to her lips and began waving her fingers through the air. The boy was delighted to see the leaves dancing with the wind, around the trees, and up into the sky. . . .

The Witches of York, they called themselves. It was the name Abigail had excitedly given them. Alice had rejected it at first. "We are so much more than witches," she said.

"Oh yes, we're 'knights' as well," Emilia said with a sarcastic edge. "But there are no dragons to slay, so I don't imagine how it could be possible."

Marian quite liked the idea of being a "knight," much more than being a witch. In real life, knights could only be girls, after all. It was what Alice had told her. So she could be one too.

But Alice was right. They weren't quite either. It didn't matter what they called themselves. No matter how many months passed, she did not and could not become used to her abilities. Living in England had already made her feel as if she were less than a human. The stares of the people around her had already made her feel monstrous. Becoming a true monster was not what she would ever have wished for herself.

She found solace, as it turned out, in one of the individuals Alice wished not to leave. One more year had passed, and Nicholas had become a man of seventeen. Over the years Marian had noticed his legs growing longer and sturdier, his shoulders broadening, his jaw becoming sharper and more defined. He was an Eton boy now, and he showed it with his manners during the dinners when he would visit the Vogels and demonstrate his knowledge.

Like one day in the middle of winter. After discussing his views on the Greek philosophers, he'd told father and daughter Vogel that he had planned to be a scholar himself, but his father was insistent upon pulling him toward the railway business. He'd be traveling to the Americas one day, he told them.

"With your wife, I presume," Vogel said as Marian topped off his wine. "You're getting to the marrying age, aren't you, Nicholas?"

Alice, who'd been listening, enrapt, to Nicholas throughout their dinner, straightened up. "Of course he is, Father. We both are, aren't we, Nick? We're the same age, after all."

Nicholas choked on his beans. Marian almost dropped her decanter of wine. Hitting his chest, Nicholas swallowed painfully, casting a nervous glance at Alice when she tried to tend to him. "I'm okay," he said, holding up his hands quickly. "I'm sorry. I didn't mean to worry anyone."

Just for a second, his eyes flitted to Marian, still clutching the decanter to her chest—a second that did not go unnoticed by Alice.

"I wonder if Nick would ever love me," Alice said suddenly as Marian prepared her for bed. "Knowing what I am."

Alice watched her from the corner of her sly eyes. Marian understood her meaning, but she didn't let her annoyance show.

"Nick—I mean Master Nicholas—will love whomever he wants to love," she said simply, fluffing Alice's pillow.

"But could Nick ever love a monster?" Alice laughed when she saw Marian's hands clench the pillow. "If I could, I would live with him forever, but perhaps that isn't possible."

"If you were worried about it," Marian said, "then you should not have made us so."

The word "monster" on Alice's lips carried several meanings, not all of which were tied to the witchcraft they now possessed. Every now and again, when Alice felt threatened and insecure toward her servant, she would use words she didn't normally. Every time Nicholas would smile at Marian instead of Alice—ask *Marian's* thoughts, pay *Marian* attention—the words "jungle" or "mud" would slip out of Alice's mouth. She would ask Marian about her coal skin and her strange gods, about cannibals and rituals and everything else she'd read from the biased, egocentric tales written by the British travelers she admired. And though Marian's blood would boil, as a servant in Alice's household, there was nothing she could do but to hide how truly isolated she felt in a land that was to her still foreign and unwelcoming. She did so now too.

"Oh, *poupée*, you know that I only mean to tease you." Alice grabbed her servant's hand before she could walk away. "I told you before that we're more than just one thing or the other. If you'd like, you can think of us as knights. Don't you love that story of knights and maidens and dragons?"

Marian couldn't deny it. Those stories were among her favorites of all.

"Remember what I once told you all those years ago, after reading you the stories of King Arthur and the Knights Templar? The fraternity of knights. Noble warriors who have powers beyond imagination, but they use it to protect. To save. And their noble cause never ends. Knight after knight. Protecting the lands. Links in a chain." Alice squeezed her arms warmly. "Remember?"

Links in a chain. It was a phrase Alice liked very much. She would repeat it like a nursery rhyme while she and the other witches played. Marian wasn't sure if they even quite understood what it meant, except Alice had said it so much, they'd simply gotten used to it. It became a mantra, something that defined their new secret coven. Marian would watch them repeat it again and again as Patricia used her power to levitate the others while they lay flat-backed on the ground.

*Links in a chain, a dangerous game. Links in a chain, a dangerous game . . .*

"Don't feel bad, Marian," Alice said. "If you'd like, you could think of us like that. You do not have to use your magic to tease or hurt others. You can use it as you wish. It is my gift to you. And truly, who knows what more mysteries our powers hold?"

Alice's power was the biggest mystery of all. She'd never shown it to her friends, no matter how much they pleaded and argued. Alice was not the type to be swayed by such things. Alice had no difficulty showing her temper to her friends, her intelligence, and sometimes even her gentleness. But at the core of it all was a secretive girl. A girl whose terrible dreams she kept to herself until the time of her choosing.

That was the side to Alice Vogel that scared Marian the most.

But right now Alice spoke earnestly, trying to comfort her. Marian wasn't sure what to make of it. "And what do you think of yourself, Miss Alice?"

Alice smiled slyly but didn't answer. And though Marian had decided to rise above Alice's callous words, their silent truce would not last. It shattered the day Alice found her servant and the object of her affection locked in passionate embrace alone in the empty servants' quarters. When Marian had met with Alice's rage later than night, she'd wondered why Alice had not simply used the stone to kill her. Wish her dead. Wish Nicholas dead, her father dead. All those who had hurt Alice, who had stomped on the girl's pride. The stone was a stone of wishes. Alice alone understood its power and how to bring it about. But she had other designs. She was waiting. Waiting to fill the stone to ask for a bigger wish. . . .

Another year passed, and Marian began hearing strange stories. Thomas Castor, Mr. Vogel's colleague, had heard in India of shadows of nightmare appearing from a shroud of darkness. He'd heard the same tale in Turkey. It was a private conversation they'd held in the living room, but Marian was listening from the kitchen. They spoke in hushed tones. Murderous shadows? It seemed so impossible. But Vogel wanted to investigate. "Chasing the unseen forces of the world," he told Castor. "Like old times."

Castor refused. "You're mind isn't as sharp as it once was, Ben."

"What?" Mr. Vogel was on his feet, but he wobbled the very second he thought he was centered on them. "Who are you to tell me such a thing?"

"Look at you!" Castor stood and pointed at his teetering frame. "You're drunk, aren't you? People are talking, Ben. Your wife disappearing. Your relationship with your daughter—"

"There is nothing strange about my relationship with my daughter," Mr. Vogel insisted, a little too strongly. "You don't understand, Castor. It's . . . it's the stone," he confessed. "Every time I go back to the study, I find it there, but there are . . . changes."

Castor raised an eyebrow. "Changes?"

"Yes, yes." Mr. Vogel struggled to find the words. "Like black streaks. Just wisps, but over the years they've become more prominent. I can't explain it. I *have* to explain it. It's my duty to!"

The man did not realize he was gripping his friend's collar until it was too late. After Castor pushed him away, Vogel knew his mind had been set.

"You've crumbled, friend." Castor frowned, searching his red face before shaking his head. "The Council won't sponsor any kind of exploration with you involved, not like this. I'll explore the situation on my own with my crew."

Castor left Mr. Vogel in the living room, a broken man. And when Marian entered his study one night to bring him tea, the man's face was redder than ever before. Tears tangled in the thick beard he'd let grow over the years. Marian had only wanted to serve his tea and leave. When he caught her wrist, she stared back into his unfocused eyes in terror. But he didn't hurt her. He asked her to sit down. He asked her to listen to his story.

"My life fell apart the moment I met them," he started. "Those monsters." And for the rest of the night, Marian heard his strange tale. A story of wanton gods and a power beyond imagination.

"I was insolent, you see." He shuddered as he remembered. "The goddesses showed no emotion, but I can tell that they weren't pleased. The intensity burned in their gaze. They told me something terrible."

He was gripping Marian's wrist too tightly, his knuckles pale. "I-it hurts," Marian said, wincing from the pain. "Please . . ."

"They told me I'd never find them again, but I refused to accept it. I wanted to learn more. I couldn't stop until I knew all their secrets. Arrogantly, I told them that if I could find them once with my genius and cunning, I would do so again. I assured them that I would never stop. That I would never allow them to hide from me forever. Over my dead body. And they . . ." He squeezed Marian's wrist. "And they told me. . . ."

The sun was almost rising when Marian entered Alice's room again in a daze. "Miss Alice," she whispered at the foot of her bed as Alice roused from her sleep. "Do *you* . . . believe in monsters?"

Alice rubbed her eyes. "Monsters like us?"

"No, worse than us. Monsters . . . real monsters. *Demons.*" Marian couldn't say more. She merely rubbed her wrist, staring down at her own shaking hands.

"There are demons of every sort," Alice said. "It was a demon that took my mother, after all." She sat up and looked out her window. "If only there *were* real monsters," she said after a while. "Real beasts like there are in stories. Like Circe, I would use them to tear down this wicked world."

It was a premonition soon to come true.

Alice never dared use her powers in her father's presence. As brazen as she was, she knew not what her fate would be if she revealed to any living soul the existence of her powers. When Marian asked why, she reminded her servant that it was not too long ago that her country had burned women at the stake, believing them to be witches. What would they do to her when they found out her magic was real?

She had decided the night after her eighteenth birthday that she would take the stone and disappear forever with the gift she'd given herself. She told Marian of her plans and warned her not to get in her way. Early the next morning, while the estate was still asleep, Alice snuck into her father's study and found the stone in the false bottom of his desk drawer, the one he kept locked with the key she now held in her hand. The stone was almost dark, and her father could never understand why. He didn't know what his daughter had done . . . how many sacrifices over months and years since her last wish were required for her to bring it to this state. The closer your connection to the victim, Alice learned, the more quickly it filled. Marian had only discovered this later, and it came as no surprise. It was the only way she could explain the sudden deaths of too many of Alice's school friends. Her father didn't know how much patience it took not to make another wish.

But when he laid his hands on her once more, her patience ran out. Marian had seen him marching toward the study but hadn't the time to warn her. He'd burst into the room and struck his daughter in the head so suddenly she couldn't use her magic—no, she was too scared to. Though she had the stone clenched in her hands, she was so scared of her father that she scarcely could remember what she was capable of.

"Stop!" Marian looked to the desk and found a letter opener. Swiping it, she wrapped herself around the man's arm, but he threw her off him before she could strike. The weapon clattered to the ground next to him unnoticed. "Stop!" Marian yelled again as he began wringing his daughter's neck.

"You figured out its secret, didn't you? All this time!" He squeezed her slender throat. "You've been making a fool of me for years. You've all been making a fool of me!"

Marian could not use her magic. What if she burned them both alive? Unlike Alice, she couldn't stomach the thought of murdering others, stealing their lives. She stood frozen in fear and disbelief, her mind blank in the face of such a horrific scene of violence.

"You're a monster!" Marian screamed. "A monster!"

"Mon . . . ster . . . ," Alice repeated with the last air she could muster for breath.

Marian did not know which stories guided the wish Alice had uttered in her mind as she was dying. But she knew it was fueled by a mounting hatred nurtured like a poisonous flower over the years of abuse, murder, and pain. Alice, who'd dreamed of becoming like the enchantress of legend and who could now lay siege to the lands of men with a flick of her finger. She plucked from the stories of her wild imagination. The plagues of Egypt. Beasts of legends. Of nightmares.

*Tear down this wicked world.*

Mr. Vogel's grip relaxed the moment he saw the stone begin to glow a soft hue. He fell back, staring in wonder as she sat up, gasping for air. "The stone," he whispered, its reflection glittering in his brown eyes. "You made a wish, didn't you? You really did discover its secret."

Alice laid her hands upon his face. "Thank you, Father," she whispered. "Because of you, because you brought this stone to me, I can be free."

As Marian watched in horror, Alice grabbed the letter opener from the floor and stabbed him in the neck.

And so the phantoms descended on York, bringing with them the fire and brimstone of the end of days.


There were too many memories. It was hot. I couldn't breathe. I had to get out. I had to get out now.

I stumbled out of the magnificent red door, collapsing onto the white stream. I thought I'd been wandering for years. I *had* been wandering for years, eight years studying the tragic lives of two girls whose fates had been twisted by the hubris of men who'd decided they had the right to learn of the secrets of the world, no matter how dangerous. I was starting to lose myself in it all, my voice, my mind.

My dark curls tumbled over my head as I knelt in the stream, holding myself up with my hands. The water rippled under Marian's footsteps.

"Alice created the phantoms?" I whispered in disbelief.

Marian's feet landed as feathers against the clear waves. "When a person dies, her consciousness is supposed to disappear. A soul should feel nothing. However, every time the stone of fate is used, it draws from the spiritual power of life, death, and fate, drawn together in the great white streams. And so the souls residing within this energy become twisted, angry. The phantoms appeared from the moment Alice began using the stone, powering it through the principle of sacrifice. However, when she made her final wish, the stone peered into her dark mind and concocted a solution from the nightmares it saw there. The phantoms became a tool to fulfill her wish—and they will not stop until the wish is fulfilled."

Alice's wish: to tear down the wicked world. The phantoms were definitely giving it their all.

"Fulfilling the wish is not so difficult for the phantoms, I suppose, given how vicious a twisted, damaged soul can be and how much bitterness they harbor toward the living. But the phantoms never belonged to Alice. They were created and driven by the Eye of Fate— and beholden to it."

"Controlled by it," I added, thinking of Saul's terrible ring.

"Although, Maia," Marian added after a pause. "We too have our own part in the blame. Our powers draw from the same source of all magic—the same stream of life and death, the substance of the universe. The power to create, destroy, and manipulate matter is fate's alone, after all. Or should be."

As Marian continued to approach me, I stared at my own hands, numb, baffled at the thought that each time I used my power to fight phantoms, I was paradoxically creating more phantoms. It was a never-ending, vicious cycle.

And not the only one.

"But why?" I asked. "Why the cycle?" I stared at my reflection in the water. "Why would your power keep reincarnating into the rest of us? Alice gave *you* all powers, not us. So why?"

Marian stopped in front of me, her plain dress floating in the water. "After the phantoms came, Alice remained in the estate while I left to see what she had done. That's when I saw them falling. The city was on fire. I ran to find the other girls, but I could only find Patricia. Her home had been destroyed, her youngest brother still inside. And when I found her, she had . . . she had drowned herself in a lake."

For a moment Marian couldn't go on. She sucked in her lips and shut her eyes tight, taking in several breaths before speaking again. "I went back to the Vogel estate. With the stone in Alice's hand, the phantoms would not attack her. She told me that there were still more wishes she could make. Such was the extent of the stone's power. There was still another wish she wanted to grant for herself. But I wanted to use the stone to get rid of the beasts forever. Alice was enraged at my betrayal—the second betrayal, she told me. The worst one of all. So we fought. It was a terrible struggle. Between our two . . . *abilities*, it was a wonder we didn't tear the estate down completely."

"But why *us*?" Standing, I looked Marian dead in her eyes, searching through the grief and guilt to find something that would help me understand why her legacy had to be my fate.

Marian lowered her head. "After the phantoms fell, I was riddled with a great sense of sorrow. If I had stopped Miss Alice before she made the wish, could I have prevented this tragedy? We were all responsible. Abigail, Emilia, Patricia, and I. Along with Alice, we all had a part to play in the tragedy that befell humanity. But then I'd remembered what Miss Alice had told me: that we were not just monsters or witches. The wish she'd made, pulled from the stories of her childhood, turned us into something more. If we really were like the knights in the stories I'd loved as a child, then perhaps I too could fight. Perhaps I could save others. And if I couldn't—"

Marian's soft face turned to stone with determination. "Links in a chain. There would be other girls like us who would be stronger than us. Who could carry on our will, our magic and responsibility, and rid the world of the phantoms forever."

"Why girls?" I asked, because in all my years of being a fan of Effigies, I never understood it.

A little smile played upon her lips. "Because I was told once that only girls can be knights. And so this place was created." Marian gazed upon the endless white space. "It was the wish I made as Alice and I held on to the stone. At the same moment she made hers."

Alice and Marian . . . two wishes granted at the same time. "What was Alice's wish?"

"Didn't Nick tell you when you were in his memories? Or perhaps Alice told you herself. Concentrate," Marian told me. "Remember."

Shutting my eyes, I searched through scrolls of memories, digging deep. Saul's mind. Two minds, two histories intertwined into one.

*Give it to me. This ungrateful wench. The thing she wanted most. Give it to me and let me keep it for eternity.*

"She wished for Nick?" The breeze rustled my hair as I watched her nod sadly.

"I hadn't even realized it myself. But it was true. I couldn't dare to dream of something so brazen, but over the years I found myself wishing . . . for a future with him." Marian bit her lip. "A future I'd never have. Because Alice took it."

And took her life. A bitter end to a dark tale. In the moment Marian created the Effigy lines, Alice created an eternal connection with Nick. The wishes became one. Nick and Alice became one through the magic of our succession.

"Alice, you see, she cared for me as a little girl does for a doll. However, though there were times that she was good to me, in truth, she never accepted my humanity." Marian clasped her hands together to keep them from shaking. "She couldn't accept that I would have my own will separate from hers, or that I could have the love of a man she felt should have been hers. And as much as she hated her father, she respected him far more than she ever did me."

Alice couldn't recognize her as an equal. No, she refused. Even as Saul, she continued to call her the name of a doll, a constant taunt to remind Marian of the attitudes existing centuries ago that would have never allowed her to be anything other than owned.

"Then what happened?" I asked her.

"The force of our two wills shattered the stone. Alice was so enraged. If I hadn't . . ." She paused. "She would have killed me if I hadn't struck first."

So Marian had killed Alice, and Alice later returned the favor. It was a feud spanning more than a century. But along the way, as Alice walked the earth in Nick's body, she was caught by the Sect and roped into the Blackwell family's terrible plan. Despite all her efforts, all her designs, all the victims she'd sacrificed for the sake of her twisted dream, she had once again become a pawn under the foot of a man desperate for power.

"The tragedies that began the day Castor and Vogel found the goddesses will never end," Marian told me. "It's a curse upon humanity. And you, Maia . . . it's you who needs to break this curse." She lifted her hand. "You need to save us. By making one last wish."

The image of a blue stone shimmered like waves over her hand. The Eye of Life. "In his despair, Vogel told me the full truth of what happened that fateful day: That when the goddesses promised that Vogel and Castor would never be able to find them again, Vogel said that over his dead body would they shut their door against him. The goddesses, with their twisted sense of humor, obliged and imposed a new rule: that only with the payment of his rotted corpse would anyone ever be allowed to cross their gate again."

A chill ran down my spine. A morbid game between gods and man. A game affecting the lives of billions.

"His carcass, they said, could be used in the place of death, whose eye had not been given. Death. Life. And fate. No one shall ever find them until the three are brought together again."

"The eyes," I said. "I could use the eyes. . . ."

"Yes," answered Marian. "Even the smallest fragment will do. When you bring their bodies together, when you call them, they will answer. That's all."

"And Vogel's body." My heart raced as I thought of Saul holding the vial of Vogel's ashes in his hands. "Belle brought it from York after scrying a memory of you and Emilia!"

"Emilia . . ." Marian smiled, remembering her. "Yes. The phantoms eventually destroyed the Vogel mansion, as I knew they would, but before they did, Emilia and I made sure to keep Vogel's body safe, buried under the ground, just in case. I did not know your friend would find it, but with it, you have a chance to find the goddesses again."

Great. There was just one problem. "Saul has Vogel's ashes now. I don't know how I'm supposed to get them back."

Marian studied me, the corners of her mouth slightly upturned. "Does he?"

"Yes, he—" Wait. I thought back to that day in the temple when Saul showed me the vial of ashes. I remember him tucking the ashes back into his coat. . . .

The coat that he'd discarded next to Harry's backpack during our fight.

Right next to where my physical body is sitting now.

"Exactly," Marian said with a satisfied grin.

Finally, I'd learned her secret. I'd learned what Marian knew that no other living soul did. There was a direct path back to the ones who started it all. I had the Eye of Life and Vogel's body, but the Eye of Fate—the white stone. I crushed it in Argentina. I smashed Saul's ring so that he could no longer use it to control phantoms. Grounded into dust. It'd probably been washed away with the rain by now.

But there was another ring.

"Blackwell . . ."

"Now go, Maia," Marian said. "Help us atone for our sins. But you must go quickly. Saul will soon make his move. Saul . . . Nick . . ."

Marian trailed off into silence.

"His move?" I frowned. "Marian, what do you—"

"He'll go to where Blackwell is. I could sense it in that moment our minds were one. Go, Maia. Go before it's too late."

The room began to shift around me, swirling like a cyclone, enveloping my body in pure energy and power. "Marian!" I cried. "The goddesses . . . What if I can't find them?"

"You will," she answered. "You'll see them. If your desire to see them is strong enough."

As my feet began to lift from the white stream, I couldn't see Marian anymore. But I could hear her voice calling to me. . . .

"Please help Nick gain peace once and for all," she begged me. "And even Alice. And all of us who bear the fate of the Effigy. Give us all peace."

# PART THREE

I' th' last night's storm I such a fellow saw,
Which made me think a man a worm. My son
Came then into my mind, and yet my mind
Was then scarce friends with him. I have heard more since.
As flies to wanton boys are we to th' gods.
They kill us for their sport.
—William Shakespeare, *King Lear* 4.1.37–42

# 30

POWER TORE THROUGH MY BODY, FLOWING
through the open doors of every Effigy whose memories I'd witnessed. My
mouth hung open as I gasped, struggling to breathe, but when I opened
my eyes, I could only see the spirits, the azure lights swirling into the sky.

Lake and Chae Rin were convulsing next to me. I could feel their
hands still gripping mine, our powers flowing through each other's
bodies as if our link was a conduit.

A stone crashed into my hand and Chae Rin's, breaking our grip—
and breaking the connection. I gasped in shock, shutting my eyes and
shivering as the power dissipated. The spirits were gone. Lake and
Chae Rin doubled over, panting. We were okay; our clothes and hair
disheveled, but otherwise we were fine.

"That was . . ." Chae Rin swallowed, touching her throat. "That was
one intense scrying session."

It was Yulia who had snapped us back to reality by throwing the
stone. She was on the other side of the gazebo at a safe distance. "I'm
sorry," she said. "I called your names, but you would not respond, and I
could not step near you."

The Deoscali danced around the courtyard, past the ruined stone walls, praising and worshipping the sign that the spirits had given them through the Effigies.

"How long have we been out?" I asked.

"Two minutes," Yulia answered. "Maybe three, at the most."

Minutes. Time really did move differently in there. Once I was able to gather myself, I dipped my hands into the pit. These shards of stone were the calcified remnants of a goddess. Only once this stone was brought together with death and fate would I be able to reach the goddesses and make one final wish. Just a fragment was all I needed. But that wasn't all.

Getting to my feet, I dove for Saul's coat, still in the gazebo, and dug out the vial of ashes. The remains of the man who had helped begin our nightmares. I couldn't imagine Saul would bother coming back for it, not if "Saul" was being driven by Nick's mind. I would have figured Alice wouldn't want it either, but then, as Saul said, Alice hadn't seemed to mind holding on to it for herself. A keepsake. Benjamin was her father after all.

But then, she'd killed her father. If Alice had retained control over Saul—if I hadn't pushed Nick so far to the surface with my goading—perhaps Alice *would* have come back for it. I held the vial up. Through the glass, Vogel's ashes glinted in the moonlight. For Alice, this would have been one final triumph over her father. Dominance over the man who had tried to dominate the path of her future.

For me, it was a way to shape my own.

"Do we want to know what that is?" Chae Rin asked, grimacing as she stared up at the vial.

"Not really." I lowered my hand, gripping the vial tight. The Eye of Life. Vogel's body to stand in for death. But even if I got my hands on fate, what if it didn't work? What if I couldn't find the goddesses?

*You'll see them. You can see them.*

"Marian . . . ," I whispered. I stared deep into the depths of the shards of blue stone I held in my palm.

"Maia?" Lake put her hand on my shoulders. "You okay?"

"Yes," I said after a while, as quiet as death, because I understood. I knew why I would be able to reach them.

Because I had died once before.

It was as Castor had written: "Only those who have died, if their desire to see them is strong enough, can cross the gate into their godly domain."

Getting to my feet, I nodded to Yulia. "We'll be off now," I told her.

The drumbeats pounded a steady rhythm, each strike as powerful as Yulia's gaze as her followers danced and sang around us.

"To fight, I presume?" Yulia asked, the fire from Deoscali's candles illuminating her pale, wrinkled skin, casting light and shadow across her heavy robes.

"As per usual," Chae Rin answered as she and Lake got to their feet.

Yulia silently watched me close my fingers around the stone shards before taking off her pendant and stretching out her hand. "Take this," she said.

I stared at the blue teardrop dangling from the golden string. "A-are you sure?"

"The spirit compels me. It's the stone you need, isn't it?"

I nodded. "It's very important."

"Too important to carry around in your hand. This will be more difficult to lose if you tie it around your neck. We will be okay here with the stones you leave behind."

After hesitantly placing the shards back into the pit, I approached her and took the pendant, tying it around my neck twice so there was no chance of it flying off.

I tilted the glass vial. "I'll still have to put Vogel's ashes in my pocket or something. I really hope it doesn't break; I don't want this man staining my pants."

I took Chae Rin and Lake's horrified expressions to mean that I would have to explain on the plane.

"Just remember, Effigies. The phantoms are not your enemies as you would presume," Yulia said. "They are but spirits twisted in agony. Life and death are connected by fate, traveling down the same road spread across the world—the road that all spirits must take."

Manipulating the course of fate had a price, just as the goddesses had told Castor and Vogel. Alice thought she'd discovered the key, but sacrificing others was just part of it. If life, death, and fate were all connected, then twisting fate would have consequences that reverberated throughout the world. Every time Alice made a wish, a soul became ruined. And when Alice wished for a plague upon the earth, the stone obliged, ruining more souls throughout history. Every action had a reaction. Every wish had the price of sacrifice.

It was *wrong*.

"Let's get back to the jet," I said to the girls. "We're going back to New York. We have to get there before Saul does."


"You guys are in Quebec? All of you?" I listened to the voice on the other end of the phone. "Yes, I know there's a giant trafficking ring over there—No, I'm not interested in the details—Yeah, I know you almost got caught, and I'm sorry. I didn't think the CSTF would—" Another lengthy pause. "Look, I don't care *how* you get them there, just *please* get to New York City as fast as you can and bring whatever arsenal you think can help—Yes, I'm *dead* serious. I'll even pay you guys, if you need it. Trust me, I know some incredibly wealthy people." I cringed at the promise. Maybe Naomi had a trust fund she could spare. "Please, I am begging you, *please* just get there!" I yelled into the phone before hanging up.

Beside me, Lake raised an eyebrow. "You really think he's going to come through?"

Giving Cheryl back her phone, I sighed. "He'd better. If I'm right, we're going to need all the help we can get."

I had the pendant around my neck and the vial in a pouch Cheryl had given me, sealed in the zipped pocket of the corduroy jacket Chae Rin had let me borrow. After I explained to the others what it was, it was better to keep it out of sight anyway.

"So far there's been no unusual activity in Greenland," Cheryl said across from me. "None at all. I can't justify mobilizing all of Sibyl's agents to New York based on a hunch."

"It's not a hunch." I tapped my fingers on the desk, watching the phantoms following us outside. "Marian told me that Saul was going to make his move on Blackwell. After the drugs wear off and those soldiers are operational, he could strike at *any* time."

"That's the problem, Maia." Chae Rin sat in the opposite row so she could put her feet up on the table. "He can attack at any time. Anywhere. We have no idea what he's planning or when he's planning to do it. Could be days from now. I know we need to get to Blackwell's ring, so it makes sense to go to New York anyway. But there are probably tons of CSTF goons in the city right now with Blackwell there. Asking Sibyl's agents to go there might just get them caught."

"She's right," Cheryl said.

"Cheryl, please. It's a risk we have to take. I'm begging you. Get those agents to New York. I just have a feeling something's going to happen." Marian's warning was lodged so deeply, I couldn't dig it back out. Saul would be on the move soon. This wasn't the time to take chances.

Cheryl hesitated but eventually gave in.

The following hours on the jet passed in contemplative silence, the clock in my head counting down tick by painful tick. We'd all spread out down the aisle to have some space while we rested. I was too wound up to even try to sleep. The memories of Effigies echoed half formed in my thoughts, tales of warriors struggling, fighting, dying under a legacy that was never quite theirs. I thought of them, of Marian and the years stolen from her. Soon my concern drifted to Rhys and Brendan in Greenland. I hadn't heard from either of them since we left for Guadeloupe. Maybe Brendan's cell phone was dead. Or maybe he was too bereaved to remember he had a cell phone at all. There had to be a reason, but some reasons I didn't want to consider. Rhys had to be okay. He *had* to be. Too many people I cared about had died already. I couldn't lose Rhys too.

I assumed I was the only one who couldn't sleep, but after an hour Lake patted my seat from behind before sitting down next to me.

"You know, I can't stop thinking about everything we saw," she said after a while, tugging the strands of her black bob. "To think our entire world went to hell because of a handful of people making bad choices."

"Isn't that how it always is?" The Sect's Council, the United Nations Assembly. Handfuls of people making decisions affecting billions.

"I've just . . . I've always wondered why we were chosen for this." Lake put her hand on her chest. "Like, why us?"

"It was fate. Literally."

"Yeah, but *why*, you know?" Lake shook her head. "Why did Marian have to be the one to go to Vogel's house? Why did Natalya have to die? Why did Belle have to suffer? Why did any of us have to—" She stopped because there were just too many "whys" to get through.

"When people make decisions, other people's lives are affected."

It was Chae Rin who'd spoken. I'd thought she was sleeping until she opened her eyes a few seats away, her legs still crossed on the table. "It's just the way it is. And what we choose to do from here on out will affect people too. That's why we have to be careful."

I touched the pendant around my neck, silently agreeing.

*Tick, tick, tick.* Time passed slowly. We were just forty-five minutes outside New York. With the early-morning sun filtering into the jet through the clouds, Cheryl watched live feeds of the news on her phone as they covered the second day of the Assembly.

"Wait." Cheryl leaned in, squinting through her glasses. "Is that . . . ? Lake, are those your parents?"

"What?" Lake jumped out of her seat and rushed to where Cheryl was sitting. I followed behind, positioning myself for a better view of Cheryl's laptop. "Why are they in New York?"

They were among the crowds swarming outside the doors of the tall building. Separating themselves from the pack, they stood next to the correspondent.

"Now, Mr. and Mrs. Soyinka, you've been giving interviews trying to convince people of your daughter's innocence. Why come to New York now? How do you feel about those who criticize you for supporting who they think is a terrorist?"

"Terrorist?" Mrs. Soyinka, in her Sunday best, looked furious at the question, so much so that the correspondent immediately flinched. "So you think it's okay to interview a mother and call her daughter a terrorist in front of her?" Her round face, expertly covered in makeup, scrunched into a vicious glare. "Is that how your news organization treats the people who come onto this show?" Her slighter-framed husband was trying to calm her down, to no avail.

"No, ma'am, that wasn't at all my intention."

"Because of people like you spreading false information and speculation, those poor girls' reputations have been ruined." She pronounced every syllable clearly and distinctly with her West African accent. "Have you ever stopped to think how their families might feel in all of this nonsense? Did you ever have any proof that all the girls were terrorists themselves? Did you present any research, any evidence, before you began talking and speculating for hours on television?" When the correspondent could only stutter a noncommittal response, Mrs. Soyinka sucked her teeth. "Very irresponsible. You should all be ashamed of yourselves."

"Wow, what a queen," I said, nodding in agreement. "She went all the way to New York to cuss 'em out."

Chae Rin whistled. "She really told them, didn't she?"

Lake was still staring at the screen, baffled.

It was her father's turn to speak. Taking the microphone from the correspondent, he stared straight into the camera through his square, horned-rimmed glasses. "We're here hoping we can talk to Mr. Blackwell on his way out. And reason with the rest of you. Please don't jump to condemning these girls before you have all the facts. At the end of the day, they are still children. Most importantly, they're someone's children."

"Your parents are pretty brave, Lake," Cheryl said.

"They're just . . . really protective of me," she said with a little smile. "I guess you don't have to wonder why I'm so spoiled, right?"

Chae Rin opened her mouth, clearly ready to make a snide remark, when the correspondent quickly took her microphone back from Mr. Soyinka.

"We just got word that Effigy Belle Rousseau is going to speak at the Assembly moments from now."

The announcement dashed the smiles from our faces.

"Belle?" As if her name itself were ice, a chill crawled through my veins.

Chae Rin frowned, no doubt remembering the brutal state the Ice Effigy had left her in. "What the hell is she up to?"

We didn't have to wait too long to find out. Belle entered the room in handcuffs, escorted by several guards. She'd been working with Blackwell as one of his bodyguards not too long ago. But to come before the United Nations, she clearly needed to show that she wasn't going to blow them all away. Maybe she was even inoculated.

She looked worn, hollowed out from the inside, like the past few days and weeks had emptied her of herself. I knew it the moment I saw her. This was her last hurrah. "There's only one reason Belle would be there," I said, and hoped beyond all hope that I was wrong.

I wasn't. Belle stepped up to podium in her black suit, her ponytail neatly tied in the back, her hands still cuffed behind her. She didn't need them to speak into the microphone, the eyes of the world on her.

She cleared her throat. "My name is Belle Rousseau." She paused. It was my first time seeing her this nervous. She didn't show it too obviously, but the way her eyes scanned the Assembly made it clear she was not nearly as comfortable as she tried to portray. The camera panned to leaders in the audience, sitting at their seats behind the long, winding tables, waiting patiently in their official, cultural garb. Blackwell was among them, sitting at the very end of one of the lower rows, his expression as serious as the others. A performance. Though I didn't know what they looked like, I knew his supporters on the Council were there too.

In the seconds the camera showed him, I searched his fingers. His usual rings were there, but not *the* ring. Fate's eye. But there was no way he wouldn't have it on him somewhere.

Steadying her breath, Belle started again, drawing my attention back. "My name is Belle Rousseau. I was born in Gisors, France. I am an Effigy. And I am also a terrorist."

As the crowd broke out into concerned chatter and whispers, the tension sucked out all the air on the jet. Next to me, Chae Rin cursed quietly, but for some reason, I didn't share in her anger. I *wanted* to be angry. I probably should have been. But all I could feel was pity for Belle as she stood in front of the United Nations and shilled for Blackwell. I had seen so many Effigies in hopeless situations on my way to Marian's memories, and they all had the same look: that wordless fear draining the hope and life out of their faces. It wasn't something that anyone other than an Effigy could recognize. As Belle swallowed, her cuffed hands rigid behind her back, I remembered the once respected Effigy, and my hatred for Blackwell only grew.

"At age thirteen, I was chosen by fate to become the *Aqua Ensis*," Belle continued. "The Effigy of Water. As an Effigy, I dedicated my life to the protection of humanity."

She stopped. Protecting humanity. Her bottom lip bobbed up and down before she snapped it shut, but the words lived on, deepening creases on her forehead as she fought to keep herself steady.

"That's right, Belle," I said. "You dedicated your life to protecting people once."

Shaking away her nerves, Belle straightened up. "However, along the way, I came to believe that loyalty to the Sect was more important than saving lives. I became disillusioned with respect to my purpose. I lost my reason for saving others. And so I became a terrorist."

As they say, the best lies always had a grain of truth to them. Belle wasn't a terrorist. She'd only allowed herself to be used by them. She still was.

"While pretending to capture the terrorist Saul, I was part of the operation secretly helping him destroy your cities. I understand that what I did was wrong. That's why I turned myself in and placed myself under the custody of the CSTF." As if to remind them, she shook her arms, her cuffs clinking. "I'm here to tell those of you still insistent upon using the Effigies as weapons of war against the phantoms. We are not your heroes. We can't be. I—"

Belle's next words died on her lips. She lost focus on the Assembly, her body arching forward as she stared at the microphone.

"What's wrong with her?" Lake asked next to me.

Aside from the fact that she was throwing us under the bus, I had no idea. And if her plan really *was* to throw us under the bus, then she certainly didn't look as committed as Blackwell probably wanted her to be. She was silent for almost too long. As the camera showed the audience once more, the screen panned over Blackwell's stiffened jaw. He was waiting with the rest of us.

Eventually, someone had to prod her before she could snap out of it. "I can't be." Her mouth pressed shut. "I can't be . . . I failed to be. It was I who failed to be a hero. But the other girls . . ."

I waited, holding my breath as she hesitated.

"They were your colleagues, were they not?" said the dignitary from Ukraine into his microphone. "You worked together closely. You were comrades. Are you telling me that you are ready to turn against them?"

Belle remained silent.

"What were they to you, then?" asked the dignitary from Botswana. "Please, tell us."

What were we to her? The question seemed to spook Belle, her face turning pale. All those months fighting together side by side. Living together. What were we to Belle Rousseau?

"I . . ." Belle paused, her eyes flitting to Blackwell, then to the other dignitaries, and finally to her own hands in chains. "I don't know." She shook her head. "I don't know."

Whispers spread throughout the group of dignitaries. Despite hiding it well, Blackwell was not pleased.

Lake, Chae Rin, and I exchanged glances, none of us knowing what to expect next. Belle clearly didn't know either. It was one thing to promise to destroy the Sect even if it meant defeating us. But now that it was the hour of truth, Belle didn't look confident at all. Her insecurity screamed across the room from the way she peered into the camera, frozen.

"The Sect must be obsolete," she said with a self-reassuring nod. "That I know. But . . . those girls . . . did nothing wrong." She'd almost whispered it. She placed her hands on the podium, curling them into fists. "I'm the only one. I watched Saul kill a man in Guadeloupe while I stood by, doing nothing."

The tourist? I'd assumed it was Belle who'd killed him. The confession filled me with some relief. Nonetheless, it was impossible to tell what was happening on that stage in front of the Assembly. Was she selling us out or testifying on our behalf? Maybe she didn't even know. On one hand, there was the plan. On the other, the truth.

"So which is it, Belle?" I whispered, narrowing my eyes.

"Blackwell's proposal is still just," she said. "The Sect needs to disappear. The United Earth Specialized Forces would take away the world's dependency on us unpredictable Effigies."

And that's what Belle wanted. To be free.

"But I am the only one. Victoria, Chae Rin . . . Maia . . . they are . . . innocent. They are . . . they were my friends." Her voice stalled on the final word, breaking just before she sucked in a breath to calm herself. "Unlike me, they don't deserve these chains."

"I don't get it." Cheryl stared into her laptop screen, shaking her head. "What's she doing?"

I straightened up. "Fighting herself." Caught between two imperatives, two allegiances, Belle had no choice but to parse through her own confused mind. Eventually, they called her off the stage. She was technically still under arrest, but in case they needed to hear further testimony, they'd have to hold her in some other room in the building, keeping her under supervision until they called for her again.

Chae Rin scoffed. "She certainly wasn't fighting herself when she was trying to beat me to death." She walked to another seat and plopped down, crossing her legs.

But even before their fight in Carnegie Hall, her confusion, her desperation was obvious. "Belle is struggling," I said. "She's been struggling this whole time."

"Aw, that's so sad." Chae Rin tilted her head to the side. "Nonetheless, if she comes for us, we have to take her out. Period."

I turned to her. "We have to help her."

"No, *we have to take her out*. Won't matter how 'confused' she is if she's still determined to kill us or put us in chains."

"Maia . . ." As the news correspondent outside the UN building babbled in the background, Lake moved between us. "You told us yourself. You were *dead*. Actually, *literally* dead. She *killed* you."

She did, though only after I dealt the final blow to kill her spirit. It wasn't a matter of forgiving or making excuses. After watching Marian's story, I knew how easy it was for someone to break. We were just people, after all. People struggling under impossible circumstances, people just trying to make it through with our hearts, bodies, and minds still intact. Everyone needed to be held accountable for their actions, but I was done with holding my friends to impossible standards. I couldn't do that anymore. I'd made up my mind of that the moment I defeated Natalya.

"I am going to save them," I whispered, and looked at Chae Rin. "Us. All of us."

Chae Rin and I glared at each other, neither willing to bend to the other.

"Wait, what is that?" said the correspondent. The girls and I turned to see the commotion outside the UN. Several black cars pulled up to the curb. The cameras zoomed in as Sibyl Langley stepped out of one in a crisp striped business suit, striding into the building with several official-looking men trailing behind.

"Here we go." Chae Rin jumped up and, pushing me aside, went to hover over Cheryl from behind her seat.

"Who is that?" The correspondent squinted. "Wait, was that—was that former Director Langley?"

The correspondent excitedly relayed what we'd just seen to the news anchor on set, and because the two had no information, they could only babble on and on about Sibyl, her dismissal from the Sect, and the persistent rumors that she was helping the Effigies evade law enforcement. They quickly switched to the feed inside the building. Sibyl waltzed into the Assembly as if she owned everyone there, in her hands vetted evidence against Blackwell.

And that was when the livestream feed cut off.

"Looks like the Assembly's not gonna let any more of this get out to the public." Cheryl picked up her phone, perking up once the dial tone stopped abruptly. "Nathan, can you get us visuals inside? We need to see what's currently happening in there."

"Yep. I'll commandeer a security cam," said Uncle Nathan on speaker. "Hold on."

Cheryl put the screen up for us to see. There was no audio yet. But we didn't need audio to gather the situation: guards pointing their guns at Sibyl's agents, who pointed their guns at them. Blackwell on his feet, striding into the side aisle while Sibyl stared him down. Complete confusion among the dignitaries.

Cheryl pulled the phone toward her. "Nathan, tell me you've got everything set up."

"Yep, I know the plan." Uncle Nathan's speedy clicking took over for the next few seconds. "Okay," he said. "I'm ready to get the visual and audio feed back online."

"Good." Cheryl flashed an almost mischievous grin. "People are going to want to livestream this."

The audio cut back in. "Sibyl Langley." Agents and security guards blocked the path between Blackwell and Sibyl, but from the way they were staring each other down, you'd think they were in each other's faces. "Are you aware of what you're accusing me of?"

"That you organized and sanctioned Saul's global terrorism to gain public support for the United Earth Specialized Forces, which you aim to control?" Sibyl tilted her head. "Yes, Bartholomäus." Her glare could have burned the wings off a fly.

Straightening his back, he looked as grim as ever. "Those are bold words for a woman who's been evading law enforcement since the attacks on Oslo."

"Attacks you orchestrated, according to Senator Abrams."

"Senator Abrams?" Blackwell laughed. "As I recall, he was murdered by the Effigies a few nights ago."

"No. He was murdered by one of the soldiers you've been secretly engineering in Greenland."

"Nathan," Cheryl prodded.

"I know, I know."

With a few clicks of his keyboard, the Assembly erupted with sounds of phone notifications. For a moment there was just rustling as everyone checked their phones. And slowly, shocked gasps rippled across the room. This was Sibyl's plan. If we couldn't stall Blackwell from the Assembly, then she could use the Assembly for maximum shock effect and maximum exposure. Put on a show with the cameras running. Use Blackwell's usual tactics against him. He knew it too. It must have been the irony that was making him fume.

But this wasn't just a show. "What you're looking at right now," Sibyl said to the Assembly, "are details outlined by former Secretary of State Briggs on plans to force Sect trainees to act as guinea pigs for an illegal virtual reality program aimed at developing child soldiers. If you look at the pictures of those dead bodies carefully, you'll see that they belong to Talia Nassar, Jessie Stone, and Philip Anglebart, who were part of the cohort Briggs mentions."

They must have been the only ones she could use. Alexander Drywater's body was too decomposed, and Gabriel was still in the wind. Blackwell flinched at each name.

"They were innocent children," Sibyl continued. "Innocent children who depended on the Council to protect them fell victim to a long con designed to grant Blackwell and his Council supporters more power and influence over world politics than they could have ever dreamed of."

"That is absolutely ridiculous." A stalky woman with short, black hair jumped to her feet in the back row, but despite her indignation, she was clearly terrified. Perhaps unconsciously, she brushed her shaking hands down her beige suit, her eyes shuttling nervously to Blackwell, who didn't return her gaze. "How dare you accuse me—"

"It's not an accusation, Betty," Sibyl said. "Those are your words. The attorney general and the director of National Intelligence have already sent agents to check out your facility in Greenland. I wouldn't even be here if I didn't know they were on board first. I'm sure you'll be getting a call from them shortly." Sibyl reached into her pocket, unfazed by the security guards who consequently twitched their guns toward her. "But first you need to hear from Abrams himself."

"This is it," Cheryl said. Each of us leaned in.

"If you know that Blackwell is dirty, then you know I had nothing to do with Oslo." Abrams. It was the conversation we had in his car.

"Aside from giving Prince the go-ahead to fire a death weapon." It was so surreal seeing heads of state react to my voice. I half wondered if they knew it was rogue Effigy Maia Finley speaking.

"I discussed it with Blackwell first. In fact, he was the one who pressed me to do it. I never would have otherwise—"

Blackwell bristled. "This is ridiculous—"

"But we were in a state of panic, and he convinced me that it was the only option. As the Council representative, he didn't have the codes or authority to do anything himself."

"That's right," said Blackwell, covering himself well. "I didn't have the authority. I guided Abrams to make the best decision we could under the circumstances."

He spoke loudly, but not loudly enough to keep the room from hearing Lake tell Abrams that Blackwell now had sole control over the satellite weapon Minerva.

"The Council voted after I resigned," Abrams continued. "There are three standing with him now: Wang Liu, a highly influential businessman in China and owner of one of the largest media providers in the world; Betty Briggs, a former US secretary of state; and Judge Antero Nylund, who is serving on the International Criminal Court."

Dignitaries were turning their heads toward the back row, which Briggs had vacated, where Wang Liu and Antero Nylund were still sitting, frozen in shock and horror.

"All people who can use their power and influence to gather legal and financial support to force Blackwell's post-Sect creation. Naomi is in the wind, and Blackwell recently assassinated Baldric and Cardinal Donati."

"*Assassination?*" a dignitary repeated, her voice cutting through the recording.

"Turn it off." Blackwell gave Sibyl a menacing look, but his warning only earned a simple shrug from the former director.

"The Sect wasn't enough," Sibyl said. "No, not with the Greenwich Accords keeping us and our resources tied up in fighting phantoms. You wanted ultimate control—control your family was never given by the Council. Control not only over the Sect but over the world. Even if that meant burning everything to the ground and starting fresh with a new organization that would grant you the military and political power you've been aiming for. Because what's a powerful, insecure man if he isn't aiming for even more power?"

"That's enough," Blackwell roared, but as he continued to face Sibyl, Cheryl's phone rang, tearing away our focus.

"Guys," Uncle Nathan said, "I just picked up a distress signal from the Municipal Defense Control Center."

The MDCC? What could possibly be going on at my uncle's old workplace?

"Why all of a sudden . . . ?" Cheryl frowned. "Nathan, can you get eyes inside?"

"Wait a sec. I'll put up live footage from the cameras in the control room."

The footage we saw left us gaping in silence. Bodies. Bloodied and broken in their seats at their computers, the computers Uncle Nathan used to spend hours staring at to help keep New York's antiphantom Needle up and running. They were being murdered by a boy whose pictures I'd seen only when compiled next to that of the other Silent Children: Gabriel Moore. His face was still coal-dark and handsome. It was his eyes that were dead. His uniform was different from the ones of the other Silent Children—like an upgraded version. It was made of white metal like the helmets they sometimes wore, though *his* helmet was nowhere in sight. A stare from his dark eyes was all it took to blow up the machines that kept New York safe. But he wasn't there alone.

"June . . ." Pushing Cheryl aside, I bent over and drew the laptop close to me, not wanting to believe what was clear on the screen. There she was wearing the same sleek white armor Gabriel had on. Snapping her fingers, she erupted fires all along the control center. Between the two of them, there wasn't a soul left alive.

"Oh god." Uncle Nathan sounded sick. "Oh god, those were my . . . June is . . ."

I could hear him throwing up over the speaker.

"What are they doing?" Chae Rin said. "How the hell did they even get in there?"

They could only be snuck inside by someone not bound by the laws of space and time.

Saul. He walked through the side door into the view of the camera, wearing a black vest, a white dress shirt, a tie, and trousers. He'd dressed for the occasion exactly how Nicholas would have back when he was alive. Before the door closed behind him, I saw the corpses of security officers lying in the hallway.

Déjà vu. Saul had been inside a control room like this decades before, only then he'd had no control over his faculties. At that time it was Blackwell's father in control. That was the beginning of the seven-day tragedy that would eventually become known as the Seattle Siege.

What would this become?

"The Needle." Uncle Nathan's voice returned, frail and terrified. "It's off-line."

There was no one left alive to sound the war siren. But it didn't matter. New York would know soon enough.

I grabbed Cheryl's collar. "How much longer until we reach New York?"

"J-just over f-fifteen minutes," she answered, pulling my hands off her.

Marian had warned me that Saul would be on the move soon, and here he was. We couldn't waste another second.

"Hey, guys—" This time it was Pete's voice buzzing out of the phone from inside Seattle Communications. "You might want to go back to the UN Assembly feed. . . ."

Saul had just appeared between Blackwell and Sibyl, carrying June and Gabriel in tow. Most of the agents and security officers were quickly disposed of with the joint efforts of June and Gabriel, Saul's personal strike team. Then they blew up the doors, which terrified dignitaries were running for, blocking the exits with the rubble. The dignitaries ducked for cover, and Blackwell and Sibyl jumped back to avoid being collateral damage.

But Saul didn't want to kill Blackwell. No. He slinked up to the man deliberately, like an animal stalking his prey. Blackwell had dived to the ground. No matter his bluster, he was no match for an Effigy he no longer controlled. With his hands propping his body up behind him and his knees jutting up into the air, he shook, watching Saul bend down next to him.

"It must be surprising to see me not on your leash, little Bartholomäus—the leash your father and his friends placed on me." Saul considered him, tilting his head to look over every angle of the man quivering before him. "You all do look alike. You, your father. I knew one of you Blackwells more than a century ago, back when I was only Nick Hudson. That Blackwell was a sniveling, pathetic man forever bitter because he was not allowed to sit at the same table as the other good old boys. I guess certain deficiencies are generational."

Blackwell let out a short gasp as Saul moved toward him. He must have thought what I did—that Saul would kill him. Instead, the Effigy merely stuck his hand inside Blackwell's pocket and pulled out the one ring not on any of Blackwell's fingers. *The* ring. The Eye of Fate.

Saul inspected its pure white surface. "It's empty. I suppose you haven't used it, have you? Nobody can make a wish with this. But it's no matter."

Saul stood, and when he looked at the dignitaries, they cowered in fear, trapped like animals in a cage. "I am the terrorist Saul," he told them. "Under the orders of Blackwell the fifth and his sniveling son shivering here before you, I was used to destroy cities and bring about terror—starting with Seattle."

A confession straight from the killer. The dignitaries listened, paralyzed. Sibyl narrowed her eyes, watching him carefully from where she stood mere meters away from sentinels June and Gabriel.

"But in actuality," Saul said, "I started out as someone quite different. My name was Nick Hudson. I was born before any of you, in 1847. I was a simple man but with many dreams. I dreamed of being a scholar, a teacher. I once had a dream of running away with the woman I loved to a place no one could find us. I dreamed of many things that were taken from me." He lifted his head, gazing up at the ceiling as if it had his terrible, century-and-a-half-long life story etched upon it. "I deserve another chance. Marian and I deserve another chance. Even if I have to reshape the world to get it."

He scoped the room, searching along the walls until he found the camera in the bottom left corner of the ceiling where the livestream's footage was being taken. He looked straight into it.

And smiled.

"Maia Finley," he said. "Are you watching?"

My bones rattled at the sound of my name whispered from his lips. Cheryl, Chae Rin, and Lake all whipped to me in shock.

"You must be watching," he continued, his loose silver hair

swinging as he shifted his head. "The world is watching. In which case, I want you to know that I plan to give you a gift. Once you get here, you'll find them . . . all over this city."

He vanished.

"Nathan." Cheryl grabbed the phone from the table, lifting it to her mouth. "We need satellite visual—now."

Uncle Nathan sounded as if he were struggling to pull himself together. "O-on it. Hey, you guys, help me out," he called, probably to the few others agents working in the center.

Various images from security cameras around the city began popping up on Cheryl's laptop screen.

"Oh my . . ." Lake covered her mouth. "Oh no . . ."

Soldiers. If Saul could warp me, June, or Gabriel from one place to another along with him, then he could warp in many more than that. Dozens, all in the same updated uniform. Using his powers, Saul left them all along the city, on streets blocking traffic, on school grounds, in front of bakeries, convenience stores. On the Brooklyn Bridge and in front of Grand Central. They were once Blackwell's enhanced soldiers, engineered with Effigy-like abilities under the direction of Grunewald. Now they were Saul's personal force.

And so were the phantoms. With the Needle down, the clouds began to crackle with energy, swirling gray into vortexes that grew darker as they began to funnel down to earth. I'd seen this before, through the windows of Ashford High, back when I had just been chosen by fate to take on a destiny larger than I could have ever imagined.

Saul. He was . . . he was going to completely destroy New York.

He appeared back inside the UN building, dusting himself off in front of the Assembly as if he'd just taken a short stroll through the city. He didn't want to show the strain the overuse of his powers had caused him, but I could see it on his face. Even though he was breathing heavily, he still had enough strength to pull out of his pocket the device he'd taken from Grunewald—the device designed to control the soldiers through voice command. He raised it to his lips—

"Kill everyone in the city. And don't stop until nobody's left."

—and threw the device to the ground, crushing it under his heel. Now nobody could call off the order. Not Blackwell. Not even him.

"What are you *doing*?" Blackwell was on his feet, his fists shaking. "You're insane. What do you think you're going to accomplish with all this? Saul! *Alice!*"

At the sound of Alice's name, Saul doubled over, grabbing his head, his screams muffled behind his clenched teeth. No one dared to go near him, not with Gabriel and June standing nearby. It was slow, gradual. But eventually Saul's girlish giggles echoed across the ceiling.

"My sweet Nicholas, you fool," Alice said, sweeping Saul's hair back. "You've completely broken, haven't you? What do you think you're going to accomplish by putting on such a show?"

Saul's face contorted, and he shook his head violently. "Stop it." Nick was clearly back, speaking through Saul's gritted teeth. "Stop it. I told you. I told all of you. I told *you*, Maia." Saul looked up at the camera, his chest heaving. "I told you in Argentina that I was going to reshape the world. But I'm going to do it my way."

It was Nick Hudson smiling now, his lips veiling centuries of a mad desperation for the freedom, the future that had been so cruelly snatched from him. "Even if that means undoing all of it. I'll turn *everything* back."

Turn everything back. I bit my lip. Did he mean what I thought he meant?

"And, Maia. Marian has already told you, hasn't she? She's told you her secret."

I suddenly felt as cold as a corpse. My neck was straining, aching from bending over, my face in pain from clenching my jaw so tight. Yulia's pendant was heavy against the tightness in my chest. I kept deathly still, watching Saul through Cheryl's laptop. Our eyes locked on each other despite being miles apart.

"My home was once destroyed by the stone. I will use it to gain back everything I've lost. Once I get the stone, this city will be saved. I can assure you of that. But, Maia, if you don't come to me and tell me where it is . . ." A serenity passed over his features, and for a moment he looked like the sweet, handsome Nick from Marian's tragic memories. "Well. It's either you come to me or you stay where you are and watch *your* home be destroyed. The choice is yours."

# 31

"I KNEW THIS WOULD HAPPEN." I TOOK THE in-ear comm that Cheryl gave us to replace the ones we'd lost.

"Phantoms are tearing through New York," Chae Rin said, checking her in-ear device. "Supersoldiers on a rampage. You really think the four of us are going to be enough?"

"No," Cheryl said from her seat. "But thanks to Maia's foresight, we already have backup on the scene."

Somehow, I didn't much feel like patting myself on the back. Saul had completely snapped, and no matter what I did, people were going to die. People already *were* dying. The only thing we could do was to get to the UN Headquarters as quickly as possible and put an end to this chaos once and for all.

"We're en route to the UN building," Cheryl said as if reading my mind. "We should get there in a couple of minutes—"

The jet began to shake dangerously.

"What's going on?" Lake said after another sudden jolt.

"Ma'am?" The pilot's voice came in through the overhead system. "We're picking up some unusual electromagnetic activity on all sides."

"What?" I slipped in front of a pair of empty seats, my leg brushing the table, and pulled up the window shade. As we hovered above New York, the skies crackled with dark phantom energy. The jet's electromagnetic armor wouldn't let it get close, but with a number of phantoms funneling out of the clouds, it may not have even mattered. Five. Ten. Twenty. It was the electric discharge crackling in the air that shook the jet with turbulence.

Lake held on to the seat to keep us steady as the floor rocked beneath us. "Will this thing even reach the UN building?"

Phantom cries echoed in the sky, pure, haunting, one following the other in an almost beautiful orchestral succession.

A phantom shot straight down like a bullet and crashed into our wing. It was so fast I almost missed seeing the phantom's long serpent body.

"We're hit!" cried the pilot. "Beginning emergency landing procedures! Hold on!"

We gripped our seats, squeezing our eyes shut and holding our breaths, and the pilot struggled to keep the jet under control. It swiveled and teetered through the sky, the emergency systems screeching danger. Lake did her best to help steady the jet, but with the rocking and blaring noises, her concentration could only hold so well. But with the combined efforts of the pilot and the Effigy of Wind, we managed to land on top of a building.

"We've overshot the UN building by about one mile," the pilot said, panting.

I checked out the window. Overshot indeed. We'd landed on top of a silver-windowed skyscraper in the middle of Times Square. Bits of debris fell down to the street where phantoms currently ravaged the fleeing pedestrians below. The carnage Saul had unleashed upon the city mere months ago in instant replay. No. I couldn't let this happen again, not from Saul or Blackwell. This was ending *today*.

Making sure my bracelet was on tight, I strode down the aisle. "Open the damn hatch!"

"Like I said, some of our agents are already on the ground, and military troops were dispatched fifteen minutes ago. I'll mobilize more backup to the area," Cheryl said. "CSTF agents, the National Guard— anyone who can help. In the meantime, I'll patch in Nathan and have him guide you to the UN building."

I nodded. "Got it."

Chae Rin and Lake were behind me as the white hatch shuddered and opened, lowering slowly into the ground. The wind blew back my hair, my clothes, and the vial inside the jacket I'd borrowed. The vial. I'd have to be careful.

Just a few meters away, a Category Four phantom descended from the skies, massive with its armor of black bones protecting its rotted flesh, covering its serpent's snout but for its long, twisting jaws. Its sights were set on the streets below.

I leapt at it from the jet, flying off the building, my scythe bursting into my hands in a blaze of fire. The blade dug through its torso, slicing through bones. I used one of bones for footing as it screamed and changed its direction back upward, crashing into one of the electronic billboards before exploding back into black mist. It was Lake who kept the debris from hitting the civilians below, using her wind to slow its fall and usher the debris and us Effigies safely to the ground. But there was only so much she could do. Another serpent-shaped phantom exploded out from the street, sending cars flying.

Chae Rin yelled, raising her arms. The dirt underneath the asphalt caught the phantom's body, forming its own set of jaws made of stone and earth to clamp onto its black torso and drag it back down. The phantom crashed onto the street, flailing as I sent a wave of fire across its length.

"Get off the roads!" I cried as the flames burned the rotten flesh. "Get to a shelter!"

But how far would they get? More phantoms were falling from the sky.

"Come on, we have to get to the UN building," Lake said as she ran up to me. "We can't stay here and fight!"

"But we can't leave them here to die either!" I fired back. "How can we—"

Lake turned. "Look!"

She was pointing down the other end of the street. Tanks were rolling in, fitted with EMA: Their bright hues gave off soft emissions around the tanks' hard, beige surfaces.

"Effigies!" A man's voice came out through a speaker from within the tank. "We have troops stationed at critical points in the city, aiding in evacuations and battle. Concentrate on stopping the terrorist Saul!"

"You heard the guy." Chae Rin grabbed my shoulder, and after I nodded, she turned to Lake. "Come on, pop princess, get us up!"

Lake lowered her head, lifted her arms and, calling the wind, raised us into the air. We flew past Times Square, leaving the tanks to shoot blasts of electrical energy to blow away the phantoms descending from the sky.

I kept my pendant beneath my shirt so it wouldn't whip into my face. I felt the stone cold against my heart.

"Travel southeast," Uncle Nathan ordered us, so we did. West Forty-Fifth groaned in agony from the battle between agents and phantoms. I figured we couldn't avoid them for long, and I was right: A spindly, serpent-like phantom blasted into the sky between Lake and me, so uncomfortably close, the force singed bits of my hair. Its sudden appearance was enough to spook Lake out of her concentration. The wind died, and before Lake could catch herself, we were already plummeting to the ground, right into the waiting jaws of a phantom burrowed into the street.

"Ugh, not this thing again!" Lake yelled, finally managing to halt our fall, as the phantoms smoky black tentacles waved back and forth into the air. A few broke pattern, aiming for us, the phantom's pulsating, rotted head splitting into a wide, toothy grin. It was just as nightmare-fueling as the one we'd seen in France.

With the help of Lake's wind, we avoided each wild slap of its tentacles. Chae Rin sent a spike of earth jutting up from below the beast, skewering its head right up through its jaw.

"Fancy meeting you girls here! You're certainly still as dangerous as ever!"

I heard his lazy, Scottish voice behind us as we landed and almost couldn't believe it. But I turned, and sure enough, it was Lucas, one of his stolen Sect-grade launchers balanced on his shoulders.

"Oh my god!" Lake pointed at him, hopping up and down. "Cute Criminal Guy!"

And he wasn't alone. Abril knelt on the hood of an abandoned car, her own trunk of a weapon aimed at one of the phantoms curled around a traffic light. I called for her, but she didn't answer even though she could easily hear us. Clearly, she hadn't changed much from when we'd first met her in Spain's Urbión Peaks. Her tanned head was still shaved, and her tongue still had few words for the Effigies. But she was here, along with other members of Jin's trafficking crew. And there was Jin, standing on top of another car down the road, his large, thick frame and black boots sturdy on the roof, his hickory beard and long coat billowing proudly in the wind as the burning corpse of a phantom crashed down from the shot he'd fired.

"It's those traffickers!" Chae Rin stared at Lucas as he caught up with us, sliding between parked cars. "So you got here after all."

I couldn't find Derrek anywhere. Jin must have left his young son behind. Smart choice. Lucas's chestnut hair was dirty and matted with sweat, which drizzled down his sharp, square jaw. His red vest was torn, and a trickle of blood spotted his arm through the slit in his sleeve where the phantom had nicked him.

"That, we did," he replied. "We were in Quebec doing a deal, but then Maia called and told us you were heading to the United Nations Headquarters. Said something bad was gonna go down and you needed the help. I wasn't completely convinced, but Jin has a soft spot for you girls. Plus, Miss Finley here can be quite persuasive. And scary." He tossed me a wink.

I put my hands on my hips. "This is the second time you almost killed us with a bad shot, by the way," I said.

"Hey, these aren't easy to use." Lucas tapped the silver trunk of his launcher. "I'm tired as hell too. We've been stuck here since the fighting started. By the way, between this, my saving you in France, and the weapons bust you pulled in Guadeloupe, I'd say you owe me a few more than one, lass."

"I offered you money," I reminded him.

"Yes, but as they say, some things are priceless."

He tapped his cheek, his pink lips spreading into an annoying—but somewhat appealing—grin. I almost considered it too, except another phantom roared from the sky. Abril fired at it.

"Just don't die," I warned him, giving his shoulder a gentle shove and starting back down the street with the girls behind me, burning phantoms as I passed before Lake took us back into the sky.

But phantoms weren't the only monsters we had to worry about. Saul's soldiers were on the move. Twenty of them stomped up Third Avenue, exploding cars and buildings as they went with merely a squint of their eyes. Grunewald had managed to mass produce

Gabriel's and June's power. Nothing escaped it—and no one. Bodies littered the streets in bloody smears.

"No," I whispered. These soldiers must have been regular people once. Whatever those scientists had done to them had killed their humanity. They didn't so much as flinch at the sight of the carnage at their hands. So this was the fate awaiting whatever military personnel naively signed up for Blackwell's "special program."

There were some plainclothes agents on the scene, shooting over a barricade they'd set up at the intersection between Third and Forty-Fifth, but their bullets simply bounced off the soldiers' white metal armor. Though their helmets had glass visors they could see through, they lowered their heads to block the attacks from the agents.

Agents . . . some of them were CSTF. I recognized a few from when we were escaping their facility upstate. And among them—

"Brendan?" I gasped. It was almost twenty-four hours since I'd seen him last in Greenland, but he was there indeed. I could see his blond hair, disheveled from the battle. "Lake, set us down! Set us down now!"

Lake looked at me. "But we've got to get to Saul!"

One of Saul's soldiers dealt with the agents, exploding the barricade.

"Okay, I see your point," Lake said before sending us hurtling toward them. Her wind knocked some of them down, but most stayed solid on their feet. Bending down, Chae Rin lifted a car above her head with her monstrous strength courtesy of sickly Abigail's wish. She threw it at the soldiers, crushing two of them stalking toward us. The distraction gave people time to get off the streets. I ordered as much as I jumped on the roofs and trunks of cars with my scythe in hand and leapt into a cluster of five soldiers. Some agents had run out from behind the barricade, but I didn't have time to focus on them. I started hacking and slashing. Their metal armor was hard, but not hard enough to withstand my blade. Before any of them could blow me up, I struck first, sending out a wave of fire around my whole body, the force throwing their burning bodies onto empty cars. But there were more coming.

"Maia!" Brendan called my name.

As did the boy running up with him.

My heart sped up, my body seizing so fast I didn't react in time to the soldier leaping behind me.

"Get down!" Rhys yelled. I dove to the side, looking up to see Rhys aim his gun straight for the glass visor. Two shots, one for each eye. The soldier hit the ground hard.

Rhys's footsteps slowed as he reached me. "Are you okay?" He crouched down, gripping my shoulders, but my arms were around him before he could speak another word.

"Rhys," I said, burying my face in his black hair. "You're okay!" Hilda's injection. It'd been meant to speed up the recovery of the soldiers she'd helped create. Instead, it'd brought Rhys back from the brink. "What are you doing here? You shouldn't be here!"

"Sibyl let me know last night what she was planning and asked for the backup," said Brendan as he reached us, gripping his gun with bloody hands. "And this guy wouldn't stay put."

"Greenland's cold," Rhys said with a shrug, and placed his rough hand on my neck. The warmth seeped in through the skin. "You okay?"

Now, *this* boy—this boy I kissed, pushing my lips into his as much as I could for as long as I could before an explosion signaled that it was time to fight again. Barely hiding his little grin, Rhys stood along with Brendan and me, cocking his gun.

"Saul's waiting for you guys at the UN HQ," he told me as Chae Rin and Lake tore through some soldiers down the road. And there were more coming up the street. "Go on ahead. We can cover the foot soldiers."

In the distance I could see a tank rolling down the streets. They really did bring an entire army here. It was the chaos Saul wanted.

"Be careful, you two." I squeezed Rhys's forearm before taking off, flinching when I heard the brothers' guns start firing again.

Chae Rin jammed her fist through the visor of one soldier, kicking his body down to the ground. "Come on, we've done enough here!"

Lake threw a barrel of wind at two more soldiers, sending them crashing into the building before lifting us up.

"You guys are a few minutes away from the UN building." Uncle Nathan came through our earpieces. "The crowd's mostly cleared, but there are phantoms still nearby. Be careful."

This time we reached the UN building uninterrupted. I thought the news crews would have dispersed, but a correspondent and one camera were still there. They'd taken refuge behind a parked truck by the sidewalk, covering the mayhem of phantoms while a few wounded from the crowd remained in front of the building—

Oh my god. Lake's parents.

"Mom! Dad!" Lake cried. They couldn't move. Her father was on the ground, his leg bleeding through the claw tears in his pants, his glasses askew. Her mother couldn't get him up, and nobody would help them, not the fleeing pedestrians nor the correspondent and her film crew, busy trying to capture ratings for their station.

We landed in front of the pair. Mother and daughter burst into tears at the sight of each other.

"Mom, you've got to get up! We have to go!" Lake tried to lift her father, but the moment the skinny man moved, he gasped out in pain, his leg wound oozing.

"Victoria, you shouldn't be here." Lake's mother wiped her plump, wet cheeks. "It's too dangerous!"

"It's too dangerous for *me*? It's too dangerous for *you*, Mom!" Lake shook her head, peering into her mother's worried eyes. "Why are you always like that? Why are you always . . . ?"

She trailed off, lowering her head.

"Lake—" I started, but a crash behind us cut me off. Three quadrupedal phantoms leapt off the four-story redbrick building it'd been destroying on First and veered toward us. Similar to the ones I'd faced outside the Deoscali Temple, they were like wildebeests, black smoke billowing off their sturdy hides and razorbacks.

"I'm not like I was before, Mom." Lake's fists shook against her knees as she sat on the pavement. "I'm not the girl who bailed on Milan anymore. You don't have to keep covering for me. You don't have to keep—"

"Victoria!" her dad cried.

The phantoms were almost on us. Lake stood, pushing past Chae Rin and me. "I'm not like I was," she insisted, the wind picking up around her feet. "I'll show you!"

It appeared in a sudden gust of wind that blew her hair and clothes to the side. A long blade, thin like a needle, stretching down from the hilt in her hand. A rapier. Lake's rapier.

"Huh?" I stepped back, thinking I was seeing things. I wasn't.

Several rings weaved around the golden handle in Lake's hands, the bulbous pommel twinkling under the morning sun. Lake stared at her weapon in awe, taking in the sight of it for the first time before putting on her game face. Lifted by the wind, she launched at the center phantom, shoving the blade into the phantom's eye. I'd never seen her call a weapon because she never *had* before. But now that she held her sword in her hands, she fought as if it belonged there. She was the knight of Marian's and Alice's imaginations, slaying the dragon as told in tales.

I had no time to gape. There were two more gunning for us. I took the one on the right, calling my scythe, leaping up and chopping its head. Chae Rin stopped hers with her bare hands, gripping its horns and tossing it aside. It was Lake who finished them off. After leaping from the phantom she'd skewered, she sent blasts of wind toward all three, condensing and pressurizing the air into blades that sliced through their hides.

"You have a sword now?" Chae Rin said as Lake, panting heavily, ran up to us. "Okay, so where's mine?"

Lake passed by us and went to her mother and father, hugging them. Neither of them knew what to say. They stared at their daughter with a mixture of pride and fear.

But more phantoms were coming fast.

"Maia, get inside!" Chae Rin lifted her fists.

"But—"

"*Go,*" she barked at me, shutting me up. "We'll wrap this up and come help you as soon as we can."

"The building's clear of phantoms, Maia." I heard Uncle Nathan in my ear. "Go. I'll stay on if you need me."

The phantoms were closing in fast. I didn't protest a second time. Leaving them behind, I ran inside the building.

I could see at least the three floor levels up from the foyer, each floor offset by thick, white walkways stretching along the wide room. My heels clicked upon the checkered tiles as I ran past the stunning artwork, eventually finding blue carpet underfoot. There were workers and tourists still inside, most likely because they wouldn't dare enter headlong into the carnage outside. Some sat on the metal staircase with their heads in their hands; others hid behind the smooth wood of the information booth. They knew who I was the second they saw me. I didn't even have to ask. They pointed me in the direction of the General Assembly, and I was off.

Not long afterward, I entered a long stretch of hallway covered in dark red carpet. The framed photographs and plaques lining the green walls seemed dedicated to human rights and peacekeeping, the words themselves hung in black letters. Immortalized in some of the artwork and pictures were the building of New York's Needle and other antiphantom devices erected to protect developing and developed countries alike. Ironic that Saul would want to stage his coup here, but as I saw the figure round the corner at the end of the hall and walk unsteadily toward me, I knew peace was what I would have to strive for—or risk tearing the entire building down from the inside with our battle.

I couldn't put it past Belle. She wasn't well. If she could let loose inside Carnegie Hall, she could do it here.

Her sword was already out.

"Belle." I stepped back, fear pulsing through me like a desperate heartbeat. She must have broken out of custody in the chaos. She couldn't have known of the new developments. I could play that to my advantage. "Belle, you know Saul's in here, don't you? He's not under Blackwell's control anymore. He's destroying the city."

"For the ring, perhaps?" Belle stopped. "Blackwell has it."

"Saul has it now."

"Ah, yes." Belle tilted her head, her eyes unfocused. "I considered killing him for it a few times myself. I'd thought, why stand by his side when I could take the ring and make my own wish? But none of the wishes I dreamed up made sense. Why wish for Natalya back when she would most likely die in battle like the other Effigies before her? Why wish for the Sect destroyed or the Effigies gone when the phantoms would continue to run amok? And if I wished for annihilation of all three—Sect, Effigies, and phantoms—the ring wouldn't be powerful enough. I wanted Blackwell's plan to be good enough, but I ruined things on my own. Because of my last-minute indecision. My weakness. I'm always *weak*." Clenching her teeth, she swung her sword at the floor, the tip slitting the surface. I stared at the weapon anxiously. "How could I do that? How could I be so . . . ?" She looked at me as if searching for answers. "We were so close. Why? I just don't understand. Maia, I don't get any of it anymore."

"It's okay, Belle," I said. Was it? Belle was trembling with self-hatred. She was volatile. I chose my words carefully. "I just need to get into the General Assembly where Saul is. If you let me pass, I can fix all of this."

Belle's steel-blue eyes were on me. "Fix it? And how will you do that?"

I couldn't play this straight. Belle wanted the "end of everything." I wanted to avoid confrontation. "Saul doesn't want to get rid of the Sect. He wants to undo all of human history."

"Undo human history." Belle lowered her head as she thought of it.

"Yes, Belle. He needs the stone. I'm going to give it to him. But you have to let me through first, okay?"

This had to work.

"All of human history." Belle's words were quiet. Cautious as she began to put the pieces together. "All of it. Gone. And you're going to him. To . . . *help* him?"

I nodded stiffly. "Something like that. But I can't fix things until you let me through."

Belle stared at the hilt in her hand, the sword just lightly touching the floor.

Then, as if not missing a single beat, she continued toward me. "No, Maia," she said solemnly. "No."

The sight of her lifeless expression as she stalked down the halls set something off inside me. The thin string of my patience snapped, fear smoothly slipping into anger that began boiling inside me. "That's enough, Belle! God." I stomped my foot in anger. "I need to get inside those chambers! Don't you get that? Didn't you hear what I told you?"

"I did," Belle said, her quiet voice packing an intensity that made me shiver. "Saul wants to reshape the world by undoing it. That means he'll end all of this." She swept her hands along the wall. The modern history of man, efforts of peace in the face of monsters human and nonhuman, all framed in the photographs on the wall. "He'll end it. The Sect. The Effigies. This legacy of death. But what of Natalya? What about her legacy?"

"What?" I stepped back. "What are you talking about?"

"This history—" Belle motioned to the wall again. "This history of peace is Natalya's legacy. It's what Natalya had dedicated her existence to. If Saul undoes everything, who will remember her? Who will remember that *we*"—she pounded her chest—"fought and died for *them*, for humanity? The Sect and the Effigies must be made obsolete, but *our memory must live on*. Natalya's life, pain, and death deserve to be remembered by *someone*."

The end of everything. It was what Belle had wanted from the beginning. What I'd *thought* she'd wanted. It was a wish bred from despair, the same kind of hopeless, angry wish that had led humanity down this ruined path in the first place. But Belle wasn't Alice. I couldn't forget how she'd struggled with herself as she'd stood in front of the Assembly. Even if Alice was too far gone, to this Effigy, there were still parts of this world that mattered.

And she was willing to kill me to protect them.

"You've got it wrong! I won't let Saul get his wish," I said quickly. "I'll stop him before he can make it!"

"*You?*" Belle laughed, high, frightening. Suddenly, I remembered the night we met at La Charte, her snarling disgust at this *nobody* who'd been chosen to carry on the legacy of her mentor. "And what if you fail? If you can't guarantee your success, then maybe it would be easier to *strike you down here*." She lifted her sword. "Then Saul. Then Sibyl. And *anyone* standing in the way of Blackwell's vision."

But despite the bloodlust in each labored breath, her confusion was clear. Palpable.

"You don't want that, deep down," I told her. "You want what we all do: peace. And that's why I can't let you stop me."

I summoned my scythe in a swirl of fire. Belle was ready. But this time, so was I.

# 32

BELLE'S HEART WASN'T IN ANY OF HER STRIKES,
though she didn't hold back. I avoided each just narrowly, my heart
beating out of my chest as the adrenaline surged through every nerve.
She launched her sword down upon my head, and I blocked it with
the pole of my scythe, pushing her back and swiping at her stomach
because I knew her avoidance of the blade would create more distance
between us. But that wouldn't deter her.

She charged at me again, yet as she tried to cut me down, with her
lifeless expression, she looked no more human than Saul's soldiers.
Unlike the last time we fought on the white cliffs of Dover, her attacks
were passionless; it was as if she were running on fumes, fighting only
because there was nothing else she could think of doing. Devoid of
hope and purpose. In many ways, those kinds of fighters were the most
dangerous.

I ducked just in time for her sword to lodge itself into the wall. It
was my chance. Her hands slipped off the handle as I kicked her back
with all my strength.

"Belle, listen to reason!" I swept the hair out of my face, breathing hard. "People are dying in the streets. How many of those people outside do you think will still be alive by the time this battle is over? Whatever you're going through, you can't solve it by letting other people get hurt. You don't have to fight me—"

"I *do* have to fight. I do. Because I don't know what else to do. I don't know how to stop this—" Belle grabbed her shirt and tugged. "This emptiness. I've been fighting since I was a child; it's the only thing I know how to do *truly* well. And that is the greatest tragedy of my life."

"Your life doesn't have to be a tragedy!" It was like I told Rhys. Even if life wasn't worth living, we had to live on. We had to *make* it worth living. I took a step forward, but Belle lowered her head. A terrible chill filled the hallway, weighing down the air. My breaths painted the air in wisps of white as frost crawled down the walls, the ceiling. It was only the floor Belle left bare as she strode toward me, unaffected by the cold.

"I will redeem myself by procuring Blackwell's new order," she said. "The Effigies will finally be at rest. The world will protect *itself* for a change. If I have to kill you to make that happen, then so be it. I've done it before." Frost wafted down from above our heads. "I'll kill Chae Rin and Victoria as well. The new organization will find the fresh Effigies and keep them locked away where they can't affect the world. That way, they won't have to suffer the pain of battle. That is *my* vision."

"And you'll kill us for it, huh?" My grip on my scythe weakened the colder it got. *You're the Fire Effigy, damn it*, I told myself before drawing heat from within, warming my body. "Pretending you don't care about us anymore is the easy way out. I already know that's not true. Otherwise, why did you try to tell the world we were innocent? Why did you try to save us?"

Belle stopped. For a moment it seemed like a glimmer of light had flickered in her eyes as her gaze shifted to the side. And then there was a sudden rush of cold, breaking my concentration, colonizing my body from skin to bone. My scythe grew too cold to hold. I let it go, and it clattered to the ground, bursting to dust.

"Belle!" I cried. "You're not the only Effigy who's ever suffered. I've seen it myself." I raised my numb hands and went back to squeezing some warmth into my arms. "But not all those Effigies gave in. Some of them fought to do the right thing until the end. *I'm* fighting until the end. You may not believe I can do it, but I *will* stop Saul and make things *truly* right. It's not about the legacy. It's about our individual choices. I've made mistakes. I've hurt my friends."

At this Belle flinched. She refused to look at me, but refused to back down at the same time. My head throbbed in pain. Yulia's pendant thawed slowly on my chest.

"There's so much I regret," I said. "But *I* choose not to give up."

A bitter scowl was not the response I was looking for. Belle stared at me with heavy-lidded eyes. "In that case, I'm happy for you, Maia."

She sent a flurry of snow through the air. I had no choice but to block it out with fire. The two streams canceled each other out in a whirl of steam, and out of the white fog came Belle, her sword in hand. Quickly, I picked up my scythe and swung, her sword clinking against the curve of the sickle.

"I guess you're just stronger than me, then, Maia," she said through gritted teeth, bringing her sword down against my blade again and again. "I guess you're just *better* than me. Like Natalya was."

Her swings were too fast. I knew I had to abandon the scythe before it broke and her sword found my head instead. The second I could, I leapt back to avoid her last attack.

"Don't." She readied her weapon. "Don't get in the way. *Stop* getting in the way of my absolution. I'm begging you, just *leave!*"

She raised the sword once more, letting it go only once she realized she'd have to if she was going to catch the blade hurdling toward her head.

Not a blade—a lance. Belle moved her head back and caught the sparkling pearl pole with her left hand. Her eyes traced a line down the short shaft to the long, curved blade at the end.

Then at Chae Rin, who'd thrown it. Lake was with her, her rapier in hand.

"Summoning." Belle couldn't help but smile, a mixture of pride and poison dripping off her lips. "So the two of you have finally unlocked the last of your psychic abilities."

Sheets of frost still cracked along part of the hallway. The mist was half clear, but that didn't make the air any easier to breathe. Belle looked at the three of us. "Lance. Rapier. Scythe. And this." She lifted her blade. "We truly are now the Four Swords."

"Belle . . . ," Chae Rin said as Belle threw her lance back at her feet so hard that the tip stuck in the floor. I could imagine what she wanted to say. The frustration was still there; she hadn't forgotten their last fight. But when she looked at me, her anger seemed to dissipate. "Come on, Belle. This is enough."

Belle whipped her blade around. "I'll tell you when it's enough."

Chae Rin took the pole of her lance and yanked it out of the ground. Lake and Chae Rin weren't as used to their weapons as Belle was, but they tried nonetheless. Belle caught Lake's hand and tried to chill it only to be met with a breath of wind straight from Lake's mouth that sent her flying back into the ground. Chae Rin and Lake pressed the charge.

And all the while I stood against the wall, watching. Trying to understand. I said I wanted to grant them peace. There was only one way I could think of to do it.

As the three girls fought, I closed my eyes.

*Hey,* I told the girl waiting inside me. *I'll let you borrow my body for a bit if you help me.*

Natalya was surprised. Usually, it was her contacting me from within the recesses of my mind, needling me from the inside out, intruding into my thoughts when I least expected it.

She least expected this.

*Why should I help you?*

*Because,* I said. *This is for Belle.*

Natalya was silent.

*I saw that memory, Natalya.* The little Fire Effigy appeared in my mind's eye, so I knew Natalya could see it too, see those lifeless eyes staring blankly into a live studio audience as her parents bragged about their celebrity daughter. *The pressure Belle put on your shoulders wasn't fair to you, but you gave her that shoulder to lean on because you didn't want to be empty anymore. Isn't that what you told me?* When Natalya said nothing, I kept going. *Belle is lost, just like you were. But she doesn't have to stay lost. None of us do. She still needs her mentor. Give her that.*

Seconds passed, but I knew what Natalya would decide in the end. We can't give our power to others. We can't use others for our own gain either.

But we could help each other.

She understood that as well as I did. I couldn't have come this far alone. And alone, Belle could never be free.

*You seem sure I won't overtake you this time,* said Natalya finally.

*You won't.*

Natalya was hesitant.

*You are her mentor. You really did help her survive. All I'm asking is that you help her one more time. This is your last chance to be a hero, Natalya.*

A pause. Lake grunted in pain as Belle ripped her rapier from her hands and threw her against the wall.

Then fire enveloped my body. As Natalya seeped through the barrier holding my consciousness, I thought I'd be thrown back into the dark, bottomless pits of my subconscious. That's what usually happened. But this time I didn't budge. I didn't step back—I stepped *aside*. It was like watching a tiny projector through a tinier window. Cramped. Uncomfortable. But I was here. I was still here.

"Belle," I said in a booming voice that felt as if it should have been several tones lower than my own.

Belle didn't stop, not until she saw the sword named after the firebird of legend in my hands. At the sight of it, she shrank back, fearful, like a child who'd just been caught misbehaving by her mother. Chae Rin and Lake backed up against the wall, no doubt terrified of the implications. They needn't have worried. I was okay. Even with Natalya moving my body, I knew that I was the one ultimately still in control. I fed Natalya more rope, and she took it, wading farther into the land of the living.

From inside my own head, I watched Natalya point her sword at Belle. "Stop," she told her. "Stop this."

"Natalya?" Belle gripped her sword tighter. She knew it wasn't a trick. I never could have summoned Zhar-Ptitsa.

"Look at yourself. Look at what you've become." Natalya shook her head, watching her once brilliant protégée, disheveled by rage and hopelessness. "Why? Because of me? My death?"

For a moment Belle couldn't speak. She simply stared at the girl—the vessel containing her scolding mentor—her lips trembling.

"Tell me!" Natalya boomed. "Is that really it? Am I the reason you've fallen so far?"

*Fallen.* As if on cue, Belle's arms slumped at her sides. She looked at Chae Rin. At Lake. At me. Then at her sword, the tip of which just touched the floor of the United Nations hallway. "I don't have a purpose anymore." This was the Belle who'd struggled in front of the UN Assembly—who'd looked lost. Small.

"Because I died?" Natalya tilted my head, peering at Belle curiously through my brown eyes. "Life is transient, Belle. We come and go like grains of sand scattered in the wind."

"It's not just that. It's *not*." Belle gripped the side of her arm with her free hand, her sword dangling in the other. "I knew you were going to die eventually. Yes, we all die. But why do we Effigies have to die like *this*?"

She pointed to the ruined walls, the broken framed photographs, the burns along the carpet from the steam we'd made. "I never asked to fight. I never *wanted* to fight, but when I looked at you, I thought I might at least die a noble death. I thought you would die a noble death. But you"—she shook her head—"you were poisoned by a friend. You died in the blink of an eye. Killed by the very people for whom you gave your life. So then what was it for?" She spread out her arms. "Why are we fighting? Why must we fight and die? When I found out how you died, I realized that nothing was worth it. It wasn't just about losing you, about being alone. I realized that I couldn't even hope for a good death. If life and death are meaningless, then what's left?"

"Hope." Natalya shoved her sword into the floor, her hand on the golden hilt, though her gaze never left Belle's face. "Hope."

Natalya was thinking of me now. Of the determined look I'd given her as I'd snapped her sword in half with the sheer force of my own will. She was thinking of me traveling the world to solve the mysteries she couldn't, wading through a hundred memories on the promise that I would save her, save us all.

I felt Natalya's sigh pass through my lips. "Hope," she said again. "To be honest, Belle, I never understood that. But then, neither did you. One has to be able to believe in herself to be able to hope, but you never could. You believed in me. You looked to me for all your answers. You mimicked me, found your strength from me, instead of yourself. You used me as a guide for your life, not knowing, not *wanting to believe* that I wasn't the savior you needed."

"But you did save me." Belle was shaking. "You saved me from Madame Bisette, from that foster home. You trained me. You gave me meaning. You were perfect. The perfect Effigy."

Natalya closed my eyes. "The first thing I did as an Effigy," she confessed, "was to murder a man threatening my father. I was eleven years old."

Belle went rigid. "Naomi Prince told me that. But you had a good reason. The man would have kept your family in his debt."

"He was a bad man, indeed," said Natalya. "But he was also a father of four, the husband of a wife who couldn't provide for them after her spouse died, couldn't afford medicine for her oldest child, who died only two years later. This is how the legend of the Matryoshka Princess began."

The hall was silent. Not a sound came from Belle, nor Chae Rin and Lake.

"Through my years," Natalya said, fighting against the sudden swell of self-loathing I could feel tingling beneath my skin, "I fought the phantoms out of duty—duty to the Sect, duty to my parents, to the people. I fought the phantoms without any hope for the future, but I fought them with every ounce of my spirit because I knew that I had to atone. I had to protect other lives in place of the lives I had taken. And now I think I understand."

"Understand what?" Belle asked quietly.

As Natalya looked at Belle, she readied her confession. "Belle. The truth is that I mentored you hoping that I could be given meaning in return. Just as I was called the Matryoshka Princess, indeed I thought of myself as a shell built only to house the other Effigies inside me. I thought I was empty. But I was wrong about myself. I *underestimated* myself. I may never have truly lived the life that I wanted. But I worked hard to live. I tried to make things right, even up until the moment of my death. I *did* hope. I gave *myself* meaning. I just didn't see it until it was too late."

"Gave . . . yourself . . ." Belle stared, slack jawed.

"Nobody can give you meaning, Belle. That's the one thing I failed to teach you. You have to find that deep within yourself." Natalya lifted her sword, pointing the blade at the Effigy. "Don't disappear, Belle. Live on. Live . . . and let me go."

Belle's sword clattered against the ground. As she sank to the floor, Natalya's sword burned up in a bolero of fire that enveloped it to the hilt.

*Thank you, Natalya,* I told her before slipping back into my body. I sank back into my own flesh, wobbling on my feet, tipping over. . . .

"Maia!" Lake ran for me, catching me before I could fall.

Chae Rin didn't follow her. While Lake lifted me to my feet, the Effigy of Earth stood in front of Belle, her feet just touching the edge of Belle's fallen blade.

"We're going to stop Saul," she told Belle. "Come with us, or stay out of our way." She turned to Lake and me. "Let's go."

Reassuring Lake that I was okay, I stood on my own feet and followed the two toward the General Assembly chambers. But as I passed

Belle—her knees planted on the floor, her hands shaking behind her—I stopped.

"Natalya's right," I told her. "There really is hope. You can find it. Please, just don't give up on yourself. Live on."

I nodded to the other girls, and we took off down the hallway, leaving the sound of Belle's quiet tears in our wake.

# 33

CHAE RIN AND LAKE'S COMBINED EFFORTS SENT the rubble blocking the entrance flying aside, opening the way into the magnificent chambers. The first thing I saw was June crouching and protecting her head just a few steps away from the entrance—a few steps away from *me*. I didn't think. The moment she stood, I tackled her.

"What are you doing?" June cried, fighting with my flailing arms.

I broke free from her grip and managed to slap her. "You! Stop being evil!" I didn't know what else to say.

"Ugh, get off me, you little *brat*."

She kicked me to the side so hard I crashed into the desk. I fumbled quickly to my feet, about to leap for her again when I heard someone clear his throat by the pulpit at the front of the chambers, his voice carried by the microphones. Saul. His silver hair lay flat against his broad shoulders, draped like silk over his black vest. Gabriel stood at his side, a dutiful watchdog. And on Saul's finger was the ring that bore the stone of wishes—newly blackened with death.

"So you were finally able to join us, Maia." He gave me a sidelong look. "I've been waiting. We all have."

I scanned the room. Every dignitary huddled by the wall on my right, past the abandoned curved rows of desks. Sibyl stood among them, some of the dead security guards and agents laid out in a corner next to her. Saul must have given them time to move the bodies. How kind.

We'd entered through the left side of the room. Blackwell hadn't moved from where we'd seen him on the livestream, near the center of the room on the left side. His back hunched, he stared between the three of us Effigies and Saul, the bloodshot bulge of his eyes indicating he knew quite well that he couldn't trust any of us. His friends in the Council were too busy cowering with the rest of them. He was in this mess alone.

"So now that you're here, I suppose we can get started." Saul leaned over, propping his head up with his elbow on the desk, tapping his fingers against the wood.

"Saul." I moved past my sister—several cautious steps forward. "Or Nick?"

"It doesn't matter what you call me," Saul said. "I'll be only Nicholas soon enough."

I looked back at the girls. Chae Rin flicked her head at the dignitaries, and immediately I understood what she meant. "You're right," I told him. "I know now how to find the rest of the stone. It's not what you might assume it is." I thought of Castor's secret story, suppressing a shudder when I realized that I had part of the eye of a goddess dangling around my neck like an ornament. And somehow that still wasn't as bad as having a man's ashes in my coat pocket. "But I'm not going to tell you anything until you let all these people go."

The dignitaries flinched as I stretched my arm out toward them.

Saul spared them a mildly interested glance. "My hostages? And once I do, how do I know you're not simply going to leave? Or attack me?"

"I won't. I will take you to the stone. I promise."

"A promise that can't be guaranteed."

But it was guaranteed. I had no tricks up my sleeve, no strategy other than to open the pathway to the goddesses because *I* was the one who needed to make a wish—a wish so grave only they could answer it. That was a hand I couldn't reveal to him yet.

"Please let them go."

"I have a better idea." Boosting himself off the podium, he admired his ring. "A white stone filled with the death of the people in this room . . . and in your city, Maia."

I clenched my teeth as he raised an eyebrow, amused at the thought.

"Alice must have been delighted when she first discovered its secret. It's gotten quite black already, but it still doesn't look completely full to me. What do you think?" He held the stone up to Gabriel, but the Silent Child did not so much as look. "If you insist on wasting my time, Maia, perhaps I should waste time by feeding this stone more souls. Gabriel, June: We can start with the dignitaries."

Gabriel was fast. He aimed his gaze, literally murderous, toward the right wall just as Chae Rin leapt onto the desk and sent a chunk of concrete hurtling up through the floor into his line of fire to explode in its stead. Everyone ducked for cover—everyone except Sibyl, that is, who was crouched near the corpse of one of her agents.

June jumped onto the table after Chae Rin, but I ran up and grabbed her foot with a dive, pulling her back down, just as Gabriel turned and glared at us. Lake was on it, redirecting the blast up to the curved white ceiling. It shook and cracked, a few cameras and lights falling to the ground and shattering in a hail of dust, but thankfully the structure held together.

Gabriel had his order, and he would carry it out. But when next he looked at the dignitaries, it was Sibyl he saw, aiming her dead agent's gun at him from across the room. He didn't have time to react.

"Gabriel!" June shouted. Two shots aimed at the head, but his arms blocked them instead. Sibyl closed her right eye, ready to shoot again.

"Watch out!" Lake screamed out as the floor exploded in front of her. Maybe it was Gabriel's injury that forced his miss—otherwise Sibyl would have been killed. But though she flew back and hit the wall hard, I could see by her grimace that she was still alive.

"Stop this, Saul!" My fury bubbling, I didn't know if I could control myself enough for a measured attack. Gabriel was ready—the moment I tried to set him on fire, he'd follow suit. A dangerous exploding match with the audience doubling as casualties. "I'm *here*. No more chaos, please. No more death."

"Are you sure?" Saul grinned evilly. "Maybe just one more to relieve stress. Gabriel?"

Gabriel was ready to follow his order. But he didn't anticipate the massive shard of ice forming from the ground beneath him, rising up and skewering him through the chest with its fine point. June screamed.

I turned to the entrance. We all did.

Belle stood by the door, lowering her hand, her chest heaving. She met each of our gazes—Lake's, Chae Rin's, and mine—but she said nothing. After one cautious step forward and to the side, she let her back hit the wall, taking in the sight of mayhem with tears building in her tired eyes. After sinking to the ground, she nodded at me.

"Do what you need to do," she said finally.

The room fell silent for just a few seconds. Though Chae Rin hesitated, Lake ran to her, asking if she was all right. In the midst of the confusion, Saul's voice carried out over the air.

"June," he said simply. "Kill that Effigy."

June leapt toward Belle, ready to fight.

"No way!" I grabbed her arm. "*No way*, June!"

June thrashed against my grip. "Let go of me!"

"Why?" I held my sister in place. "Because you have your orders? Because Saul said so? Or because you really want to kill us all regardless?" It crushed me to watch June struggle hard so that she could murder on Saul's command. And I knew it wasn't just the kill chip. Saul reminded us both.

"June," he said. "You remember my promise. You know I'll bring your parents back. I'll make everything as it was."

"He won't," I told her. "He was under Blackwell's control when he promised you that." Blackwell returned my glare with his own. "He used you to frame me and turn the world against the Effigies. It was all to make sure Blackwell's plan passed at the United Nations. Now that he's free, you think he gives a crap about you? He said it himself; he wants to turn everything back. Undo everything that's happened after the stone was discovered and get his old life back. If he gets his wish, our parents may never be born. Even if they are, even if *we* are, that fire might still happen anyway. All those people you killed—it was all for nothing."

"Stop it!" June gritted her teeth. "Stop it! You don't know what it's like! You don't know what death is like! You don't!"

She pushed me back so hard, I thought I'd twist my foot out of shape when I stepped back to steady myself. Her face flashed with a dangerous kind of anger that mangled her anguished features into something almost grotesque.

"I don't remember everything. But I remember feelings. Anger. Hopelessness." She pounded her chest right above her heart. "Deep, deep loneliness. Why was it *me*? Why did I have to die, Maia? Why did Mom, Dad, and I have to die like that?"

I trembled, biting my lip in silence because I didn't know. It was "fate," but that answer didn't seem good enough.

When I died, I was gone for only a few moments, my soul safely carried to the parallel world of the Effigies. How must it have been for June then, dead for a year, disembodied, erased? As Marian had said, we were not supposed to feel anything after death, but Alice's wishes had warped everything, twisted innocent souls and made them suffer. If Saul hadn't resurrected June, she might have ended up as a phantom. She certainly had the anger of one.

Gripping her head, June turned to Saul at the pulpit. "I can't take this. You have to help me. You have to bring back my parents. My mind is always in chaos. I can't stop it. You have to make me well again. And not just in here." She patted her head.

"What does she mean?" Lake exchanged glances with Chae Rin, who'd remained where she was.

"My body won't hold up." June lowered her hands, staring at the palms that once smoked with fire. "The stress these powers are causing . . . I can feel my body breaking down a little bit each day."

I noticed out of the corner of my eye Blackwell lowering his head, his fingers clenched into fists at the mention of her body's degradation, but my focus was on June.

"I know," I whispered. Gently, I held her hand. She didn't move at the touch. "June, I get it. I'll help you. But you have to trust me."

June remained silent.

"Maia," Saul said. "Every second you waste here, more people die in your city."

"He's right," said Uncle Nathan through my earpiece. "We've been monitoring the situation through the city's street cams—whichever ones are left. Our side's holding up, but between the phantoms and the soldiers, it's not looking good. . . ."

He trailed off. Rhys and Brendan. Lucas and Jin's crew. Were they still out there fighting? Or had they succumbed to the battle? There'd been too much death already. I didn't want to lose anyone else. I sucked in a breath and walked to the front of the chambers. Saul's gaze followed me as I took the short white steps up to the platform. And for a moment we stood, gazes locked on each other. I wondered if he could see her when he looked at me: Marian. I wondered if he knew she'd begged me to stop him.

After unzipping my jacket pocket, I brought out the velvet pouch. Benjamin Vogel's ashes pooled over the now shattered vial. Saul smiled when I told him what it was.

"I guess I can never be rid of you Vogels," Saul said as he considered the pouch in my hand. "I'll have to make sure I include that in my wish."

I imagined Alice would react to the comment, fight back at the prospect of being erased, but Nick's rage and hatred was too strong now. He held her at bay, Alice's indignation revealing itself through a mere twitch of his left eye and the slightest of grimaces. Trapped. Helpless. If this was to be Alice's end, it was an ironic one for the girl who sacrificed others to be free.

"Before we get started," I told him, "you should know, the stone exists in a dimension separate from ours. When Vogel and Castor were searching for it, they realized that they would be able to see it only with 'eyes of death.' In other words, they had to be dead. Those are the rules. Only those who've died can do this."

"That's no matter," said Saul as he moved closer to me. "I already am dead."

"I mean that literally."

"So do I."

Saul lifted his vest over his head and threw it to the ground. Then he took my hand into his metal grip, courtesy of Grunewald, and slipped it inside his white shirt, letting my fingers unhook one of the buttons. I flinched as he pressed it against his chest, the hair prickling my palms. I could feel him breathing. What I couldn't feel was his heartbeat.

"It's strange, isn't it?" he said once I looked up at him, surprised. "I shouldn't be able to breathe, shouldn't even be able to function. But for Alice's wish that she should have me forever, I somehow still do. Together we walked the earth until my hair turned gray and my body died. And I remained as Alice remembered me—as Alice wanted me. My body preserved, because this Nicholas was the one she'd wanted to steal from Marian forever."

I yanked my hand away from him, staring at the bare skin my hand had laid upon.

"Show me, Maia," Saul said. "Show me the way to my wishes."

"Not so fast." With a sweeping majesty that contradicted the subtle desperation twisting his expression, Blackwell stalked up the stairs. "The stone is mine by right. It was my plan that set this in motion. Wherever this realm is, you will take me with you."

"Are you sure, Blackwell?" Saul lifted his metal hand, and when he pressed his fingers together, they sharpened to a point. "Because if death is your wish, I can grant it."

Blackwell stopped a safe distance away from us, but he was undeterred. "You won't move against me. I still have the codes to Minerva. It's aimed at this city as we speak."

Fearful chatter erupted from the dignitaries. Abrams's recording was true after all. With the camera and thus the livestream down, we in this room were the only ones who'd be able to vouch for this. But we had to make it through the morning first.

"They're waiting for my command as we speak." Blackwell touched his ear where there must have been an in-ear communications device, like mine.

"And what will you do, Blackwell?" Saul laughed. "Eradicate your-self? Please. Stop interfering as if you still have a card to play. Your role in this is finished, irrelevant—just as your fathers were before you."

Blackwell shook with anger as Saul's laughter continued to echo against the high ceiling.

"Little Bartholomäus. Did you think that by amassing godlike power, you could escape your fate as a man? How much longer do you have left to live, I wonder?"

As Saul scanned his body, I frowned, staring back at Sibyl, who only returned my confusion with an unreadable expression.

"The illness is called Huntington's disease, am I correct?" Saul stroked his chin. "The same as your father died from, or so I heard while I was in Greenland. I learned of the research they were conduct-ing there to save your life."

Hilda's division. The cellular regeneration stuff. She'd told me it was a personal project for Blackwell, but I'd had no idea it was because of this. In many ways it was hard to believe, and in other ways it made sense. I knew that for Blackwell to inherit his father's plan to over-take the Sect, there had to be something else driving him, something personal beyond his fury and jealousy, beyond his thirst for the seat of power denied his family. Now I understood. He was dying.

"It's no matter, Blackwell. When I make my wish, I'll grant all of you peace," Saul said.

"Peace," I whispered, Marian's plea echoing in my mind.

"Yes, Maia." When Saul gripped my shoulder with his human hand, I could feel his ring pressed against my shoulder. "Peace."

*Please . . .* , Marian cried from deep within me.

It was time. I wasn't quite sure how it would work exactly. If they had to touch, or if there was some special pattern they had to be arranged in. Perhaps it was Marian compelling me to act, guiding my fingers as I slipped the chain of Yulia's pendant over my neck. Saul narrowed his eyes, confused as I held the blue stone in my palm, but eventually he seemed to understand. After shifting the ring so that the stone was facing downward, he placed his hand below mine, at an angle, so that we could both still see the stone's shining white surface. Then I emptied Vogel's ashes over our hands. Yes, this was enough. They were here: fate, life—and Vogel's body to fill in the absence of death. We had gathered the Three, as the goddesses themselves had commanded.

The white ring, the blue pendant, and the black ashes illuminated at once, fueled by our desire to see the fates. And then a brilliant white light appeared. It was what I'd witnessed in death: great white lights filling the atmosphere. They flowed into the room through the walls, sparkling like clear water, enveloping us. I could feel my soul being pulled from my body. I could feel the flesh collapsing in a heap on the floor.

"Maia!" Belle, Lake, and Chae Rin all called, but their voices were fading.

"Maia!" Uncle Nathan this time, his desperate cry filling my ear. "You're shorting out, Maia. Maia? *Maia!*"

The room was fading, the people in it disappearing. Belle on her feet. June running toward me. Chae Rin hopping off the desk. Blackwell pulling a gun out from behind his jacket and pointing it at himself.

And as they faded out of existence, a single white door materialized in kind. It looked handcrafted and exquisite, the imperial gate to a mansion or a palace. Like the door to an Effigy's memories. It appeared behind Saul. He hadn't had time to turn and look. We were awash in white light. It was already drawing us in. . . .


No. This couldn't be it.

But this was . . .

This was the white stream, the one I saw whenever I scried. My feet waded in the familiar waters, not hot and not cold. But we weren't in my consciousness. Or at least, I didn't think we were. Were we?

"This place." Saul looked up at the endless, pure white sky. He looked like he recognized it. Well, as an Effigy, he would. As Nicholas, he would have spent time in this realm. A century. The fear in his eyes told me as much. "Why here?" Rounding on me, he grabbed my shoulders. "What did you do?"

"What? I don't know!" A grunt escaped my lips as I fought against him. "I've never done this before."

Somehow, I knew my body was still in the General Assembly chambers, alive, though just barely. What I was now . . .

These limbs, these clothes. They felt real, but I knew they weren't. This was an astral body projected out of the physical. My soul. My consciousness. Though the pendant, Saul's ring, and Vogel's ashes had crossed over with us, our flesh had remained behind.

How could I be sure I'd return to mine like Castor and Vogel had? "Maia?"

I turned, baffled. June walked up next to me, gazing around the vast emptiness in wonder. "June? What the hell are you—"

Only those who've died could cross the gate. June had been dead once. Her soul was called in with the rest of us. But if that were the case, then what was I to make of Blackwell, who'd slid up next to Saul, much to the dead Effigy's surprise?

"You followed us in." Saul gritted his teeth, his metal hand whirring as he squeezed it into a fist. "You killed yourself."

The gun.

"To see the door at the moment of my death," Blackwell repeated, his lips spreading into a satisfied grin as he took in the sight of endless nothing. "It was as Vogel and Castor predicted in the secret volume—or what part of it my people were able to translate. But I don't need to simulate my death. I will regain my body with the wish I make." He turned. "From the goddesses."

A sudden chill swept across my body, followed by a hollowness so vast I could fall into it and never be found again. The hairs on the back of my neck singed from their power, though they themselves did not speak, did not make a move against us.

They'd appeared. I felt them behind me. We all could. A quiet but insurmountable power that killed the feeling in my hands. I turned slowly.

Yulia's pendant fell from my ash-covered hand into the white stream.

Larger than the rest of us, but still human. In front of their magnificent white door, they sat, three silver goddesses on three silver thrones. Golden leafs trickled down their white hair, draped down their white robes, spilling into the forever-flowing stream from which their thrones stretched into the skies. The three were identical. Same heart-shaped faces, sharp jaws. Same colorless lips and unreadable expressions. They were the same—except for their unblinking eyes. White like the stone of wishes. She sat in the center. Blue like the stone of life. She flanked on the right. And the goddess on the left— her eyes were black as obsidian. Her eyes were the only ones I'd never seen. Their lips did not move as they spoke in unison. I heard their voices reverberating in the empty chamber of my mind.

—*You've come at last*—

# 34

*—IT HAS BEEN MANY YEARS SINCE WE HAVE GAZED upon human eyes—*

*—And since that day, we have seen with our eyes the curious desire of man—*

*—Tell me, then, what is it now that you seek from us?—*

I couldn't tell which one had spoken and when. Blue, Black, or White? Their voices were identical, the same dispassionate words sinking to the ground, cold like winter crisps of ice. Insane. Impossible. They were impossible. I've never been religious, never thought much of a higher power. When Uncle Nathan read Castor's story, I'd simply taken everything in stride. After all, if the Effigies are possible, other weird crap must be equally possible. But seeing them here. Seeing these . . . beings in front of me. It was as if they were cut out of the white nothingness, partially dissolved into the space that surrounded. Neither here nor there. My legs didn't move an inch. Their presence was so thick you could wade in it. And though they looked at us with the curiosity of a child, it felt like I'd die if I dared to move an inch.

"Who . . . ? What are you?" It was Saul who'd spoken, his human fingers twitching. So even he was afraid.

—*Created to watch over the fates of humankind*—

—*Created to measure lives of humankind*—

—*Created to determine the deaths of humankind*—

Fate. Life. And death. "Then who created *you*?" I covered my mouth with my hands, surprised at myself for having the courage to even ask.

—*There are many secrets still unknown in this world, Maia Finley*—

—*The secrets of the world*—

—*Stories left unwritten*—

—*But your story will soon come to an end*—

—*Your path. Your destiny*—

They were looking at me as they said it. The stone gaze of Black pierced straight through my flesh and soul.

"I know you." June rubbed her face down from her lips. "I felt you. Where . . . ?" She shut her eyes, trying to remember. "It was . . . when I was . . . when I was . . . dead. . . ."

A shadow passed over June's face. She was silent. We all were, but there was something different about hers. When she lowered her head and bit her cheek, I knew she was trying to control something within herself, something fighting to be released.

Anger. She began to shake with it.

"Who controls fate?" she whispered, as if remembering a question she'd asked long ago. When she raised her head again, tears brimmed in her eyes. "So you're the reason my parents and I died."

—*What is born must die*—

—*Such is the fate of all life*—

"Bullshit!" June's yell echoed into the endless white sky. "*Bullshit*. You killed my parents. You killed *me*." She pointed at them, her arms trembling in the air. "It wasn't fair. It wasn't *fair*."

*—It was a fate that was unavoidable—*

It was White who'd spoken. I was starting to hear it now . . . the slight variations in their voices. The way her head twitched just slightly though her lips didn't move.

"Unavoidable." I wrapped my hand around June's, lowering her arm. "Maybe. But some fates are avoidable."

"My fate, for example." Saul. He stepped forward, raising his ring. "Because of this. This stone . . . You gave it to Benjamin Vogel, didn't you?"

*—Benjamin Vogel—*

*—Ah, yes. So he's come back to us at last—*

A mocking statement, but without a hint of emotion. As I stared at the ashes covering my hand, Saul continued. "Vogel took the stone home. The stone *you* willingly gave him. And once he did, my fate was destroyed. Why? How could you allow such a foolish thing to happen?"

*—We asked him his wish—*

*—He wished to see what we could see—*

*—And so I gave him my eye—*

White—no, Fate. She'd spoken. Neither of her eyes were missing. If I weren't so creeped out and terrified, I'd have asked her how many she had to spare.

"You gave him the power of fate. But it was his daughter who used it. It was his daughter who destroyed me. Created the phantoms. Created the Effigies. Took my life, my spirit, my love. So why? Why did you allow it? Look at me!" Saul boomed, his hands outspread. He caught his reflection in the mirror, and the sight leached tears from his eyes. "Was this my fate? Was this to be the fate of Nicholas Hudson? Why?" He bent over, his hands clutching his head. *"Why?"*

"You have to understand what you've done," I said as Saul's tears fell. "What you did changed the course of human history; it could have destroyed us entirely! Don't you . . . ?" I swallowed, searching their blank, oval eyes, wide and shining like jewels. "Don't you care?"

We waited in the silence that followed.

*—Why did we give the stone?—*

*—Because we were curious—*

Curious. It was what Castor himself had written, but the word sounded much more frigid from them. Inhuman. The fates of Marian, Alice, and Nick. The fates of mankind and all the people torn apart by phantoms. The fates of the Sect agents who'd given their lives to protect society, of the final cohort of the Fisk-Hoffman facility who were transformed into monsters long before the Devil's Hole burned down.

The fates of the Effigies fighting under a bloody legacy none of us could escape.

All to satisfy their *curiosity.*

June's hand shook in mine. Or was it mine that shook in hers? I couldn't tell. My teeth clenched shut against words that held too many painful memories in them. Evil memories that could have been avoided if only this place had never been found.

*—Keep your rage for yourselves—*

The goddesses's response.

*—It was the hubris of humankind that led the travelers to seek this place—*

*—The hubris of humankind that led them to change their own fates—*

*—What would humankind do with the power of fate they desired so?—*

*—Who would they sacrifice to allow their dreams to come true?—*

*—We observed and saw for ourselves your actions—*

*—We allowed you to architect your own fates—*

*—And so the power of life, death, and fate became a child's game—*

*—A game that has brought you to us once again—*

The breeze blew our hair and clothes. But not the goddesses'. They remained still. Unmoving. Eternal.

*—So we ask again. What is it now that you seek of us?—*

I hadn't realized I was holding my breath. I released, sucking in another breath greedily. Ridiculous. Even as an Effigy, this was way above my pay grade. But I couldn't forget why I was here. I had to speak first, but the words wouldn't form. Nobody could speak at all, not even Blackwell. The pompous man had desired to become a god himself, but in the face of gods, he remained still and small like the rest of us.

*—But of course, it is another wish—*

*—Even while in the depths of despair, humankind does not learn—*

*—What is your wish, then?—*

*—Or is it another power you seek?—*

It was then that Black moved for the first time, lifting her white-robed arm, her silver fingers bending, twitching, as they reached for her eye.

I looked away, covering my face with my hands. And by the time I looked again, one of the goddess's sockets was empty, smooth like the marble that paved the floors of palaces.

And in her hand was a black stone.

It was much larger than the pendant in the stream at my feet or the stone in the ring on Saul's finger. The size of an egg, but sharply cut like a diamond. It glittered in the goddess's hand, whispering death.

Fate followed suit. Taking out her eye, weighing it in her hand.

*—Questions left unanswered—*

*—What would humanity do with the power of fate?—*

*—What would humanity do with the power of death?—*

Their movements matched exactly. They threw the stones. Rolling, rolling in the white stream. They came toward us, unpinned bombs nearing the front lines.

Blackwell, Saul, June, and me. Each of us exchanged glances.

Then we ran.

It was a mad dash for the white stone. Saul was fast. I had to take him out first. I grabbed his hand, but it slipped out of my grasp, leaving the ring in my grip. Even if I wanted to use it, I didn't have the opportunity to. Saul punched me in the face. The ring flew from my grip as he swung his metal hand toward my heart. But then June was there, tripping him, giving me time to chase down Blackwell.

*Don't let him get the stone*, I told myself, my legs pumping as hard as I could manage. Blackwell was sluggish, and I was an Effigy. I was already gaining on him. I could catch him. I could do it. *Don't let him get the stone!*

We dove for it at the same time, but it was Blackwell's hand that reached it first. I tried to snatch it before he could realize it was in his grip, but he held out his hand to stop me, holding the stone in the other like a grenade.

Silence. It took a few seconds for everyone to understand what had just transpired. June's scream of anguish and Blackwell's laughter brought the reality crashing down hard. The stone was his. Blackwell had the Eye of Fate.

As he rose to his feet, he couldn't stop laughing. He stared at his shaking hand closed around the stone, his eyes wilder than I've ever seen them. He laughed, long and hard, his pitch rising into the sky above. He was undone.

"The feat that not even my father could accomplish. Not the Council. Not Prince. Not the Sect." His whole body bent and trembled as his voice grew louder. "Nobody since the famed Castor and Vogel. I am the first. And the *last*." He opened his hand. The white stone glittered in his palm. "So much power." He closed his eyes. "I can feel it pulsating through me."

"Blackwell," I tried, rising to my feet. "Come on . . . Don't do anything stupid."

Blackwell smirked. "Are you afraid now, Maia? Do you finally fear my power? If so, then you've learned from the mistakes of your elders. Arthur Prince. Sibyl Langley. They will learn soon enough. I told you, Maia. I told you that I would achieve the impossible. With this, I can even conquer death."

I understood in that one, awful moment, as I looked at his magnanimous frame arched backward in near ecstasy. He was the soldier gripping the sword, standing on top of the skeletons pleading for mercy as he tipped the blade to their skulls. The painting in his mansion was a promise to himself that he would accomplish what no man before him ever could.

"You always did talk too much, Bartholomäus. But your stone still needs a sacrifice."

Saul stood at a distance behind me. Saul.

With the Eye of Death.

"It's over," Saul whispered.

Time slowed to a crawl. June was screaming. I was running, reaching for him. Saul lifted the stone to his mouth.

I felt it. I felt my body laid out by Lake onto the floor of the General Assembly chambers, disintegrating into dust. I felt my soul being pulled out of the realm of the goddesses with no physical flesh left to tether to. The white light of fate washed my spirit away. I was traveling. Traveling to the next girl . . .


"Oh."

A new red door. Erected behind me. The same white stream below my feet. I wondered why. It didn't look like anyone else was here. Not

Saul, not June. Certainly not Blackwell—well, his soul washed back into the same place we're all supposed to go after death. Thanks to Saul, we were both now dead for good.

No goddesses here either. Good. Screw them. Even if I *was* painfully lonely in here.

Natalya had said once that this room was a manifestation of the connection we all shared, all of us Effigies, dead and alive. Our connection existed in the first place only because of the twisting of fate that kept our souls from traveling the same path as others. We didn't enter the great white river that spread around the world, taking us along until it was time for us to be born in another form. Our souls were carried by fate to the next girl. A cosmic chain all on our own. If I was here, guarding a door of my own, then that meant my soul had already found the next Effigy. I could only imagine who the poor girl was.

What would she see if she scried and came here? If she wandered into this space, begging to see my memories?

She'd see me fail.

I'd been trusted with one task. One simple task. To give everyone peace. To save them all. And now, in Saul's hands, they would all be undone. Lake, Belle, and Chae Rin. Brendan and Rhys. Sibyl and Cheryl. Uncle Nathan. Their bodies, their souls, their lives were probably unraveling as I stood here—as I would stand here. For eternity.

Tears began to leak from my eyes, dripping off my chin. I would never see any of them again. The friends, the sisters I'd gained. My family. A love of my own. I would never have the life I wanted. Is this the despair that Natalya had warned me about the last time I died? Time moved differently here. More slowly. How many centuries would I wait here? How long would it take me to lose my mind like Natalya had?

My knees buckled, hitting the white stream. No. I didn't want that.

I didn't want to be here. "Please, somebody." I buried my face in my hands. It couldn't end like this. It couldn't end like this! "Please! *Please!*"

"Hey, Lil Sis."

An unbelievable sound. An unmistakable voice. My body twitched as if I'd been shocked by an electrical current, my hands lowering slowly from my head. I didn't dare to look up.

I looked up.

"June?" I whispered, standing. "That can't be you."

But it was. June in the uniform Saul had given her. June, with Saul's ring in her outstretched hand. I wanted to ask how. But I already knew.

"I took it while Blackwell was monologuing," June said, giving me a little wink. "Then, when I saw Saul with the stone, I had to think fast. He's so used to me being his lackey that he's not even bothering to pay attention to me. That's his mistake, seeing as I wished that I would be the next Fire Effigy. And that I'd be able to see you again." With her thumb, she launched the ring up into the air and caught it again. "Guess it brought me here. Funny how this thing interprets wishes."

I collapsed to the ground, crying. I didn't know why. I was just so tired. It was all too much. Why had this happened to us? Why did one sister have to die while the other was alive? I'd tried so hard. Fought so hard. But June was right from the beginning. None of this was fair.

"This isn't what I wanted for you." I gulped in air, my tears slipping into my mouth as I inhaled. "Not this legacy . . ."

Her arms wrapped around my body. "Don't cry, Lil Sis. We still have a chance."

"What does it matter?" I looked up at her with tearful eyes. "Saul is going to kill everyone."

"Not if we work together." June cupped my face, her own tears brimming. "You were right, Maia. Seeing you die again, I—" She shook her head. "You don't have a body anymore. You don't deserve that. You don't deserve anything I did to you. And I want to stop." The tears fell. "I only wanted us to be a family again, but look what I did instead."

"You can't live at the expense of other people," I told her.

"I know. I *know* that." June trembled. "I did wrong. Seeing you like this, I know that now more than ever. I just wish I'd understood it before it was too late."

"June . . ."

"So many people." June shut her eyes against the memories, against each charred body begging for mercy. "My *god*. I've hurt so many people. And I can't take that back."

I shivered as I watched the realization dawn on her. The weight of others' souls bearing down on her until she buckled and doubled over.

"I was just so . . . so angry," she confessed, eyelashes wet. "I woke up so *angry*."

Angry. An angry soul, perhaps, courtesy of Alice. But thanks to Saul's resurrection, she ended up a different kind of monster. It was a fate she didn't deserve.

She wiped her eyes. "But you, Maia—you've saved lives. You sacrificed yourself to save lives. You used to look down on yourself so much. You used to worship the Effigies, thinking you could never be like them. But look at you." She pointed at me; my heart fluttered as I saw the light in her eyes. "You've surpassed every limitation you or anyone placed on yourself. You're not that kid on the bus anymore, Maia. I'm so proud of you. And I'm sorry for everything."

Finally. *This* was June. *This* was my sister. With a sob, I pulled her into my arms, and then we were both crying—tears of pain, sorrow, and joy, finding solace in each other's arms.

"Don't give up," June begged me. "Please. I'm here now. We're both here. So tell me what to do."

June, waiting for my direction. Looking for me to lead. I never thought the day would come. But she was right. I *was* different now.

And I couldn't lose hope.

"June." I breathed her name. "You trust me, right, Big Sis?"

June ruffled my hair. "I'm here, aren't I? I trust you with my life. Naturally."

A strange sort of peace settled into my bones. A silent power, stronger than any Effigy, rested there, waiting for my command. At her words, her affirmation, my lips trembled into a smile. "Then you're going to have to let me borrow something."


Time moved differently in the land of dead Effigies. Saul had only just lowered the black Eye of Death from his mouth by the time my consciousness reemerged from the depths of my twin sister's flesh, her body dragged out of the physical realm and into the spiritual realm with a wish from the ring. The Saul standing before me did not yet realize. He was laughing, walking toward the white stone that had already sunk to the ground. The stone of wishes. The Eye of Fate he'd fought for, died for, and killed for. The power he thought was finally his.

Nick Hudson's life was indeed a sorrowful one. As was Alice Vogel's. Neither of them had wanted their lives to become twisted so. I was sure even Alice would take it all back if she could. Her father's beatings. Her mother's murder. Nick's rejection.

But our actions were our own. The goddesses had already proven that by giving us the power of the heavens. This fate was always a choice, the consequences of humanity's hubris brought down upon humanity's heads. Alice had chosen murder long before she became like the witches she'd admired so that she could escape a powerless fate. Nick had chosen to kill others to regain his life and his love. And this was the end those choices brought them to.

Flames erupted around June's body. True flames born from the power of an Effigy. It was not just my power. It was June's. Our pure energy dissolved the nano-network embedded in the back of June's brain stem, freeing her body of its contaminants at last. The combined wills of the Finley twins working together. It was a power neither of us could have imagined. A magnificent, glorious broadsword, jeweled from the red-tassled golden hilt to the tip of the blade, formed in our hands. Our sword.

We were already running forward, the sword drawn. We had become the knight of Marian's dreams and Alice's stories. The perfect knight whose sole purpose was to bring an end to the Effigies' suffering, to close the curtain on that tale of blood and death. Because Saul had turned, we could see his sea-blue eyes and his handsome face—

Just as we plunged the sword through his heart.

He gasped, blood surging out from his trembling lips. The Eye of Death slipped out of his hand and into June's.

"I'm sorry." It was I who whispered as Saul reached for my face— the face of the one who held his lover. "I'm sorry . . . Nick . . . Alice. . . ."

As Saul's flesh turned to dust, Alice Vogel's and Nick Hudson's souls returned to the white streams at last.

June and I bent over, our body suddenly heavy. The breath came out of our throat in painful rasps. Saul's blood dripped from the tip of our sword into the quiet stream.

*—The stone is yours—*

It was Fate who'd spoken.

We picked up the Eye of Fate.

*—Then? What is your wish?—*

The stone was as light as a feather. But its terrible power quaked within us, just from the slightest touch. We'd have to be careful.

I spoke first from June's mouth, wording my wish carefully.

"Marian asked me to give all of us peace. I promised Natalya, too. This is how I want to do it. I wish for the Effigy line to end." I gripped the stone tighter in my hand. "No more Effigies standing in front of a red door. Their souls should find peace like they were meant to. No more Effigies. No more phantoms. All the evil Alice did with the stone needs to be undone."

The goddesses watched us with curiosity.

"But that's not all!" June spoke next. "There are enhanced soldiers destroying New York right now. They used to be people, so we can't just get rid of them, but we want their 'enhanced abilities' gone. Oh, and we want our parents back. I want my sister back. Oh—and world peace!"

Wow, June was really going for it.

The goddesses continued to watch us.

"Is that . . . ?" I gulped. "Is that okay?"

—*Humanity's eternal peace cannot be granted by us. Some wishes cannot be granted even with our power. Such is the fate of the world*—

—*For Vogel's folly to be completely undone, a sacrifice is required. A sacrifice is required for all such wishes*—

—*A sacrifice of death*—

Death stared at us with one remaining black eye, unblinking.

"We can't sacrifice anyone else," I said.

—*The girl, Alice, chose to sacrifice, and so her wishes were granted*—

"That was *her* choice," I said. "I won't make her mistakes. Please. I can't kill anyone else. But this one wish. It has to be granted. *Please.*"

The goddesses thought.

—*Your parents will remain as souls. Such is the sacrifice we require to save humanity from its own wicked choices*—

June's anguish was the same as mine, maybe more. But no matter how we pleaded, the goddesses would not change their minds. It was their offer. Our parents, for the lives of billions for centuries to come.

We agreed.

*—However, Maia Finley. Should the Effigy line end, should the Effigies of old find peace as souls waiting to be reborn, then you too will disappear—*

Life. Her voice always sounded lighter than the others. For a moment I wondered if she was genuinely concerned. I could feel June's restless consciousness stirring within her body. "That's why I asked for my sister back," she said. "Let Maia live again!"

*—For the Effigies' line to end—*

*—For the sister to be resurrected—*

*—It is an inherent contradiction—*

*—For the Effigy line to end, the sister must die—*

So this was it. My true swan song. June's despair began to bubble to the surface, forming a protest on her lips because she already knew my decision. But I was the stronger Effigy. I kept her at bay, borrowing her mouth to speak.

"That's fine," I said.

I didn't know why, in that moment, I was so filled with serenity. I didn't want to die. Even though I knew my soul would be free, I didn't want to die so young. There was still so much I wanted to do. But I had my mission. I'd promised them all, all the Effigies whose stories had played before my eyes. I would release them from their prison. I would give them all peace. Natalya, Marian. They were waiting for me . . . waiting for release.

"June," I said with her lips, her tongue. "I always thought that you were the sister who was meant to live. That you were the one who should have become an Effigy. But I did good, didn't I? I used to think I couldn't do anything right. But now I get to save the world." I smiled.

"You said you trusted me. Well, I trust me too. I believe in myself . . . enough to give myself up. I said I would give them peace. I want to give you peace too. I can sacrifice myself to do that."

For a long time the goddesses said nothing. Nothing, until Life spoke, her blue eyes shimmering.

—*It is a pity. The Effigies who protected humankind. And you, Maia Finley, standing as light in the darkness*—

She fell silent.

—*For a wish to be granted, a sacrifice is required*—

—*Your sacrifice has been noted*—

—*Your wish will be so*—

I could feel the weight of their power growing, filling the white stream with an electrifying force that buzzed up June's body. I dropped the stone into the stream, stepping back. The white space began to turn around us, June and me, funneling like a cloud. I could feel myself disappearing, out of June's body, vanishing from reality. My third death.

*Live on, June*, I told her, hoping my thoughts would reach her at least one more time. *Live on for the both of us. For Mom and Dad, too.*

And as I disappeared, the goddesses watched. Curious.

—*A girl who sacrificed others*—

—*A girl who sacrifices herself . . . to save others . . . how curious*—

I could feel the coils of history unraveling, the bricks built up being set down one after the other. The wishes of old unfurled, vanishing into the dark. The wishes uttered in the Vogel household were being undone.

—*But perhaps not everything should be undone*—

*After*

*Three months later*

*Late October*

*New York City*

I sat in Mr. Whomsley's algebra class, staring out the windows, my eyes locked on the giant red construction cranes spread out along the city. The efforts to restore the city were still going strong—more than a few contractors were going to make bank off this.

What I didn't see were those little bright streaks of the most obnoxious metallic blue running up and down New York's sky-grazing Needle. It was off-line. It'd been off-line ever since people realized that the phantoms were gone and would never return.

Out of the corner of her eye, Missy Stevenson was staring at me. Kids stared at me these days. It made sense. Ashford High didn't get too many ghosts. This one had returned with her head held high and her curly brown hair tied up like nothing at all had happened. Of course they'd be freaked out. Some days they swarmed around me asking questions, and other days they just stared at me. But growing up in a world where knights and dragons were real, they'd long ago learned to accept the unacceptable. Returning Missy's stare with a wink was all I needed to get her to focus back on the incomprehensible equations littering the chalkboard.

I counted down to three thirty, because I had a few stops to make. And I was excited about all of them.

The bell rang.

"Hey, Finley—" Rick Fielding tried to approach me. A bunch of students were already crowding me, but I didn't have time for the usual twenty questions.

"Sorry, guys, gotta go!" I weaved between students and desks and practically fled the classroom.

I opted to take a cab back to South Slope, and like I suspected, it took almost an hour to get there with construction ravaging the city. Well, the broken roads were a better sight than dead bodies.

"Oh good, you're back from school!"

Uncle Nathan had his suitcase open in our brownstone's living room, except his clothes were practically everywhere but inside. He had some dress shirts and sweaters strewn about the sofa, three different ties lined up along the coffee table next to the remote control. The pressure cooker on the kitchen counter was still steaming, and because there wasn't a wall between the two rooms, the smell of brown rice filled the air. Rice made with beans, just like my mom had once taught him. And there was the cook, standing beyond the kitchen next to the staircase, fighting with his tie in front of the mirror hanging on the wall.

Once he heard me come in, he turned and spread his arms. A button-down blue shirt, a black tie, and black dress slacks. Plus, a gray sweater to top it off.

"How do I look?"

"Is this for your DARPA interview tomorrow?" I walked past the bag of fan letters I kept by the shoe rack because I didn't want to lug it up to my room. The television was on but muted, glued to the news as it almost always was in this household.

"Yeah. I'm trying to figure out if business casual would work for it, you know? I mean, business casual's what I usually do for interviews. It worked at the MDCC when it was still up and running, but this is the Department of Defense. Different rules, don't you think?"

Uncle Nathan paused, and as if suddenly overcome by a rush of insecurity, he started fighting with his tie again.

Walking over to the kitchen with a sigh, I took a bowl out of the cabinet and started dumping in some rice. "You look fine. They want your brain. They're not going to reject you because you're wearing the wrong tie."

"I guess." Uncle Nathan slunk toward the kitchen.

"You should lose the sweater, though."

"It's gone." He flung it off and tossed it onto the couch with the rest. "Hey." He sat on the stool on the other side of the high marble tabletop, where I'd just placed my bowl of rice. "I just want to make sure you're okay with the possibility of moving to Virginia. I mean, I may not even get the job. But even if I do get the job, I'm keeping my options open."

"It's fine, Uncle," I reassured him around a mouthful of rice. "I've gotten used to new starts. And stop saying you may not get the job. You helped save the world. I think that makes you qualified—oh, look!"

Dropping my fork, I ran to the living room center table and clicked on the television's volume. In a round conference room, a familiar woman was fielding press questions from behind a podium.

"Yes, the International Counter-Terrorism Agency has taken the doctors and scientists in the Greenland facility into custody. We've since taken them in for questioning."

Sibyl Langley's sharp eyes could have been enough to scare the reporters out of asking questions, but they wouldn't be deterred.

"What will be done about the research program the late Dr. Grunewald was in charge of?" asked one, though the cameras wouldn't let me see his face. "I'm referring to the program fronted by former Attorney General Betty Briggs and former Sect Council representative Bart Blackwell."

"You mean the enhanced soldiers," Sibyl said.

Uncle Nathan shivered from where he sat. The entire city of New York remembered their carnage. After they had turned back into normal, weaponless men and women, they were rounded up rather easily by the combined forces of agents, the military, the National Guard, and so on. But by the time they'd been taken in, the damage they'd done to the city was almost total.

"Three months ago Blackwell proposed that the program could be used for a joint international military effort. Even with Blackwell dead, can you tell us if this program is still on the table?"

Sibyl ran a hand through her short black hair, her milky white suit as well cut and stylish as ever. "You all already know that the United Earth Specialized Forces was dead the moment Blackwell died. And when the General Assembly met last month, it was final. That includes the enhanced forces."

And the Sect. With the phantoms gone, people like Uncle Nathan weren't the only ones who had to find new jobs. But the criminals who'd helped Blackwell were still out there, roaming all over the world. Someone had to catch them and bring them to justice. The United States voted on the creation of a temporary force dedicated to the task. Blackwell's Council friends were already in custody, with more yet to come. It was a good way for people like Sibyl to get their hands dirty.

"There will be efforts to funnel that research—particularly the medical research—into projects that would help society. But those details aren't for me to provide. Thank you. That will be all."

"Langley! Langley!"

Sibyl walked off the stage as the reporters called for her.

"She's still as busy as ever," Uncle Nathan said as I turned down the volume. "Guess she has to use that skill set somehow." He sighed, looking down at his clothes. "Everything changed so suddenly. I know we all have to adapt, but everything's different."

He watched me as I walked back around the counter. "Society was formed around the logic of its own protection against the phantoms. Now they're gone."

"They are indeed." Picking my fork back up, I shoved some more rice into my mouth.

"Sometimes I have no clue how I'm going to adapt," Uncle Nathan continued. "What is the world even going to be like without the phantoms and the Effigies?"

Leaning over, my mouth still filled with rice and beans, I gave him a kiss on the cheek. "Safer," I told him.

Uncle Nathan smirked, tugging at his tie.

The food was sticky going down, tangy and hot, just like I loved it as a kid. "Speaking of change, after I finish eating, I'm taking a bus upstate."

"Oh good." Uncle Nathan was distracted by his tie. "I know she's getting antsy in there. Last time I visited, she said she was trying to pass the time by writing fan fiction in her head. She actually started reciting the lines by heart right then and there." He looked up. "I'm a bit worried about her."

"She'll be fine. She turned herself in; she knows what she's doing." I tapped the fork against the bowl in slight irritation. It still bothered me to think of her in there. "Besides, her trial's in two weeks, and Naomi Prince got us a good lawyer, the same one she used in her sons' trials. They can't possibly fault her for everything she did."

"But they'll have to fault her for *some* things," Uncle Nathan said. "She won't get off clean. It may be years before she comes back home.

And even then, she'll have to rebuild her life." Uncle Nathan rested his arm against the marble counter. "That's not a small task."

"True." I set my fork down. "But she'll be alive."

Uncle Nathan smiled. "Also true."

The two of us talked while I ate, and Uncle Nathan continued to go through ties. Upstate was just one of the stops on my list. If I could brave the traffic, I'd have to find my way over to Manhattan to see him. My face flushed with excitement. I made sure to fix my face first, powdering out the sheen of oil, brightening up the dark red lipstick faded on my lips. A fresh blouse, a cute skirt. It was not every day he was in town.

"I'm off, Uncle Nathan! I'll be back before midnight! Hopefully not alone!"

"Okay, can't wait. But really, come before midnight, all right?" Uncle Nathan pointed at me. "Not a minute later or I think I'll be fined by social services. See you, Maia."


I checked Doll Soldiers on the subway because Lucas was sending me texts again asking me to meet up, and I wasn't going to answer any of them. As much as I wanted to see Jin's crew again, I was pretty sure Lucas's intensions were not the purest—I still owed his crew a favor, after all—and there was no way in hell I was popping over to the Alps for a rendezvous. I was done with cross-world traveling for a while.

My shades made searching through the website a bit difficult, but it was better than getting chatted up by one of the few people on a New York subway who'd bother to give a crap. As expected, my name was all over the forum, but only for positive reasons. It was nice to be vindicated. Users had been piecing together all the mysteries born from the United Nations Assembly on that day three months ago. Briggs and the mysterious facility. The enhanced soldiers. Blackwell's plot and sudden suicide. The death of Saul. The existence of two Maia Finleys. And my body, obliterated and then re-formed. Many explained what they could and left the rest.

[+500, - 103] Now that Maia wasn't a terrorist after all, we Fireflies are still waiting on our apology from everyone else on this board who dragged her for weeks.

[+438, - 89] Still can't believe the whole evil twin theory. That's some crazy shit.

Yeah. It was. Crazier living it.

"Ooh, the music video for Lake's new single!" some girls were cooing a few seats down.

I could see in one of the threads that it was finally out. "You Wish I Was" had already blasted past GBD's tumbling release to snatch number one on the Billboard Hot 100 its first week out. Then again, it wasn't hard to believe the world would be thirsty to hear the whisper-vocal, pop-light, R & B stylings of an Effigy formerly accused and newly acquitted of terrorism. With the song murdering every chart, Lake was ready to sweep the AMAs next month.

I sent her a text: OMG your new video is FIRE. JO WEEPS! GBD is dead in ditch lmao!!

My phone bleeped several seconds later.

SCREAMING. Can't wait to see u later!! ♥♥

That reminded me. I typed Belle's name into a search and scrolled through posts. But nothing had changed since I checked last week. Budapest was still her last-known whereabouts. I'd sent out the place and date to all the girls. Who knew if Belle even had her phone anymore. So I asked Sibyl, who was traveling all over the world and who had networks everywhere, to pass on the message. That was a month ago. Even Chae Rin had torn herself away from her mother and was on a flight here from Vancouver. I was sure she'd come. She had to, after everything.

I left the subway and traveled through Queens. Rhys's apartment wasn't very big, and the rent was more than manageable for a Prince with money. There was a weird smell here, but no less than any other apartment building. One of his neighbors was an old lady who always gave me the evil eye when she saw me, like I was there to steal something. Sighing, I rang the bell, straightening out my skirt, suddenly wondering whether it was too long or too short.

"What are you doing?"

Rhys caught me shifting around awkwardly, tugging at my skirt. Leaning against the door frame, he stared at me with his eyebrow arched.

"Nothing!" I said, straightening up quickly.

"You're doing the 'I need to go potty' dance."

My face flushed. "I am *not*." I pushed him out the way, catching his little grin as I waltzed into the apartment. Even with the Sect gone, he still lived like a Sect agent. The small living room was pristine, the vinyl albums he'd moved from his old place perfectly alphabetized on the shelf next to the beige cabinet. The framed photos on the deep yellow walls were mostly of his mother and his brother. None of his father yet. That would probably come with time. But there were the two of us on the table in between the wood-framed chair and the sofa. And on the counter next to the tall lamp, another framed picture featuring La Resistance—he and his brother, Brendan, reunited with their joyful mother. Dot and Pete still in their lab coats. Sibyl and Uncle Nathan. The Effigies minus Belle. We'd taken it after coming back to Seattle to celebrate a job well done.

"That was a good time," he said, walking up to me. The sun filtered in through the violet curtains of the window.

"I remember lots of booze. Booze I can't legally drink but drank anyway and then got sick and threw up."

And I wasn't the only one who'd gotten drunk. Poor Brendan had even tried to challenge Pete to a duel to the death over the young lady Victoria's heart. It was weird.

He laughed. "You saved the world," he said with a little shrug. "You've earned the right to break a few rules."

Rhys hooked me by the waist and drew me closer to him. My heart rate skyrocketed. I still wasn't used to his casual kisses, like the one he gave me on the side of my temple before sitting on the couch. I'd never done anything like this before. Not that I was against it, but the opportunity had just never presented itself. I still sometimes felt like a robot learning to feel, but some things came easily with Rhys. When he put his feet on the coffee table, I curled up next to him, satisfied by the shy smile he returned.

"What's that?" I pointed at the file next to his feet.

"Oh." Rhys cleared his throat, pushing it away with his foot. "It's not important."

"Oh, come on." Since secrets weren't really my thing anymore, I leaned over and picked it up. The thin, pointed face of a morose-looking woman stared back at me from the first sheet, pale blond hair framing the pair of sunken eyes adding to the fatigue of her expression.

"Irina Volkov," I whispered, reading the name on the file. "Vasily's mother?"

Rhys sighed when I looked at him. "I . . . wanted to know where Vasily's grandparents lived. It wasn't in his personal file, but I figured it'd be in his mother's. It turns out that his grandmother lives alone in Ukraine. She doesn't have anyone to help her. From this file it seems she's barely living on the severance pay the Sect gave her after her daughter died."

Vasily's grandmother. After Rhys was acquitted, Sibyl, who'd strongly vouched for him in front of a jury, offered him a spot on her task force. To catch the rest of Blackwell's criminals, she needed the best agents. But he'd rejected her.

"Is this why?" I asked him. He knew what I meant immediately.

Rhys picked up the file, staring at the forlorn woman. "Vasily cut ties with her after Greenland. She doesn't know what happened to him. Probably doesn't even know that he's dead. Somebody should tell her. I've been too scared to, but . . . it's been three months. I think it's time."

The fate of the two were still connected, even separated by the veil of life and death. The bond forged during their stay in the Devil's Hole probably could never be severed. But maybe this way, they'd both have peace.

"I'm still not sure what I'll say once I meet her—or how much I should explain about Vasily and our relationship. But I know I have to see her. I have to help her out. Maybe stay with her for a while, if she'll let me. I can set her up in a better place, make sure she has everything she needs for as long as she needs it. And then maybe . . . maybe I'll take Sibyl up on her offer."

"Sibyl and Rhys, together again," I said. "Stopping the bad guys."

"The bad guys . . ." He set the file back down with another sigh. "During that trial, the lawyer explained to everyone that I was just a casualty of the Fisk-Hoffman facility's cruelty. A casualty of my own father's abuse. But that's not enough for me. I have to atone. I'm going to dedicate my life to protecting people from now on."

"Sounds good," I said, giving him a pat on the back and an exaggerated nod I hoped was a little cute. "Very Aidan Prince–like."

"Well." Rhys slipped his arm around my waist. "You're the one who said I have some karma to work off."

I smiled at him. "You know what, Aidan? I think you'll turn out just fine."

He kissed me, deep and warm, his lips enveloping mine as he pulled me in by the small of my back.

Actually, I could get used to this.


Since it was the end of October, the sky was already dark by the time my bus arrived at the flat building of the CSTF upstate—well, formerly of the CSTF. It'd been converted and passed over to the International Counter-Terrorism Agency, which meant, actually, that quite a few people who'd worked for the former agency were now in the very jail cells they'd packed full of Sect agents.

I passed through the metal detectors in the lobby for what felt like the hundredth time. A hundred times for a hundred visits. Being here again was a painful reminder of Eveline and Howard. Since Howard's death, she had dedicated herself to the agency, devoted to tracking down the very people who'd led her husband toward the path of his demise. She never blamed Rhys, of course. She'd told him as much at Howard's funeral. But I knew it'd be a while before she could lay eyes on him again without being reminded of those painful memories.

Rather than being taken to the jail cells, I was ushered into a different room with booths set up behind walls of glass, on the other side of which the prisoners would shuffle in. The officer seated me in one of the chairs. It wasn't until June walked in, in her orange jumper, her feet and hands chained, that I picked up the phone, tears prickling my eyes.

"You have to stop crying every time you come here," June said with a little smile. "I keep telling you to suck it up, and you never do."

I couldn't help it. I'd cried after I awoke again on the floor of the
United Nations to find that we'd both returned from the realm of the
goddesses. I'd cried when June then stood and confessed her crimes in
front of the UN Assembly. I'd cried as she'd requested to be taken into
custody, as they'd hauled her away in cuffs.

Sacrifice. Sacrifice is needed for a wish to be granted. June sacrificing her sister bought the Effigies their freedom. And somehow, in the
strange eyes of the goddesses, my sacrifice of myself apparently bought
me my life.

I'd asked for June to be at peace too, and thankfully, mercifully,
they'd given that to us. June no longer had the urge to kill.

But I couldn't sacrifice myself for her anymore. And June didn't
have any nanotechnology in her anymore. She wasn't the Fire Effigy
either. Just a regular human girl. She couldn't blast her way out of here
like she did in France. She would have to face her crimes like others
had. All I could do was hope for her and cry with her.

"And I keep telling you that you had nanotech in you," I reminded
her, the phone cold and hard against my ear. "You can use it as a
defense. You don't need to tell them the other stuff."

"What other stuff?" June raised an eyebrow. "You mean the stuff
about how I *wanted* to help Saul? How the kill chip they put in me
was just a fail-safe in case I went off script? You know very well that I
helped Saul because I thought it meant having my family back."

I bit my lip. I already knew, but if it meant saving June, I'd rather
her lie. "I mean, it's understandable," I said. "Isn't it?"

"Maybe. Maybe not. But I've done too much damage. My heart
won't feel at ease until I've been tried in a fair court of law."

I shook my head, letting out a little incredulous laugh. Even after
having gone through hell and back, she was the same old righteous
June. I was so glad when she'd taken my suggestion to seek some kind

of therapy for her experiences. The doctors they offered here were okay, but I knew she'd do even better if we could get her into a care facility. Anything but a lifetime in prison. If Naomi's lawyer could get Rhys off the hook, then hopefully he'd do the same for her. But it would be a tall feat considering the cosmic forces at play in June's decent into darkness.

"Don't worry, Lil Sis. I have faith." She pressed her hand against the glass. "So should you. After all, you shouldn't even be here. Neither of us should. You could call it fate, or you could call it luck. Or mercy. But we're here. I wouldn't count out the Finley sisters."

I touched the glass where she had, cool to the touch, returning her smile with a determined nod. To be honest, even with my sacrifice, I didn't know why the goddesses had given me a second chance, and I doubted I ever would. But I wasn't going to take it for granted. We were here. We'd had to let our parents go, and it was the hardest decision we could make—the sacrifice we'd made for the sake of the world. But we were here. As long as we were alive, we could hope for the future.

"You know, it's almost eight," she said. "I thought you had somewhere else to be."

"I do, but I've got time." Lowering my hand, I settled into my chair. "So tell me about this fan fiction you've been writing...."

June rubbed her hands, excited.


I waited in Brooklyn Bridge Park, the bridge once ravaged by Saul now fully operational. There weren't a lot of people around. The long row of benches overlooking the East River was mostly empty except for a couple I could see in the distance if I squinted. The heavy construction still happening around the city may have deterred a few from night visits to the park. But I came nonetheless. Eleven o'clock. I was the first one. Sitting on the bench, I took in the sight of the Manhattan skyline and that eyesore of a needle we'd never need again. I shut my eyes, breathing in the not-so-sweet air, still comforted by the knowledge of freedom. Humanity's freedom. No longer bound by our cages, we were free to roam the earth, the seas, and the skies without fear of the monsters lurking there. The Effigies' freedom, having been released from the Effigy line into the great stream of life, their souls able to find rest. And my freedom. There were no more sacred duties to die for. No more destines of blood and battle. I could be what I wanted to be.

A pair of hands shook my shoulders from behind.

"So you saw my video, did you?" Grinning, Lake jumped over the bench excitedly and started poking me. "Which part did you like best? Ooh, did you catch all my digs at GBD and my witty, ironic lamp-shading of my past eras?"

Lake was dressed like the pop star she now was: designer shoes, pants, and a long fake-fur jacket probably still worth more than our month's rent. I shrugged.

"I didn't know you *had* eras."

"Well, yeah. I had my reality-TV-show era, my Girl's By Day era." She counted them off with her fingers. "My Effigy-training era, my saving-the-world-as-an-Effigy-and-solo-artist era—"

"We get it," said Chae Rin, behind us in a pair of jeans and a worn-out jean-jacket coat that looked stolen from a thrift shop. She hopped over the bench, plopping down next to Lake. "I met her at Grand Central, and she's been annoying me ever since."

"But you loved my video." Lake nudged me. "She loved my video!"

"It was big budget." Chae Rin shrugged. "They spent way more money on you than I thought they would."

I checked behind the bench. "Where are your suitcases?"

"Already at your apartment." Lake whipped out her phone because she probably wanted to play her music video for the ten hundredth time. "Your uncle looks lovely as ever, by the way."

"I'm really happy you guys decided to stay over." I turned to them, pulling my legs up on the bench. "It's been so weird not having you guys around."

"You mean it's been weird not being around each other twenty-four seven, fighting for our lives." Chae Rin laughed. "Weird, but not missed."

I scoffed. What a lie. She totally missed us. She'd texted me every day from Vancouver, even in the middle of dance class when she was pissed off at her vicious instructor. Now that our great battle was over, Chae Rin could concentrate on refining her skills to one day rejoin Le Cirque de Minuit—now this time one hundred percent phantom free.

"Well," Chae Rin said, "I've been helping my family get the restaurant up and running again, so I really only have the weekend to spend here."

"That'll be enough!" Lake tapped her phone. "Ooh, I can't wait to go shopping in SoHo. I've already called the paparazzi in advance."

I searched behind me again.

"Belle, right?" Chae Rin gave me a sidelong look. Sheepishly, I nodded. "Anyone heard from her in the past three months?"

"I mean, she's been going through some stuff," said Lake, pausing her video and setting down her phone. "I really wouldn't be surprised if she wasn't up for a sleepover."

"Not a sleepover." I folded my arms because I didn't want to look childish. "It's an overnight get-together. An Effigy weekend. We're warriors. We don't do sleepovers."

"That reminds me—I can't wait for you guys to see my new pajamas. They're so cute!"

Lake squealed so loud and began chatting up her plans for the weekend, so the three of us didn't notice the footsteps behind us. But when she cleared her throat, Lake and Chae Rin were the only ones who looked surprised. I stared at Belle, her clothes covered by a long red jacket that swept the ground. I lifted an eyebrow, my arms on my knees.

"So . . ." I searched her hands. "No suitcase?"

Belle looked over the East River, shifting nervously.

"It's okay, you know," I said, when nobody spoke for too long. "All the Effigies were acquitted of any perceived wrongdoings. You don't have to stand there looking like a criminal."

She lowered her head.

"Belle, I heard you've been helping people resettle in Dead Zones all over Europe." Lake brimmed with pride. "That's pretty great!"

"Yeah," Chae Rin said. "That's pretty impressive. There might be some hope for you yet."

A moment of understanding passed between both girls as they looked at each other. The imperceptible nods of Belle's and Chae Rin's heads were as close to burying the hatchet as the two would get.

"Maia," Belle said to me at last, her voice barely a whisper. "Can I talk to you? Alone?"

Chae Rin and Lake couldn't hide the hint of worry that flashed across their faces. But I wasn't scared. And somehow I knew I didn't have to be. Not anymore.

So this was trust. I smiled at her. "Sure."

We walked farther down the strip along the river, far enough away that the other girls couldn't hear us.

"So, is it true?" I asked her as she turned from me toward the river. "You're helping people now?" I thought about it. "Well, it's a lot better than trying to erase them from existence."

Funny. Belle was the one who'd asked me to talk, and yet she responded with silence. Then again, this was Belle.

"Why help them?" I knew the answer, but I wanted to hear it from her lips. So I waited.

And finally, Belle spoke.

"Do you remember when we met in the temple, Maia?" Her coat fluttered in the breeze. "You told me that I wasn't the only one who'd suffered."

"Yeah, I remember."

Belle stretched and closed her hands as if she couldn't decide what to do with them. "When I see those families, those children in need, I'm reminded of that." She shut her eyes. "I'm reminded of why Natalya kept fighting. Of why so many do despite the pain. And not just Effigies. So many people around the world fight. They fight for others." Opening her eyes, she turned to me. "*You* fight for others. Because it is right."

"I fight for others . . ." Truthfully, I wanted to keep fighting. I hadn't told Uncle Nathan yet that I was planning on studying criminology after graduating high school.

"But there are so many ways to fight," Belle said. "I want to try it again. I want to try helping others rather than hurting them. Natalya told me to live on. This is how I'll do it."

"It's a good start," I said. "Like Natalya said, there's always hope, right?"

She fell silent again, and for a moment I wondered if I'd said something wrong. But then it came.

An apology.

"I'm sorry I killed you," she said.

The words had come out in such a matter-of-fact manner that I couldn't help myself. I burst out laughing. Belle stared back at me, shocked. I was a little shocked too. But after three months of sitting with the past, pondering all that had happened to us, to *all* of us, I'd come to the conclusion that it was time to move on.

We all needed to, to be free.

"It's okay," I said, wiping a couple of tears from my eyes, tears formed from more than just laughter. The clumsy apology was like a trigger that released the knots from my neck, a balm upon old scars. "Just don't do it again."

My laughter brought Chae Rin and Lake to where we were standing.

"Belle told a joke?" Lake said as they caught up to us. "Oh my god, did Belle tell a joke?"

Chae Rin looked skeptical. "Is she malfunctioning?"

"Th-that's not . . . ," Belle stuttered, clearly embarrassed.

Chae Rin smirked. "Yep. Malfunctioning."

Lake and I placed a hand on Belle's shoulders.

"It's okay," Lake said. "You're allowed to be human."

"Yeah." I smiled. "And no matter what, we're still in this together."

As if on cue, Lake stepped back and lowered her head.

The air shifted, moving around her arm until a thin rapier appeared in her hands. She buried the point into the asphalt.

Chae Rin laughed. "So we're doing this? All right." She wasted no time, kicking the ground. The magnificent white pole of her lance flew up from inside the broken stone, launching into her hand. She dug the bladed tip into the ground with Lake's sword.

I was next. The girls stood back as fire erupted from my hands, stretching down the length as a marvelous scythe. I couldn't count how many times this weapon had saved my life. Now I trapped the blade into the earth.

"Well?" I said, grinning at Belle.

Belle shook her head. "Ridiculous," she whispered. But she called her sword anyway, summoning it from within a flurry of snow. It was the final blade in the circle we'd made.

The Four Swords.

It was as the goddesses had said: Not everything had to be undone.

We stood in the circle, each girl looking to the other. Silent, but for the legends we'd written brimming behind our delighted eyes. The world had changed. It was changing as we stood there by the East River, blanketed under the stars. But we four—we would remain, for as long as we lived, as we were in this moment.

The final Effigies.

# ACKNOWLEDGMENTS

I want to thank the Simon & Schuster team, especially my editor, Sarah McCabe, for guiding me along this amazing journey. With this being my first-ever series, there was a lot of self-doubt and nerves involved on my part. But it's endlessly wonderful and encouraging to know that there are people cheering for you no matter what. Thank you to Simon & Schuster Canada for doing so much to promote the series. Thanks to my agent, Natalie Lakosil, and my former editor, Michael Strother, for being the first in the industry to champion the series.

I am eternally grateful to my family and friends for having my back, but I especially want to acknowledge my mother and my two brothers. No matter how difficult things have been, I can continue to walk forward step-by-step because of you guys. And most importantly, I want to thank the fans who have continued to support this series, sending me letters and tweets and e-mails letting me know just how much you love the Effigies. I wrote these three books with joy knowing you were always there, hungry for more of the story.

In my life I have seen how easy it is to fall on hard times and how people will start to treat you once you do. But these books in print are proof that you should never count yourself out. Thank you to everyone who taught me that.

# ABOUT THE AUTHOR

Sarah Raughley grew up in Southern Ontario writing stories about freakish little girls with powers because she secretly wanted to be one. She is a huge fangirl of anything from manga to sci-fi/fantasy TV to Japanese role-playing games, but she will swear up and down at book signings that she was inspired by Jane Austen. On top of being a young adult writer, Sarah has a PhD in English, which makes her a doctor, so it turns out she didn't have to go to medical school after all.